SADDLED
WITH
FINESSE

ZEA KAYLEIGH GALAN

Saddled with Finesse: An Alpenglow Ridge Novel

Copyright © 2024 by Zea Kayleigh Galan.

www.zeakayleighgalan.com

Cover Artwork by Wingu Studio

Book designed by Zaji-Kali Galan

Formatting by Zaji-Kali Galan

This book is a work of fiction. Names, characters, businesses, organizations, places, events and incidents either are the product of the author's imagination or are used fictitiously. Any resemblance to actual persons, living or dead, events, or locales is entirely coincidental.

For information contact :

zeakayleigh@gmail.com

First Edition: April 5, 2024

To you,
You don't have to earn it,
it's yours.

Listen to the Official Playlist

Tanner Adell - Buckle Bunny
Jimmie Allen - Best Shot
Reyna Roberts - Lawless
Stevie Wonder - As
Megan Thee Stallion - WTF I Want
Ms. Lauryn Hill - Ex Factor
Rihanna - Same Ol' Mistakes
Beyoncé – TEXAS HOLD 'EM
Sam Cooke - You Send Me
Tanner Adell - Love You a Little Bit
BRELAND – Natural
Emawk - 18
Shaboozey - Let It Burn
Zanski - Fool
Kiana Ledé - Deeper
Carter Faith – Wild
Destiny's Child – Girl
Rodell Duff – Tell Me Twice
Ariana Grande – pov
<u>Listen on Spotify!</u>

Join the Newsletter

NEVER MISS AN UPDATE about Zea Kayleigh, newsletter exclusives such as freebies and giveaways, first looks at new books, upcoming series, and events.

SIGN UP HERE!

Hi Friend!

This is a romantic suspense novel that is suitable for mature audiences only. There are darker themes in this book that may be sensitive to some readers. For a full list of potentially sensitive content, visit my website: www.zeakayleighgalan.com/cw

SADDLED
WITH
FINESSE

CHAPTER 1

Riesling Mason

COLD SWEAT COLLECTS DOWN my back. Holding the phone with both hands, I lean onto the serving station. My elbows sting against the grooves of the rubber tray beneath them. This table's bar drinks are currently sweating and getting watery.

"You gonna run these or what?" My manager, Jamie, snaps me out of my state of panic.

A *while.*

Nine months is more than a while. And if I have any say in it—which I do—to say I never want to see Teddy again is an understatement.

"Relax, Jamie! I'm going." I slide the phone into the middle pocket of my standard Peak's Restaurant apron. Each drink gets placed strategically on my tray so that I can carry them all to my awaiting table. The last thing I need is to be doused with whiskey, coke and beer tonight.

Oh how the bougie have fallen.

In the time it takes to walk these drinks over, my mind has begun to wonder about the text. Why is he messaging me now? I've stayed out of his life. Asked for nothing. I've said nothing to anyone. I've been good.

Why now?

After I place the drinks on the table, I go into my spiel about the specials for dinner today. Twirling a bit of my blonde ponytail around my finger as I pop my gum. Peak's isn't known for its culinary prowess. *Mostly* men come to this place for the beautiful women in tiny, tight tops and shorts. I knew that and *they* know that. Given this information, it also does not shock me that I'll be carrying nearly one hundred and fifty fried chicken wings back to this table... accompanied by an equal amount of fries.

I read back the order to them, "Six Quarter baskets with extra crispy fries, extra ranch, coming up!" I look back to my notepad, "Scratch that, one with extra blue cheese." The man sitting in the far corner winks at me.

I'm used to how these guests treat us, at this point. They think that because I'm in this skimpy uniform I might give them a happy ending with their fried chicken.

This isn't a strip club and I'm no dancer.

Somehow talking about blue cheese has elicited this skeevy wink. *Gross.*

Tips are the reason I'm here though. I just smirk briefly before turning on a heel to enter the order in for the kitchen.

Better for them to think they have a chance... before the bill comes out.

The night drones on this way as the dinner rush picks up and I get into a rhythm of constant movement. Bouncing from table to bar, to putting in another order with the kitchen, to table to bar to putting...

You get it.

I'm thankful for the influx of guests. It means I can keep my thoughts off of the phone currently burning a hole in my apron. Every time I thought I had a second to check a notification, I would get a new table before I could even unlock the screen.

I couldn't check, but that didn't mean my mind wasn't going over every possible reason why *he* would send that message. The last time I saw him face to face, I was wiping blood from the corner of my mouth.

Never again.

My sidework to close out my shift flies by with my mind spinning over what sparked his message. Marie and Karla don't mind filling in my silence with talk about how their tables drove them crazy tonight. I nod at the appropriate times and walk out to my car with them after we lock up for the night.

Driving in the silence of my Mustang and trudging up the three flights of stairs all blur with how exhausted I am. I have no plans to move from my bed until the sun comes up.

Thanks to my infatuation with Teddy, a man who was never any good for me, I'm living in Denver. I like it here, but it's not home.

I toe off my work-mandated, slip-proof black sneakers at the door of my tiny studio apartment. Promptly flopping face-first onto my bed, drained from how busy the night was.

The stack of cash from the tables I served tonight goes into the jar I have under my nightstand. Thankfully, I can reach it from where I lay sprawled on the bed. Sliding the apron from under my body, it thunks to the carpet. I had completely forgotten my phone was in there. I'd been on autopilot the whole way home.

With a huff, I scooch my body close enough to the edge of my bed using as little energy as possible to retrieve my phone. I could use some mindless scrolling until I pass out.

My social media was once glitz and glamour. Pictures of me at this five-star restaurant. Pictures from this fancy trip wearing the shoes everyone was salivating over, but could never afford. Selfies of my flawless beat at the dinner party only six-figure men could afford to attend. Everyone in my hometown thought I was living a charmed life because I did my best to show it that way. Leaving out all the darkness behind the scenes.

Now, I barely post anything outside of the occasional thirst trap.

What?

I'm still fine as hell. Just broke.

Likes and comments from a post I shared earlier today line up neatly down my screen. It was an old picture of me at the ranch surrounded by the staff and my parents. The horses moseying about in the background of the photo twist my heart in knots. The last day I was in Alpenglow Ridge. Maybe the last day I was truly happy.

> **Teddy : I want to see you. Are you home?**

Home?

My tired brain finally makes the connection. I hardly ever post about my past. It's too painful and unattainable after everything I've done. But, I felt homesick this morning.

I missed my family.

I missed my friends.

All the people in this photo mean so much to me and I barely get to see them now. The last time I did was when my father was recovering in the hospital after a massive heart attack. With tearful eyes, I gave and received hugs from every one of them who came to visit.

This picture had been the last we'd all taken before my father's health took a plunge. Like the shitty daughter I am, I left before the lies I told could catch up to me.

That was six months ago.

I don't respond to his text. There is nothing to say. I clear the notifications with a flourish. Reaching blindly for my charging cable, I plug my phone up to charge and slide it onto the nightstand. Wrapping the comforter around my body like a burrito, I give into the drooping of my eyelids. I let my exhaustion overtake me.

◆◆◆◆

MY RINGTONE BLARES INTO the small space, waking me with a start. Pawing the general area of the nightstand to find my phone is not as effective as I'd like it to be. I hear it thunk to the ground. *Great.* Fully awake and frustrated now, I kick with ferocity at the blanket to free myself.

At least, the sun is up.

I don't check to see who's calling before I answer the phone. "Good morning, honey! Did I wake you?"

"Mom, you know you did. I work nights." I try to keep the eyeroll I'm doing out of the tone of my voice, but she knows me better than that.

"Well, we're on ranch time here so I've been up for a couple of hours. You do remember what time we get started right?" The playful teasing in her tone makes my heart squeeze a little too tightly. I rub at my chest.

Sighing, I respond, "Yea, I remember." Looking at my phone to see if there were any texts I missed from her before I picked up the phone, I ask, "Is dad alright?"

"Oh yes! I didn't mean to alarm you. Or maybe I did... since this was a wake-up call." She chuckles at her own joke. "It's nothing that dreadful, thank God. Your daddy wants to talk."

"And you're sure it's to me?" My huff is long. I love my dad, but my refusal to work at the ranch is a major point of contention for us. When I left, I didn't give any reasoning or time for him to adjust to the abrupt decision I had made. The opportunity for more came to me and I did everything I could to take advantage of that as quickly as possible. I had always felt that the things that cost at least a comma and, or, have some sparkle were what my life should consist of. Ranch life though, doesn't come with the same razzle-dazzle I was after.

With his heart, I hate being the focus of his attention and causing him more stress. My choice is the same. It makes me feel twice as bad for letting him down.

"Yes, Riesling. Your dad is being cryptic with me and I can't stand it. I tried to use a little back rub to get him to give me any sort of details. I barely got this irritating task of trying to get my only daughter to come home for once."

I was there last month to get my hair done. There for the appointment and left shortly after, but I was there, technically. I just didn't see them.

"Okay... Please don't ever share about you and dad rubbing anything with me. It's... strange. Definitely too much information at—" I pull the phone from my ear to check the time. "—eight AM on a Tuesday."

"Honey, you know how you were made, right? It was not by immaculate conception, you know." The smile in my mom's voice makes me smile as well. I miss her. It's been so long since I've seen her happy.

I'd driven to Alpenglow Ridge in a blaze of tears and panic, thinking I only had a sliver of a chance to see my dad again. The drive is just over an hour away. Each second moved at a glacial pace. I had her on speakerphone in my car for the entire drive. Neither of us said anything. The sounds of the bustling hospital whirred over the sound of my tires ripping the highway up. The cold from that lobby waiting room followed me from the hospital for weeks after.

I couldn't shake that chill.

To hear her smile again, erases that guilt I had felt for coming back to Denver. They were more than surviving in my absence. There's no way I can be in Alpenglow Ridge for long stretches of time since I left. It's too risky.

But this smile. This small little bit of happiness in her voice is enough to make me smile too. Still, I can't picture myself even packing that suitcase I've laid out on my floor now without remembering the last fateful time that I tried to pack it up. Going back to Alpenglow Ridge is probably the dumbest thing I could imagine doing.

It's not smart. And in most things, I would consider myself to be smart. Except when I was younger and made the worst decision, over and over and over again.

"Mom, please." I start grabbing clothes from my laundry basket and throw them into the luggage. From the clean clothes basket, instead of my dirty clothes laundry basket, of course.

"I want to know why dad couldn't call me. Why can't he just call me like you're doing now and tell me what's up?" I walk into my small bathroom across the open studio space. "Toothbrush, toothpaste, face wash, face creams, toner..." The ones *he* preferred ran out a long time ago. I could likely repurchase the bottles I'm packing all for under fifty dollars. But, I don't have fifty dollars to spare.

I throw them into my smaller toiletry bag. My eyes snag on the gold wrappers sticking out from the bathroom drawer. It's not like I've needed them for months. I pick up the roll of condoms considering how necessary it would be to pack.

Why second guess? Better safe than sorry.

"Honey, I don't know what your dad wants. Only that he asked me to get you up here. I take it that you're packing so I can tell him you're on the way, right?"

I brush through my extensions. The tangled mess I woke up with is almost untamable since I went to sleep without my scarf on last night. *Scary.* A little hair oil couldn't hurt. I rub some argan oil in my hands before smoothing it over my blonde ends. It almost looks perfect.

Plugging in my straightener, I answer my mom, "Yea, I guess. I'm working a double on Friday. I'm not staying long." I press the straightener over my hair, flipping the ends just how I like them. "Tell him that because I don't want the guilt trip."

She chuckles. "Of course. Because that's going to do something. Your dad has his own plans. I'll have breakfast waiting for you, honey."

I hang up after we exchange I *love yous* and stare at my phone a little longer.

I'm going to Alpenglow Ridge. Fine. Just a few days. No big deal. He'll never know. I repeat it in my head as I carefully apply makeup and lashes.

Shoes are the last thing to get thrown into my suitcase. My tank top and skinny jeans are cute enough for the ranch. But my chucks? Oh no.

Definitely need my boots.

These wine-red cowboy boots were a present from mom. It's been a few years and I only wore them on the ranch a few times before they sat here useless in my closet.

They aren't who I am anymore.

I shrug to myself in the full-length mirror on my wall. Turning to get a view of my backside, I do a little twerk. Confirming, "It's still fat, baby!" I smack my ass and blow a kiss to myself. All the happy times with my friends and family are taped along the edges of this mirror. Including the photo I posted yesterday.

I focus on the one I took after Mel's twenty-first birthday party. We had spent the better part of that weekend miserably hungover, but it was the best night. It's been a while since we all hung out. Things aren't the same anymore. On the off chance I spend some time in town there, I've decided to throw in something other than tank tops... just in case.

Satisfied with what I've packed, I drag my small suitcase down all three flights of stairs. I'm Alpenglow Ridge bound.

CHAPTER 2

Cory Whitfield

"IT'S NOT FAIR FOR our teachers to stay here longer than they are expected to. The school year is almost over and they are tired, Mr. Whitfield." *I'm tired.*

"I know, it's my wi—their mother's day to pick them up and I guess she just forgot or something. I'm coming as quickly as I can. Give me fifteen minutes… tops! Please."

She sighs a heavy sound that presses down on my shoulders. I try my best to be safe, but also quick, making it through rush hour traffic in Denver. "Fifteen minutes, Mr. Whitfield."

I arrive at the school in fourteen minutes where Cory Jr. and Brendan are sitting on the curb in the pickup line. Their vice-principal, Alison Blackburn, waits behind them with her arms crossed. I park and get out of the car to open the back door of my truck for them. I'm fully prepared to give her the long speech. The one about how I'm trying to make things work with the custody agreement I have with their mom. I still haven't been able to get in touch with her and she didn't tell me that she couldn't make it to pick up the kids today.

My mouth opens to begin my story, but Alison holds up a hand. "It's fine, Mr. Whitfield. They're good kids and were no trouble at all, but you must find a way to prevent this from happening so often. I've made a note in your file about it, but with just three days left of school, I'm certain you can figure it out." She gives me a stern look with an eyebrow raised. Her teacher's tone makes me feel like a chastised student... instead of a thirty-year-old man who is drowning in his own life.

I nod. "Yes, of course." She nods back to me and heads over to her car, parked behind where I pulled up and drives off like a bat out of hell. When I turn back to my truck, CJ gives me a lopsided tilt of his lips. I scrub a hand over my neck. I have no idea what to tell them. None of this conversation should be happening in this after-school pickup line. I hustle back to the driver's side and check my rearview. "Everybody buckled?"

"Yep" they both respond. Bren from his booster and CJ from the other side of the car seat for my youngest.

"Alright. Let's hit it." The daycare that Gabriel, my two, almost three, year old is at stays open until six for pick up. It's five-thirty, so I should make it there well before they close. It's only around the corner from my two oldest's elementary school. "How was taekwondo?" I look at them in the rearview again.

"Today was the last day. We just had a party to celebrate," CJ responds.

"That sounds like fun. Was there cake?"

"No cake. But we got juice and snacks! They had my favorite rainbow Goldfish, dad!" Bren adds in with a bounce. He pulls, a now crumpled, piece of paper from his backpack. "And our certificates of completion! Can we hang it up in the living room?"

Before I can reply, CJ speaks up. "That means we will need to be picked up at three-thirty tomorrow... And Thursday and Friday." He reminds me, just a hint of bitterness in his tone. My heart squeezes at being judged by my oldest. He knows too much. Has felt the hurt of our separation the fiercest, as well.

"I know, son. I know." I consider throwing Vanessa under the bus like I very well deserve to do. That doesn't change the fact that my kids were the last ones to be picked up today. I keep my mouth closed.

We arrive at Sunshine Tots with time to spare and I get my toddler situated in his car seat.

Back at home, my phone vibrates on the dining table. I ordered something to be delivered for dinner when I acknowledged there was nothing in the fridge worth trying to combine for an actual meal. The screen shows a picture of my aunt Janet and me when I was eighteen. I smile with my whole face as she looks down at me. I pick up, saying, "Hey, auntie."

"Hey, Cory. How are you?"

Considering how to respond, I go with the truth. "I'm tired as hell. What about you?"

"I've been better. You know what today is?"

It takes me a second, but I realize that today is *that* day. The day that changed my life forever. "How can it be that twenty years have passed?"

"I don't know, but I miss her every day. Even your dad too." She pauses like she's choosing her next words with care. "You doing okay?"

I scoff, wiping a tear she can probably hear in my voice but I respond, "Yea. I'm good." I look in on the boys getting ready for bed. Bren and CJ are following their routines and Gabe sits happily in the room on the floor in his pajamas. He's rolling a truck on the carpeted rug that looks like a series of roads overlapping all in dizzying patterns. Stepping back into the kitchen, I start putting away to-go containers and wiping the table down.

"You sure?"

I sigh. "No. I'm not, but I'm too tired to think about something else that I need to be handling better. Van forgot to pick up the boys from school. I have to give away two of my properties this week because I can't chance that she will forget them again. I have no idea what I'm going to do with the boys when school is out. Somehow, I forgot to find some sort of activity or camp or something for them. I've been up since four this morning. I'm tired, Jan. I'm really fucking tired."

"You can always come home." *Home.* My aunt moved to Alpenglow Ridge about ten years ago after I graduated from high school. She's built a life there. Found the love of her life, Sammie, and seems happy. Hell, I'm happy for her. But... "I don't know if that's a good idea."

"And why not? You say that every time I suggest it. The boys will be out of school. I know you're paying that condo month to month. Denver is still the worst place to buy a home. Just give them the proper notice and come stay with me."

"I can't just leave, Jan. How am I supposed to feed my boys or myself with no job? We'll eat you out of your house and home. We would be too big of a burden on you there. You do remember I have three kids right?"

"And I have three guest rooms. How is that any different from your condo there? As far as work goes, you think Alpenglow doesn't have lawns and such. Let me ask around, I'm sure I could get you something started."

Could moving in with my aunt be a good idea? There are so many reasons why it could be. For one, I need a damn break. A full day of hauling soil bags, digging holes, sweating in the sun... trying to make everyone else look like they have the picture-perfect house. It's as much as I can take.

Vanessa still hasn't responded to any of my texts or calls. How do you... Just forget to pick up your own children? I mean really... What the hell? She doesn't want to be with me? Fine. Our marriage was not the best thing in my life, but it was ours. She wanted out, I let her go. But the boys? She can't decide to be in and out whenever she feels like it. I'm there for them in the good and bad times.

I'm not usually one to complain, but I'm reaching a breaking point.

"It'll give you a break and you can start somewhere fresh. I work from home, I can watch the boys for you. I miss my littles anyway. Christmas was so long ago and I came to you all." I start to respond and tell her all the reasons that I think this is a bad idea. But, she's right. A break sounds nice.

"I don't know, Jan."

"What about starting your own landscaping company? That used to be your dream, the goal. Is it not anymore?"

I had been working for Mark for the past five years. It's nice to have a little bit of direction in what and where I go day to day. I love not having to think about anything. I simply show up and do my job. It's easy.

What if I did have help though? Starting my own business could be...

"It is something I want. I want that very much so. But I don't know. Janet, that's a lot of work. And with the boys..."

"I said I've got them. Only until you figure it out."

"I'll think about it."

"I love you, nephew."

"I love you. Listen, I need to finish putting the boys to bed. I'll call you later okay?"

"Take me in there so I can say goodnight on speaker."

I do what she asks and let her go.

Laying in bed that night, I think over her proposal again. It's not that far-fetched of an idea.

Reaching into my nightstand, I pull out the old worn envelope and look it over. The edges have long been rubbed away. The small sticker that used to keep it closed is no longer sticky, but I've since used Cellatape to hold it in place.

> *To my son on his birthday,*
>
> *First, I love you. You are the best present that your father and I ever received. How lucky is it, that on my birthday, I gave birth to you? We are so blessed to have you in our lives. Everyday that we get to watch you grow has been the best day ever. Never forget that you are loved and will always have someone on your team as long as we are around. Our wish for you is to keep that love in your heart for your friends, your family and this earth. We know you will make us so proud this year! Your dad says that he still expects you to make the honor roll. I do not doubt that you will. The big 1-0! Enjoy your party tonight and make a splash!*
>
> *All our love,*
>
> *Mama and Daddy*

I stare at the ceiling for a few minutes. Wiping the tears from my eyes, I return the card back to its spot. The last handwritten thing I ever received from them. How many times have I read it? Vanessa never understood why I still held onto their memory so tightly. But how could she? She's never lost anyone.

It's only me who is always losing. My life—a series of losses. People don't seem to stick around as far as I'm concerned.

Seems like the best thing for me is to go where I can have even the smallest bit of support. To be closer to my remaining family. I've got a bit saved away. Not enough for long, but enough to make it work for a few months. I've made up my mind. Come Monday, I'm putting in my two weeks. Alpenglow Ridge, here we come.

CHAPTER 3

Cory

THE SHOVEL BREAKS INTO the surface of the dirt with a crisp sound.

Music to my ears.

Throwing the unearthed soil into a pile, with a satisfying plop. I continue digging the area for a flower bed. My cart is set up off to the side of the long drive and I get the occasional wave from locals driving by.

A Buick slows to the Mason Ranch sign I'm digging around. I recognize the older woman's voice before Sammie Portillo rolls her window down and I see her wide grin. "Cory! I didn't expect to see you here! I was just headed to Janet's house. I hear your boys are giving her a run for her money!"

After school ended for them, I brought them here to stay with my aunt. I've only joined them in town a couple days ago. This town is even smaller than I remembered. My old neighborhood was probably bigger. Alpenglow Ridge is beautiful with a clear view of the mountains from everywhere you go. There are no large skyscrapers or apartment complexes obscuring the view. On the other hand, only a few shops are in town. If there is something you need, that isn't carried in the grocery store, convenience store, or any of the family-owned shops in town... you'll have to drive about thirty minutes south or north to get it.

The beauty does make it so that I can see the appeal of living in the middle of nowhere, though.

Ambling over to her car, I prop my chin over my hands on the shovel I was using. "I told her as much. Nobody listens to me though. They see three cute faces and get completely blindsided." I laugh because my boys are a handful on even the best days now that school is over. I wouldn't trade them for the world on a silver platter. My ex-wife didn't feel the same.

"Well, I guess I'll be her reinforcement then. I brought lunch and a little treat. They'll love my green chili. Janet sure does." She adds a wink because my aunt does love Sammie's chili. They've been dating for the last three years and it's the happiest I've ever seen her.

Nodding, I say, "Oh, I know. She wouldn't let me have any of the leftovers last time. I almost lost my hand when I pulled it from the fridge. She closed the door so fast that I think it might be on a pressure sensor. X-ray vision or something. Still don't know how she knew I picked that container up from the other room." I make little holes in the gravel with the shovel and shake my head at how protective Janet is of Sammie's food. "Hey, when you gonna move in already?" I give her shit because it makes no sense to me, or anyone else in this town, that they live apart after dating for so long.

"Quit meddling. Old people like things how they are. I'm right around the corner and that's close enough." Her tone is sure, but I know she would have moved in with Janet yesterday if she offered.

"Call me a hopeless romantic then. I—" My words are drowned out by deep bass blaring from a hot red Mustang pulling up to where Sammie and I are talking. Long blonde hair whips out of the window and she gives us a cursory hand toss as she speeds by. I guess that's supposed to be a greeting. She makes the quick turn down the Mason Ranch driveway. Dirt and gravel kick up under her tires making me shield my face with my forearm. The crunch of her tires can be heard over a woman rapping about how she does what she wants. I'm still staring after the red car, mouth open when Sammie clears her throat.

Turning to my aunt's girlfriend, I also clear my throat, neck blazing with irritation rising to my ears. "What was I saying?"

Sammie just laughs and shifts in her seat, moving her elbow off the window. "You weren't saying anything. I'm going to Janet's. I'll see you tonight." I agree that I'll be seeing her later and throw a hand up at her exit.

Who the hell was that?

I get back to digging the flower bed. Each stab into the ground brings my nerves down. I find the peace I feel when working with my hands in this way. I begin mapping out where each flower will go and make holes just large enough for each flower to fit into. The cart I'm using today has the palettes of the flowers I'll be planting. It takes me a few hours, but I'm happy with how the crisscross rows of blooms stretch out in front of the bricked pillars of the gate.

The only thing that makes me happier than flowers arranged beautifully in the ground, is arranging them in bouquets. I don't want to be a florist or anything. I like the appeal of an immaculately decorated home or business, complimented with the greenery and florals to match. The feeling of presenting a place in its best light. A close second would be the perfect bouquet for a coffee table or someone's hands. Too bad it's been years since I've been able to present anyone with that kind of gift without coming off as clingy or as if I expect more.

I shake my head, trying not to think about the number of times I have made that very mistake in the past. My cart squeaks the whole way up the long drive back to the main house. I pass the house, to my blue truck parked off to the side between the barn. The sexy little Mustang sits crooked and half on the grass where the paved parking area ends.

She's gonna get a flat like that.

I don't know who she is, but no one should disrespect a car this nice. It's a shame really. On that note, it could use a wash too.

I'm loading up the empty palettes and the remaining bags of soil into the bed of my truck. This gig at Mason Ranch is a huge help and it's something to keep me busy. I will need more like it to establish something worthwhile in this town. The small town gossip train needs to travel about me in my favor to bring in more clients.

My aunt warned me about how quick news travels around here. I'm already the poor divorced dad of three who gets those stupid–and by the way, not at all comforting–back pats and pitying looks. I'm divorced. Not dying. You could never tell that by how they've looked at me when Janet introduced me to people.

Danny Mason, the man in charge around here, told me he wanted more commercial and professional landscaping for his Ranch.

I can do that.

There's some other maintenance like cutting and baling hay that he would like for me to do. I'm not super familiar with that kind of work. He assured me that there would be someone to help me. Apparently, it isn't too different from cutting grass, just learning new equipment.

For the summer, I'll busy myself with his renovation and trying to get a few new clients, as well. I don't know how long I will be in Alpenglow Ridge, but sitting on Janet's couch won't change my circumstances. I already feel better after a half day's work.

More like myself.

"Cory! Honey, did you bring a lunch?" Chandie waves to me from the back patio steps. Her bracelets and rings send sparkles dancing across every surface. It's more like a light show with how icy Mrs. Mason is.

She steps off her sidewalk and continues her stride to my truck. She tsks under her breath at the parking job on the Mustang. "Daughters, right?" She chuckles at her joke, but I just stand here awkwardly smiling and nodding because I clearly can't relate. I have three sons. All of which are under the age of seven. Chandie seems to notice my lack of true confirmation and chuckles a little harder. "I suppose you wouldn't know much about that, now would you?"

"No. Not really" I admit rubbing the back of my neck. "I thought you had a son..." I'm sure Janet said they had one kid called Reese.

Chandie laughs in earnest now. Bending over at the waist and holding her thighs. The movement makes the sparkles from her bracelet dance across my truck and I shield my face. She wipes at the corner of her eyes. "Oh, Reese would love this." She puts her arm in mine and starts walking us up the stairs. "You didn't bring a lunch did you?" She asks, repeating her question from earlier. She interrupts my inspection of the large patio that wraps around the entire backside of their house.

The sun is high now, but I know the sun sets right behind the mountains that are off in the distance. The view must be incredible from their porch.

Add the horses grazing in the pastured area or training in the fenced-off area and it's a slice of country heaven. There's a patio swing swaying in the breeze with cushions and a blanket. I imagine how nice it would be to sit out here and take in more of the small town beauty. Leaves rustle and birds chirp. The percussion of the hooves just off to the side. It's idyllic.

I shake the daydreaming from my head and pat her hand on my arm. "I didn't. I thought I'd go grab a couple of tacos from the stand over on Main and come back later. Would you mind if I used your bathroom before I head off?"

"Of course not. But I would mind if you went to that taco stand! I made way too much food since we have a few new people working here and it's going to go to waste. I'll even introduce you to Reese, our daughter." She winks.

"Okay." I say slow and careful because I don't want to be rude. My stomach makes a gurgling sound now that I smell the food coming from the direction I'm guessing is the kitchen. "I'm starving."

She smiles big and bright at me. Everything about this woman is bright. We only talked for a few moments when I met with Danny before. She came into their home office and fussed over him. Chandie put a water bottle in his hand, urging him to keep his water intake up for some medication or the other. She gave him genuine smiles and soothing back rubs, while he took his medication and gruffed about doing it. On her exit, he smiled at her backside and returned to the stern man he had been with me before her entrance. I couldn't understand how they worked, but nothing seemed to dim that light in Chandie.

She points me down a hallway and says to take the third left that has the guest bathroom. I do what I need to and leave. My phone vibrates with a text and I check it on my way back to the kitchen for lunch.

Van: I know it's my weekend but I can't.

The sigh leaves my mouth before I can check it. My ex-wife is... I'd never disrespect her. But my patience is thinning more and more with each time she cancels on our boys. She is off "finding herself"—AKA robbing the cradle of some other mother, who is actually concerned with their kid. The guilt I felt for her unhappiness dissipated as quickly as she did. Vanessa made her decision. She signed the papers. Sometimes, I wonder if she thinks she divorced more than just me, but our children too. This is one of the three texts she has sent me after forgetting them at school.

Me: Right. What do I tell them?

Them. CJ, Brendan and Gabe. My life. Everything I do is for these boys. I want to be strong and support them, but this is the worst part of my life too. Feeling like I failed them. How do I tell them that their mother is canceling her plans to spend the weekend with them?

Like it's some brunch she's taking a raincheck for.

Like they aren't her priority.

Like they aren't her whole life.

They deserve to be first. My boys should have a mother who shows them love outside of the scheduled time the court required of her. Her bubble with three dots pops up on the screen a few times before finally disappearing.

It doesn't come back.

Stupidly, I stare at my phone, hoping she wouldn't let them down. Hoping like the fool I am, because I know her better than that.

She isn't going to respond.

A catcalling whistle rips down the hallway I'm standing in, startling me out of my guilt spiral.

"You look like prey."

The woman from the Mustang earlier prowls over to me. Her hips sway and her hand shoots up to flip her hair from one shoulder. The light in the hallway is sparse only filtering in through the doorways of the other rooms that are open. Each step clicks with her red boots. My eyes trail her curves from her strong thighs to her pouty lips. There's a dainty necklace that drops down the swell of her chest. My gaze follows it down, down, down…

She is stunning. Like an angel with how she radiates some healthy glow. Striking in a way that's devastating. Everything about her is a tease, that much is clear from seeing her only once.

Her beautiful dark eyes are assessing me in a way that makes me feel vulnerable and lain bare. Honey blonde hair falls over her shoulder again and she plays with it now. Flicking the ends over her chest, drawing my attention there.

"Oh no… More like roadkill." She pouts. The angel lifts my chin with a finger. "Eyes up here, prey. It's a lot easier to talk to someone that way."

My eyes lock onto hers, registering that I'm ogling her like a creep in this hallway. I felt entranced though. Even my heart is beating faster like I've run a marathon with the impact of her attention on me.

I'm doing a great job of making myself look like a complete jackass right now. On the plus side, she has to work here, so I'll see her again. Get it together, Cory. This is not the first attractive woman you've seen in your life.

I clear my dry throat, croaking out, "Sorry? Prey?"

"Yea." She pitches a thumb over her shoulder at the wall behind her. Mounted there is a big stag stuffed on a plaque. The horns are sprawling to create shadows along the wall.

My brows furrow, "I look like a stuffed deer?" I question aloud.

Is this a compliment?

No, right?

That thing is dead.

She just compared me to a dead thing, mounted for decoration. Someone, maybe Danny, shot that creature.

She shrugs with a smirk like it's the most normal thing to say to someone. "Yea. I think it's the disappointment in the eyes." She points back and forth between my eyes and adds, "A deer in headlights if I ever saw one."

Before I can sputter or respond in any kind of meaningful way, she's already down the hallway with her phone to her ear. "Melly Mel! What you doing girl?!" She turns into the last doorway on the right and kicks it closed.

The main house is where Chandie and Danny live. Many people work on the property, but I don't think they are that welcoming to employees.

She is not just someone who works here.

She has to be their daughter.

Reese.

Chapter 4

Reese

 on telling me that you were in town?" My friend's voice comes through the speakerphone. It's hard to take Mel's anger seriously when she sounds like what I imagine Tinkerbell's voice would be like. Small bells tolling and ringing. "Notice via selfie with Chandie is not acceptable. And that was from Facebook. Not even IG Stories."

Kicking the door shut, I flop down onto my bed. The black pillows flop onto the ground along with my boots. "Yea and what kind of friend are you? You saw Chandie with me in her clutches and you didn't try to save me. She's been catching me up on town gossip." I look over my manicure and reach for a file from my purse beside me. "All while acting like this visit is not supposedly *so important* that I needed to be woken at eight AM." Laying back onto the bed, I stretch my toes trying to get them to loosen up after being strangled in those boots. I've not worn them enough and they need much more breaking in.

"You should have called Chloe. She's always looking to fill up her gossip tank." Our friend, Chloe, is a hair stylist. The best in this town. Possibly in Colorado, but don't tell her that. She'll likely raise her rates and I'm barely able to stay on her schedule as it is. Her appointments are booked at least three months in advance. I know that because she is the only person I have ever trusted to keep both my hair and my extensions, the signature honey blonde tone I love. She doesn't make any exceptions to that rule. *Heifer.*

"Let's fix that then. I'm only telling this story once." I huff a sigh as if it pains me to gossip with my girls, but the news I just learned was too juicy not to share. "Lemme call you right back."

We've kept in touch over the years, but we aren't as close as we once were. Occasional calls or texts keep me somewhat in the loop on what's going on with them. Thanks to social media, we're able to share all the big stuff with photos included.

I dial the two of them on FaceTime. "Well if it isn't the black cat? Rumor is that you just slunk back in town." Clo's voice booms into my room.

I turn the volume down because there are all kinds of people roaming the house right now. Like that little snack I saw on the way to my room. Correction, big snack! Strong shoulders and big hands. Definitely over six feet. The man was thick. How's that saying go?

How do you eat an elephant?

One bite at a time.

I'm sure every morsel of that man would be scrumptious. I shiver thinking about what it would be like to have those big hands on me...

Those eyes though. He looked like a kicked puppy.

Prey, indeed.

But not my kind of prey. If he's working here, I can't see what my efforts would even gain me.

Flipping my hair over my shoulder, I look at the girls on my screen. "It almost sounds like you don't like my slinking." I make a pouting face into the camera and bat my eyelashes.

"The slink in, I don't mind. It's the slinking out that I hate." Clo rolls her eyes. I know she's upset that I will come back to get my hair done and then dip out within the hour. I never stay longer.

She found happiness here. Married her high school sweetheart and they have an amazing life together. That's not here for me.

Gotta get Sally on the road as soon as my necessary upkeep is done.

Sally is my Mustang.

She is fast and sexy.

Just like me.

Clearing my throat with a flourish, I say, "That's kind of the topic for today's discussion, ladies."

Melody bounces in her seat and Chloe puts the phone on her station's table against the mirror. "You're lucky I finished Pam's hair early then. I've got like 20 minutes until my next cut and color."

"This is actually important, you two. Danny is adding a camp to the Ranch. Like an actual camp—for kids."

They both stare into the screen blinking for a moment, waiting for me to continue. "Okay. I knew that. How is this juicy gossip? I think Chandie might be losing her touch." Melody's soft voice chimes in.

"Yea. I did too. What am I missing?" Clo says.

"I have been begging my dad for years to make this a camp for kids! And every time he told me he would think about it. He told my mom that he was thinking about the addition before... before the heart attack." I stutter into the last bit of that sentence. The fear I have over losing my dad is still present. "But, now that things have changed, he wants my help."

At breakfast, he sat me down at the dining table. My mom hovered at the doorway. If I hadn't been panicked before—that had gotten my attention. This was the position they took when I was in trouble all through school. I was a fan of sneaking out without their permission. This was a common occurrence.

"*Time is not on my side. When something like this happens to you, you get to think about what you would have done differently. And you are always what comes to mind. Maybe it is bait because we want you here more. But I don't care. You had this dream and I want to help you make it come to life. We know you're not a horse girl anymore, but maybe you can get us going... Your mom and I want your help starting Masons' Horsing Around.*"

"It's finally happening," I say.

"And he's putting you in charge of it?" Mel beams into the phone now holding it closer to her face. "That's amazing! Congratulations, Reese!"

My face falls a bit at her excitement. Since this was my dream, I can see how that would be her conclusion. Her deductions were the same as I had, as well. But, you can't run a start-up when you don't even live in the town it's starting up in. I start combing my fingers through my hair, nervously perfecting the strands in my tiny rectangle of the call.

Chloe notices before I can recover quickly enough. "He didn't. Did he?"

"Not exactly. He said he would like my input on some of the plans he has for the place. There's a lot to do before this can be real, you know? And with how tired he's been... He just needs some help in the meantime."

"So, what does that mean? I think I know, but I don't want to get excited again." Melody's impatience is palpable through the camera. I feel a little bad letting the silence stretch for effect. "Hello?!"

"He asked me to move back home. Just for the next couple of months." I hold my hand up as if it can hold back their whoops and cheers. "Temporary. It's temporary! I stressed that with him and I'm stressing it with you two, as well. Drea's included in that too, but she's working so I'll fill her in later. None of that scheming either! I see it brimming in your eyes, Mel." I laugh thinking about Melody and her love for Alpenglow Ridge. She moved here when we were juniors and though it was kinda rough for her, she made it through because of us.

"Stipulations aside, we still get to celebrate right?!" Mel tentatively clarifies.

"We're dragging you out if we have to. Cinnabon, close your eyes and ears." Cinnabon is a nickname Chloe has been calling Melody since we were in school.

"What for?" Mel asks.

Chloe sighs, "I'm gonna talk about Mack."

The silence is quick to take over the line. Mel nods once and then a couple more times before saying, "I need to get back to work." She hangs up without waiting for our response and now it's the one video coming through the chat.

"That's one way to do it." Chloe winces. She's bumping the ends of her bob under with a curling iron, looking at the phone like it stinks. "She says that she's happier now that they're separated and everything is normal." Raising an eyebrow at me, she asks, "Does that seem normal?"

"No. It does not. How is Mack holding up?"

"Oh, he isn't. He is a mess and what's worse is that Mel won't talk to him anymore. He says she just woke up one day and was... different. And I agree with him. Mel is so weird about Mack now. She won't talk to me about it. From the looks of it, I'd guess she isn't talking to you about it either."

"Well, Mack was more mad than you two were when he found out I signed that lease in Denver." Signed... Accepted the keys... Same, difference for this conversation's sake. "I haven't talked to him in a couple of months since everyone was visiting Dad." He had been really cold. Mack's family owns the land next to ours and he had been my friend... probably since birth. "You think he'll take my call?"

"Yes. He's too nice not to. It might cheer him up to know you're back. Outside of moving back, which is huge news, what else happened at this ominous breakfast?"

"Temporarily." Checking my teeth in my tiny reflection on the screen before I say, "Apparently, they hired Janet's nephew to redo all the landscaping on the property and some other stuff. Mom said he was cute and single."

"Did you see him?"

"Nope. I'm sure I will though. He's not for me either way. Man's got three kids. And where there's kids—there's a mom. Possibly more than one mom. That just sounds like a bunch of drama I don't want to be a part of."

Chloe laughs, picking her phone up again. "Girl, you don't want to be a part of anything. Stop lying to yourself. Cause you're not lying to me!"

I scoff at her assessment. "Whatever. I'll have you know I had a date just last weekend."

I recall the boring dinner I went on with the guy Garret? Grant? Maybe it was Gareth? I don't remember. The restaurant was incredible though and he had me picked up in an Uber black. He won some cool points for that. But...God. He was so boring! I wouldn't call him back if he was the last man on earth. Money does not equal personality even if it did equal privilege.

"On second thought, what's it like here? Anyone interesting grabbing beers at QB's?"

"You know I don't know. I only go when it's closed. Quincy will have me slinging beers if I'm in that place during open hours. I'm not playing with him like that." She sprays something onto her hair and brushes it again. Quincy is the high school sweetheart I was telling you about earlier. He owns the sports bar in town. When he first opened, Chloe was his main bartender until it got enough traction to hire a full staff. Now, Drea and Mel work there. Mel is only there on weekends since she works at AR high school during the week.

Chloe's salon, Tuft, is in the apartment space above the bar and they could not be more different. Where her salon is sleek, modern and sophisticated; QB's is all exposed brick, industrial pipes and sports pennants. Suits them perfectly.

Laughing I say, "I don't blame you! I remember those days."

The bell over Chloe's door rings. Excited chatter from her next client increases in volume the closer she gets to Chloe's booth. "I'm gonna call you later okay? We need to figure out how to celebrate! Text me."

Agreeing, I hang up with Chloe. New notifications for texts from Teddy are waiting for me when the call ends.

Teddy : {Picture MSG}

Teddy : I picked something up for you.

I would normally be happy to see a little LuLu Lacey bag. But not from him. Never from him anymore. I clear the messages again and try not to think about the fact that I will have to face him for defying his demands. I won't be able to avoid him forever while I'm here, but I will prolong it as long as I can.

CHAPTER 5

Reese, Eight Years Ago

"Oh, you scared me!" Startled, I jump back. My arm catching on some leads hanging from the hook on the outside of the stable I'm checking. I love to come say good night to our horses after everyone else has gone home.

"I'm sorry." His smile is small. He appraises my body in a way that I can feel, like he's touching me. The heavy canvas jacket that I'm wearing billows in the same breeze that rustles the leaves around the barn. "I was coming to say good night to Legend." He reaches out a hand to give his tan horse in the stall before me a treat. Legend wastes no time in poking his head over the door to take the treat from his owner's hand.

I look over his dark grey suit. The legs are stuffed into rubber work boots for him to come out this far into the working area. No doubt because he didn't want to scuff up his loafers on the wood chips over here. "You come here often to say good night?"

He chuckles and the sound makes me feel a little less uncomfortable being this far from my house alone. "Not always. But tonight seems like a good night to do it."

"Why is that?" I look up at him and his blue eyes sparkle with mischief.

"Well…" he seems to consider for a little while before continuing, "Danny is taking quite a few of the horses up to Estes for the big wedding this weekend. I heard, let's say around town, that my son is planning to throw a birthday party here in our absence."

My face heats because I'm no rat. If I tell him the truth, I won't be doing my friend any favors. "Mr.—" I begin, but he cuts me off with a finger to my lips.

"Call me Teddy. It's a nickname." I stand there not knowing what to do. My eyes dart to the house. He turns my face back to his. "I'm not mad. I want to make sure he's safe. You only turn eighteen once, right?"

I nod slowly, still a little unsure if I'm safe out here with my father's friend.

"And how old are you these days?"

"Seventeen," I answer.

His eyes sparkle even more and the small smile he wore has grown much larger. "You have definitely grown from the last time I really saw you." Another breeze whips through the narrow walkway. I pull my jacket tighter around me, though I don't think the chill is coming from the wind. I don't quite know how to respond to what he's saying besides maybe... yep?

His smile never wavers when he adds, "Like I said, I just want him to be safe. You two have been friends for a long time. My wife tells me about how you are at the house often." He pauses as if he's thinking about something. "You know? We could be friends, too. No one calls me Teddy anymore so that can be a nickname just for you. What if I were to call you Ree? Does anyone call you that?"

"Not really."

"Perfect." His smirk is admittedly charming. I have no doubt that for a man his age, he is attractive. I've never been much into suits and gelled hair, but on him, it works. "As my friend, I could help you with the party, just a little bit. I don't want this thing to get too out of control. You can imagine how bad that would look for me." He smooths a nonexistent wrinkle from his suit jacket. "Here let me take your number down." That's when I realized that he wasn't trying to straighten a wrinkle, but instead looking for his phone. "I think I left it in my car." He turns for the driveway. When I don't move, he says, "Come with me." The command came from his mouth easily. Something in his tone makes me comply.

Following him to the driveway in front of the barn, my jaw drops at the beautiful convertible parked haphazardly in the gravel. Its sleek black lines glint in the safety lights on the outside of the barn building. I am no expert when it comes to cars, but this one has to be fast. Most importantly, it was sexy and… expensive. Everything about Teddy seemed pricey. Though he is never around much. Anytime I've seen him in passing, there was something affluent and alluring in his mannerisms. He presses a button on a fob he produces from his suit pocket. The lights of the car, illuminating in time with the small chirps.

I was riveted in place by the luxury.

He runs a hand down the hood before opening the door. He sits in the driver's seat with more grace than I could imagine from a man his height. Teddy grabs his phone from the cupholder, but I was too busy still gaping at how beautiful this car was. He chuckles again, and this time it sounds more pleasant than before. Stepping from the car again, he hands me the phone.

"You like cars?"

"I don't know. But this is way nicer than my pickup." I throw a thumb over my shoulder to the silver F150 that's parked on the concrete drive by the house.

"That it is." Not exactly an insult because anyone with eyes could tell that these two cars did not compare.

I take the phone from his hand, but I hesitate. "What exactly do you want me to do with this?"

"Save your contact. Send yourself a text. That way we can talk." Looking from the phone to his face, he adds, "About the party, of course."

I nod slowly, doing what he asked, and handing his phone back to him. He smiles at me and gets back into his car. "Whatever you're doing out here, you probably want to hurry it up. I wouldn't want anything to happen to you." He says with a wink before leaving me there, watching his car go.

A COUPLE OF DAYS later, I can hear the voices of people talking, coming from the kitchen. It's not uncommon for my mom to have people over, especially on a Sunday. The sweater dress I'm wearing feels itchy when I walk into the open space and see Teddy sitting there with his wife. They're with my mom and dad having eggs and bacon. The smell of coffee mixing with the combination of bacon grease in the air.

I stand there guilty though I don't know why I feel so guilty.

Just two days before, Teddy met me at a liquor store right outside Denver to load the half keg of beer into the back of my pickup truck. This was my friend's dad after all. How could I be in trouble when it was him who provided the alcohol? Though he had good intentions, my friend still ended up getting completely wasted. He and his girlfriend had a huge fight and I'm pretty sure they're broken up now.

My thoughts are spinning through my head, but I resume my path into the kitchen before anyone can notice that I'm acting weird.

Teddy and I have a secret.

It feels kind of naughty... and I like it.

I grab a mug from the cabinet above the coffee maker, allowing it to slam, announcing my presence.

"Reese, honey! You're up. Good morning!" My mom comes over to squeeze me by the shoulders and kiss my forehead. "These look beautiful! Did Chloe do them?" She runs her hands over the long honeyed single braids. "I love them!"

I shrug. "Thanks. I think the blonde suits me. Plus they are so much easier under a hat." I use a hand to flip the hair over my shoulder.

My dad grunts in approval, still sipping from his coffee. No doubt wishing he wasn't entertaining people this early in the morning. It's only nine, but if I'm honest, there would never be a time that he would approve of people visiting. He much prefers the company of cattle and horses.

Teddy's wife comes over and holds the braids up by the ends that graze just the top of my butt. "This is really beautiful. Babe, doesn't she look beautiful?" Teddy's eyes meet mine and I blush under his gaze. He looks me over for a moment and the itchiness I was feeling before, returns. I scratch at my arm in response to my rising body temperature.

"Very beautiful." His approval rings like a bell through me. No one notices his wink. Both my mom and her guest continue chatting to each other at the coffee pot, refilling their cups.

I take my cup and walk towards my side of the house. I don't get past the living room before I feel his hand on my arm. I turn and meet his piercing stare.

"Did you have fun this weekend?" he asks.

I assume he means at the barn rager. Tapping my fingernails on the mug, I think about how best to answer this question. "I did. It will definitely be one to remember... for a long time. I think your son and his girlfriend are broken up because of it though."

"So that's why he's been holed up in his room." Teddy seems to be thinking aloud. He still hasn't let go of my arm. His grasp isn't tight, but the heat from his hand is not helping with how overall hot I feel in this dress right now. Looking up from my arm to his face, I can see that he's watching me again.

"Do you have a boyfriend?" He asks.

"Tame me? I think not. Though I'm sure many think they are."

His eyebrow lifts, "Interesting choice of words." He releases my arm. "Why would they think they're your boyfriend, if you don't?"

I consider my answer for a bit. "I like nice things. Really nice things. But, I would rather not be the one to spend my money on them. Like my hair. Chloe may be my friend, but getting into her chair isn't cheap." I roll my eyes. "No friends and family discount. So, boys will pay for that stuff so that I'll spend time with them."

He chuckles, blue eyes sparkling. "That's all it takes?"

"Sure, I guess. My time costs money. If I'm not training horses, I'd rather be doing nothing." I shrug. "Dad's pay is shit, also." I flip my hair over a shoulder again just missing his body with the swing of my braids.

He sits on the couch and I sit on the chair opposite, liking where this conversation could be going.

"So hair? What other kind of stuff do these boyfriends buy you?" He puts air quotations around boyfriends. The gesture is so similar to one I've seen my friend do. It makes me smile just a bit thinking about how they must be quite similar.

"Umm... let me think. Josh buys me lunch so I'll sit at the table with him. Allen G bought me some really nice snip toes. I barely had to break them in the leather is so soft... I don't know just some stuff I like."

He scratches his chin. "You know I'm an expert at making deals." The full weight of his attention settles on me as he leans forward onto his elbows. His voice is lower now. "What if we had a deal?"

I lean over the coffee table, whispering, "Like another secret deal?"

He mimics my posture, leaning over the coffee table too. Up this close, I can smell the deep, clean cologne he must use. "You tell me what you want and I'll get it for you. I can do better than a couple of school lunches."

Skeptical, I ask, "And what do you want in return?"

"Let's start with time."

"Time?"

"Yes, Ree. Time." I smile at his nickname for me. Now, I like it. I like it a lot.

CHAPTER 6

Cory

"YOU OKAY, CORY?" CHANDIE touches my arm softly, a look of concern etched between the lines of her eyebrows.

I've been staring at the cheesesteak sandwich she made for far too long.

What happened in that hallway?

And why did I like it?

I'm fairly confident that Reese read me in that moment more clearly than anyone else has.

Prey.

What would a woman like that do with a man she considered prey? Her keen eyes took me in and I didn't mind it one bit. Out of my league doesn't even begin to describe what she is to me. A woman like her would never go for me. I barely have time to think let alone date someone.

Date? Definitely not.

I'm starting over in this town. I need to be focusing on getting more work done and not on trying to date anyone.

Women think babies are cute, then they find out you have three and they run for the hills. She would likely be the same, anyway.

"I'm sorry. What were you saying?" I take a bite out of the large sandwich and put it back onto the plate. Concentrating hard on keeping the concerned look off my face.

"I asked how the boys liked small town life. Janet tells me they're a handful. Especially Brendon."

"Oh, Bren? Bren is a fun little guy. I call him the blur. One day I'm gonna get him on a track and see what that time looks like." If I ever figure out how to schedule that kind of stuff with my own schedule.

She laughs. "With that many boys, your sanity would probably benefit from some activities like that." She pats my arm again since I've been looking down at the sandwich, picking small pieces off of the bread. "I don't know if Danny told you about what we're doing here, but I would love for them to join us for the summer."

Her eyes are soft with understanding. I know in this moment that Chandie is a truly good person. Good people are hard to find. My own mom used to tell me about how hard it was to find good people in the world. If you were lucky enough to find one, keep them in your life. Simple enough advice.

I have failed to do that in the past. I don't have room for any more bad people in my life.

"I'm sure I will find something for them to do besides driving Jan up a wall. I really appreciate the offer, but you don't have to do that."

"Oh, honey. It's not an offer. I am an amazing friend. My friend is currently going insane with those boys running through her house. I simply can't allow that to happen." I wince at her words though they aren't malicious. "She doesn't want you all to feel rushed or unwelcome, so she is too nice to say it. We're opening the camp on a small scale, somewhat like a trial run. Just the kids and the Mentors group on the property to see if this is really possible. I can hold the spots open for your boys to join us. It will give you some peace of mind knowing they're right here. It will also give them something constructive to do. Little kids need to run around and soak up the sun in the summer. Let's allow them to do that, huh?" She holds my gaze and I'm certain that this wasn't a conversation at all. Chandie had already decided.

"I just don't know if I can afford to do that for them, Chandie. I'm not really established in this area and I'm still—"

She cut me off in the middle of what was going to be a long list of reasons why I couldn't accept her kind offering. "I'll take care of it. I said I was an amazing friend, right? Not just to Janet." She gives me a wink. "I'm gonna go see if Reese will join us for lunch." With that she leaves me at the table, sparkles skittering off the walls of the dining room on her exit.

When Danny explained what he was looking for, I didn't ask much about the project itself. It was very standard and similar to a few other requests that I was familiar with. Somehow I had not thought about getting my boys involved in it.

Opening my emails, I check the correspondence between Danny and me for more information. I don't find much. I'll have to ask Chandie when she comes back. I spend the next ten minutes eating the rest of my sandwich, so I can get back to work. There is still plenty of time to figure things out before anything happens with the boys.

"You out in the stables with us?" I look up to see a tall, dark skinned man making himself a sandwich on the kitchen island. He holds a plate with two hoagie rolls open to pile in beef, peppers and onion with the tongs Chandie left out for everyone to use. The spray cheese makes a low hiss as he coats the tops of the grilled meat and onions.

"Uh... No. I'm doing the landscaping."

He moves to the next catering dish and piles steak fries onto a new plate, but pauses when I answer him. "By yourself?" He looks at me sympathetically.

I guess I'm not going to escape that look today. I grit my teeth against the, now rising, irritation. Is *Pity Me* stamped onto my forehead or something? This man does not know me or the shit I've been through.

"Yes. For now." The words are muffled by my clamped teeth. I take a slow breath before continuing with less tension. "I'm putting a team together. Been in town just a few days."

He picks up his two plates backing toward the doors leading to the porch. "Well if that's the case, I know a couple of people who need the work. Take my number down."

My previous frustration quickly switches to elation at a lead on a team. He was right to be worried about me trying to do everything myself. If I am to make this into a real business, I'll need more than my two hands. "Yea.

Okay! That would actually be a big help." I go to add a new contact on my phone realizing I don't know his name.

He chuckles a bit realizing what I have. "Name's Anthony Dupont. Everyone calls me Tony. I'm the Ranch manager."

"Cory Whitfield. You don't understand how much this helps me. I appreciate it."

He nods. "Don't thank me yet." He rattles off the number and adds, "Send me your name in a text and I'll pass it along. Cool?"

"Cool." He leaves out of the door, back first, grabbing a fry with his teeth.

I clean up after myself and reload my cart to work on the other side of the sign out front. The squeaking of my wheels gets quickly taken over then by the pounding of hooves as a brown horse cuts by me.

"On your right!"

Honey blonde hair ripples in the wind. Her round ass bounces as Reese leans forward on her horse, willing it to run faster. Red boots gripping the side of the horse's body.

There's such precision in how she commands the horse. I watch her the whole way over to the fence. She slows the horse and hops down to unlatch the gate there. She gives the horse so much affection, leading her through the gate, that I feel a little jealous. I have no business feeling jealous when I don't even know this woman. But, having her attention for the short period of time I did was intoxicating and I want more of it.

Where the hell is she going?

"Better not let Danny catch you drooling after his daughter like that," Tony calls from near the barn. Sitting on a folding chair, he's down to the second sandwich.

"I wasn't drooling." *Maybe a little bit.*

"Check your chin, brother. Want a napkin?" He laughs and lifts one in the air from under his plate.

I can't be mad because she is drool-worthy. I exaggerate wiping my chin before I stack the pallet of ornamental grasses onto the cart. Looking back to where Reese rode off, I can see her tying up the horse now. There is something sexy as hell about a woman on horseback. And this woman knows exactly what she's doing up there.

"Man, you're really making it too easy to clown you right now. You gonna daydream the rest of the day or are you working?"

"Hey, you're not my manager," I toss out at him. "I'm going." Besides, it will be far easier to daydream about her when I don't have an audience to witness all the thoughts I'm having.

There's no harm in thinking, right? I could never have her, but a man can dream, can't he?

CHAPTER 7

Reese

I STUFF MY FEET back into my boots, on a mission. The dial tone drones on in my room on speakerphone.

Voicemail.

I expected as much despite what Clo said. I grab my keys, charger and purse off the dresser, in a hurry to get across the property.

Swinging my door open, my mom stands there with her hand up, like she was about to knock. She chuckles, "Going somewhere?" Her gaze is appraising as it lands on my face. "In a hurry, too." Squeezing my shoulder, she asks, "You okay?"

"Yea." I grab the small bottle opener that's also a switchblade off my nightstand. Returning to the doorway where my mother stands, I say, "You know you don't have to ask to come in here."

"Sure, sure. You look like you're headed out anyway. I was just going to see if you wanted some of this food I made." She waves a lazy hand down the hall. "Or I can pack it up for you, too."

"Oh, that's perfect actually. Maybe Mack will be more willing to see me if I bring food."

"Mack?" My mom's eyebrows shoot up. We share a look that from me means, drop it, but from her means that she won't drop it. "Why are you going over there?"

"I can't visit an old friend?"

"You usually don't."

I flinch at the words. She didn't mean for them to be an attack, but the words hit me in the chest all the same. Mack was my best friend growing up. Before I started middle school with Chloe and well before he met Mel. We were still close until he and Mel started to have problems. He shut me out convinced that I was taking Mel's side. Which is ridiculous because Mel won't even address their relationship with us. Outside of saying, "I just don't want to talk about it." Moving from Alpenglow Ridge only made the distance between us easier to grow. When he came to visit us in the hospital, it was the first time I had seen him in almost a year. All that changes today. He lives next to me and, honestly, I miss my friend. "I will see him today."

"He needs that."

Needs.

Mack was the heart and soul of our friend group in high school. He knew everyone and everyone loved him. When Mel came to Alpenglow Ridge, he fell for her and dude was obsessed. I thought he had only a chance in hell with the new girl. I first met her as he walked her to our English class. When she agreed to date him, I was... nervous. He just always seemed to love her more than she loved him.

"You're probably right. If I'm gonna be here for the foreseeable future, I should try to—" What? Cheer him up? I'm in the middle of this truthfully. Being in the middle can work to my advantage. Since I'm not entirely sure what I can offer him to help, I settle on, "—reconnect. It's been a while since we just talked."

Mom gives me a small smile and brushes some of the hair from my shoulder. "I'll pack the sandwiches then. And maybe a little something extra for Mack-attack." He is a grown man, but my mom still calls him the same nickname she has since we were little. She strides down the hallway in her signature sparkle. I grab a couple more things from my suitcase before I follow down the hallway my mom just left.

My boots click on the tile as I slowly walk down the hall. I take time to actually look at all the frames hung up on the left side. Pictures of friends and family are artfully arranged between nature shots my mom has taken from her phone. Nostalgia overtakes all my senses as I'm transported through the memories these photos unlock.

There's dad on his favorite horse, Aries, and a smaller version of me being held up by my mom. A cloud of black curls surrounds my cherubic cheeks as I squeal with delight being this close to the horses and my daddy. More pictures of the three of us hold my attention as I take all the memories in. Photos I had given mom from high school also hang on the walls.

Candid shots of my mom at various events, selling the large costume jewelry she makes. Her passion for sparkles had made her wildly popular in the state. Once I finally convinced her to make a website to sell online— it took her designs from appearing at a few artisan craft shows to being advertised in magazines and even garnering the interest of several local celebs looking for ethically made pieces.

The one picture that really made me pause was of the six of my friends and me, all laid out on the lawn at ARHS. It was just a grassy knoll on the east side of the building, but we affectionately dubbed it The Lawn for ease. Also, who wants to call it a knoll? I didn't.

I lay on Mack's stomach, he lays on Melody's stomach and Mel lays on Ty's stomach. Andrea is throwing up a peace sign. Chloe takes the picture from Quincy's lap and we all have the most exaggerated smiles on our faces. Eyes are crinkled tight and every tooth is on display. We all look so happy. I take the picture from the wall and put it into my bag with the other things I grabbed earlier.

"Here and I put some brownies in there too." I jump, startled like I was doing something wrong with the picture frame half hanging out of the top of my purse. My mom nudges me with the reusable tote she's filled with plastic containers and...

"Jack, mom? I said I was going to talk, not get drunk."

"Honey, getting drunk is a choice. Just a little might take the edge off. I put some napkins in there, too. Just in case."

"A choice, I won't be making. Thank you for doing this. I'll be back later." I give her a side hug between my two bags and hustle out to the barn.

I wave at Tony as I'm prepping Heather. He's sitting on a fold-out chair watching the other hands do work I'm glad doesn't fall to me while I'm here. I've had my fair share and it's only a matter of time before I'm out here with them again.

I swipe some cut carrot pieces from the bucket just inside the stable doors. I stuff a couple into my bag and some into my pocket. Crunching through wood shavings to get to the stable, where my favorite girl is already chuffing softly as she sees me. She bobs her head side to side over the doors sniffing at my hair and face.

Unhooking the latch, I throw my bags on the large hook on the side. I make quick work getting her saddled. Heather sniffs around my back pocket trying to nip the carrot I have stashed there. Her hot breath tickles me. "Behave," I tell her.

She knickers back like she knows what I'm saying, but doesn't agree.

"Later. Okay, baby? I didn't put those carrots in the pocket for me."

That seems to earn her approval. I mount her and we walk slowly from the building toward Mack's house. There are no gates stopping us until we get to the edge of the property closest to the Stewart's land.

Once I get past the barn, I shout, "On your right!" At this point, Heather and I have set off into a trot. Gravel and dust still fly up around me creating a low cloud of dirt from the speed we're going. I don't slow down to make sure they hear or care to make small talk right now. I need to get to my friend because it's been too long.

Chapter 8

Reese

"As far as you know, I'm not here." My booted foot is wedged in the doorway preventing Mack Stewart from closing the door in my face. *Rude.* "How did you even know I was here?"

"Where else would you be licking your wounds?" I reply, giving him a knowing smirk.

A scoff puffs from his lips before he turns from the door, allowing it to slowly creak open. He walks off toward the back of the house I practically grew up in, too. His long frame lopes towards the kitchen. Following his lead, I see he already has a tumbler of something sitting on the counter.

It's two in the afternoon.

Now the bottle of Jack Daniels feels less out of place in my bag. Chandie does know just about everything about everyone in this town, after all.

I take a seat at the island on a plush leather stool. Tossing what I've brought onto the counter, my purse slides across the surface toward his glass. He has the wherewithal to grab the glass before it goes crashing to the ground. So maybe he's not drunk. Just starting early.

His sharp look lands on me. He finishes the contents of the glass with a tilt of his head. Barely wincing at the burn of what had to be three fingers of whiskey.

Oh.

So, it's like that.

"This only confirms what I already knew was true, to begin with." I push him for conversation since he will be unsuccessful at peeling my face with his chilly stare alone. Mack looks... intimidating.

Mean.

This is not the kind of look I can ever remember receiving from my happy-go-lucky friend. A frown on his face would have been hard to conjure from memory. He was cold and standoffish at the hospital, but understandably so. The silence that chills the space around him is different and very new.

I sit there.

Just waiting for him to take the bait.

C'mon, Mack. This isn't you.

In this silence, I take in my friend. I didn't feel like that much time had passed since I really saw him.

I was wrong.

The man before me is haggard. His sandy brown hair is greasy and sticking up in all different directions. Stains and deep wrinkles are abundant on an Alpenglow Ridge High School t-shirt, that I'm positive didn't occur from today's wear. Dark circles ring his eyes and he just seems gaunt, and hollow.

With how easily he finished that liquor, I'd say his pledge to stop drinking has also been voided. The promise was to Mel, after all.

"Why are you here, Reese?" His voice is monotone and somehow irritated at the same time.

Nope. Not taking the bait then.

I allow the topic change since kidding around won't be the way to win him over. "Can't I visit a friend while I'm in town?"

"Is that something you do?" *Ouch.* Okay. That's what we're doing.

My voice is more shrill than I would like when I respond, "Why does everyone keep saying that?"

"Let me guess. *They* told you," He sneers they. His fingers make air quotes around his words. "*Mack's not holding up well.*" He pushes off his stool, walking over to the fridge to pull an identical Jack Daniel's bottle from the top. Unlike the one mom packed for me, this one is nearly empty.

Now it's my turn to scoff. "What's that voice and the fingers? *They* do care about you. Chloe is worried." And Chloe is not a worrier. More like a plan-and-execute type of lady. The concern was enough to set off alarm bells in my head.

"So she sent *you*?" The indignant tone he takes makes me feel like the shitty friend I clearly have been. His throat works as he polishes off the last of the whiskey, tipping the bottle way back. He throws the bottle toward the trash can against the wall. It goes in and clinks against what must be other bottles of alcohol. I choose to ignore the urge to question if that is the case.

"Just think of me as special forces. I brought some food. Let's have some lunch. We don't even have to talk." I shrug like it's no big deal. I'm lying through my teeth because I have all the questions and they are increasing exponentially the longer I sit here.

Have you been drinking like this the whole time?

Since when did you hate my guts?

I left to prevent something like this from happening.

Okay, that last one was not a question.

"Whatever. You know where everything is at. I'm going out back." He leaves the kitchen, but not before grabbing a Coors out of the fridge.

This is going well.

Said no one.

Good thing I'm not easily deterred because the way Mack is acting makes me see why no one has really talked to him. The switch up is not one I would have believed if I didn't see it with my own eyes.

I heat up the sandwiches in the toaster oven behind me before going to the back patio to find Mack again. He rubs Heather's neck and I knew my instincts were right bringing her with me. The crease in his forehead has softened to a somewhat content smoothness. He whispers something to my horse that I can't hear. He's offering a carrot piece in his hand for her to nibble.

It's kinda sweet. He looks younger. Like he did when we were just teenagers stuck working at the Ranch together. We used to get so territorial over who could ride which horse. Mack's family grows all types of produce and sod. The only animals they had were chickens. Not nearly as exciting as the fast and powerful horses we have. They really are the best way to keep the cattle in check. Mack loved walking across the property lines to play with them. We would spend the afternoons watching them graze in the fields if no one was there to help us ride.

We have plenty of our own horses, but we stable a few horses for others in town. Oftentimes, we're training the horse to ride and cooperate in the stables. It's a win-win situation to have so many horses at our disposal. My dad is one of the best trainers in town, and I'd like to think he passed that skill on to me. Though, I haven't been here in years, this is the kind of thing that doesn't fade with time. He taught both of us and we worked together side by side. Earning whatever little pocket change we could when we were still in school. Up until I left.

I was kind of a little shit when I was younger. When we got Heather as a yearling, I marveled over how I would finally have my own. Her red bay coat shined in the sun with her black mane blowing in the breeze. She has two white half stockings on her hind legs with matching white hooves. She was perfect in my eyes.

Mack made the *unforgivable* mistake of calling Heather *ours* instead of *mine*. I was so upset that I ran to my dad to tell him about the whole thing. It was a big blowout between the two of us back then. We fought, but we found our way back to friendship then. I'm determined to do that again. Find our way back. Horses are the way to both of our hearts.

"She's mine, you know?" I repeat the words I said to Mack all those years ago. I walk over to where she's tied up letting out the knot. I lean on the banister overlooking the large yard that's separated by low fencing. Just beyond is one of the many open fields designated for Stewart's sod production.

He scoffs loud enough for me to hear, responding, "Horses belong to no one." With a sigh, he finishes the silly little saying my dad would tell us.

"Their hearts choose you and you simply protect them." He shakes his head, resting his forehead against Heather. He gives her another piece of carrot from my saddle bag before loping back to the porch.

All our houses face away from the range on this county road. We have spent many nights watching the sunset after working hard all day, eating on my patio or his, just shooting the shit. Talking about what life would be like when we got out of Alpenglow Ridge. It's still early right now and the heat is starting to increase for Colorado in June. It's perfect weather for a sit down with my oldest friend.

"Don't go crazy, I'm trusting you." I tell Heather and drop her lead from my hand. She walks off grazing at her leisure in premium Stewart grass. Walking over to the porch, I take the seat across from Mack at the white powder-dusted metal conversation set. I'm pulling everything out of the bag, choosing to leave the whiskey and frame in until...

Hell, I'm not pulling those out until it is absolutely necessary.

"It's true you know."

"What is?" He eyes me speculatively.

Now, I see it. The hurt. It swirls in his eyes with an intensity that I was not prepared for. It's so hard to resist the urge to hug him, but I'm not. Because, one, I know that's not at all what he would want. And, two, I'm not sure if that shirt is even sanitary.

"About the horses. My dad was on to something."

"Oh, I know. When we were fifteen, he gave me that same speech, but modified it for young ladies." He does the air quotes around "young ladies", no doubt the exact words Danny used.

A laugh bubbles up out of me, uncontrolled. "He what?!" I exclaim. The laugh takes over my body now and I'm doubled over my lap. Mack begins to eat his sandwich, but a small smirk plays on his lips. Feeling composed enough to get a full sentence out, I ask, "Please tell me that it wasn't me that he was comparing to a horse?"

"Oh yes. It was you who could not be *metaphorically* tamed like these mares." He sits up a little taller mimicking my dad's serious conversation posture. He always leans to one side with his gesturing arm propped on one knee. It's a pose that says, *lean in I'm sharing trade wisdom.* "It will take far more to convince a spirit like Riesling to stay in your pasture."

"Gross," I fake like I'm throwing up in my mouth with one finger pressed to my lips, blowing my cheeks out. "He used my full government too. He meant it." I shake my head. "Why can't men and women be friends? Everyone is always trying to set people up just because they want to see you 'settled already' or even worse 'you deserve to be happy.'"

"I'll cheers to that." Mack raises his beer conspiratorially before realizing I have nothing to clink his bottle with. He shrugs and takes a big gulp anyway. "All these people come to the house saying how they know just the person to help me get over..." He pauses. Refusing to say her name, I reckon. He waves the bottle in front of him like the gesture is a substitute for the person. "Why would I want to do *this* again?"

I want to say something encouraging. This is the time to say...

What? I don't know... I am in no way in a better position than he is. How can I be encouraging? Especially with the one terrible long "relationship" I had, that I'm still paying the consequences for.

Instead of saying anything, I grab the bottle of Jack and open it. "Relationships are overrated. Either you're lucky—" I take a swig from the bottle. "— or believe in that mushy shit and are willing to ignore how much they really suck." I take a heavy swig from the bottle and pass it across the table. Giving a single nod of my head toward the bottle, I add, "Compliments of Chandie."

He grabs the bottle without hesitation, taking a swig himself. "I did think it would be us for a long time, Reese. By the time Danny sat me down for that talk, I was self-aware enough to know he was barking up the wrong tree. We weren't meant to be together in that way. Not ever. We're tied. When you left here, it felt like my sister abandoned me." I can't stifle the flinch. "Out of sight and out of mind, I stayed here. When she left..."

He speaks in a low tone. I open my mouth to cut him off, but he puts up a hand, putting the bottle down on the table. I pick it up because *this*, I will need the alcohol for, I'm sure.

"Let me say this because I don't want us to have this conversation again. You are like my blood. I don't know why you left. Why you were running, *are* running. But, I know a scared horse when I see one. When you're here in town, I don't see you. I had to hear from Chloe the last three times before Danny's heart attack. He's like an uncle to me, you know. And dealing with *her*, I couldn't be there for him or for you. And I beat myself up for that. But I know, you wouldn't let me anyway. Reese, you're still running. You come here today, looking at me like I'm broken. You might look nicer than I do right now... be more put together, Reese. But this? This is your reflection too." He gestures to his crazy hair and stained shirt.

I look down to my hands, refusing to make eye contact after he's said all that.

"I miss the silent Mack from earlier." I huff a laugh and stand. I can't sit here any longer. I may get too emotional or drunk and tell him the answers to his questions. "Just read me to filth, huh? I'm supposed to be here helping you." I throw my hands in the air while I pace a little. Finding no relief in moving, I plop back into the patio chair and kick my boots up on the table. I reach for the bottle, but Mack stops me by grabbing the bottle too.

After all, a little more brown liquor couldn't hurt.

"Why are you here, Reese?"

How do I answer this question?

I could tell him about the camp addition and how my dad offered me this opportunity.

I could tell him about the little panic I had at Peak's with the texts.

I could tell him about the conversation with Chloe, leaving out that Mel was on the call.

But, I don't think any of that is the real answer he is looking for.

The real answer is exactly why Teddy doesn't want me here. He was worried about me running my mouth and here I am considering doing just that.

I don't answer his question. Instead, I pick up my tote. Just one item remains. I grab it carefully, like the precious thing it is. Placing it on the table and spinning it to face him properly.

He stares at the frame for a moment before picking it up. The glassy glint in his eyes makes my own burn in anticipation of tears. This picture from eight years ago must feel like a lifetime to him as well.

"I miss us too." My voice is barely a whisper. If I acknowledge the loneliness I've felt any louder, the tears may actually roll. I wipe at the corner of my eye with a knuckle before standing again. With more conviction, I add, "Jack's yours, but you will be back at work tomorrow. If you aren't walking back through the gate at seven, I'm coming with the bullhorn. I'm not bluffing either. I found it in my closet earlier." I call Heather over and give her a rub on the neck. "Be there," I say to Mack before I walk her over to the gate just knowing I'll see my brother bright and early.

CHAPTER 9

Reese

"To Reese finally moving back to Alpenglow Ridge! Cheers!" Mel's pixie voice shouts as she brandishes the shot glass into the air.

"Temporarily!" I add over the clinking of shot glasses. The blue liquid sloshes over the rims of the four glasses before we all take the AMF shots. Each of us puts our empty glasses on Andrea's tray she has sitting on the edge of our booth at QB's.

"For the longest time in existence, since you high-tailed it out of here more than four years ago." Chloe sips from her pale beer. Her bright orange jumpsuit and matching dangling earrings glare neon in the dim lighting. I glare right back at her little comment. "What? Don't act like it ain't true. I love you to bits, but you act like the law is on your tail for murder when you come upstairs. Checking windows and shit. It makes me nervous."

"I wasn't checking windows. You're exaggerating." I sip from my White Claw flicking the pull tab back and forth until it comes off. Looking up, my three friends are looking at me with incredulous faces. I put my "don't push me" face on because this is not the conversation I'm having right now. "I agreed to come out tonight because we are supposed to be celebrating! Celebrating me—not accusing."

Andrea ignores me to share her evidence alongside Clo's. "Once, I saw her in the lot leaving before my shift and she didn't even get out of the Mustang. She talked to me through the window like I was begging her for change. She did call me while I was doing my opening duties. Girl, you are more slippery than oil! I can count on my hand the number of times I've seen you in here." She laughs before she slides out of the booth and picks her tray up. Mel, Chloe and Andrea share a look between each other. *What is that look?* "I'll be back with fries and onion rings later." She winks at me and pats my hand. Like she didn't just give Mel and Chloe plenty of ammo to have this talk I clearly said I didn't want to have.

"Look, that's not what tonight is. I see you building your smirking little wall up." Mel points to my face. "We are just happy you're back." She sips from a Long Island iced tea.

I've never seen her drink like this, so I'm confident this night will be entertaining at the very least.

During our senior year, Mel made a pact with Mack that they wouldn't drink except for special occasions. They were limited to one drink when a party at his house got out of control and he nearly O.D. from alcohol poisoning. She was distraught and refused to talk to him again. To see them both drinking again makes me feel like their separation is real. Like it truly is over. And what kind of friend am I to just now see it for what it is?

In the past week, my daddy and I have been ironing everything out for the camp to integrate seamlessly. The trick is scheduling with the operations already commencing on the ranch. With any luck, in a week's time, we should be ready for that trial run. It will be a fun place for kids in town who are old enough to join the horsemanship program. My mom has a list of young ones interested.

Not only will we be teaching them to ride, but also how to care for the horses. When they aren't with the horses, our partner has their own Colorado-based nature activities the kids will be able to do. There's also games and activities to keep them entertained with something other than their screens. I haven't been that involved with that part of the planning, but I trust that my parent have done the research in picking a partner.

Mack was there at 6:55AM to open the gates for the other hands on Wednesday. He went to the stables to start his day with the newer four years that are ready to be trained properly. It's not my main purpose on the ranch, but soon enough I'll have the hang of things. There will be time to be able to teach young kids to ride just like my dad taught me. There's so much more to running a cattle ranch than playing with the horses. I loved training the new horses when I didn't have all this new business information on my plate too. Teaching people to love these magnificent creatures for all they are is where my heart will always be. It was all I wanted to do when I was younger.

"Did you hear me?" Chloe waves a hand in front of my face.

"Yea. I'm happy to be back."

"Not even close." She shakes her head. "I said, I invited a couple of the hands to have drinks too." She tries to nod her head toward Mel inconspicuously, and my eyes shift to where my friend is sitting. Her pink top shimmers in the light. The short puffed cap sleeves and ruffled peplum stick out as much as the nearly neon ensemble my other friend has on.

I start doing the quick math in my head. "Oh, no. Chloe, please. I'm like their boss, now. Why would you do that? How are they gonna take me seriously?" My words feel a little garbled. They must sound that way too, but I don't ask. I really don't drink anymore. Starting with Adios Mother Fucker shots plus a White Claw might have been a mistake.

"No one told you to dance on the table tops. Besides, you are not their boss, just boss adjacent. Like any of them care anyway! We all grew up here, Reese, they know who you are."

They think they know who I am. "Right. And so now I can't enjoy myself tonight." I shove the tall can away from me and Chloe pushes it right back toward me.

"You're still out with your girls. Just relax. Keep sipping your low-cal, low-sugar seltzer water. Pretty soon, the edges will be fuzzy enough for you to actually sit back in your seat."

"I am relaxed." I make an effort to sit back further in the booth. Men, I can handle. Piece of cake... when I'm sober and have my wits about me. Being in a place like this, where virtually anyone could share information about where I'm saying and what I'm doing... I swallow more mango-scented bubbles. Good thing I packed my switchblade.

"Seriously, what is up with you? We're celebrating" Melody whines and playfully pouts. "We're single! I want to mingle. I know you hate it here, but just give it a chance. Next time, we can go someplace more of your scene in Denver. I need practice first."

"Practice?" I laugh more at the ridiculous notion than at what she's trying to do. Chloe gives me a kick under the table. "Um, ow! I'm sorry, but do you think the hands from Mason Ranch will be good *practice*? Melody, you're basically rubbing yourself in bacon grease to stand in front of wolves. They will devour you."

"Maybe I want to be devoured! Have you thought about that?" Her cheeks deepen in color at her own outburst. She drinks more from her glass and leaves only ice behind. "Maybe *sweet, little* Melody wants to have some fun too."

"Hey hey! Absolutely no judgment from me!" I put my hands out in front of me. "These men literally break mares for a living. I don't want you to get dickmatized and then we have a different heartbreak to clean up."

"Don't worry about her heart. It's just little Mel we're trying to fill up." Chloe teases.

Mel bunches her shoulders. "I need another drink. Where did Andrea go?" She looks around the bar trying to find our other friend as she makes her rounds.

"Come on Cinnabon, how long has it been? Were you and Mack even fucking at the end?"

Mel continues to get more flustered. Her brown eyes are wary at the directness of Chloe's question. She opens her mouth to respond, but I cut her off. "Gross. That's my brother. You don't need to answer that question. I will be your wingwoman. No problem." Taking another sip from my can, I turn to Chloe, "Who did you invite?"

"Just the ones I like…" Chloe pulls her phone out of her purse. There's a big grin on her face.

I circle my hand in front of me, urging her to continue. "Like who, Clo?" She's not paying attention to me at all, completely focused on whatever just popped up on her screen.

"Fluff, Mel. They all came in Tony's truck." Clo says, avoiding my question again.

Mel checks her lipstick with her phone and arranges her curls to frame her face more intentionally. I'm not really concerned anymore since Tony's coming and he's cool.

At least I will have someone to talk to.

No doubts in my mind exist about where Chloe will be. Andrea takes over the bar top with Sarah Jane. They both benefit from the after-work crowd and Quincy can be with his wife.

"Chloe said you were here, but somehow I still thought you'd bail." Anthony Dupont wears tight wranglers and a button-down shirt crisp enough to cut. The way the sleeves hug his chest and arms are the main reason why this man was my very first crush. He came to work for my daddy when I was fourteen and he was twenty. Originally from Louisiana, his southern accent was enough to earn him a starring role in many teenage dreams of mine. Unfortunately, he always saw me as Danny's daughter, so I was put in that little sister category before I ever stood a chance. His tight curls flop around his head and just over his eyebrows. They must still be damp with product from his shower after work.

"You better not touch Melody." The words came out more venomous than I intended, but I couldn't handle this man. Melody would likely never survive.

His bright white smile glistens with mischief. "You're barking up the wrong tree, little girl." He leans his forearm onto the booth to get closer to my ear. He says in a low tone, "There's only one person for me." He backs away again and I follow his gaze to the bar.

"Quincy? Interesting choice since he's married. But, I can't say I hate that picture. Though... Chloe is kind of possessive. I wouldn't cross her if I were you." I tease.

Chloe points two fingers between her eyes and back to Tony in mock suspicion. "I'm watching you, Dupont."

He shakes his head, laughing. "Don't play with me. You know I'm talking about Drea."

I laugh with him too because of course, I knew that. Anyone with eyes could see that. Except maybe, Andrea. I tap my chin, pretending to think my response over. "Do you think she knows?"

He glares at me. "I ain't on the clock, so I don't have to laugh at your little jokes."

I stand from the booth grabbing my nearly empty drink and bumping into him. "It's a good thing you're patient then." He chuckles, but offers his arm to me and I hold on for balance. The three drinks I've had are enough to make me a little bit more than tipsy.

We walk over to the larger table with tall black vinyl stools. There are a few baskets of fries and onion rings, which must have been the ones we ordered earlier. They are strewn across the table with dips of all kinds scattered among them. Two pitchers of that light beer Chloe was drinking are being passed around, as everyone pours themselves a mug.

Melody sits at the short end of the table looking like the sweet dance teacher she is. Chloe and Quincy sit across from me, though they could be sitting on the same stool with how closely they're pressed together. Taylor is at the other end of the table opposite Mel. Their girlfriend, Ashley sits in their lap, sipping daintily from a shot of some clear liquor. I chose to sit at the chair to Mel's right. From the vibe of our previous conversation, she won't need my help as wingwoman, but I'm here for moral support either way. Tony sits next to me, immediately pulling a basket of fries and a basket of onion rings in front of himself.

I nudge him in the arm saying, "Hey! They're for the table. We're all sharing."

"Nobody is gonna eat these, they're all boo'd up." He gestures around the table with a fry before he swipes some dips closer as well. "Why would I let good food go to waste?"

"I hear ya, bruh." A marginally familiar voice says from behind me. "Shots! We're celebrating and Andrea at the bar said we're drinking AMFs. A round on me!"

I spin on my stool to face the speaker. Something kind of clicks, but the connection is too foggy. "You?" My fuzzy brain can't place his face right now. "I know you." His big body is close to mine and I resist the urge to pull him even closer. The man smells good and that beard is so full and soft-looking. The combination makes me want to purr and rub myself against him like a barn cat.

"Reese, this is Cory. He's the one who's been making Mason Ranch look like someone cares about it." He smiles and gives the man a clap on the back. "Glad you could make it."

Tony introduces everyone at the table and they all turn to give him a wave or acknowledgment.

This is prey.

My prey.

No, not mine.

Just an easy mark and not one worth taking.

I remember seeing him working this week and dismissing the potential. Even if he did look good out there in his cargos. When I realized Janet's nephew is the single dad that my mom said they'd hired, it was an immediate off-limits sign branded to him. A hard-pass. A complication I do not need now... or ever. But, especially not now. My overheated, AMF-soaked insides just haven't caught up to that same realization yet.

I can't keep my eyes off him.

Cory walks around treating everyone fondly, handing them a bright blue shot with each greeting. My shot glass is the last one he passes out. "To new beginnings." He raises his glass in the air and we all clink in the middle. I take the shot quickly before I can second guess the decision. This one is not as horrible as the last.

A bad sign.

Mel sets her shot glass down first, saying, "I'm gonna sit at the bar and look available." She does a little shimmy towards me which means that the alcohol is working. Her pink strappy heels and pink purse that matches her pink poofy top is reminiscent of Teresa Barbie. She stands out in contrast to the gaudy blue and orange decor all hung up for Bronco pride. In a nightclub in Denver, she would be more appropriately dressed.

Mel sits on a stool playing the part of a lost damsel in confusion about sports. *Atta girl.* Andrea's at the bar. I trust she'll be in good hands.

Tony grabs the tray that Cory brought drinks over with and begins collecting the empty shot glasses. He puts what's left of the fried snacks on the tray and gives me a nod. "Holler if you need me. I'll be a the bar." With that, he throws a hand up and goes to the barstool at the farthest end. He stacks up the empty shot glasses in the sink just behind the counter and the tray in the rack they belong in. Making her job that much easier. He's on his phone, but I don't miss the looks he gives Drea when she gets close enough to see him. I sigh, just thinking about what it would be like to have a man love me like that.

Not him. Tony has made that clear and I'm not so secretly hoping Drea will pull her head out of her ass long enough to see it.

But someone.

My phone buzzes in my hand and I check the notification.

Teddy : It's been four days. You visited him but not me. Don't upset me, Ree.

Suddenly, I feel sick. The meager contents of my stomach are too heavy and the alcohol has made things too blurry. I grip the phone harder, wishing that I hadn't been drinking.

CHAPTER 10

Reese, Eight Years Ago

I THINK ABOUT OUR conversation for a long time. The one Teddy and I had.

I love the Ranch and training, but I like nice things too.

He tells me about how he found success in Alpenglow, but he also knew he wanted more. He went to school to become a lawyer while still honoring what his family had done for generations. I admire how he improved his small town family business, but created something bigger for himself in Denver. I actually like hearing him talk about his life with me and how he tells me that I deserve more. That I'm worth more.

There isn't that much money in working the Ranch with dad right now. I love to do it. I have never once complained. The horses have always been why. They make me so happy. Our house is nice and I know we have nice things. Being an only child has made my life comfortable. There's nothing I've asked for that my parents haven't gotten for me.

My spoils aren't as nice as the things Teddy has. I don't have many, but I know that I like designer things the best. My affinity for shiny jewelry was fostered by my mother. I have a list in my mind that's a mile high of things I've seen online. Things I've seen my favorite artists, rappers, and posh women in magazines draped in, the finest things. I want to be like them and exude that same sense of exclusivity, elegance, and class.

I know I can't just go from a horse-training hick to a high-class bombshell overnight or something. I'm cute. I know I'm just as attractive as those women, but the main difference is money and opportunity.

Teddy could be my link or the start to a demure and elegant life that doesn't involve dusty clothes and long days wrangling cattle.

My opportunity.

In class, I'm thinking about it. In the stables, I'm thinking about it. At dinner, I'm thinking about it. When I'm sitting on The Lawn eating fast food Kenneth or Nick has gotten me to get me to go out with them, I'm thinking about it.

I try my hardest to decide what I should ask for. And also what kinds of things that Teddy would want to do if we spent *time* together. Thinking about it only makes me more anxious about spending the time. Because what I want, is worth more than I can truly comprehend even spending.

It's six PM on the following Thursday and I don't have anything to do. I decide to FaceTime him since it's way better than texting and calling.

I look at myself on the phone screen, making sure I don't look as nervous as I feel until he connects. His face fills the screen. Strong jaw, piercing blue eyes, and just a bit of scruff dusting his chin. His hair is still impeccably styled.

What would a sexy man like this want to do with me? He could easily get any woman he wanted. I suppose being married is a hard stop for so many women. What he and I have isn't a threat to that. *I don't want to be his wife.*

I just want what he can give me.

"Ree." he answers.

I try to see where he is, but don't recognize anything around him. I can tell it's nice though. Wall sconces provide dim lighting and the low classical music are a dead giveaway. I can see he's moving somewhere else though.

"Teddy." I put on a demure smile. "What are you doing?"

"I'm at a bar." His commanding tone still makes me shiver a bit.

"Oh. Do you wanna let me go?" *Please say no.*

"No." He puts a headphone in. "Are you okay?"

"Duh. I'm just sitting in bed." I hold the phone up higher, so he can see where I'm laying.

"And you called me? I like that." He gives me his small smile. Approval. I like that too.

"I thought you might." I return his small smile, feeling more confident in my choice to video call him. "Are you drinking at the bar? What's your drink?"

He smirks. "What do you think it is?"

I roll onto my back. My braids fan out around me and I spend some time arranging them around my face. He waits patiently for my answer like he has all the time in the world. I bite my lip and respond, "Cognac." The fanciest alcohol I could think of.

"Final answer?" Teddy raises an eyebrow.

"Final answer." I nod.

"Wrong."

"Wrong? I thought I had the best answer. You look like a brandy man."

He laughs. "I will try not to be wounded by your guess. Gin is my drink. Never with tonic, but maybe chilled."

"Ew. I've had gin before and it's gross." I stick my tongue out and make a face. "I think I would have preferred the cognac."

He laughs more robustly now. The sounds of the bar intensify as he goes back to the area he was in before. "Settle it," he tells the person on the other side of the phone.

"You're leaving?" I ask.

"Of course. I have something far better to do." He gives me a wink. Butterflies flutter in my tummy at his response. I've never felt the kind of excitement like the kind he has elicited in me.

"What's that?"

"Talking to you, Ree."

I feel my face heat and I put an arm over my face so that I can see him over it. My cheeks are hot on my forearm and I don't want him to see how he's affecting me.

"Have you thought about my deal?" He says

"Maybe." *Um, yes!* I can't think about anything else but that. It's been easy enough to conceal in the texts and the few short phone calls. Thoughts of what I should ask for are the biggest topics on my mind, all the time.

"There's nothing you want, baby girl?" *Baby girl. Ah! Squeal.* I never heard it sound so possessive as it sounds from his lips. *Like I'm his. And I love it.*

"I want all kinds of things," I admit, removing my arm from my face.

"Tell me just one thing."

"It's going to be too much, Teddy."

"You insult me," he says. Eyebrows slanting together. "You want it and it's yours."

I pause and ponder over my answer for a bit longer. Gathering up the courage I say, "Well... I've been looking at a purse at the mall for a long time. It's cobalt blue and the leather is quilted to perfection. It's so pretty! I could probably stare at it all day."

He nods slowly like he's thinking it over. "Let's go get it then."

I sit up in the bed. "Right now?"

He shrugs, "Why not?"

"I don't know... Are you being serious?"

"Of course." He puts his phone into a mount in his convertible. Teddy leans his head back against the headrest. It's hard to see in the car with only a bit of lighting from the garage he's in, illuminating his face. He unbuttons his collar to remove the tie he's wearing. I watch him for several moments, considering my options. Each move he makes lures me deeper into the intrigue of this situation. Each button he unbuttons... My thoughts race and he catches my fascination. Giving me a stern look he says, "I don't enjoy repeating myself."

Decision made. "Okay. I'll get ready." Placing the phone on the nightstand, I flitter around my room in and out of the camera. Grabbing a henley and jeans, it takes me no time to throw on my tennis shoes, not my dusty boots, and get into my truck. After I told him I was on my way, he told me to be safe. We meet at the mall I saw the purse in.

I showed him the display case the purse was being shown in. The shiny blue leather glints from the display lights. He tells the sales associate to get it and before I could blink, I'm sitting in the food court eating an ice cream sundae with my orange shopping bag sitting next to me.

It was that easy.

I basically pointed and he swiped.

This—I could very easily get used to.

Putting my cup on the sticky table, I tell him, "Thank you, Teddy! I love it so much. I'll never be taking this purse off. I'm gonna sleep with it right next to me."

He leans back into the plastic seat with his arms crossed, making a point not to touch the table. He says, "You could sleep next to me instead. I'll keep the purse safe." He winks, but I feel those butterflies come back to me.

I cross my legs under the table and poke around at the chocolate and caramel swirls in the ice cream with my spoon. "I couldn't do that. It's a school night. My parents would ask me all kinds of questions..."

"I'm sure you could find a way." He leans a little closer to me, saying in a low tone, "After all, you love this bag so much, right? What's one night?"

"I guess you're right..."

Soon after, I follow his car to the older neighborhood that he lives in. This is the first time I have been inside of his condo. All the cars, lined up on the narrow street were fancier than any I'd seen in Alpenglow Ridge. That was just from what I could see outside of the garages.

True to his word, he did sleep next to me in his large king-size bed. We started off on separate sides of his bed. At some point in the night, he was right behind me holding his body close to mine with an arm draped over my waist.

It's the first time I ever slept in a man's bed. Everything smelled like that deep, clean scent I would always associate with Teddy. When I felt him move to envelop me, I didn't sleep for the rest of the night. Staring at the wall, I waited for my alarm for school to go off at six AM. His hardness was insistent on my back in the morning. He couldn't argue with me about leaving, since school was a priority he could understand. I got out of there as quickly as possible and to school on time.

Everything had changed that night, though.

At school, everyone noticed and was awed over my thousand-dollar handbag. Chloe and Drea were impressed by my new treat. Mel was always quieter than the rest. I felt like what I had done the night before was worth it. The exhilaration from that feeling alone was worth the night at Teddy's.

I couldn't see a possible downside. I had made my first steps to the life I knew was meant for me.

CHAPTER 11

Cory

"WOAH. YOU'RE GONNA CRACK it." I gently press the phone down from so close to her face.

Her eyes snap to me.

Nothing could prepare me for Reese's full attention. She lazily, or maybe just drunkenly given how she sways on her stool, takes in my face. When her eyes meet mine, she blurts, "You're that prey from my hallway before."

My eyebrows scrunch, in discouragement, not because I don't remember the only words this beautiful woman has spoken to me.

Reese adds, "And you're doing the landscaping." I chuckle at her slurred garble of a realization. She presses her index finger to my chest. Little sparks and tiny prickles of awareness fizzle where she makes contact with my body. I look down at her hand, lightly grabbing her wrist. That doesn't deter her from the touch. More confusingly, she says, "Off limits." She finally pulls her hand from me, making an X with her fingers.

"Off limits?" I'm always asking her to clarify her assumptions about me it seems. The prey sentiment has stuck around either way. I've had no chance to rectify it. I thought over that moment more times than I can count and each time I liked it more. What is prey if not something desired? I could be way worse things than be desired by the angel in front of me.

"Yes." She lifts her chin. "And I won't apologize for the pansies Heather ate out front. They are her favorite."

I laugh, "I wouldn't be foolish enough to think that you would." This woman doesn't seem like the type to apologize for anything.

Not that I would ask her to. She could have trampled me with her horse and I would say thank you.

How pathetic am I?

Even in the garish lighting of QB's, Reese looks radiant. The light gleams off her golden waves that bounce with each movement she makes.

Dark eyes, so intense, that look up at me under thick black eyelashes. She considers me for a moment longer, biting the corner of her shiny lower lip before she asks, "What does that mean?"

"Nothing." I cough into my fist. Needing to change the subject before I say something stupid... and expose how much I'm feeling her. "Why were you about to Hulk smash your phone?"

She doesn't get a chance to answer me before another voice chimes in. "Did you two want to get burgers or some chicken tenders?" Turning to Reese, she asks, "When was the last time you ate? You look sick." The bartender, Andrea, holds Reese's arm, rubbing circles with her thumb. Reese doesn't look sick to me, but I am a bit biased.

Something about the moment feels significant, though I can't place how yet. The look in her eyes was raw and fragile when she was checking her phone—not the consuming and calculating look she gives me.

She shakes her head and responds to her friend, "I'm good. I just need some water. You know what?" She sways. "Actually, let me get some tenders, too. And tell Tony, I'm not sharing these." She points at the man at the bar and he gives her a salute.

Andrea rolls her eyes at Reese, but smiles, responding, "I'll bring water for the table, but I'm not telling Ant shit." She sticks her tongue out at Reese just a little. I tell Andrea that I'll have the same and she circles the table gathering everyone else's orders.

"They're in love you know?" Reese whispers loudly to me.

"Who?" I drink a little of my tea relishing how easy it goes down. That disgusting blue shot was my maximum for the night.

"Anthony and Andrea. They're a cute couple, huh?" She follows Andrea with her eyes and I look over to glimpse what she's seeing. Andrea's short black bob covers part of her face as she enters the order to the kitchen on her tablet. Tony watches her and their eyes catch. Even if Reese had said nothing to me, I would have seen it. Andrea's eyes hold regret and it makes her freeze in place like she's caught in his gaze. Anthony's face stays neutral, but the intensity in his eyes could mean anything.

When I look back to Reese, she grabs my chin with her cool hand to turn my head back to them. Her friend has returned from the kitchen now, carrying more of the ramekins full of dips, a burger and fresh onion rings. "Okay? What am I missing? She brought him his order. That's her job isn't it?"

She shakes her head back and forth. Each motion makes her seem more unstable but she says, "Andrea never takes his order. He comes here every weekend she's working. He stays for her shift and sees her to her car safely." She ticks off each action with her fingers.

"So, she's his girlfriend? Is she in some kind of trouble?"

Her laugh comes out breathy, just louder than the announcers all talking at once from the tvs in the bar. I want to bottle that sound and keep it for myself as it gets louder and more free. Golden hair brushes her bare shoulders. The dark purple of her crop top stands in contrast to light brown skin that I know would be soft as silk if I ran my hands over it. She's wearing that little treat of a gold chain again. It shimmers, taunting me. It's hard not to let my eyes travel the path, but she is too busy laughing to notice my attention on her chest. Thank God.

"He wishes." She says when she catches her breath.

I wish she would hold my face again.

Her smile is mischievous like she knows a secret I don't. I like this smile, too. She throws a thumb over her shoulder vaguely in the direction of the other men at the table. "They had no problem catching me up on all the fucked up love stories in town. Tony's getting no play."

The gossip around the stables and at lunch is enough to let me know that she's right about the ranch hands. They love to get into each other's business. Tony sees and hears it all, but I've never heard them say anything about him when we have lunch.

I have never been more grateful to have run into him on the way home today. He said a bunch of them were coming to this QB's place. I hadn't been yet.

Casually, I asked if Reese would be there. Tony chuckled knowingly and told me that it was her friends we were meeting here.

Sitting and just talking with Reese feels easy and natural. She is a little tipsy maybe, but it softens her in a way I don't think I've seen in the short time I've been in town. Admittedly, I've only seen her in passing on the ranch, but she's always in motion. Either walking to the pasture or riding over to, what I've learned is Mack's house.

All the hands eat whatever lunch Chandie makes, in the barn. I've been eating with them though I never see her eat out there. When I asked about it, Tony said it was because she ate her lunch with her dad.

Though Danny has recovered well from the severity of his heart attack, he is a proud man. I saw that clear as day. He can't ride anymore without assistance. I can't imagine going through that. Reese loves her dad, that much is clear. She walks the pasture with him in the morning, so he can ride with her assistance before the hands all arrive for work.

As soon as I got home, I asked Jan if she would mind me stepping out for a bit tonight. She basically pushed me out the front door. Looking me over, she changed her tune telling me to look less like I had been playing in dirt.

Quickly showering and changing, I spent the rest of my time listening to the boys catch me up on what they had been doing all day. Jan had apparently taken them to a park in town.

My oldest, CJ, was still in a mood. He had been looking forward to seeing Vanessa tonight. I think it's hard for him because he remembers her the most. Vanessa's absence couldn't be replaced by anything and I knew that. My younger sons haven't been a part of a world where she is a strong memory. I'm grateful for that.

I know I shouldn't be, but having to soothe three boys in the absence of their mother is more than I can take, when I feel her absence too. Not the woman herself, but the partner missing from our lives. I feel the sting of that every day.

I stayed to help them get ready for bed. My guilt thinking about CJ's sad eyes before I said goodnight makes me check my phone to see if Jan needs anything.

Me: Everything okay?

"It's that look again." Reese's gentle observation is accompanied by her lifting my chin with her cool fingertips. She studies me and I feel exposed. Too exposed.

Reaching up, I cover her hand with mine. I'm finding out that I love for her to touch my face. I think it will be safer for me to just hold her hand in mine. If she keeps finding ways to touch me though, I won't be able to ignore how my dick is stirring at her concern.

I focus on her fingers. Though she works with the horses quite a bit, her hands aren't as rough as I expected. They're somewhat smooth but strong. "What look?" I ask, still tracing lines over her hand's deep creases and scars.

A man's voice booms over the chatter in the bar, "You son of a bitch!" The crashing of glass breaks my focus from how I've been memorizing Reese's fingers. She jerks back from me unstably running over to her friends crouching on the ground.

Tony is helping Andrea off the floor. She's covered in the drinks and fried food she was carrying. Collapsed burgers, fries, chicken tenders, and sauces slick the ground. Other guests in the bar are moving out of the way of the commotion. Some slipping on the food that's fallen. Mack is holding Ellis, one of the hands that I recognize from the Ranch, by the collar. He rains punches into his face without any remorse.

Reese holds Melody back, who stares dumbfounded as the fight continues mere feet from her. Ellis is restraining Mack from throwing any more punches. Blood gushes from his face in a few spots and Mack's lip is cut open. People in the bar are scattering from the chaos, still watching from a distance.

Quincy hauls Mack off Ellis. "Get the hell out, Mack! What the fuck are you thinking? Not in my bar." Mack doesn't fight him or look back at the mess he's made. He spits blood from his mouth at the man on the ground. His friend tries to pull him to the exit now, but he shrugs off Quincy's hold. He walks out of the bar staring down anyone who dares make eye contact with him. The front door slams closed behind them.

I take the opportunity to check my phone again while Mel and Reese talk in hurried, hushed tones.

Jan: They're sleeping, just like they were when you left.

I put my phone back into my pocket. The scene before me is starkly different from the chill not-date date I was on with Reese. I look around for the signature blonde mane, but I come up empty.

Chloe is helping clear some of the spills with towels on the table. The heavy rumble of a rolling mop bucket over the concrete floor comes from Tony. He's watching a flustered Andrea try to pick up larger pieces of the glass from the floor. He shakes his head, handing her the broom he was carrying and the other bartender takes the mop bucket.

"What the fuck?" Quincy exclaims into his bar. He puts his finger in Ellis' face, "You know who Mel is. How could you do that to Mack? You two are boys! And this is how you treat him? You couldn't go to him as a man and let him know this was how you're moving? If I had known it was like this..." He shakes his head with a disgusted look on his face. "It wasn't my business until you brought it into mine! All this bullshit drama. Get the fuck out too."

Ellis looks just as pissed with a towel to his nose, but he doesn't say anything. He reaches out to touch Mel's arm and thinks better of it. She sits at the bar quietly sobbing with her face in her hands now. Reese isn't with her though.

Ellis gives her another look, saying, "I'll call you tomorrow, Mel," before walking toward the door.

She says nothing before running off toward the bathroom and he leaves. Chloe rushes off after her and I'm the only one left from our shared table.

These aren't my people. I don't belong here with everyone murmuring and recovering from what happened. After searching the bar a little longer, I go to the parking lot praying that she didn't try to get behind the wheel.

I'm rounding the corner of the building to the back lot where just a few tall lamps are illuminating the lot. Her red Mustang is still in the same spot that I saw it in earlier.

But she isn't in the car.

It's not until I get closer that I hear the low voices.

I stop my advance when I see Reese is locked in an embrace with Mack.

Chapter 12

Reese

"No fuck that. And fuck him! How could they do this to me?"

I'm too tipsy to be having a serious conversation like this. Due to Mack's rage, my dinner is probably being swept up into a dustpan as we speak. I was really looking forward to the sobering effect of fried chicken and potatoes. I'm a saint for not asking *how he could do this to me*.

"Mack," I say his name with as much patience as I can muster. "What are you talking about?"

"The second *friend* who has gone behind my back to try and get at Melody. Fuck." He's pacing back and forth in front of the Mustang. He licks his split lip and curses. I'm sitting on the trunk, trying to will the two Macks in front of me to sync up. He pulls at his hair as a stream of curses pours from his lips.

"Wait. What?"

"Tyson. Remember him? And now, Ellis. What is it about me? Fuck!"

"Tyson has nothing to do with this. Just calm down, Mack. Maybe it's just time." Chloe's stepbrother, Ty, was the first to leave AR. He got into CU and never looked back. They were in some weird love triangle when we were in high school and Mel had just moved here.

"Time?" He questions incredulously, pausing his pacing for a brief moment. His face is even more red as the word spears into me. I try my best not to sway sitting here when I feel his misplaced anger piercing me. "Time for more people to trample all over what I have to give?"

He shakes his head and takes a deep breath. I can see my friend is struggling and I don't know how to help him. Of all the gossip I've sat through, I have no idea what it was like for them since I left. What I do know is that it's not my place to say anything right now.

He knows it and I know it.

If anything, I should be offended by his words. My face screws up around the rebuttal I'm containing, but I say nothing as he paces some more. I cross my arms instead against the cool night breeze.

"That's not fair. Fuck, that's not fair, Reese. Just..." His words break off and he struggles to decide what to say to me. "I'm gonna go home. I shouldn't have come." He unlocks his car with a honk and rips the door open. Hopping down from Sally, I scurry over to stop him from slamming the door closed. He doesn't yank the door out of my hand though I know he could. I know he wants to.

"Please don't do something you'll regret. Mel is trying to move on. You should do the same. You can't keep beating yourself up *or* beating up any guy who looks at her. That's not fair. If she wants to leave, then you have to find peace in letting her."

The daggers he's staring at me soften as I speak. The look of defeat replaces all the anger etched into his brow from earlier. "I don't want to hear about her moving on when I can't. I was the luckiest guy in the world having her." He gets out of the driver's seat and comes to hug me. In our embrace, I feel like we're young kids again. The nostalgia hits me, turning my stomach more than the toxic blue liquid I ingested at the bar. "But I wasn't lucky enough to keep her," he whispers into my hair. The pain in his words makes me stiffen in the embrace before I step back from his arms.

"Is that what you think? That you're not enough?" I search his face for any signs that this is an exaggeration. I'm shocked to see in his eyes that he truly feels that way. "Mack,—"

"This isn't about you, Reese. I mean, it kind of is. She's not the only person desperate to get away from me. Everyone sided with her like I was in the wrong somehow. No one comes to see me, just because. But, I see you all go to the bar and hang out and shit. I came here tonight, not because I was invited. No one invited me to what was supposed to be *your party*. I want to celebrate you being back too but no one called me." He looks to my face and it's me who put the hurt there now. "When she left, I didn't just lose her. Everyone is gone." He fidgets with his keys around a finger, getting more distraught.

I worry that I'm not helping at all because quite honestly, maybe I'm not. Though I haven't been with them, I haven't been here either. He's right. I didn't tell him about tonight. How could I when I knew Mel would be there and it was her idea to have this party? That's just one of the many reasons why I hate coming back here. I can't please everyone and there's not enough time to make everyone happy.

The guilt that I already have plus this town's admonishment for me wanting more is too much to handle. My relaxed buzz is truly gone replaced with this need to defend myself. I wanted to say something earlier, but I thought I was protecting Mack's feelings. I thought I was being a good friend. He does not think so.

There are no good feelings now.

"Don't throw your guilt at me! I had my reasons for leaving. I never saw a text from you asking to come see me or to hang out, you ass! I was in Denver—not another fucking country. When I moved away you acted just like they did. Like it was a personal attack. Like I abandoned you. And fuck that! Communication and travel work both ways. So don't lump me in with your pity bullshit. When you were happy with her, it was fine that I wasn't here. You never batted an eye. Now that she's gone, it's not.

"I feel for you. I really do and I know it's gonna be hard. One thing I won't allow you to do is have me going down with them in your mind when I'm the one here with you now. Chloe has got Mel, just like she always does. Drea and Tony have... whatever that is they have. But, we always had each other. I'm here trying to support you, *brother*." I sneer the last word just as he sneered at me the first day I went to visit him.

"Bullshit! You're here because you feel like an outlier. Like me. If they wanted you there—you'd be there." I jerk back from him, feeling insulted and attacked.

Mack doesn't care. He gets back into his truck and starts the engine. Slamming the door, but rolling down the window, he says, "I'm gone. I'll see you at work Monday."

I flip him the bird as he reverses out of his spot. I see a figure step from the shaded side of the building coming over towards me now. I'm seconds from scrambling to my car before the figure calls out my name.

"Reese!" The figure picks up their pace and the parking lot light catches the sheen in his hair and beard. "Reese, wait up!"

Chapter 13

Reese

"It's you."

I look him up and down. "Well, I'm going home. Tell them good night for me." I'm in a foul mood after everything that just happened with Mack. I don't need to add in resisting the drunken urges my body has right now. I don't know that I will resist them at this point. I'm pissed and hungry and tipsy enough to be very horny.

In this unflattering light, I can make out the hesitant smile on his face. This man looks at me like he cherishes the sight of me alone. My heartbeat quickens and I decide to get into the car either way. I don't need any more difficult situations tonight.

Nope.

No!

No.

Cory may be cute and his smile may make my own inch higher, but he is still a *no*. I'm trying to put my key into the car door to get it open when his warm hand stops me. With that soft touch alone, I'm recalling how he studied my fingers in the bar. His rough hands left little tingles that ran up my palms and arms. I'm unsuccessful in thwarting the urge to shiver at the memory. Turning in place to face him, I don't take my hand from the key in my car door.

"Why is it that you feel comfortable touching my body as if it were yours?" My tone is more clipped than I wanted, but he doesn't even flinch at the words.

Our bodies are close enough to touch since he hasn't moved his hand from mine. Whatever product he puts into his beard wafts in the breeze making it difficult not to move my face closer to his.

I want to breathe him in and inhale more deeply.

My grimace is immediate with how hard I'm working to not look at his full lips... Or how his handsome face is sprinkled with haphazard freckles like he had been kissed by the sun and dusted in its joy. I'm lost in the mix of hard and softness in the features of his face, each detail fitting more perfectly into the next.

His dark eyes are heated and confident like he knows my secret. "Should I be uncomfortable?" The smirk in his tone, makes my traitorous eyes travel up to his mouth. I could see he cleaned up before coming out tonight. I make no mention of it to him because he would no doubt take it as permission to continue whatever *this* is.

He pulls the keys from the door at that point and puts them into his back pocket.

I huff, frustrated. "Yes. You should. You don't know me, for one." I straighten from my car to lean around his body. "I have no problem grabbing those. It's just a butt." I attempt just that when he presses me closer to the car. He covers me completely and the warmth from his body is just as intoxicating as his delicious, masculine smell.

"Careful." He whispers close to my ear, his breath brushing across the shell. His lips brush against me and I can't help the shiver now. With how close he is, I know he felt it. "I might think you want to grab for them."

I use my index finger on his pec to create some space between us and he lets me. I would never let a man be this close to me without paying the price. And Cory, has paid nothing.

I may still have a little alcohol in my system, but I'll never forget myself. This is *not* how I operate.

I hear people leaving the bar and make a point to step around him. His reflexes are quicker than my still semi-buzzed movements. I'm tripping over myself and falling before I can get a hand near his back pocket. His arm wraps my waist before I can reach the fob and he's ushering me in the opposite direction of my car.

"Hey, give me my keys!" I seethe trying to ignore how good his strong arm feels around me all while trying to dig my heels in. "I'm not going anywhere with you." The words hiss through my clenched teeth.

"Do you honestly think I'm going to let you drive home when you nearly face-planted trying to grab these?" He dangles the keys in front of me like bait. "Taking you home. It's on my way and I'd just feel better knowing you made it."

I huff again. "I'll just ride with Clo and Q or Mel or something. I don't need you to do this."

Or want you to. Any nice thing a man does for you comes with a price. I almost say, but catch myself.

Though something about Cory just feels inherently good, easy. He's still a man and I can't trust him. I barely know him.

Psh. Easy? I know that has to be wrong because how could things be easy when nothing about him or his life is simple?

He doesn't relent until we're standing next to the passenger side of his truck on the other row in the lot. Cory's opening the door toward me, but I'm leaning onto it with my full weight. My back is to his front and it doesn't take long for him to give up against my stubbornness. The door closes with a satisfying thunk.

He leans close enough to my ear that I can feel the brush of his soft beard against it. "Do you think cockblocking your friends is going to make you very popular?"

He has no idea what he's talking about and that makes me laugh from deep in my chest. I can't stop the howl of laughter that breaks from my body. I bend over under the weight of the absurdity and my ass pushes against him.

He doesn't give me more space, instead he moves us closer to the truck with his large body pressing mine to the door. I don't give into the urge I have to align our hips in the delicious way my pussy is just throbbing to feel right now.

I'm never drinking AMFs again. Too easily this could escalate to something more.

Reese, he has not earned that kind of entertainment.

Instead, I tell him, "You think a fifteen minute drive is going to deter those two from a good night? Did you see how Chloe ate Quincy's face? In the bar? At a table full of people? I've seen Quincy's dick more times than I can count. I got lumped into the lies they told their parents back when we were in school. I'll be fine."

He looks me over, considering me for a few moments before letting out a sigh that flows over my neck and shoulders. "Will you just let me be a good guy tonight?" His hand is now at the small of my back, dangerously close to the waistband of my jeans. He leans down to whisper in my ear again. "Get into the truck, Reese." His calm command sends more shivers down my spine as the words fall over me like summer rain.

"Fine." I push my ass into him, expecting him to be the *good guy* he claims he is and back away. He grabs the sides of my waist, pulling my body away from the door as he opens it. With a sigh, I flop into the seat and hold my hand out. "Can I have my keys, now? I'm in your truck." I'm being a brat, but I can't help it.

His forearm rests on the door frame and he leans his forehead against it. The darkness of the night makes it feel like it's only us in this place. The light from inside the vehicle has stark shadows marring his face.

Why am I noticing how different all his features look in different lights? Stop that.

The weight of my keys presses into my palm. I hesitate long enough for Cory to close them and my hand in his. He pulls me unhurriedly towards him by the grasp and my body follows without resistance.

Our faces are close enough for me to feel his breath over my mouth, when he asks, "Who cares for you, Reese?"

A few moments pass where I try to understand what he's asking me. A smart response isn't forthcoming. There are so many things that he could mean. All of them are too much for my fuzzy brain right now. He tracks the emotions that are probably all flashing through my eyes.

I don't truthfully know how to answer this. The last person that I thought cared for me, didn't.

He looks into my eyes more earnestly than I deserve. The look he gives me makes me feel like I am the only woman in this town. In this state. Maybe in this world.

I've never had someone convey this kind of concern or sincerity with just their eyes like Cory does.

Undeterred, he rephrases his question. "Will you let me care for you?"

Damn.

He doesn't know what that means—to care for me. No one does.

He has three kids. He's living with his aunt. He had a wife. I need... I don't know, but he doesn't need me on his mind. On his radar. And definitely not to care for.

"No." I respond. I have too many things to figure out right now. Adding anything else could tip my scales too far out of balance. Moving too far from going forward to going backward. "That's not a good idea... Whatever that means."

"It doesn't have to mean *anything*. I'm not even sure what I want it to mean, but I'm drawn to you. I think you're beautiful and I know our lives aren't... compatible." He leans back from me, seeming to take my whole body in. I've turned toward him and he readjusts my legs so that they bracket his thick thighs. "I have no expectations. Can you just count me in?"

No expectations? Doesn't have to mean anything? "Count you in for what?" I ask with a disbelieving chuckle because if he's asking to hook up right now...

I should be thinking no, but my body is hoping I say yes.

Though I don't know if waking up in Chandie's house together will be the best idea. I don't think waking up in Janet's house is any better. His truck is pretty spacious... The rumors about Reese's fast ass would make town gossip easily before Monday.

Once a hoe, always a hoe.

Ugh. Why am I even considering this?

Off limits. Off limits. No, no, no.

"I don't know." He gestures between our two bodies. "This. I like being around you. Don't you like being around me?"

Did I? I guess I do. The usual hesitation I have around men isn't there. An anomaly.

By now, I would have already tried to secure my next meal. Demanding a pricy toll of some kind in the form of gifts, trips or direct deposits. With Cory, I haven't even thought about doing any of that.

I'm sure he's heard what people say about me. I've had boyfriends and all the things in between that particular label. One, of which, is still texting me though I won't respond. I don't actually remember liking any one of them. Trust was not my strong suit before Teddy and it definitely isn't after him.

Maybe it's the liquors swirling in my blood.

Maybe it's how good his lips look despite the garish lighting in here.

Maybe it's the five month dry spell I've been going through.

It has to be that last one, because I close the distance between our mouths.

His kiss is soft at first. His warm lips sliding over mine tenderly. The little sparks of energy that crackled all between us are running down my chin, my neck, and my arms.

That's when I realize that it's Cory's fingertips tracing lightly along my skin. The heat I feel from his body is more intoxicating than the AMF.

I just want to get closer to him.

My keys fall to the floor as I wrap my arms around his neck, dragging my nails down the back of his head and neck bringing his face even closer to me. The desire to feel what his weight would be like pressed against my body overwhelms my sanity for a moment.

My brain plays the scene out in technicolor for me and my back arches into him searching for more pressure. His hands find my waist again, pulling me flush with his hard length. I lean back to make it easier for him to kiss my neck, but also so I can feel more of his dick against my center. Cory's soft kisses wander purposefully down my chain and over the tops of my breasts.

Goosebumps chase his mouth over my skin and I feel too hot. It would be so easy for him to pull my top down and take that next step. But, he doesn't take it.

And holy hell, why isn't he taking it?

He rubs small circles over my nipples all while kissing slowly along the edge of the bra I'm wearing, driving me crazy. My hips are moving over his erection in time with his mouth. Maybe I should feel embarrassed to be so willing and wanton for this man, but when he pinches a nipple through the stretchy fabric my thighs lock around him. With the heel of my boot pressing into his ass, he gives me the pressure I'm yearning for.

His teeth leave little fissions of pain that he soothes with licks as he nips around the thin gold metal dangling between my cleavage. Muttering something like *this damn necklace*, he takes a deep inhale like he's gathering strength. The feel of his beard brushing the sensitive skin of my heaving chest causes me to flush impossibly hotter. Cory kisses his way up to my collarbone and neck to kiss my lips again.

His tongue swipes the seam of my lips, asking. I meet his tongue with my own before I nip at his bottom lip. No, it says.

I don't trust myself though I know I can trust him, somehow. It's not a choice I can voice aloud right now for fear that I'll regret this all.

He chuckles under his breath leaning his forehead to mine, looking into my eyes. Cory smiles at my own kiss drunk and drunk-drunk one, looking satisfied with himself.

There is no denying that he was right. This feels natural. He runs his thumb over my bottom lip with reverence. "Let's get you home before you maul me in this parking lot."

I splutter trying to make a rebuttal come out, but I can't find a suitable lie. I was one hundred percent contemplating it. Matter of fact, I was moments from doing just that. His smirk makes me smack him in the arm before he adjusts himself and ducks out the door frame to drive me home.

CHAPTER 14

Cory

Her.

I would never get her scent out of my head. Sure, it could be the perfume she wears or it could be just the essence of a predator. Everything working to pull you in. I like it either way and that is a problem.

I've heard murmurs from the gossips at Janet's house about the return of Danny's girl, the man-eater. At her crochet club meeting last Sunday, I overheard the end of a conversation my aunt missed. She was grabbing a platter of deviled eggs from the kitchen. I was going to grab a movie to watch in the room I was staying in. I stopped just short of turning the corner into the living room when I heard Reese's name.

"Did you hear Riesling Mason is back. I guess I better warn everyone to hide their husbands and probably their sons too." The first woman says with a barely contained giggle.

The other woman snickers, "If they can't find them at night anymore, we know where to check first. Did you see how her ass was hanging out of those shorts? In public, no less."

"No class. Though she a high dollar hoe." Rude gossip number one says. "Only the men with money are who we should be looking out for. I ain't saying she a gold digger, but..."

"Do life insurance policies count?"

They both laughed until my aunt came back into the room, pretending the gossip didn't happen. My fists clenched at the crass way they talk about the actions of a woman they don't even know. I don't know why my aunt puts up with them. I hope she disinvites them next month. If I were to hear them again, I don't know if I would hold my tongue. I had only seen her in passing a few times before, but now that I've tasted her skin, been inebriated by her scent...

Regardless, I told Janet that I didn't want whoever those foul women were around my sons when I was not there. She seemed confused, but told me that she would respect my wishes. It was likely because of the look on my face or maybe it was the finality in my tone.

The things they said—the person they described just doesn't seem to be the person sitting in my passenger seat right now. This was a ridiculous notion considering I barely knew anything about Reese. How can I know if what they said was true or not? One thing I did know is that I didn't like it.

I closed her door and walked around to the other side of my truck. I check my phone again to make sure no other updates about the boys have come through. They haven't. What could happen to them in BFE anyway? I shake my head.

"Can I use this?" Reese holds up the charging cord connected to my console.

I nod. "Yea. Just don't play anything too twangy." I wince at how that sounded rude, but I really don't like country music.

"Too twangy?" She laughs. "One day I'll show you what good country music is. Not just the "classics", but there so many up-and-coming artists making hits you'd enjoy."

"Uh-huh."

"I'm serious, Cory. Broaden your mind."

"Uh-huh. Miss me with the banjos." I tease.

She gives me a quizzical look before saying, "You really don't know me, huh? Fine. Rap it is." A playful jab, but one that I know she feels will put space between us. Women like her want to be "figured out".

I will figure her out.

I'll learn anything I must to be around her more. I saw how she looked at me when I stopped her from getting into her car. She was shocked that

I would even say a thing to her, in a good way. A woman like her was well out of my league. I was out of my depth, but she saw me, studied me, and under her attention, I felt like I was just a man. Not a dad. Not a divorcee. Just a man... that she wanted to devour.

In the past, I would never be seen kissing a woman I barely knew in a parking lot, grinding my dick into her like I had a right to. Damn. When she kissed me, something snapped. The years of being a consolation prize and the pity dates were over. The heat in her eyes made me feel wanted in a way that I could become addicted to.

It took everything in me not to expose her soft tits and find out just where that necklace led to. It was even harder to stop kissing her. I had to. I wanted her, but I didn't want it to be some liquor-fueled one-night stand. That will never be my style.

"I could say the same to you." She flips her hair over her shoulder and puts on a song. The music makes the bass thrum through the cabin space and jangles the change in my cup holder. A female rapper spits on the track and she seems to relax into the seat once the music is playing.

We drive without saying much because I know the way to Mason Ranch. I don't want to break any of the ties pulling us toward each other. When I talk to anyone these days the only thing I have to talk about is my kids and what relocating has been like. Before the move, it was the same—the boys and work. She and I could talk about work, but it just doesn't seem appropriate given how close my lips were to her stiff nipples just moments ago.

The kids conversation... I know it's off limits right now. She knows about the boys. With the way she kissed me a couple of minutes ago, I would say it's a discussion for another time.

She likes me. Likes me enough to dry hump my dick with her strong thighs holding me right where she needed me. Let me damn near mark her chest in that parking lot. Her gold hair splayed across my center console and her back arched. *She was ready.* She was still intoxicated. That kept me from going any farther. If she wants me—wants this—she's going to remember it with full clarity. Without the excuse of alcohol for her to hide behind.

The metallic voice of the hands-free assistant chimes with a new message from my truck. Reese, who was once relaxed and melting into the plush leather of my seats, goes ramrod straight and then frantically tries to make the speakers stop dictating her text. She turns the stereo off, but the assistant isn't a part of the music system. She only clears the screen for the text to glow brightly from the center display. "From Teddy, bear face emoji, Stop fucking around Ree. I know where to find you. Do you want to respond?"

Gone is the woman who was clenching me closer. In her place, this Reese stares at her phone like it may bite her. In the light from her screen, I can tell that she is panicked. I can see how she is even more freaked out with the text being clear for me to read from the navigation screen.

To my credit, I only grip the steering wheel tight enough to hear a faint groan from the leather in the now silent cabin. Holding my tongue takes effort. I find myself refraining from saying anything, or worse, the wrong thing.

After all, I know what she looks like.

Damn. She's gorgeous. The kind of beauty that is only enhanced by the flawless way she presents herself in photoshoot-ready makeup and not a hair out of place. The hypnotic way she sways her hips when she commands the attention of a room. Any person, man or woman, probably wants a piece of her for themselves.

I knew there had to be a roster. Other men trying to get at a woman like her. It still pisses me off to be hit with that fact so clearly in black and white. The message is long gone from my screen, but I still see it. It's burned into my mind though I still say nothing.

And Ree? I've never heard anyone call her that.

Okay... So, I haven't known her that long, but even around her friends tonight... Where she was chill and unguarded. No one called her that.

If I could calm down long enough—I would ask the right questions. I don't know if I would say something stupid and kill any chance I have of getting back to where we were before. I breathe in slowly through my nose, chancing a glance at Reese. Her head is propped on a fist as she stares out the window at nothing. She's not relaxed. It looks like she'll bolt as soon as we get to her house.

I turn the radio back on with the controls on the steering wheel. The soft sounds of R&B fill the car. Most of what I listen to can be classified under oldies by my sons, but it consists of the music from soundtracks of all the best 90's movies my parents loved. I started listening when I was in high school to dredge up the happier memories of them. With my boys around all the time, I'd rather have this music playing than the inappropriate garbage they play on the radios now. Just because they censor the curse words, does not make it good for all audiences.

The rhythmic music is helping me to be more relaxed and at least loosen the grip I have on the wheel.

Could I be upset with her?

No.

She's not mine.

We aren't anything.

This wasn't even a real date that I was bringing her home from.

It still makes me angry as hell to think about another man putting their hands on her. I want to be the only man who deserves to touch her perfect body.

"It's not what you think." Her voice is quiet. We're turning onto her long drive, but I don't respond with how tightly I'm clenching my jaw.

She's... nervous. Maybe even terrified from the look on her pretty face. She shoves her phone into her bag and looks out the window when I keep my mouth shut.

I park in the same spot I always do when I get here for work. There is something rote about the action and I exit the car robotically to open her door. How I manage is all muscle memory of some sort. I can't stop how this Teddy person is needling my brain.

I open her door, stepping back to give her the space to run how she looks like she wants to do.

She shocks me by quietly saying, "Cory." Reese grabs my wrist. I look down to where her grasp burns me like a brand though her fingers are cold. She tugs my arm gently, trying to get me to face her. I can't help feeling like a damn child throwing a tantrum.

As I said, she's not mine. I have no right to be upset.

"Cory." She tries again, but this time her voice is louder, more firm. "Would you just talk to me?"

"About what?" I grit my teeth at my own response. *Get it together, idiot.*

"He's…" She starts and I prepare for the blow as she tries to find her words. She fidgets with the strap of her purse for a bit before meeting my eyes. Starting again, she says, "It's complicated. Teddy is this guy I used to mess with. He's been texting me because I'm back in town and he thinks we will hook up again." She covers her mouth, rolling her eyes and scoffing. "I don't know why I'm telling you that. I just wanted you to know that he's not my guy. I'm not going to hook up with him or anything." Her eyes are sincere and I believe her, but it doesn't make me feel any better.

I remove her hand from my wrist, but she covers it with her other hand. I stare at them together. I think about how simple it was to imagine holding them for a very long time at the bar earlier. She raises gentle fingers to my face, burying them in my beard. Her touch is light. I still feel the weight from her hand all the same.

I meet her gaze. "Right," is all I can clip out. Reese's searching eyes tell me that there is more that she wants to say. Everything in my mind wants to find out what or who put the anguish in her eyes. My heart doesn't know if it is even worth it.

I see her outside of work once, and what I thought could be something—circles down the drain. I have a family to think about. I don't need to get tangled up with someone who has "complicated" situations with their ex or whoever that man is to her. He had a bear emoji by his contact for fuck's sake. That has to mean something.

"He doesn't matter," she says in that soft tone again. I wish I could tell my stupid brain and heart to let go of whatever wishing they came together on in that parking lot earlier. This is a red flag I should be wary of. "Will you still take me to get my car in the morning?" She asks me shyly.

Will I? Her mom or friends could take her. That would probably be best. For me.

I can't stomach being that much of an asshole to her. I was the one who forced her to leave it there. Her hand still burns on my face and I have the good sense to step back. It falls to my chest, right over my heart. The stupid thing skips with her being so close.

I sigh. "Yea. I'll take you tomorrow." I feel like such a simp fool. Still running her errands when she probably has someone else.

She leans up to kiss my cheek and walks to her door. Hips swaying and purse swinging. She slips inside to the foyer and turns the porch light off.

I get into my car and swear I see something moving in the backyard. I ignore it since it's likely a tree shadow and I need to get back home to my boys after the most confusing night I've had in a really long time.

Chapter 15

Reese

My stomach grumbles loudly and I remember that I still haven't eaten anything.

One of the perks of being back home is the abundance of food that Chandie always has in the house. I look through the contents of the fridge and settle on some pasta dish my mom made. Walking over to the living room, I put something on to watch as I eat pasta from the large Tupperware with a fork.

Did I heat it up? No. I need food and I can't be bothered. The tomato and Italian sausage mixed with the carb-y goodness of Fusilli pasta do wonders with the tilt-a-whirl feeling my gut is currently experiencing after this night.

First, Mack. The last person I expected to get into a bar fight, but the only person that I've actually known who's done it. I've seen him fight before, but this was different. That same anger and hurt I saw the first day back was growing inside him and I could do nothing to help my friend. I might have made it worse with whatever tonight was. My semi-drunk "see reason" conversation was the worst decision I've had so far.

How many times have I seen that I truly don't know what it's like in Alpenglow Ridge anymore? And then proceed to put my foot in my own mouth anyway!

Temporary. I'm here temporarily.

I sigh. The low conversation of the rom-com starring Tatiana Ali I put on barely distracts me from my own thoughts.

The second, and likely the biggest, *what the fuck?!* of the night was Cory. Despite how fervently, I have said that he is off limits and the exact opposite of what I'm looking for, I was drawn to him.

Fine. I was a little bit tipsy... and my little pussy was missing the attention of a man after months of going without. But seriously... What the fuuuuuck, Reese? I have no good excuse for my behavior.

Men are good for one thing and one thing, only.

Okay, maybe two.

One: what they can do for you. Relationships are overrated. Over the last few years, I've gotten anything I could have possibly wanted by simply looking like the type of woman they only fantasize about being with. Made a living, vacationed, and went to nice events with some of the most influential people in Colorado. I lived comfortably in Denver up until the last year, when things became...

Well, when my circumstances changed or maybe when I realized my circumstances needed changing.

Hence, why I'm currently slinging wings and fries for a meager tipped wage, in the shortest jean shorts they make, at Peak's forty hours a week.

Two: dick. And I'd argue that one doesn't even need to be coming from a man because I know plenty of people getting it done without one. In fact, Karla had been the one to introduce me to my most recent method of sexual fulfillment. I thought she had lost her mind when we all ended up in a sex shop after a shift. She was more knowledgeable than the person working there. I left with a smooth pink number that had been enough to sustain me and the least problematic part of my sex life.

A toy cannot replace a person. *Full stop.*

I haven't had a man show me anything impressive since well before I stopped letting them touch me in that way.

I click off the TV and replace the pasta in the fridge. I'm grateful my parents are both long asleep when I tiptoe back to the other side of the house to my bedroom.

I need a shower and I need to come.

Maybe then, I can rid myself of thoughts that want to creep in about the single dad that I should not be having. It was embarrassing enough to have Teddy talk to me the way he had and then for Cory to see it.

Why should I care if he thinks anything about him?

Cory is not my man. He is off-limits. But I can't lie and say that the kiss we shared earlier did not light my body up. That I wasn't hoping for more.

He worked me up with precision. He knew just what I liked and how I liked to be touched. We weren't naked, but I felt the effects of him under my skin like a fever. Even now, the ghosts of his touch redden my neck and I feel myself flushing hotter. There is nothing better than a big man taking care of you like a priority.

I could never be his priority and I refuse to settle for anything less—ever again.

I shake my head and grab my toy before going to the bathroom.

Steam closes around me as I step into the blistering hot stream of water from my shower head. The eucalyptus and lavender of my body wash overtakes my senses. Inhaling deeply, I lather up my body. I still feel sort of unstable. With each minute that passes the water kneads the tension from my back and shoulders. The stress abates to a small throb in my head.

Thinking of throbbing has my mind racing back to the moment in Cory's truck when I had hoped he would push for more. Literally. What's the harm in taking that technicolor fantasy to the next level with a little help? Here, alone in my shower.

I lean against the shower wall and put a foot onto the soap holder. Sliding the toy along my slit, there is no resistance. I'm wet and ready.

A little gasp escapes me as I imagine it's Cory penetrating my aching seam. The steam makes my breathing feel shallow as I work myself just like I imagine he would. Slow and steady, building my pleasure and drinking in the show I'm giving him. Nothing is fake about the way I'm clenching this toy with each memory of his lips and teeth making contact with me. "Cory," I exhale shakily into the steam. It's not long until I'm coming harder than I have in a long while. I pant and grip the shower door handle until the rush of my orgasm subsides again.

Setting the toy in the top rack of my shower caddy shelves, you'd never know it was there. "I'm coming back for you later," I say to the toy and not to the man I have now used for an orgasm that I am still feeling in my toes.

There is no way he will want anything to do with me after how our night ended anyway. I don't feel rejected, but Teddy's message had changed everything between us.

Rookie mistake connecting my phone like that.

No one hits me up that late unless it's about shifts at work. I just saw my girls, but there's nothing embarrassing they would have said in a message. I can only be lucky that Teddy didn't say anything more incriminating about us. Definitely a mistake to connect my phone like that.

At the bar, before talking in his car, or even before at the table—we had something. All I know is that when I am around him, it feels like it's just us. Time stands still.

Under his gaze, I feel like more.

More than the scared girl who fled town when her choices caught up to her. More than the town tramp coming home to lick her wounds. More than the woman who is still lying to all the people who love her.

He can't see that person. He just sees me... and to be seen by Cory could be dangerous. For us both. I could never forgive myself if I dragged him into what could only be described as a mess.

This mess keeps getting bigger the more I try to clean it up.

Have you been trying?

Teddy is threatening you now.

Situation NOT de-escalated.

Scrubbing my makeup off, I stop the flow of water from my shower. Applying lotion and face cream on autopilot in the mirror as my mind spins. How can I make Teddy go away for good without actually talking to him again?

I slide my slippers on with a towel wrapped around me to walk across the hallway to my room from the bathroom. My hand pauses above the door knob when I see the door is already opened a crack.

I remember closing it before I went to shower. No one in the house should be up. It's nearly one-thirty in the morning.

Clutching my towel with one hand and pushing the door open slowly, I gasp sharply at what sits on my bed. Or rather, who.

I scramble inside the door closing it behind me. My panicked movements are unnecessary since I have established everyone else in the house is asleep. Clumsy fingers brush over the light switch, illuminating the room.

The light is also unnecessary because I know who sits there. From that aroused, heavy breathing alone. "All clean for me?" he asks.

Crossing to the drawer, I move with a kind of confidence that I don't truly feel. I'm still that dumb girl from the past and under Teddy's stare I feel just as small. Naive.

I pull out a camisole and sleep shorts letting my towel drop to the ground. He tracks my movements with heated blue eyes. My stomach roils as my sobriety smacks me hard in the face.

He's still handsome, as always. A wolf in sheep's clothing.

Looking over my shoulder, I catch his fists balled tight in his flat front pockets. He says nothing while I dress with my mask firmly in place.

"How did you get in here?" I ask with a sickeningly sweet purr that I know he likes to hear from me. I'm hoping my tone doesn't give away the accusation there.

"Side door, Ree." He stands from the bed. Each step he takes curls something tighter in my gut. His pressed attire creases at specific points making him look stuffy and more put together than it should.

I was fooled by his facade and all the things he hides behind. I'm frozen in place thinking. Foolishly allowing this man to cage me against the dresser with his arms bracketing my own. His cologne burns my nostrils with memories. I absently touch my mouth thinking about the blood.

He watches me touch my lips with rapt interest. All I can think about is how shocked I was that this man could hurt me so much. And that I allowed him to for far too long.

He leans toward me trying to take a kiss I did not offer. I lean my head away from him, instead asking, "What are you doing here, Teddy?"

"You weren't responding to my texts." Taking another step away from him, he clenches his fist. I chance a glance at my blade on the nightstand. He blinks and the blatant menace subsides in his eyes when he says, "I missed you."

He closes the distance between our hips and my nerves are shot.

He came in here without my permission.

To my parent's home without their knowledge.

He's trying to push up on me when I haven't heard from him in months. By my request, but I'm tired and ready to crash. The disrespect is too much to grin and bear. I won't play nice for him anymore.

"Bullshit." I push away from him. "Please just go without making a scene."

"Don't act like you have some choice here."

I'm irritated by his casual response. My eyebrows pinch. "The fuck, Teddy," I hiss out. "Are you off your rocker? I don't want you or anything associated with you."

"I don't remember you saying that on your knees..." he pretends to think it over before continuing, "or your back. Should I remind you? For old time's sake."

I grind my molars. My options are limited. I place both my hands on his chest trying to create space between us.

I manage to get to my doorway again. Placing my hand on the knob, ready to kick him out as soon as possible. "What do you want?"

"I want to know who else you're talking to." *Of course.*

"Why would I tell anyone about you, fucking psycho?" *To shame myself further in this town.* I think not.

"So what? You're staying here again?" He looks around the room like he's seeing it for the first time.

"What does it matter to you?"

"The thousands I'm spending on your apartment? That matters to me. When were you going to tell me that you weren't living there anymore?"

I flinch. "It's only temporary."

"And yet," he taps a finger to his chin contemplatively, "Teddy Bear is the last to know."

"I haven't told anyone about you," I say in a hushed tone. I feel self-conscious and I fidget with the big braid I put my hair into before I showered. He stops my fingers by grabbing my hand and yanking me toward him. Some of it is still between my fingers and a whimper escapes my lips when a few strands are yanked, too.

"Move all your shit out this weekend. I want it gone. You have until Monday. I'm not paying for an apartment you're not living in. We'll have to figure something else out when you're done here." He presses his groin close to me in emphasis. A shiver races down my back. He takes it for something other than the disgust and fear it is. "And you will be done here soon. I don't want you in town for too long. Understood?" His smile is sinister and wicked, but I nod my head.

Maybe the fear is exactly what he wants to see. A flash of teeth peeks from his smirk for the briefest moment. "I'll be seeing you." With that, he leaves the room and I hear the hiss of the screen door closing behind him. I turn off the overhead light and turn on my lamp.

Flopping onto my bed, I hear the distinct sound of a paper bag crinkling under the weight of my pillows falling. Kicking them out of the way, the glossy black design shines in the dim lighting of my bedside lamp.

How could I have missed the signature white and black bag that Lulu Lacey is known for?

Ripping the black tissue paper out as fast as I can I pull out the smooth, shining black box. There's a small note lying snugly under a sheer white ribbon tied in a bow. I carefully untie the ribbon and remove the note.

I know this is from him because he's the only one who ever spent this kind of money on lingerie for me. I should have recognized this same box from the text he sent me earlier too.

My hands tremble as I open and remove the note from its envelope.

> **Ree,**
> **I prefer you black and blue.**
> **T**

The note falls from my hands onto my bed.

With shaking fingers, I pull the top off of the box. In it sits a black lace lingerie set with straps and loops that would only look like bondage over my curves. The sheer cups add coverage only by the way of intricate blue lace flowers the color of bruises. They're positioned over the nipples and along the straps in various places. The crotchless thong and garter belt have a similar design with the same deep blue lace flowers.

I'd love something like this from anyone else. Scratch that. I'd love the lingerie period. If I had a love language, it would be expensive clothes that make my body look even more appetizing.

But... that note.

The important word missing rather intentionally sends a shiver down my back again.

Quickly replacing everything back into the bag, I shove it to the back of my closet behind some of my old winter coats.

I clamber to my purse and pull my blade out. I go to lock the side door checking that he isn't waiting outside for me.

When I feel satisfied, I tiptoe back to my room though there is no one on this side of the house. Now, I'm feeling unsettled and paranoid and the sneaking around can't be helped.

I take my blade and slip it under my pillow, turn off my light, and stare at my door until my exhaustion overtakes me with a fitful sleep.

CHAPTER 16

Cory

"YOU DON'T HAVE TO sneak in here. I know you were out drinking." The giggles from Sammie join Janet's gruff chuckle. When I turn to see them both sitting on the couch, I stop trying to sneak past the living room. The TV audience joins their fun with laughter cueing up on the late night show they're watching reruns of.

"I know, Jan, and I wasn't drinking. I had one shot. Hey, Sammie." I lean against the door way swinging my keys around my finger.

Janet was always my cool aunt. I wasn't known for being a particularly mischievous teenager who sneaked out or anything. I thought it would be best to be quiet coming home, to respect the house. It's late and even if my boys are happily sleeping. Slamming a door to wake them up would bring about questions I am in no way able to process right now.

What would I tell them?

What was I doing tonight?

When I left here earlier, I thought I had an opportunity to spend time with the beautiful woman who has been just out of reach. Then chaos broke out over that jackass Mack fighting someone at Quincy's bar.

Nothing went the way I thought it would.

Why did she go to Mack and not Melody?

Seeing her try to comfort him... and then that text from Teddy.

Who is Teddy?

My mind circled around the complicated woman that I just wanted to get closer to despite all the obvious reasons that I shouldn't.

And the biggest question of why?

"How was your night?" Sammie gives me a knowing smile, which tells me the news has already traveled here. I laugh to myself and grab the back of my neck. The memories of leaning over Reese in my truck come to the forefront of my mind.

Sammie pats the spot on the couch next to them. She clutches the bowl of chips she's eating from before it goes flying. I drop into the spot jostling them both.

"It was alright." Not a lie. Not really the truth. I need more time to give an answer that's more candid than this one. I sink deeper into the couch with my arms splayed around the back. I'm exhausted and not because it's late.

"Well there's no beating around the bush in this house. Sheryl saw you taking Reese to your truck." Jan's eyebrow raises and I know she heard more than just that. "You dating this woman? Is that why you took so much time getting all shaved up and smelling nice before you left?"

I have not been interested in dating anyone since Vanessa left. I didn't have time for the bad blind dates I was set up on and dating apps are hardly any better. No one made me feel like they were worth the effort required.

The hurt of losing my wife to a younger man... Then the hurt of being the bearer of bad news to my sons that they had essentially lost their mother... It was too much.

I should be focusing on making what I'm starting here in Alpenglow more stable and making it last, not on Reese. She may be beautiful and her unexpected compassion may have sparked something in me that I haven't felt in... well, I don't know if I even felt that with my ex-wife. I just don't know if pursuing her is worth it with so many unknowns floating around her.

"Is it?" Janet's voice cuts through my thoughts and I stand from the couch.

"No. We're not dating." I scarf down a quick sandwich before popping my head into the living room. "I'm gonna go shower and get to bed. I've got an, um, errand to run in the morning. Do you mind watching the boys til I get back?"

"What kind of errand? I don't mind. Sam bought all the stuff to make big breakfast in the morning. The boys will love it."

No sense in lying because it will likely get back to her via Chandie anyway. "I've got to take Reese back to her car in the morning."

Janet and Sammie share a look. "Okay, baby. We'll see you tomorrow," Sammie says.

After my shower, I lay in bed unable to sleep. I rip my t-shirt off feeling hot and the sleep pants I'm wearing don't feel that comfortable either. My fan is going full speed, but there is this persistent heat down my spine that won't subside.

Cory, think of any other woman and get it over with.

Any other woman.

There are millions on this planet.

I close my eyes, hoping for someone reasonable—a celebrity or something.

Instead, I'm assaulted by the images of the woman I left wanting tonight.

I can feel the heels of her boots digging into my ass and before I know it, my hand is wrapped around my dick and I'm tugging. The way she gripped me with her legs could only be a preview of what it would be like to actually...

My grip tightens as I thrust into my hand. A small drip of precum, runs down my fist as visions of her delicate neck and soft skin play in my head. I stroke faster, find a rhythm that matches the way she was grinding on me.

My biggest regret at the moment is not getting the chance to see what was underneath that strapless bra. My hand speeds up as I think more about how hard her nipples were and if she'd like me to lick or suck on them more. I lick my own lips, hoping for the faint traces of her lipgloss to be there when I know it's not.

In my mind, she says, "Cory. Make me come," in that breathless way that causes my balls to tighten in anticipation. The thought of her ordering me to take her send me over the edge. My sweet angel coming apart for me. I thrust more fervently and come into my hand.

The sticky mess spilling between my knuckles and fingers, when she might have let me make a mess all over her... It would have been easy to get my nut off in the backseat tonight. It took everything in me to step away from those luscious curves. Even harder knowing that she might not give me the time of day again.

Did I make a huge mistake in *not* letting her maul me in that parking lot?

I reach over to my shirt, clean myself up with it, and feel fucking pathetic.

After what I saw tonight and not knowing what's going on with Teddy—the last thing I need is to be jerking off to thoughts of her. I've got it out of my system now and that's what matters.

She's out of my system.

She said that she and Teddy were nothing. It felt honest. True.

The next morning I pull up to my usual spot in the driveway at work. Just like last night. But Reese's Mustang sits in its usual spot, much to my surprise.

I look at the house and see that she's coming out carrying several flat cardboard boxes.

I step around my truck.

When she sees me, she freezes. A curse leaves her lips and her cheeks redden. "I'm sorry, Cory. I completely forgot!" She's loading the boxes into the back of an old silver Ford F150.

"You moving back already?" My voice sounds dejected and hurt.

Yea. She's out of your system.

Reese flinches and then shrugs trying to cover her reaction. "No. I'm not moving back to Denver."

"So, what's with the boxes?"

She considers me for a moment. I feel her eyes roam over my face and then assess my clothing. The cargos and t-shirt I'm wearing passed whatever assessment she was making. She nods to herself, "You busy today?"

"Wasn't supposed to be, but today is for my boys." Coming over here for nothing was not a part of my plan after what happened last night. She nods again and I fling an arm out to her car parked properly. It's so unlike the haphazard way she normally parks it. "Who brought it home?

"Oh. Yea... Quincy came this morning with Chloe to drop it off. They left just before you got here. I meant to text you but I don't have your number." She starts fidgeting with her hair, taking her eyes off me.

I feel the loss of her gaze immediately.

The jeans and cropped tee she wears clings to her body like a second skin. The top says Peak's on it with two mountains placed in the exact spot over her chest to be suggestive. Her thin gold chain sways from the shirt under her ribcage on either side. Forever teasing me that I don't know what it looks like under her tight little tops. She continues, "I could have gotten your number from my mom, I guess, but I've been busy getting ready. I've got a shift tonight, but I thought I'd start packing up my apartment before I need to be there." She meets my eyes again looking a little embarrassed at her chattering. "Don't know why I'm telling you this."

"I think you know why." She holds my stare and we stay silent for a while. After leaving the house with three very sugared up young boys, the silence is not only appreciated but welcome for me. I can tell that Reese is uncomfortable by the way she starts to fidget with her hair again. "I meant what I said last night."

She looks confused, asking, "About taking me to get my car?"

"No, about counting me in." And I did mean it. She's not out of my system because I don't want her out of my system.

I can't expect the next woman I'm interested in to not have a life before me. I can't fault her for having previous relationships. She said that Teddy was not her guy. And she doesn't want to see him. As for Mack, it's clear that he was all torn up about his ex and not trying to be with Reese. I caught the end of that nasty argument they were having so that's a conversation for another day.

I have an ex-wife, that doesn't want anything to do with me, but she will be a part of my life. We have children together. Sometimes life is just messy. Why would I ignore the interest that I have for her when no other woman has even piqued it in years?

She laughs. The sound of it makes me internally pat my own back because she doesn't do it often enough. "I still don't know what that means," she admits.

"It means that I just want you to give it a shot." I shrug my shoulders like its no big deal. "To give me a chance. It can start with you asking for my number."

Reese sits on the bumper of the silver truck and I sit next to her. "I don't think I know how to do that," she says rubbing her hands along her thighs without looking up to me.

"Easy." I pull my phone out of my back pocket and mimic her posture on the truck. "Cory," I say looking into her eyes, "I need your number, so we can keep seeing each other because I had a really great time with you last night."

She laughs again, this time doubling over and flipping her hair back. When she leans up again, the strands glimmer in the morning light along with her smile. I smile to myself at being able to get her to relax. "I wouldn't say it was a great time but having your number could have its merits..." She holds both her hands up lifting one and then the other like she is weighing the options.

"Oh, there's merits." I raise an eyebrow and let the innuendo play into my words. Holding my phone between us, I will her to take it. Just hoping for her to take the bait that I'm dangling.

"Fine," she relents. Taking the phone from my hand she puts her number in and calls her own phone. I hear it vibrating in her pocket before she pulls it out and ends the call.

I take my phone back and see that she's saved her contact as Reese with a yellow heart emoji. "With a heart and everything? We're basically going steady now." I lean over to bump her shoulder with mine, playfully.

"Oh, it's serious," she teases before turning her phone around to show me her phone where she's saved my name with a green heart emoji next to it.

I pretend to be shocked as I gasp and clutch at my heart. "It is serious!" Standing from the bumper I walk backward toward my truck. "Should I get my letterman jacket?"

She rises from the bumper as well, taking long strides to grab the front of my shirt and pull me toward her. "How about your lips instead?"

I don't resist her advance and meet her lips for the briefest moment before my arms wrap around her waist and bring her flush to my body. She feels good in my arms.

I could get used to this feeling.

I swipe my tongue along her lips again, like last night. This time she tastes like vanilla and allows my tongue to brush hers.

With her body fitting perfectly against mine, I want to keep her here and take her back to my truck, all at the same time. My hand finds her waist and I rub small circles over the exposed skin above her jeans. She's so fucking soft. I squeeze her even closer to me. Whatever magic her lips are laced with, I'm under their spell.

Getting to be this close to her... with her *this* unguarded, feels like a gift.

The kiss is over before I want and she nips at my bottom lip just like last night. Stepping out of my embrace, her thumb swipes the gloss from my mouth.

"I like the merits." Now it's her walking backward away from me. "You'll text me." She tells me, not asks, before turning to jog toward the Mason house.

I smirk the whole drive home, tasting her lip gloss long after she left.

CHAPTER 17

Reese

"Hot Food!" Jamie yells down the hall at the other servers all waiting for their drinks at the bar.

I've changed out of my jeans into my tiny work shorts for my shift tonight. Karla and Marie are closing the restaurant with me like usual. We all know Jamie hates working the double on Fridays. Yelling is his default volume by the time the dinner shift rolls around.

The seven other servers are on the floor with guests. Between the three of us waiting here, we play Rock, Paper, Scissors to see who is going to grab the tray piled with food waiting to be run to the tables. I made the unfortunate mistake of picking rock when both of them picked paper.

"And that's what we're here for! To make some paper!" Marie drags out the word paper. She finishes with her tongue sticking all the way out, "Ahh." She mimics Megan thee Stallion's signature adlib.

I scratch my nose with my middle finger pointedly at her.

"Whatever, I'm going!" I say to Jamie. Karla and Marie go back to talking about what club they're gonna hit tonight after we close at midnight. My plans will include getting the rest of my things packed away before I have to deal with Teddy showing up unannounced again.

Will I miss my tiny studio on the third floor that had no elevator or pantry? No. But moving back to my parent's ranch home comes with its cons as well. The pros do outweigh quite a few of them, like my mom's cooking, the horses, and being close to my girls... and now, Cory.

He's been texting me cute memes all day about horses and gardening.

I've never had a man who cared about *me* more than my ass or what my mouth can do.

I learned far too young that men were easy to manipulate if you could distract them with the prospect of sex. I've received clothes, shoes, purses, jewelry, makeup, alcohol—you name it—just for being cute or for a suggestively teasing selfie.

For one date, I could likely get all these things in addition to an Uber black picking me up and dropping me off at my own place at the end of the night.

When it came to Teddy though, I was stupid.

God, I was so stupid and I paid the price. Now, I never leave my house without a weapon. Self-defense classes had been my first priority when he left.

For a few months, I pretended like nothing had changed. That I hadn't changed. Keeping up my same finessing. Collecting what I wanted in exchange for my time, my body. I had to stop that too.

But it's been nine months since Teddy and I came to an understanding. One that he completely ignored by showing up at my parent's house last night. He had taught me what it means to have your trust and confidence in someone broken.

Something tells me Cory is different. He and Teddy couldn't be more opposites.

So here I am, mindlessly taking orders and flipping my ponytail around my finger for the rest of the night. I'll be needing these tips for the foreseeable future. My dad is getting better. He is, but taking a bigger role in the ranch's addition will mean more time in Alpenglow Ridge and less time in Peak's. Though Chandie and Danny would make sure I want for nothing, I can't keep living in their house forever.

I've been serving at Peak's long enough to go on autopilot and think about what it's like to not be Riesling Mason from Alpenglow Ridge. Thinking about Cory's soft kisses and rough hands is enough material to daydream about. Instead of the long leering looks from the patrons here to watch the basketball game and grab a handful.

With Cory, he treats me like someone new. Someone different. He has no expectations of me and hasn't asked for a nude once today. And honestly, that is a big step up from the individuals usually hitting me up.

If I'm honest I'd send him one if he asked, no problem.

The man is sexy and capable and the way he fills out those work cargos... Your girl could definitely be swayed into wrapping herself up in just a bow for him to untie after work. What he's packing could be enough to have me dickmatized as I had previously warned Mel about.

I have been messaging her to see if she's okay after what happened at the bar but all I'm getting is the silent treatment. She hasn't texted me back but I know she's been reading every message.

I get it.

I went to Mack, which in hindsight did seem like I was taking his side.

I wasn't...

Not really.

She said she was fine and when I saw how hurt he was, I just went after him.

That completely blew up in my face.

Ugh. I thought being in the middle was an advantage...

It wasn't.

Mack hasn't texted me back either.

I'm no marriage counselor so my meddling days are over for now. I'll just wait for them to come to me.

I remember my apron buzzing at some point during our rush but never got the chance to check it. I'm out back getting some air. All my checks are paid out so I wait for the last guests to leave out here. It's nice to smell the crisp Colorado breeze instead of fried food and beer for even the briefest moment. I look at my phone and smile at the text there.

Cory : When will you be back in Alpenglow Ridge?

I smile at his message and text him back right away.

Me: Miss me already? Maybe tomorrow. I've got so much left to pack.

I shove my phone back into the apron. When I reenter the dining area, most of the guests have left. A few guys are lingering by the bar, watching the last TV that's on. Some basketball game has gone into overtime. Ignoring them completely since they weren't from my tables, I started stacking chairs and rolling silverware.

Karla plops down onto the booth next to me to roll her portion for the night. "We're gonna go to Wave after. Wanna meet over there? Marie's boyfriend is bringing his friends," she singsongs.

"They're cute, Reese!" Marie joins us across the booth to roll silverware, as well. "You'd have fun. Plus, free drinks!" She sticks her bottom lip out with her hands together in a praying gesture.

"I've got to pack ladies. Landlord wants me out before the weekend." *Demands it, actually.*

"Does that mean you're not working here anymore? What the hell? You didn't even say anything. Lucky bitch." Karla tosses her napkin bundle into the bin with a playful huff.

"I'm gonna try to keep my Saturday night and Wednesday shifts for a bit. AR is not that far, guys."

They look at each other and then to me they say, "Lucky bitch."

I roll my eyes and focus on my task.

"Who is he?" Marie says. When I feign ignorance, she elaborates, "You've been smiling at your phone all night. What trick is treating you?"

I laugh and stack my silverware into the tub for tomorrow's lunch shift. "No trick. Just some small town cutie." I wink.

"You're living a Hallmark movie! Let me guess, his wife died and you're the only one who can make him feel alive again. Big city girl helping his business and all, with your incredible marketing skills to save his Christmas tree farm." Karla giggles to herself clearly proud of the picture she's painted. Marie gives her a high five as she joins in on the giggling.

"First, I'm *from* Alpenglow Ridge. How could I be the big city girl helping him? Also, I don't know shit about marketing! I'm working at Peak's with you two."

"But he is a Christmas tree farmer?" Karla questions.

"And he's a widower?" Marie adds.

I throw my hands up, leaving the booth.

Giving the restaurant a final walk through, I make sure everything is closed down properly. I lock the door behind the two guys from the bar, who have finally left now that the game is over.

The girls follow me out to the employee parking lot in the back. My hand is on my blade in the purse as we walk into the dimly lit area.

"Give us something Reese! You've had the best luck with men out of all of us." She pauses and taps her chin, adding, "Well you used to... New purses, new shoes! Hell, I know someone is paying to keep you that blonde and there was always some new guy to pick you up after work for a while there. Marie's boyfriend works at a bank. No way he's starring in Hallmark's next big hit." Marie gives Karla a pointed look but Karla just shrugs. "What? It's true!"

There is no way I'm going to tell these two anymore about Cory. And besides, I don't know much more than what I've said. I don't know if his wife is still alive or not.

Actually, there's a lot I don't know about him.

This is all really new.

"Earth to Reese? Is he packing at least?" Marie asks.

"I don't know. We haven't fucked," I respond.

Now the look they share is definitely accusatory.

"You were there for a week and nothing?" If I were anyone else, I might be offended. But, I have been in an uncharacteristically long dry spell. I did have a few guys I was seeing—I didn't let them touch me. Teddy showed me that my body was property and I believed him. I had kept up my usual techniques, but I found that there was nothing I wanted more than to be left alone.

When I started dating it was even worse. I didn't want to go to a fancy dinner with some guy who bored me to tears, for any reason at all. What's the point when they flake after you express that you don't want to sleep with them? And I would rather go without than have company that did nothing for me. Especially, if they were only after their release and mine came second, if it came at all.

Gareth, or whatever his name was, only proved me right after I finally went on a date for the first time in four months. It was awful. And totally unsatisfying. No way was he getting between my legs.

Sigh.

I love sex. That is no secret, but my pink Satysfyer is the only package I've been receiving. A little buzz can go a long way. Pinky has been going the distance and gone farther than ever before last night. I'm not gonna tell these two that either.

Instead, I say, "He's not like that. He's sweet and I only saw him outside of the ranch once. Last night..." I trail off getting distracted by the notification on my phone.

I haven't checked them since I responded to Cory earlier.

"And you're smiling like the cat who got the cream already?" Marie walks from her car to where I'm standing next to Sally. I've thrown my apron and purse into the passenger seat so all I have is my phone in my hand.

She's right, I was smiling at his text again. "What's Sunday CineFlix?"

I hug my phone to my chest. "It's a movie night the town holds behind the senior center. They play old movies for the seniors in town to socialize." I spin to face her with my eyebrows pulled together and a hand on my hip. "You know it's rude to read over people's shoulders?" I throw my phone into the passenger seat with my other things from work.

Marie holds her hands out in front of her. "I just find it hard to believe that you're going for a "small town cutie" who wants to take you to an event meant for old people instead of going out with us."

"Leave her alone, Marie. We need to get ready if we wanna get into Wave before the guys leave." Karla slams her door and drives off.

"Alright. I'll see you on Wednesday then, I guess." She eyes me speculatively before getting into her car.

"Yea. Wednesday. Have fun though. Take a shot for me!" She agrees and blows me a kiss, leaving the lot at top speed.

I sit in the driver's seat looking over the text from Cory in peace without their prying eyes.

> **Cory : I do want to see you again. Maybe we could get food and Sunday CineFlix? Is that cheesy?**

I smile again before typing my response and head back to the studio.

> **Me: Cheesy? Maybe… Pick me up at 5.**

CHAPTER 18

Cory

THANKS TO TONY, I'VE had three guys reach out to me about working with my company over the past week. After speaking to them, it seems like they'd be a good fit for the part-time work I'm offering. The best thing about landscaping is that if you're able-bodied, pretty much anything can be taught or is just common knowledge.

With being related to one of the town's largest communicator (AKA gossip), I already have a few residential properties lined up that need some basic maintenance and upkeep in addition to the commercial property I've got with Mason Ranch.

My fingers sink into the soil of the raised plant bed I put together for Janet. I scoop out a hole large enough for the transplant with my fingers. The cool dirt is damp enough to not need much watering for the new plants I've gotten. This edible garden is a present for both Sammie and Janet. In this box, I've got cucumbers, tomatoes, several kinds of peppers and some hardy greens. In the other box on the other side of the back patio door, I filled it with herbs of all kinds that I know Sammie uses the most.

Yesterday, I took the boys with me to the nursery, about thirty minutes south, to get all the materials and plants we would need for this project. They had fun helping get the materials, but not as much with building or transferring the plants. They are playing on the playset Janet had built for them instead.

The next thing I need to do is find someplace for us to live. One of the best things about Alpenglow Ridge is that there are few newer developments that have been built. Most of them have no significant amount of land they sit on. Renting one for the time being would be a lot better than sneaking in and out of Janet's house.

Not that it has been happening much, but I would like to have some privacy again. I love Janet and am thankful for her help. If I'm actually going to make this place my home, I need to get a spot sooner or later. Preferably sooner. I have a bit in savings. We're not in a place financially to move out just yet.

Satisfied with the progress of the plant beds, I try to make sense of all these life changes. New career, new place, new life.

I want to be the man that can handle all this.

Vanessa's financial contribution to our household was the only thing she helped with in the past. I don't miss her, but I do miss not worrying about whether we will be able to afford all the things we need.

I just couldn't stay in Denver anymore. Van's punishing me for the decision, and in turn the boys. By not being there. Making the one-hour drive is too taxing on her perfect life with Davis. At least, that's her excuse. Never mind how she has been absent from her commitment to them even when we did live in town.

Being close to the only remaining family I have left is better than any half-life I was living in the big city. I just need a couple more gigs before I can get that house.

For them.

For us.

For me.

"Everyone wants burgers?" I call out to them and Brendan comes running the fastest to where I'm sitting on the bench rubbing my hands on a towel.

"I beat! I beat! I'm the winner! I want burgers, Daddy!"

"Whoa slow your roll, Bren. One burger for you. Your brothers need lunch too," I tease.

"Yea, but I got here first! Gabe can only eat a half burger anyway, daddy."

CJ carries Gabe who is sucking on his t-shirt collar to the bench I'm sitting on. "You only won because I have a twenty-pound weight in my arms." He tells Bren as Gabe uses the back of the bench to walk toward me. I pick him up and pull the shirt from his mouth. "Burgers sound good to me." CJ adds. "Can we get ice cream too? The DreamCreamery is right next to Joe's, dad!"

I pretend to think it over, but it was my plan all along. I don't want to spoil these three rotten trying to fill the hole Vanessa left. I can't help but think about what they would be doing if she had picked them up when she was supposed to yesterday. They would likely be watching TV all day, which I know they would enjoy.

"Okay, we can get some ice cream after, but only if everyone finishes their dinner." I point at the three of them and they all agree emphatically. Everyone piles into my truck. I carefully buckle Gabe and give him the little bean bag lizard he likes to play with. Me, not so much.

Rounding the back, I hop in and put on the playlist I like to listen to. CJ reads a comic book in the passenger seat as we ride to the small strip of businesses on the main road in town. He pushes his glasses up and I think about how much he must be dealing with. I dread the talk I'm going to have with them at Joe's Burgers.

We park out front and Gabe gets excited seeing the large ice cream cone painted on the window outside of The DreamCreamery's window! "I-cream, daddy! I-cream!" His chubby arm swings about and the lizard toys sails into the front seat knocking CJ's book out of his hand. It falls into the side crevice between the seat and the center console.

"Hey!" CJ complains. "It's gonna rip!"

"Ha! Gotta have faster reflexes like me, Ceej!" Bren teases from the backseat as he and CJ unbuckle their seatbelts. CJ rolls his eyes, hopping out of the truck to dig around under the seat to try and get his book.

I'm unbuckling Gabe when CJ holds a glittery tube up to me and says, "Dad, who's lipgloss is this?" He hands Gabe his stuffy while I stand there saying nothing...

Do I tell him it's Reese's?

No other woman has been in this car and Janet doesn't wear any makeup, let alone glitter lipgloss.

What lie could I tell? I don't want to lie at all but I don't want to have this conversation either. Those seem to be piling up at the moment.

"Um, it's a friend's," I reply, rushing everyone toward the burger joint. Bren has already decided running will be his only method of motion, so it's just me, CJ and my toddler walking to the restaurant at once. "She must have left it in here," I murmur to my oldest. I take the tube from him and put it into my back pocket.

My son looks like he has more questions, but thankfully we reach the cashier and she asks us, "What can I get you today?"

Bren orders three cheeseburger meals and one kid's meal as fast as he can, barely taking a breath between words. The cashier looks to me for confirmation and I nod, swiping my card when she tells us the total.

CJ picks up Gabe to put him in a high chair next to the booth Brendan is already sitting in.

Wasting no time, CJ asks, "Is she the friend from work that you saw last night?"

"I saw a lot of friends from work last night, buddy. She must have dropped that when I took her home." His eyes get very big behind his glasses and I know that I've made a bad choice in sharing that tidbit of information. Backtracking, I add, "It was late and sometimes it's safer if you drive someone instead of letting them drive themselves."

"She was drunk?!" CJ exclaims, eyes growing even larger.

I'm fucking this up, badly.

"That's not the point. I actually have something I wanted to talk to you three about. Well, you and Bren more than Gabriel."

"Oh no. Is this drunk lady going to be our new mommy?" CJ asks with his hands on his temples.

I choke on my water. Coughing for a moment before I shake my head saying, "Don't call her a drunk lady, CJ. She's not a drunk and no, she is not your new mommy. Her name is Reese." He nods slowly, but still seems hesitant.

Bren is barely listening as he dances the lizard around for Gabe, who is back to sucking on his shirt collar.

"The property that I am currently working on, will be offering a summer camp for kids your age. They have some spots open for you and Bren. Do you think you'd like to do that this summer instead of staying at Aunt Jan's all day?"

"Oh yes! Summer camp sounds like fun daddy! What do they do at camp?" Bren responds, but CJ remains quiet, picking at the straw paper wrapper from his fountain drink.

"At Mason Ranch, they'll teach you horse safety and how to ride and care for horses. There are other games, like kickball and scavenger hunts in the woods. They'll have different activities throughout the day. It will focus mostly around the horses, I think."

"That actually does sound pretty cool," CJ admits looking up from his shredded paper pieces.

"And I'll be a cowboy who can go fast?" Bren says pretending to ride a horse, circling a pretend lasso in the air.

Gabe bounces his lizard on the table, "Horsey!"

"Gabe, you're gonna be with Aunt Jan while Bren and CJ go to camp but we will visit the horses too, okay buddy?"

He dances his lizard around some more. Bren is still riding his imaginary horse when the cashier drops off our food and the boys get to eating.

"When are we going to be going to camp?" CJ asks when most of his food is gone.

"Next week, if you want."

He nods, and more tentatively he asks, "And Reese will be there?"

"Umm, I don't know Ceej. She trains the horses. I don't know if she works with the kids all that much." This conversation is actually going way better than I thought it would. I didn't know if they would be interested in something like this. They had spent their time with Van's parents for the summer in the past.

"Like the peanut butter cups. Is she made out of chocolate?" Bren asks around a mouthful of burger.

I laugh and shake my head. "No, she's not made of chocolate." Though she is sweet.

Thinking back to the kiss she gave me, I'm happy I saw her this morning. How long had it been since I kissed anyone like that? Years, if ever. I would hate for more years to go by without a kiss from this woman. Her soft curves and little teases. That gold chain I've grown accustomed to finding on her...

I drove home half hard and I could only think about when I would see her again. The tube of lipgloss burns in my pocket. I have a thought to send Reese a picture of it when my phone vibrates on the table with an unknown number.

"Everybody clean up and let's head next door." I pull out my wallet and hand CJ my card. "One scoop and one topping. A half scoop for Gabe. Okay? I gotta take this." He nods, helping his brothers get ready to leave. I answer my phone stepping outside of the restaurant.

"Whitfield Landscaping. What can I do for ya?"

"Hi, this is Rebecca Stewart. I got your number from Chandie. Are you free to talk right now?" My boys are walking out of Joe's and ambling into DreamCreamery. I move over to in front of the ice cream shop and give them a thumbs up as they wait in the short line to order.

"Yes. I am. Did you have a residential or commercial property request?"

"Actually what I'm asking for may be a little unorthodox. My husband has recently let go of a couple of employees we had working on our sod properties. They mostly run themselves, but we're approaching our busiest season. I was hoping we could partner with you for the harvest and distribution. I know it's not specifically what you do but Chandie speaks highly of your work ethic. I'd be able to compensate you fairly for the short notice."

"And you say there's a few properties? What would our timeline look like for this job?"

"We have three lots outside of the one behind our home. I have overseen the growth and watering myself and our cutting machines are already set to go. We'd need about four guys by the end of next week preferably. I'm happy to have you over to talk about it more. Could you come on Monday?"

"I could. You said your name was Rebecca?"

"Yes. Let's try for eleven. I'll send you the address."

"Perfect. Thank you."

We hang up and I let out a true sigh.

I'm getting closer and closer with each new piece of business coming my way.

The bell from the ice cream store dings as I enter to find where my sons are sitting. I see them in the back corner.

A pink mess covers Gabe as he tries to eat the strawberry scoop from his mini cone. "I-cream!" He exclaims as he tries to share some of his dessert with me. I dodge the dairy attack and opt for grabbing napkins instead to get some of the mess off his face and hands.

"No thank you, buddy. Is it good?" He nods emphatically, taking another lick and more drips from his cone onto the table.

"Who was that dad?" CJ asks eating his vanilla scoop from a cup.

"I think the answer to my prayers," I respond.

I suppose it's time to celebrate. I know exactly who I'd like to do that with. I send Reese a text.

Me: When will you be back in Alpenglow Ridge?

CHAPTER 19

Cory

"Are you gonna be okay on your own or do you want to ride with me?"

I gulp and look up at the massive, striking beast in front of me.

From where I was laying flowers or fresh sod, he always seemed... well, smaller. I am not a small man. At six foot one, there are very few who would use any word other than big to describe me. Hauling heavy materials for my job has served me well as far as muscle tone goes. As humble as a humble brag can be with these facts considered.

But standing next to him with his head looming over mine... I always thought horses were docile and friendly. Artemis looks like he might eat me.

"Don't you think a trail ride might be a little advanced for a beginner? Scratch that. A novice." I inch closer to the large white and brown horse and he bobs his head enough to startle me.

Reese laughs and I can't enjoy it because Artemis could chomp my hand off at any moment. "Don't be scared. They can feel that." I resist stepping any closer to the horse and my hesitation seems to amuse her even more. She holds a bigger laugh behind her hand. "We haven't gotten to the hard part yet. Are you sure you don't want to just ride with me?"

Ride with her? Tempting. So very tempting, but I doubt that will help my concentration at all. "No. It's fine. I'm trying to hold on to a little of my pride here."

She lifts an eyebrow. "I thought you were groveling?" *Oh right.* I had to cancel our Sunday night date because Bren wasn't feeling well. It must have been something he ate because he was sick as a dog the whole day and a bit yesterday. Janet might have been able to handle everything, but it didn't feel right to leave her to do the job.

I apologized to Reese so much. She told me it was no big deal since she was packing up her old place. I felt awful and told her I would make it up to her. I was surprised that she did invite me to go riding with her today. Reese is not the kind of person I would imagine to give someone a second chance. I'm not complaining.

"On horseback?" I ask, fidgeting with my key ring. I debate whether to ask her if I can meet her there with my truck or something, but keep my mouth shut instead.

She snickers, "Preferably. Look, I won't tell anyone if you're too scared to ride. Artemis has been on this trail plenty of times. It's going to be more about you not falling off than anything else." She pats his side and hands him a treat from her bag. I have the urge to protect her small hand when he grabs it with his big tile teeth. She gives me a look, not even paying attention to how close his mouth is to her hand. "It's no problem."

"Alright. And you promise he won't just take off and leave me dragging behind by the reins?"

She scoffs. "Are you questioning the integrity of mine or my dad's training abilities?"

Backtracking. I need to backtrack. "No. Not at all. I, um... I'm the inexperienced one... Maybe we could walk next to them. That would still be fun, right?"

"If you're really that nervous, you can just ride with me. It would be pointless to bring Artemis if you aren't gonna ride him. I'm not walking the ten miles this trail includes." She picks up the second bundle of equipment headed back from the tack room. Setting them on the small bench by the stable, she says, "Those are your options."

I think it over for a little while longer. Reese stands next to her horse, rubbing her side and cooing softly.

The jeans she has on have been a distraction this whole time walking over here. With her bending over to brush the horses' coats... Those thighs and the tiniest peek of her ass from a carefully cut and frayed hole under the back pocket are enough reasons to get onto this horse.

I don't think I'd last with her tight ass bouncing on my dick for ten miles of trail riding. But at least I'd be able to watch it bounce from my horse and not risk that embarrassment if I rode behind her.

She snaps her fingers pointing up to her face. "Eyes up here, prey. Which one? We're gonna miss the sunset." Her smirk let me know that she was entirely aware of where my thoughts had gone.

"If you say it's safe, I'll ride the beast." Artemis's large head ducks down to the side of my head and I catch the movement out of my periphery. Before I cringe, I can see that he is mirroring the position Heather is in with Reese, asking for scratches, too.

"See! He likes you." Reese reaches over to place my hand on the side of Artemis' neck. I give him a few rubs and he seems to be pleased with that.

Maybe this won't be so bad.

<hr>

REESE HOPS OFF HER horse to open the fence at the west side of the property. I've never been this far back on the ranch. There is a lot of new grass here where they have kept the cows from grazing over it.

Heather follows her through the opening and waits patiently for me to pass through on Artemis. After locking the gate, Reese re-mounts with ease, clipping her helmet back into place. She said she didn't normally wear her helmet, but she's got one on today in solidarity with me. She's sweet in that way.

It was hot with the sun beating down directly on my neck for the ride here. I'm not taking my helmet off until I am safely on the ground again. Seeing the small beads of sweat roll down Reese's back takes my mind to the fantasies. The ones I said I wasn't going to give into ,but they have been helping me get through the lonely nights.

Usually, I didn't have this problem. For her? I needed extra time with my fist lately.

My mouth waters and I shake my head to clear my thoughts. There is no way it will be safe for me to get distracted on the back of this gigantic horse.

It took some adjusting but I will admit that it was pretty cool to be on horseback. She showed me some basic maneuvers like how to hold the reins and my legs to make Artemis move. I do feel more confident, though the trail in front of me is not the same flat grazing land we had been crossing before.

Reese looks back at me when I'm still in the same place after she's progressed into the wooded area. "Come on, Cory. It's the same as before, just prettier."

"Yea. I, um… I'm on my way," I say, gripping the reins tighter in my hands.

"You sure? You're not moving." She chuckles, turning Heather to face where I'm still beside the gate.

Swiping a hand over my brow under the hot helmet, I say, "Oh. You noticed that."

"I thought we were past this. Artemis has gone on this trail a thousand times. He's not going to let anything happen to you. Do you want me to ride behind you?"

"No." I say more loudly than I meant to. Clearing my throat, I add, "It's fine." I press my legs in tight to Artemis giving him the go-ahead to take to the trail. Large trees shade the area and it's much cooler here than before. The relief of that alone has already made this journey worth it.

To her credit, the ride isn't that much different. The ground is clear and I only have to brush branches out of my way every now and again. I'm thankful to the fact she's in front of me so I know just when to be on the lookout for them.

Colorado is beautiful this time of year. It's lush with small pops of yellow, pink and purple blooms breaking up the monotony of green all around us. I've been hiking before. Hell, I used to hike all the time. There is something so different about seeing these familiar plants from horseback.

I smile to myself that Reese wanted to share this with me even after I flaked last weekend. We have been texting ever since. I've been made aware that she was nervous about the fact that my boys signed up for her clinic. I think she isn't giving herself enough credit.

Feeling confident enough with Artemis to carry on a conversation, I ask her, "So, are you looking forward to camp starting next week? I know it's just the soft launch, but Chandie was telling me about how excited she is for the boys to be a part of it."

I see her back stiffen. Expected at this point. This woman has avoided talking about my kids with expertise. I fully intend to open that door today. She brought me to do this with her and that means something to me. I know she has nowhere to duck off to or a way to truly distract me.

"Yea." She responds after a moment. " I am looking forward to it. Things on the back end have been going well."

"That's good to hear..." I push my luck, adding, "You'll have two of my sons in your program. Is that gonna be weird for you?"

She halts abruptly. Artemis stops as well, having the good sense to not run directly into Heather. I pull the right of my rein back anyway causing him to do a tight turn on the trail. Once I am back facing Reese, she smirks at me.

"What? I'm doing what you showed me," I explain.

"He would have stopped anyway. They aren't stupid."

I don't tell her that he did stop and it was me. "Just in case. It was only a precaution."

She gives me a placating nod. "Sure, sure." We continue down the trail under the cool canopy of trees. Birds scatter from them, adding to the peaceful ambiance. It honestly is a much nicer experience than I could have hoped for. Artemis isn't all that bad.

"Ah. Well, I forgot to tell you the other night, but CJ was the one who found your lipgloss under his seat. I told them who you were at lunch that day. It was also when I got the call from Rebecca about the other gig I landed."

She turns to look at me with Heather keeping her pace as before. "What did you say?"

"I landed another gig. I'll be working with Rebecca Stewart on the sod properties they own. I met with her yesterday. It's actually a pretty sweet—"

She cuts me off, stopping in front of the creek we've just approached. Reese is off of her horse quickly and coming to stand by my side. "No, that part about finding my lipgloss."

"Yea. What about it? I told them that you train the horses."

"And that was all?" She takes a water bottle out of her saddle bag, drinking deeply from the bottle before handing it over to me. I take it and drink deeply not aware of how thirsty I really was.

"Thanks, I needed that." Reese makes a rolling motion with her hands encouraging me to answer the question. "Nothing more than that. It's not like we were going steady when this happened," I joke, hoping to lighten the mood.

She smirks and walks over to where the horses are drinking from the creek and gives them both scratches at the base of their necks. She coos to them both, turning back to me. "Is that what we're doing? Is that what you want?"

"I've lost count of the number of times I've told you that I care for you and want to be the one who cares for you. I haven't wanted to get close to anyone after Van left. She was the only serious relationship I had ever been in. She gave me the greatest gifts before she decided that I wasn't what she wanted." I fiddle with the strap on my helmet before removing it from my head. Taking it off has given me something to do with my hands and I need something to focus on if I'm going to talk about this.

When I look up, she's toeing some rocks on the edge of the creek into the stream of water. Her response is hesitant and I can tell it's costing her something to ask this next question. "Is it hard?" She meets my eyes, clarifying, "Do you miss her, your ex-wife?"

I tut and rub a hand furiously over my hair. "Nah. She was... never for me, I guess. We were young and CJ was a surprise. I thought I was doing the right thing by asking her to marry me. Her family freaked out about her having a kid out of wedlock and it just... Nah, I don't miss her. But my boys—" I can't stop how my voice breaks. I don't talk about this with anyone. All my friends were her friends too and they chose her, which I can only see as the blessing it is. "My boys miss her. CJ the most. Bren and Gabe were too young to know much besides the fact that she was there and then she wasn't."

Wiping a hand on her jeans, she touches my arm. It's hesitant, but I lean into her tenderness. I thought that no one besides her horses received this kind of open affection. No one is here to witness it. I see the difference between me and them.

Maybe I am as pitiful as she assumed me to be in that hallway.

My heart softened because this woman was showing me attention. I don't give a damn. The look in her eyes feels like more than pity though. It's free of pretense and full of compassion. I don't know what I did to earn this from her, but I will take it either way.

I use my left hand to grab hers from my bicep to intertwine our fingers. She gasps softly when I pull her into my body.

We're both a little hot and sticky from the summer heat. Nothing could stop me from letting her know that she can have me. If she wants to touch me, to ground me in her affection—here I am.

It might be reckless, but I know this is the start of something. It takes her only moments to wrap her arms around my body and I settle my chin on her head. She says something into my chest, but I don't quite understand it. Leaning her head back from my body she says, "Is that why you looked so hurt when we first met? For them?"

"Yea." I brush a few strands that have escaped her braid from her lashes and tuck them behind her ear. She shudders. My fingers continue their path down her neck to her collarbone. I hook the necklace with my index and middle finger pulling it from under her tank top strap. Placing a kiss in the hollow of her neck and breathing in her warm scent mixed with the sweat of exertion to get here.

She places a hand over mine and I meet her eyes again. There's a vulnerability in their chocolate depths. "Are you sure?"

"About being with you? Absolutely. Do you want me to go get my letterman? I told you it was in my truck." I motion toward the general direction of where my truck is.

She chuckles before stepping away from my embrace, my arm falling limply to my side. "Telling your sons about me... About people knowing we're together. You may not have been here for very long, but people don't say the—" she pauses seeming to think about the words for a moment before continuing, "They don't say the nicest things about me. Are you sure you want to be associated with that? With me?"

Reese appears ready for me to answer in a way that would be the opposite of what I just said. It makes my chest hurt because I already know what they say.

"Reese, baby." I lift her chin to look up at me. "I don't give a damn what they say. If you commit to me, I will commit to you. Fully. When I said I wanted to be the one to care for you, it didn't come with conditions. What we do is between us. Our relationship would be for us. Everything else is just that. Everything else."

I give her some space again. What I'm going to say next could make all this fall apart if she doesn't tell me what I need to hear. "Are you sure that this is what *you* want? I have three boys. I have an ex-wife. I don't even have my own place right now, which I'm working on. But, this is me. My sons aren't going anywhere and I will never keep their mother from being in their lives, which might mean our lives too. I need to know that you are really in this."

Chapter 20

Reese, Seven Years Ago

"Do you like?" I run my finger through the now straight and honeyed strands. Feeling a little bit unsure of the drastic change. I'm standing in the doorway of a condo I have become all too familiar with.

He looks me over, taking in every inch of my frame. For a moment, I'm not sure he will actually invite me in. I didn't tell him that I was coming over, but I figured he would like the surprise.

Teddy finally cracks a grin and pulls me into the house by my waist, closing the door behind him with a slam. "I love it. I've always said blonde suits you." He nuzzles my neck and I shiver.

"Thank God! I spent way too many hours with Chloe fussing over it to make sure my hair was perfect. Thank you by the way. It would not be possible if not for you." I give him a wink. Especially when the bundles of extensions are factored into the whole cost of bleaching and dying to match, as well. I look as close to Beyoncé on tour, as I possibly can with this honey gold hair, flowing down my back.

It has only been a few weeks that his credit card was burning a hole in my pocket. Swiping it never felt so good.

New dress? Compliments of Teddy.

My brand new tool-worked rhinestone cowboy boots? Also compliments of Teddy.

And let's not forget the stunning new teardrop diamond and turquoise earrings dangling from my ears. They really bring out the color of my hair against my skin.

You guessed it, also compliments of Teddy.

My birthday celebrations would not be complete without a new outfit. Cough, *compliments of Teddy*, cough.

Everything matches my bag, perfectly.

Hell, even I can't stop staring at me in the mirror. I feel and look like the bougie bitch I was always meant to be.

He frowns a bit. "You didn't tell anyone how you paid for that right?"

"No. I used the app, like you said. Easy and convenient." I trace some patterns onto his chest with my finger.

His smile returns. "Good. I had planned on seeing you tomorrow, but I think you can have your surprise now."

"Awe!" I squeal bouncing on my tiptoes as I follow him into the kitchen. "What did you get me?" My new designer ankle strap sandals click in the most satisfying way across his kitchen tiles. His open-concept kitchen is minimally decorated and it's obvious that he never cooks in here.

"It's a surprise, Ree. I had them wrap it. You can open it now if you want." He slides the gift over to me on the counter.

"Of course, I want!" There's gold wrapping paper on a rectangular box with a shiny gold ribbon tied on top. It looks almost too pretty to mess up. The excitement of a gift from him outweighs the time and effort that went into the wrapping.

I pick the box up and it's decently heavy. Once I get the paper off, my eyes widen in surprise.

"D'usse." The cognac is highly coveted by the rappers I listen to and I remember thinking that it would be something Teddy would drink.

"You don't like it." He says, not asks, his response. He hangs his head, small strands of his brown hair flopping into his face. Teddy leans onto the counter and I barely registered before that he is still in a suit. It was a work day for him today. However, I know he's been home for at least an hour.

I never thought it was unusual that he seemed to live in these suits. It's kinda sexy. As a lawyer, excuse me, *named partner*, he represents not only his clients, but the reputation of the firm. I've seen him in casual clothes twice since we started talking that night.

We video chat pretty often but mostly text back and forth. He talks to me more than the boys at my school. I've stayed at his house a few times too with Chloe or Mel covering for me so that I can spend the night.

Gone are the Joshs and Allens. I have *a man* on my line now. One who is always sending me lunch, buying me things, and asking me about my day.

Not just trying to feel me up after class or hook up at some party.

All the girls in my grade are jealous that I'm being spoiled so thoroughly. I can't blame them, I would be jealous of me too.

I cross the short distance to him, tucking his hair back in its place, waiting for him to meet my eyes. When he does, I say, "I love it. So thoughtful of you." Raising my eyebrows, I ask, "Wanna be a cognac man with me tonight?"

His face brightens. "Very much so." He turns to grab two glasses from his cabinet. The well-dressed man opens the bottle with ease and pours us each some of the dark spirit.

At first sip, the brandy is a little bit spicy, but still smoother than the *rubbing alcohol* my friends are usually able to nab for parties I've been to. I take another sip watching him as he watches me intently.

"Do you like it?"

"It's nice. Feels warm in my body." I let a hand skim down my curves and his eyes are drawn to the motion. He sips from his glass again and I ask, "Can we watch something? I told my parents that I'd be at Chloe's tonight since she's going to be at Q's. We're each other's alibi." I wiggle my eyebrows and do a little jig, proud of myself for making the time to spend with him.

"You pick something. I'm gonna order food. Is that okay?"

"Of course," I respond before flopping onto his plush leather sectional couch. I start scrolling through the streaming options before settling on a cheesy rom-com. I want to see if he'll say something about the selection.

He unbuttons his suit jacket and hangs it over the back of the dining room chair just off to the side of the luxe living room. When he comes to sit, I arrange us so that I'm laying back over his arm. He doesn't comment on the movie I picked as I had hoped. We watch together until the delivery person rings the bell out front. Teddy gets the bags and I meet him at the table to get some food.

"I have kind of another surprise for you." He holds up a green paper bag for me to see.

"Is it extra rolls? I am obsessed with those things. I could probably eat my weight in bread right now. I'm starved." I finish the glass of D'usse I was drinking, setting it on the table. Teddy picks up the glass and returns with it filled again.

I have no idea how much because I'm already feeling a little bit tipsy after the first. I live in the country and we don't have much to do besides drinking and fucking shit up, but I usually just stick to beers. This stuff is much stronger.

"No, Ree. It's not rolls. It's chocolate, actually," he says.

"Even better! I love chocolate!"

"Infused chocolate." He laughs. Teddy takes a few moments to open the confusing package and hands a couple of pieces to me. I eat all three pieces before I think out loud, "Infused with what?"

"It's canna-chocolate. You ever had it before?"

No.

No, I have not.

I've maybe taken a hit of someone's joint here or there, but I have never had an edible before. Not wanting to sound dumb and inexperienced though I totally am, I lie and say, "Yea. This is yummy! Tastes like chocolate oranges." And it did. It tasted like chocolate oranges with maybe a bit of dirt. Strange but familiar.

I didn't feel any different from the earlier tipsiness. But... I have no idea how long it will take to feel the effects of these.

We both sit at the dining table and I shovel food into my mouth because I wasn't lying when I said I was starved. I'm still drinking alcohol because I never asked for water and Teddy didn't offer any to me either.

After I'm done eating, I feel even more dizzy and lightheaded than I did before. I remember him asking if I wanted to lie down and I nodded to get to the couch and try to watch the movie again. He hands me more chocolate and I take it because I didn't think that I should stop eating them. I end up falling asleep on the movie before it's over.

When I wake up the next morning, I feel groggy and like I'm on a boat just bobbing in the water.

I'm still high.

Rubbing at the crust in my eyes, I try to get my bearings. It's dark in the room even with the first rays of sunlight coming in from the large windows here. I try to sit up as slowly as I can manage because I'm like a hair's breadth away from throwing up right now. I can feel the uneasiness in my gut already.

I look for my phone and I stop moving entirely when I notice that I'm naked.

Naked, naked.

There is not a single piece of clothing on me.

The panic builds and builds as I can't find my phone and I'm still feeling like the room is spinning. I try to think back to whether I had taken them off myself but I don't remember anything.

There is deep breathing from the other side of me where Teddy sleeps. He's lying across the chaise of the sectional, only in boxers now.

I start to feel around my body to check for any indication that something happened between us. The more I panicked the more I realized that something definitely happened between us. He—

I can't say it.

I won't say it.

There's got to be an explanation for this because he wouldn't do that. I know he wouldn't. I'm just not thinking straight right now. I find my dress on the floor at my feet. I tug it on and curl up under the blanket though

I never found my underwear. I try to sleep off this awful headache and uneasiness a little longer.

When daylight comes through the room, I wake with an even worse headache. I stumble to the bathroom and do my business. I stop in front of the mirror because my hair looks like a complete rat's nest in the back. Upon further inspection, there are little hickeys down my neck and chest. Afraid to look, but needing to know I take my dress back off. I gasp when I see the bruises at my waist in the shape of fingers.

I can't say it.

"Ree. You up?" His voice sounds like razor blades in my head. Not just from the headache but from what I now suspect happened last night.

I quickly redress and wash my hands.

Leaving the bathroom, I see he's standing in the kitchen pouring himself some coffee. He holds a mug to me, but I shake my head stuttering out, "Did we... Were we... Did you fuck me last night?"

"Hi, good morning," He says with a chuckle like something is funny.

I scoff. "Good morning. Now, answer the question."

"We did have a little fun last night." He smiles into his phone as he scrolls emails.

"A little fun?!" My voice is shrill as it echoes through the kitchen space. "I was passed out. I don't think it can be fun for me if my boyfriend is fucking me while I'm not even conscious!"

"Boyfriend? Ree." His tone is condescending like he's talking to a toddler and not an eighteen year old woman. "I'm not your boyfriend. We had a deal. I just collected on my part of it." Face as hard as stone. Not one emotion crosses it. As if I am the one being irrational.

I sputter for several moments before I can choose my words more effectively. "Not my—You had sex with my unconscious body last night."

"And was I present while you were charging all sorts of bullshit to my card? I think not." He sets his coffee on the counter and gets into my face. "I'd say we're even for now. You can take a shower upstairs. I ordered breakfast and it should be here in the next twenty."

"Even? For now?" I stand there in utter shock at what I'm hearing. I cross my arms over my body to stave off the chill seeping into my bones. I still feel a little queasy and like my brain is about to pound out of my skull.

"Yes. Shower upstairs. I assume you brought a bag since you planned to stay the night." He raises an eyebrow.

I did pack a bag to stay the night. When I packed everything, sex had crossed my mind. I didn't think it would happen like this. I had at least thought I would remember what we did. And maybe even enjoy it.

He is acting as if this is all normal. And maybe it is normal. I'm not a virgin but I've never stayed the night at a guy's house for this type of thing before. I've also never been that drunk or high before. I probably wanted to have sex with him and said as much, but just don't remember because I was so messed up.

I grab my bag and shower before I come back downstairs in leggings and a tank top. The food is waiting for me because he has already served us both breakfast hash with an omelet. There's also orange juice and under any other circumstances, I would think this is kinda sweet. My head is still throbbing with the headache of everything that happened last night.

He said he wasn't my boyfriend, but he's taking care of me like one. Maybe he just doesn't like labels or something. I continue to think as I eat the food in front of me.

Teddy breaks the silence and I startle out of my reverie. "I had planned to come and pick you up today for this, but we can go after you finish eating. If you still want."

I sip my orange juice and ask, "Go where?"

"Your choice. It's been almost a year since your last. Nordstrom is your store, is it not?"

My entire mood changes. No mention of a budget. Or a time limit. It only takes me moments to realize what is at stake. I've known him long enough to know that anything he wants to stipulate, he will. My curiosity and need for luxury just like the women I admire on glossy covers and in all the music videos I consume outweighs any previous distress I had before.

Like a moth to a flame, I nod my head.

He raises an eyebrow. "And our agreement stands?"

I swallow several times around nothing. *Our agreement.* When he said "time" before I didn't think that included sex. I suppose I knew a grown man would want more. I just thought it would be... different.

We had been spending time. Talking, spending the night, and a date occasionally. I actually enjoyed Teddy's company. He didn't make me feel like a child. He made me feel important. Dared me to dream of more from my life.

After all, what's the difference between a grope here or there and what happened to me last night? Teddy is getting me far nicer things than Taco Bell and boots. The stakes are simply higher. That's all.

Besides... I'm not hurting. I feel... normal.

Look normal.

Outside of a few hickeys and bruises, I feel the same.

Could it be so bad to have an agreement like this when I get a new handbag out of it too?

"Our agreement stands," I say.

Chapter 21

Reese

I NEED TO KNOW *that you are really in this.*

I should have taken more time.

This is the opposite of temporary.

The opposite of casual.

And I haven't even begun to figure out what I'm going to do about Teddy. I can't hurt Cory. I'm selfish enough to ignore all those things and answer him. "Yes. I want this. I want you."

Cory steps into my space again pulling me so that our bodies are flush against each other. I'm helpless to how I melt into him when our lips meet. He kisses me softly.

I feel the tug of my braid as he wraps a hand around it. Moaning into his mouth, I feel even hotter than before with him growing harder. The longer we kiss, it's as if oxygen doesn't matter. I've never been kissed like this. Cory makes me feel like I'm seventeen again.

Like every kiss is a first one.

I can't get enough of how he lets me pick the pace and respects my wishes and even my demands for more.

I want more.

I want this man and what he could give me.

Not designer accessories or money or gifts of any kind.

Just him.

I like him.

I want more of Cory... and this feeling.

That should be scary, but it isn't.

My fingers dig into his back and shirt as I work to bring him closer though our bodies are already touching. When I reach for his pants, he lets me. I palm him reverently and a groan rumbles from his lips into my mouth and it tastes like assurance. I'm trying to work his belt free from his cargos. He's hard and ready for me and I want nothing more than to let him slide into my body to...

I don't even know... Solidify that he wants me.

Just me.

"Is this all we were meant to see?" He says breaking my lust-blown haze.

"Huh?" I say, panting.

"On the trail ride?"

My lust clears for a bit and I register what he's talking about even though my body is still humming on the one-track thought of having him inside me.

Suddenly, I feel embarrassed.

Rejected.

Deeply ashamed that I was going to try to fuck him right here, right now.

This is the second time that I have offered my body to him and he's stopped my advances.

He doesn't want that.

I'm basically assaulting him because I don't know how to do this.

Sex is always expected of me. And he... he doesn't want it.

I step away from him, feeling how hot my neck and face are with the feelings coming to me more quickly than I can stop them. I back away, away, away until my body hits a tree.

I hear the jingling of Cory's buckle but my face is in my hands.

No tears.

No tears.

"Baby." He tries to remove my hands, but I shake my head trying to avoid his attempts. He doesn't allow me to get far and I can't see anything with how my shame is still flaming up my neck. I slide down the tree trunk, not caring about how my shirt catches the bark and scratches at my skin.

Don't cry.

Hoe.

Golddigger.

Slut.

Don't fucking cry, Reese.

The words circle and circle and circle. I'm spun up and humiliated. He just asked me to be in an actual relationship with him. To be a part of his life. He told me that he didn't care what they said and that he wanted me anyway.

What am I doing?

God. He deserves better.

He at least deserves someone who can process simple affection like a regular woman would.

I took his sweet kiss and made it into something completely different.

"I'm sorry—I just... I'm proving them all right, aren't I?" My voice sounds weak and watery.

"Proving who right?" Cory asks me as he sits next to me on the ground. He plucks a leaf from my hair, smoothing more hair from my face. My skin still feels hot and sticky.

Not in the same way as before, when it turned me on. I want to crawl out of it and be anywhere else, but in this situation.

"Them." I flail my arms about knowing the names but not wanting to speak them. For fear that they will pop up to spread more gossip about the golddigging husband stealer. "Like I said, it's town gossip that I am—"

"I told you that I don't care about that. What's really going on? What did I say?"

What did he say? I shake my head. "No. It's what I did. I was trying—"

"Don't apologize for that. And as for the gossip..." He holds my face in his hands but I've already covered it again with my own. "Hate knows love's the cure," Cory says. "Stevie Wonder said that. As long as you resist what love tells you, the hate will always be louder. There are so many people in your life who love you, Reese. You are loved." He wraps his arms around my body and says into my hair, "Anyone with eyes can see that. You have eyes, don't you?" He jokes and nuzzles my head some more. "As much as I would love for us to do that, I would rather spend this time doing something that you love. You mentioned a sunset..."

He releases me from the embrace and I peek hesitantly between my fingers. I see his eyes are open, and there is no judgment there. It's only because he doesn't know me or what I've done.

He strokes my hands with his thumb and I take deep breaths grounding into his touch. Feeling each rough path of his thumb soothe me. Finally, I trust myself not to cry enough to drop my hands from my face.

"Hey, pretty girl." He keeps stroking my hands and I feel less embarrassed. He looks at me the same way he had before. No ill-will. No expectations. "Do you want to go back to the ranch?"

I shake my head. Using the hold he has on me to pull him back into me. The mix of his fabric softener and cologne makes me smile. I can feel myself relax further into his chest. Just like before, his head rests on mine. "We can go where I planned before." Cory's chin rubs my head as he agrees.

Reluctantly, I release our embrace and go to Heather, running my fingers through her mane. She nips at the side of my face and I scratch her some more knowing she can sense exactly what I'm feeling. "It's okay girl. You wanna keep riding?" I pull a treat from my saddlebag and give her one and then one to Artemis.

Cory has his helmet back on and is trying to mount Artemis by the time I've got onto Heather's back. "You need some help?"

"Um... nah." He grunts before I see his leg finally swing over. "See? I'm ready. Lead the way, pretty girl."

It shouldn't make me feel this giddy, but I like that he calls me that. I smirk and lead the horses over the shallow water. The sun is already getting lower in the sky. We should make it to the spot I've picked before the sun sets with some time to set up everything I've packed.

We ride in silence, taking in the scenery. Every now and then I sneak a peek behind me to see if he's keeping up. He's doing pretty well. Or Artemis is keeping him close. Either way, it makes me happier and happier to see him there smiling at me each time I turn around.

Why he hasn't run in the opposite direction is still beyond me. I'm not accustomed to having a breakdown like the one I just had in front of anyone. Cory took it in stride. What did I do to deserve a man like him?

We keep riding for a bit until the trees thin and a much larger clearing stretches out before us.

"Oh wow! That's…"

"Stunning," I say, hopping off Heather for the last time looking at what he's seeing. The creek we were at before leads to the Poudre River which is much wider. The water rushes over large boulders in the river. It's loud enough to be calming and not drown out regular conversation.

Cory dismounts from his horse and walks over to the river. He shocks me when he takes his shoes and socks off before rolling up his pant legs to his knees. I join him, taking off my boots and setting them next to his. When I get into the water next to him, the immediate cold of the water makes me shiver. He pulls me over to him and we stand on a flat rock with his arms over my shoulders.

The sky is open and clear this evening. The foothills are only a few minutes from here. The striking way that the peaks cut across the sky would take anyone's breath away. We sway in the water sharing hiking stories until our legs get too cold. Mine from when I lived here still and his from when he lived in Denver.

I packed a blanket for our ride and laid it out on the grassy clearing near the river for us to sit on. The horses meander by the water and nibble on some grass just to our side. Everything about this moment feels special. With my legs crossed, Cory lays his head on my lap.

"Thank you for bringing me here." I look away from the mountains to look at him again. My fingernails are running over his scalp and he looks utterly at peace.

"There's more," I say. "Stay here." He lifts his head from my lap and I return with the insulated lunch box and thermos I packed earlier.

"Damn. Now, I know for sure that you like me."

I chuckle, arranging the fruits and cheeses I brought for us on the blanket. "Is a sunset picnic, really a sunset picnic without food and drink?" I wink, reclining onto the blanket carefully, trying not to spill any of the food I've arranged.

I offer him the thermos and he sniffs it. "Is this lemonade?"

"We can't exactly ride home drunk. Definitely not safe for a—what'd you call yourself? Oh yea. Definitely not safe for a novice horse rider."

"Thank you for bringing me here." He repeats but this time grabbing my hand.

"I figured that it's my job to show you the very best Alpenglow Ridge has to offer." I shrug. "My parents used to come out here with me when we were young. It felt like we went so much farther than this, back then. Like we had traveled across some great long distance. Funnily enough, everything was just in our backyard." I get lost in the memories of a time when things were so magical.

"How old were you when you started riding?" He traces the lines on my palms and over the creases of my knuckles. The touch is so soothing and gentle.

I close my eyes before responding. "I think my dad let me on a horse by myself when I was seven or eight. Not for long periods at a time and he was by my side for most of it. He never was the same protective with Mack. But, I think the first time I came here was when we were nine."

"That's kind of incredible. I couldn't imagine the boys riding this far. Would you bring them here?"

I think over what he's really asking. "When they're ready, sure. Maybe you could wear Gabe on your back." I giggle and feel the shadow over my face as he leans over me. I open my eyes again. Warm browns connect with mine and I reach up to touch his face. Cory nestles into my hand.

"You really want to bring them all here?"

I scratch into his beard feeling the coarse, yet soft hair underneath my nails. "Sure, why wouldn't I?"

He closes his eyes. I miss his attention, but he seems to be thinking over his next words. "I didn't have this for so long. Parents. I never know if I'm doing enough or making the right decisions for them."

"When did you lose them?" I don't want to prod but I want to hold all the weight of his heart in mine like he did for me. I will back off if he doesn't want to share. I have to try.

"Ten." He swallows several times before looking at me again with watery eyes. "They were hit by a drunk driver when I was ten years old. After going to dinner one night. I was with my grandma."

"Cory," I sit up resting a hand on his shoulder. "I'm so sorry. I can't imagine what that was like for you. When I nearly lost Danny, I did not cope well. I'm so sorry."

"Yea. It's alright. I never talk about it. I, also, never drink more than one if I'm out. I don't even drink at home. I still remember talking to them before they left that night." He gives a short chuff. "I complained about how many kisses my mom was giving me before they walked out. My dad was just telling me how I needed to finish my homework before I could watch TV."

And he never saw them again. My eyes sting a bit. I ask, "What's your favorite memory of them?"

"Easy," he sighs. "Breakfasts with them. My mom wasn't that great of a cook. My dad mostly cooked and my mom supervised. But she and my dad made breakfast every morning. Together. They fit each other perfectly, even at a young age I could tell that what they had was remarkable. I never saw them fight or raise their voices with each other. They were always touching like it would hurt them to not be joined in some way."

He's lost in the memories. I can't help but smile at his soft smile as he recalls, "I knew I wanted a love like that. They told me that I was the greatest joy they ever received. Eyes just like my dad's, my mom's nose and mouth. Even after all these years, I still miss them so fucking much."

His voice breaks at the end and I wipe a lone tear from his cheek with my thumb. He locks eyes with me again and the vulnerability there takes my breath away.

I crawl closer to him, needing to be closer. Straddling his lap, he grabs my thighs and rests his head against my collarbone. The smell of his shampoo beckons me to rest my chin on his head, happy to be connected to him... A man who deserved so much more from his life.

So much more than me.

Can I really be what he wants?

What he needs?

"I bet they would be proud of you, of the man you are."

His voice is slightly muffled as he talks into my chest. "Why's that?"

"You're raising three beautiful children, and well from what I can tell. What the town says. You're chasing your passion. You still have such a positive outlook on life. What more could a parent want for their son?"

"Mmmh. But, I failed at one thing."

"At what?" I question.

"I'm working on it right now."

Leaning back, Cory lifts his head. His hands hold me at the waist, not tightly, but firm enough that I can feel each of his fingertips.

Breathless, I ask, "What are you working on?"

He kisses along my jaw and down my neck. "Finding my match."

CHAPTER 22

Reese

WHEN I THOUGHT OF bringing Cory here, I could only hope that he would make out with me. That maybe I would receive more of his sweet kisses.

After what I said in the trees for just us to hear, I didn't see him accepting me or revealing his own hurt to me.

But here I am, looking into the eyes of this beautiful man who wears his heart on his sleeve. Who exposed his loss to me with the reverence saved for only someone whom you can trust.

Maybe that's game, but I will play it until he's done with me. Whatever he wants I would happily give in this moment.

When he catches my gold harness in his teeth, I shiver. My nipples hardening in anticipation. I swear this man has already trained my body. Already shown me that when he wants me, this is the first of his advances.

His lips trail lower and I can't help but grind down on his lap to feel his growing erection. In this light, his freckled brown skin glows as he runs his hands down my waist and thighs.

I want more but I don't want to push him. I do it anyway. "More. Cory, please."

"I got you, pretty girl. Let me show you what it means to be mine. There is no part of you that I won't cherish." He punctuates each promise with a kiss that makes me feel more restless than the last. My hips rub over him more deliberately as I chase the arousal building in me from his words.

Cherish.

Have I ever been cherished before?

With my breast in his hand he circles my stiff nipple with his thumb and I drop my head back. His other hand is on my ass, and I feel too hot. I'm buzzing with the need to touch him, but I don't want to embarrass myself again... or make him uncomfortable...

I want to be cherished by him.

To be treated like I'm precious and important to him.

This tender man with family on his heart and compassion in his caress.

It's me that he wants.

Just me.

"Can I take this off?" He asks, pulling up on my tank top. I nod emphatically, *please* on my lips. He chuckles, "I mean do many people come over here?"

"Oh." I brush the hair out of my lashes, sitting up." No, not unless they are coming from our property. It's difficult to cross the river here and people couldn't see us from the other side." I move my hips back and forth more quickly now. "Cory, please." I feel needy, sound needy and I might die if he doesn't put his mouth on me again.

His sultry eyes light with desire and I shudder as he lifts my top over my head. Pulling my soft bra down, he lowers his lips to my nipple. Licking all around the brown peak until I'm truly aching. Pinching it lightly, he moves to the other to give it the same sweet kisses. I hold his head to me all while I'm still grinding my hips onto him. Desperate.

I had gone months without the desire to even be near a man this way. Somehow, around this man, I can't keep my hands to myself. I don't want space—I just want him to touch in every way imaginable.

He lays me back on the blanket and pulls his own shirt off. His big body shades my own as I look up at him. Unclipping my bra, I throw it onto the pile of our clothes and watch him. Enchanted by how even his body is kissed with the same delicious freckles and more ink I couldn't see before. His broad chest flexes as he runs his hands over my exposed body, holding my breasts with both hands.

There has never been a sexier sight than Cory kneeling over me with the sun beginning to set behind him. His shoulders bunch, bouncing the tattoo that trails down his right arm. I can't make out the design, but I'm not really trying because I'm too distracted by how he's kissing down my chest and stomach. I refuse to close my eyes for even a second for fear of missing anything. I love how he takes his time with me.

There is no hurry or rush.

When he gets to my jeans he pulls at the waistband with his teeth. The brush of his trim mustache against my sensitized skin makes goosebumps rise across my middle.

All I want is to hold on to this moment for as long as possible, when he says, "You want this, beautiful? Do you want my mouth on that needy pussy?"

"Should I mail you a formal request, Cory? Please." I whimper and he unbuttons my pants. Lifting my hips, he works them down and off. The cool breeze on my thighs and calves feels as sinful as the warm breaths Cory takes admiring the little cotton thong I'm wearing.

"How did you know green was my favorite color?" He asks just before nibbling at the waistband. He kisses over my hips and the elastic of my panties, driving me crazy. I'm so worked up that I feel how damp this thong is getting by the second. I'm feeling frenzied and I want more than just these kisses over fabric. My hips buck up toward his mouth, begging for more.

He was right. I am so needy for him. So desperate to get more than this. "More. Please, please, Cory. I need your mouth."

"In time, pretty girl. I want to savor every taste." With that, he licks right over my clit through the fabric again. My heedless moan rings loud in my own ears and I try to be good. To listen to his words.

He smirks up at me, pulling my thong down my legs. He doesn't take them off, just pulls them low enough to put his head between my thighs.

"Oh, baby." He moves his focus from my center to my face again. "You're dripping. Is that for me?" His deep voice rumbles over my throbbing clit and I squirm with restraint. It would be too easy to pull his face to me with my thighs.

"God, yes. Touch me." *Please, please, please.*

He rubs a finger through my lips and watch his finger slide easily through my wetness. He looks into my eyes from between my legs. "Perfection warrants patience," he says before he dips a finger in, to the knuckle and pulls it out again. I whimper as I try to stay put. I try to stop squirming.

"Don't move." Teddy's command resonates in my head. Words of domination and I adhere. I squeeze my eyes closed and clear his voice from my thoughts.

No.

No, I'm here with Cory.

This is different.

A second finger pushes into me and I'm back on this picnic blanket with Cory again. I moan at his thick fingers sliding in deeper and deeper. His mouth descends to my clit and I cry out from how good it feels to have his hot mouth on my sensitive bud.

"Cory!" I cry, grabbing onto his short hair as best I can. I settle for scratching my nails at his scalp while I hold his head right where I want him. He hums onto my clit in approval and I melt under his ministrations. "You're going to make me come. Please, baby. Lick my clit, I need your tongue."

All the blood in my body rushes with my quickening heartbeat as he flicks his tongue over me back and forth. I can feel my pussy gripping his fingers and he curls them up, hitting my spot. The pressure is perfect, the pace has me panting and I'm—"Cory, I'm going to come just like that. I'm gonna—"

"Like this, pretty girl. Is this what you wanted?"

"Yes, yes, yes." I chant as my orgasm crests and throbs. My back arches off of the blanket and I soar on the high of elation Cory has given me. He drags out my pleasure slowly thrusting in and out of me with his fingers, watching me with hooded eyes.

I relax onto the blanket again. Taking in the man in front of me who just made me come harder than I ever have with someone else. His dick strains in his cargos so hard it looks painful.

I'm too sensitive and I grab his wrist to halt his movements. He pulls his fingers out, slow and deliberate. I sit up to bring his hand to my mouth, but he stops me.

"Ah, ah. This is for me." He licks his fingers, not missing a single drop of my release. I shudder again. I could come again from the satisfied look on his face alone. "Haven't I earned dessert?"

I flop back on the blanket feeling boneless and satiated. "Wake me up when I get a turn." I feel my lids getting heavier and heavier. I feel a little bit selfish just lying here, but it isn't long before he lies at my side.

"When I take you, Reese, it will be at my leisure. Not some quickie in the woods."

Being a bit bratty, I say, "I don't think this counts as the woods," rubbing my chin, like I'm deep in thought.

"Whatever it is, I realized just now that I only want those sweet sounds for myself. Not even the mountain lions can have them."

I sit up with a hand to my chest. I gasp. "Do you think the horses are scandalized now? Heather probably can't wait to spill all the dirty details of what we did here to her stable mates." I'm still completely naked and Cory has on his pants. Something about my state of undress and his relaxed face does something to me.

A corner of his lips quirks up, "You think you're funny, huh?" I nod, biting my lip before reaching over his body to grab my clothes. My nipples brush across his chest and I lean in, knowing that I'm only tempting him further.

He's still hard.

Licking my lips, I run my hand over his straining erection hoping to tempt him.

His voice comes out controlled and even but the threat of reprimand lingers there. "Pretty girl, you're playing with fire."

"Maybe I like it hot…" I did. I wanted to ride him slow in the sunset.

"Not tonight, pretty girl. We need to get home." He gets up from the blanket, adjusting himself, to get the water bottle. He takes a big swig and offers the bottle to me. "Feeling thirsty?"

"Feeling like jello." I respond reaching for it with as little effort as possible.

"Good." He smirks and nods to himself.

He holds me for a few more moments on the blanket before we re-dress and I untie the horses for us to get back home.

Later that night when I'm lying in bed after a long session with Pinky in the shower. My phone buzzes with a text from him that makes me feel giddy and irrationally excited.

Cory : Can I take you to dinner tomorrow night?

CHAPTER 23

Reese

"SHOULD I TELL HIM you'll be another hour?" I check my phone and see it's 5:30 PM.

"Ha ha. Very funny, mom. I just need to put my clothes and some perfume on now." I top the dark pink liquid lipstick off with some gloss. I lean into the mirror making sure my makeup looks as good up close as it does from farther away.

Chandie smiles at me in the mirror. "You look beautiful, honey." She gives my hair in the back a fluff. "I knew you'd like him."

My brows pinch. "Like him? What makes you say that?"

"Probably the fact that you're getting fully glammed to go have dinner... on a Wednesday." I unplug the curling iron I used before to put loose curls in my hair and turn to face my mom.

"If I'm leaving the house, I need to be stunning. Simple."

"Uh-huh. Sure, baby." She leaves the bathroom as I'm putting the makeup bag I'm bringing with me into my purse.

She returns with a small red box in her hands. Looking at her face, my look asks *what is this?* She gives me a look back that says *open it and find out.*

I take it from her and open the lid. Inside sits a small charm that has three stones dangling from their own short chains.

"What's this?" I take the small piece and look at the stones more closely.

"For your harness." She closes my hand with her own, bringing our joint hands to her lips and kissing them. "Polished to a shine, I made this charm so many years ago and I've not made any like it. I had hoped it would be for a pendant but I think you could use them tonight."

I'm taken aback by her words. For my twenty-first, my mom asked me if I wanted a necklace as a present and I requested this gold harness instead.

"Do you remember what you said to me?"

"Yea. I wanted to protect my heart. We both know I love this harness because it's sexy. Permanent jewelry is still very fashionable, mom."

"It is, it is. And I've never made another one of those either."

"It's not really your style."

"True. But I know why you wanted to protect your heart."

I step back from her, panicked by what she might bring up. I am in no place to have this discussion right now. "What do you know?"

"Baby, I saw how you shrank away from us long before you moved to Denver. Your dad may not have been as vocal as I was, but we knew you were going through something. You moving out was the real sign. I wish I had said more. I regret that all the time." She shakes her head, "That's in the past, and when you're ready to talk just know that I'm here for you. This charm is to be worn close to your heart."

"Okay. Thank you for the charm. It's beautiful." I don't know what else to say because Cory will be here in a short while. Whatever my mom thinks she knows will have to wait. "It's just dinner." I shrug, turning back to the counter to fluff my hair some more, feigning nonchalance that I don't feel. "I'm gonna get dressed." I grab my phone and purse from the counter, walk to my room, and leave my mom in the bathroom.

Closing the door behind me, I pick up the dress I let steam from my shower. A shower I desperately needed after loading and unloading the last of my boxes from the apartment into the house earlier.

The burgundy material is soft and buttery under my fingers. It's the same shade as the crop top I wore when Cory brought me home. I hope that he will think of our first kiss, then what we did last night. And maybe more...

As I'm sliding on my chunky heels, I hear the doorbell ring.

I check my reflection once again and smirk. Running my hands down the sides of my breasts and hips, I blow a kiss in the mirror. "Slim thick and he knows it!"

The charm my mom gave me falls onto the floor from my nightstand and I pick it up. Years of being my mom's little helper when I was not allowed to ride on my own helps me recall what the stones are: Red Jasper, Rose Quartz, and White Jade. I smile to myself and pull my harness up through the plunging neckline of my dress. I open the lobster claw clasp and attach the pendant. The cold metal tickles my sternum and I feel them tap against me with every step I take down the hall.

Cory's eyes drink in my every detail from head to toe as he stands from the couch where my Dad sits with him. I caught the end of their conversation before my dad noticed that I was in the room. "—I brought that stag down, and I doubt that you are much faster than him."

Cory laughs nervously as I look from him to my dad sitting in his recliner. "Message received, Danny. I'll have her home before midnight." He brushes his dark jeans and comes to stand next to me.

"She's a grown woman, Danny. Leave her be!" My mom slaps at his arm and turns to me from where she's standing by the mantle. "Come home when you're ready. Just use the side door." She winks. "I don't want to be woken up before sunrise."

"Wow. This is not junior prom you guys. Please let's go before they try to have the birds and bees talk with us." I grab Cory's hand, "Bye, parents. Don't wait up."

I waste no time leading him to his truck. He's still chuckling but it's much more relaxed now that we aren't getting the third degree from good cop/bad cop in there.

"Don't be embarrassed. They care about you," he says.

"You wouldn't be saying that if it were your parents' doing this." I slap a hand over my mouth not realizing what I said until the words already left my lips.

"I would love to have them still looking out for me." He gives me a small smile looking up at me through dark lashes. I'm leaning on the passenger side door like the first night we spent together. Tonight, things are different. The sun is out, but just barely. "That's heavy. You don't have to pick it up."

My brows pinch. I take in the dark button-down he's wearing that's rolled up over his forearms. Tentatively, I rest a hand on one of them and use my other hand to raise his chin to meet my eyes. "I'm sorry, I didn't mean to say that."

"I know what you meant. Seriously, it's fine." He shakes his head clearing the drab thought and my hand drops from his face. He takes it again, rough callouses catching my knuckles, but he's raising my hand back to his face. "I love it when you do that." His smile is almost boyish. The gold in his eyes seems to brighten when I hold his face in earnest now.

"I don't know why I keep doing it. I'm really not like this." I bit my lip and he uses his thumb to pull it from my teeth.

"Don't be embarrassed. You're in Cory's care now. There's probably nothing you could do that I wouldn't enjoy." He opens my door for me and I get into his passenger seat again.

"Cory with the green heart emoji, right?" My smirk is hard to contain. "I forgot how serious we were. I mean you met my parents and everything."

"That's right," he responds. Not missing a beat. "The heart emoji is binding." He winks and I feel my face heat.

I let careful fingers curl into his soft beard and my thumb brushes over his plump bottom lip. "Since we're going steady, can I kiss you before the date?"

I can't take another moment without it. Without him. It hasn't even been a full day since I last had my lips on his, but I need to feel them like I need my next breath right now.

He leans down to press his lips to the side of my mouth. Intentionally, missing the kiss I wanted. "If we don't leave soon, I'll have you straddling me in the passenger seat again." He pulls me close to him, but not close enough. "You look stunning. I haven't said it yet and I couldn't let another moment pass without letting you know."

In this dress, it's easy enough to swing my legs to pull him into me just like at QB's. For a second, I think he'll let me have what I'm asking for. "Reese. Let me take you to dinner." He chuckles at my persistence and I sigh.

The pout I have on is childish, but I've never had a man resist me so easily. I get what I want or leave.

For some reason, I trust what Cory has in store for us tonight.

"Fine." I cross my arms over my chest. He chuckles some more, but closes my door and gets into the driver's seat.

We pull out of the long drive and he takes the left instead of the right, which would take us into town, and heads toward the highway instead. "I hope you don't mind, I wanted to go somewhere a little fancier than Alpenglow Ridge's Town Grill."

I place my hand on his knee, "I don't mind at all. Where are we going?"

"Rossi's. I haven't had good Italian food in the longest."

"Rossi's is my favorite! I love the alfredo tortellini." At his smile, I ask, "Did you know that? How did you know that?!"

"A little birdie told me."

"Is that little birdie, Clo?"

He looks over to me quickly and returns his eyes to the road. "And what if I did have a little help?" His gaze flicks back and forth from me to the road only making my smile grow. This man put more effort into this last minute date than I could have expected. I'm so happy that I spent the time I did getting ready today. The bodycon dress I chose is just nice enough to be appropriate for the place we're going to.

I've ordered takeout from this restaurant more times than I can count. But a date there? Not once.

I give his knee another squeeze. "I wouldn't say anything about it. It's perfect, Cory."

CHAPTER 24

Cory

"Whitfield, party of two."

The hostess calls us and I walk behind Reese with my hand on her lower back. I just know that she wore this little dress only to show me how toned and long her legs are. I already know. I remember how she held me in place with her thighs on that picnic blanket. How could I forget?

The curves that I'm fighting hard not to imagine getting lost in are distracting to my bigger agenda. I brought her to dinner for the sole purpose of getting to know her better. To find out more about what lies beneath that pretty sadity persona everyone else gets from her. I know there is something softer and sweeter at her core.

Yesterday, I said I wanted to know if she was all in. Maybe it was too soon to ask that of someone but that's where I am in life. I don't have the desire to be messing around with someone who isn't interested in more than hooking up. Being between those long legs yesterday had been more than I could have hoped for… I need to know there is more to our connection than that.

I won't lie and say that I wasn't tempted to run my hands up her thigh the whole ride here. Just to see if she's as wet as she was yesterday.

I won't even lie and say that I haven't been picturing what that little gold chain looks like over her laid out on my bed.

There's no point.

No one would believe that lie.

I crave Reese more than anyone I've met before. There is more to us. For the sake of my sanity, hitting and quitting is not an option. This woman would make me forget my own name if I let her.

Her delicate hand on my knee, while we waited for our reservation, was enough to have me counting to one hundred in my head. I had to focus on breathing through my nose and thinking about ogre toes... Anything to not pop a boner with her hand so close to my dick.

Do I want her to touch me and feel me? Yes.

But, not for some quick car fuck. I want to take my time with her. To earn a spot behind the wall she gave me a glimpse of.

Now, if my hand could remember that, I would greatly appreciate it.

By the time we get to the table, it's migrated close enough to the generous dip above her ass. She doesn't seem to mind it at all.

When I pull her chair out at our table, she smirks saying in a low tone, "I could have sworn you were a titty man, but going for the ass on a first date... scandalous, Mr. Whitfield."

My neck heats up to my ears and I chuckle at being caught. "It slipped..." I lie unbelievably, coughing into my fist before taking my own seat.

"Relax. I'm not mad. Just making an observation." She smirks again this time pouring water from the carafe into my glass and then her own.

"Oh, that reminds me..." I reach into my back pocket to take her lipgloss out. I hand it to her across the table and she looks at it confused at first and then the realization dawns on her.

"Thank you!" she says. "I was looking for it when I was getting ready tonight."

"Probably should have given it to you yesterday, but I forgot all about it by the time we got to my truck." I was too busy focusing on not pulling her into the bed of my truck.

She blushes and drinks from her glass. "Oh," she responds. Fidgeting with the rings on her fingers.

"Oh?" I ask. Not the response I was expecting. She seems uncomfortable. "What's going through your mind right now, Reese?"

The waitress arrives before Reese can respond, asking for our order. She orders a Cabernet asking if I wanted to share a bottle with her.

"Nah, I'm good." She hesitates, unsure if she should decide against her wine, but I add, "It's fine for you to have one. I'm driving. Better safe than sorry."

"Okay, a tall glass for me then."

The waitress leaves and Reese meets my stare head on. Her bare foot rubs against my leg under the table. How has she gotten her foot out of her shoes without me noticing? Her toes brush my calf and I trap her foot against my thigh before it can go any higher.

"What were you saying before?" I ask.

"I wasn't saying anything," she purrs. Looking at me under her lashes, while she wiggles her toes closer to my crotch. "Are we going anywhere after the restaurant?"

I eye her, trying to get a read, but I let her foot go. She returns to brushing her toes over me, sending little sparks of desire up my leg. "What makes you think we're going anywhere after?"

"Isn't that what dinner's for?" When I give her a confused look, she clarifies, "To fuel up for later... You know? Energy for getting horizontal..."

I choke on my water. "Did you just say *getting horizontal*?" I laugh with Reese who hides a devious smile behind drinking her own water. Wiping at my beard with my napkin, making sure I don't have any spills, I ask, "That's why you think I brought you here?"

"Yea," she responds simply.

The waitress returns with her wine. Reese orders us both the tortellini she loves so much with grilled chicken. When the waitress leaves, Reese continues, "Maybe we could get a hotel, there's a couple of really nice ones that will let you book for a single night. It would be easier than driving straight to Chandie's." She lifts a shoulder like it all makes sense. But I'm not sure I follow.

"What would be easier? You don't know what we're doing after dinner yet."

Reese narrows her eyes at me and sips deeply from her red wine that matches the color of the tight dress she's wearing. "Okay. I'll bite." She places the glass back on the table and looks up at me through her long lashes. "What else is in store for us tonight, Mr. Whitfield?"

Mr. Whitfield. I like that.

"There's a lounge nearby, actually. On Wednesdays, they have an open mic for local comedians. An old client of mine is performing and she's pretty funny. Her name is Grace French. Maybe you've heard of her." At her pretty unimpressed expression, I keep going. "Well... I was thinking that I really love your laugh, and I think you would enjoy her show. And maybe... I could hear it some more." Feeling like a complete simp by the end of my admission, I start to twist my water glass in circles. Allowing the condensation to make shapes on the white tablecloth.

I started to doubt whether this was a good idea or not. I don't even know if she likes stand-up comedy. It was a stab in the dark and a blind one at that.

She stops my hand with her own and I meet her gaze. Her eyes sparkle with excitement and she says, "That sounds amazing. If I had known you were going to be this thoughtful, I wouldn't have even put the thong on." She winks.

I laugh at her crass joke and flip my hand so that her hand rests in mine. "A thong, huh?" Images of her ass cheeks consuming a thin little strip of lace flicker in my mind. I could peel it off slow enough to make her squirm...

I feel my face heat and pick up my glass. Wishing that maybe I had ordered a beer instead. Reese does not make it easy to think about anything other than her delicious body and I'm only human.

She giggles and rubs her thumb over my fingers, which only makes my dick respond more acutely to how I want this woman.

The planning is worth it though. The bare minimum of showing her a good time is the least I could do. Her smiles and being able to surprise her with what I've done tonight are only the beginning of what I can see for us.

If I'm not careful, she'll eat me alive. I don't mind the prospect of having my life consumed by her.

Our main dishes arrive and she was right. The pasta is incredible. We get onto the subject of Denver traffic, sharing our worst experiences of sitting in our cars. We laugh about our misery and also times when it has come in handy to miss some appointments.

"I am never mad to miss the first hour of the lunch shift. It's usually slow as all get out. If I'm late, then I can get there when the tables are really coming in." She shrugs a shoulder. "If I'm working til close anyway, why waste time doing nothing but twiddling my thumbs?"

I nod and try to picture what Reese would be like working at Peak's. I've never eaten in the restaurant. It's famous for how small the uniforms are and how strict the hiring process is. Sexy women only. Reese fits that requirement, but I can't understand why she would leave Mason Ranch to do that instead. She loves the horses. "Do you like working there?"

"It's alright, I guess. Better than what I was doing before."

My brows bunch and I set my fork on the plate. "Working the Ranch?"

She takes another sip of wine and picks at a folded noodle for a bit before she answers me. "No. I left the Ranch four years ago. I just started working at Peak's about eight months ago."

Now I really am curious. "What were you doing before Peak's?"

"Uh... Something way different." She finishes her glass of wine and the server is already at the table with the bottle before I can ask if she wants more. She sips deeply from the glass and returns to eating her food.

Am I grilling her?

Shit.

Chill, Cory. It's not a job interview. I change the subject since it seems she is done with this one. "Did you like living in Denver? You're all moved out right?"

She nods, chewing her last bite. "Brought the last box in from the truck this morning actually. My old apartment wasn't that far from here."

"Oh yea? My condo was like forty-five minutes west from this place."

"Damn. Mine was like fifteen minutes. I used to get takeout from here all the time."

"Why not eat inside? Seems your speed. It's nice here." I smile at her taking a bite of my own food.

She drinks a little deeper from her glass before she responds. "I don't know. Just never came up."

"But it's your favorite?

"It is."

"So, I'm the first date that you've had here?"

She nods with the corner of her mouth inching up a little.

I beam. "Makes me feel kind of special." My smile stretches my cheeks, feeling like I have accomplished something.

"You are." Reese's eyes are lowered to her near empty plate. When she looks up at me with a kind of reverence and gratitude, I know what I need from her at that moment.

"Come here," I say. She stands from the table and sits in my lap. I don't care that a few of the other guests have started to look at us. Our table is not dead-center, but there are few tables in this area we're in. The large booths line the perimeter walls around us. The way the ambient lighting glows in her golden hair along her shoulders is magical. She looks angelic and I can't believe how lucky I am to be here with her. Holding her face gently, I ask, "Can I kiss you?" She smiles softly and presses her lips to mine. It was a chaste kiss, but I needed to feel her lips on mine, if only for a moment.

"I'm very glad you brought me here, Cory," she whispers in my ear, just for me to hear.

"I am, too." I whisper back. "Our night is just getting started."

"Good." She responds and goes back to her chair. Amanda, the waitress, returns and I order the triple-layer chocolate cake sundae.

"This dress has some stretch, but I think you're trying to test the limits of just how much with all these carbs tonight. I'm gonna pop a seam."

I lift an eyebrow at her. "You thought the cake was to share?"

"Obviously! It's my favorite."

"Nah. Can't be. Cause it's mine." I wink at her and she rolls her eyes with a smile on her lips.

She wipes her mouth with her napkin and asks, "So, are you liking AR?"

"It's a big adjustment. New place, new career path and a new living situation. I'm handling it as best I can. The boys are taking it in stride though. They're happy and that makes me happy."

Twisting the rings on her fingers again, she looks at her hands. "How old are they?"

I reach across the table to take her hand in mine, again. "Cory Junior is seven. Brendan is five and Gabriel will be three in a few months."

"Were you on a schedule?"

I chuckle. "No, I wasn't. I just always wanted a family and at the time it felt right. I never would have guessed that I'd have all boys, but it's kind of perfect."

"What do you mean?"

"Well, it's just me now. I'm barely able to keep up with the boys. I would probably lose my mind if I was raising a girl by myself, too. It's not easy. I'm thankful for my aunt. Without her, I don't know what I'd be doing."

"You weren't working landscaping before?"

"Oh yea. I was. But I was working for someone else, for their company. That was simple, no problems. Janet is actually the one who pushed me to build something for myself. It was my plan before I had these three."

"Building something for yourself. An entrepreneur."

I scoff. "Something like that. Caught a break with Alpenglow because there isn't any competition for me. I've got a small team now. My contract with your dad is the only reason I'm able to do that."

She smiles. "He saw something in you. Danny might be rough around the edges, but he's a softie."

"Danny? Soft? Do you not remember how he threatened me before I brought you here tonight?"

"Yea but that standard country daddy talk. Everyone has a shotgun out there."

"That doesn't exactly prove me wrong, Reese."

She considers me for a moment. "Maybe not. But, if he didn't like you, you'd be at the end of the barrel, not just hearing about how he would use it."

I laugh and am about the respond, but the cake comes with two spoons. Reese snatches one of them and gets a bite of the cake into her mouth before I can object. She moans her appreciation and I watch her fascinated by how she pulls the spoon clean from her mouth.

Fuuck. "That good, huh?"

"Best thing I've had in my mouth all week."

I raise an eyebrow at her. "Careful, Reese."

"Yea, yea. I'm playing with fire. But... as I said before, I like it hot." She says before I feel her foot drag up my leg to my thigh again.

CHAPTER 25

Reese

"YOU KNOW, I HAD a really great time tonight."

And I really, really did. Cory took me to have my favorite meal and the show was amazing. My sides hurt from how much I laughed. At one point, I almost spit my water out over the table and Cory. Grace French just made herself a new fan tonight.

I never thought I would like it so much and yet, he surprised me. He showed me something about myself that even I didn't know.

I look over to Cory and he's still holding my hand. All night he's allowed me to touch him however I liked, never pushing me to do more than I've initiated and it's... nice. Unusual, but refreshing.

"That makes me really happy." He smiles back at me. "It's almost like... I planned for you to enjoy yourself tonight." He teases, leading us to the parking garage we came from. The narrow alley between the garage is dimly lit. The brick pavers sparkling a bit with the residual rainwater from last night.

I sway into him feeling light and content with our night together. Our hands swing between us. I'm happy I wore these shoes so my heels aren't getting stuck in the grooves between bricks. "Well, it was a very good plan."

I waste no time directing us closer to a part of the facade outside the garage where the streetlights don't reach us. Cory allows me to pull him closer. Close enough for him to cover my body from anyone who could walk by us. Though there aren't many people walking on this side of the building at this time of night.

His hands find my waist and I arch into his touch, craving the closeness he's giving me. Grabbing his waistband, I trail my fingers under his shirt. Up his flat stomach and around to his back, relishing the goosebumps I'm creating on him. He looks into my eyes and at that moment, I feel it.

The desire there isn't carnal like I expected. There's admiration in his soft, brown eyes.

Our lips meet with a promise. The same one we shared on the trail yesterday.

I'm not saying with my words, but with my heart that I will hold his with the utmost care. This adoring man who spent time making my evening more memorable than any I can recall. Not because he spent the most or because he took me to the most lavish event. Because he cared whether I enjoyed it.

And I'll never forget that.

The kiss turns more urgent as I pull his leg between mine. I brazenly roll my hips on him chasing more friction.

The groan that comes from his chest when I place my hand over his growing length has me shuddering against the wall.

I want to hear it again.

I break the kiss only to whisper in his ear, "I need you inside me." Scratching my nails along his neck, he leans into my touch.

Cory closes his eyes and I can see he's fighting for control to think clearly and make a decision. In my heels, I can lean up enough to nip his earlobe and trace my tongue along the sensitive spot just below. "Don't think. Take me home."

I lean back and he meets my eyes again. His pupils are fully dilated at this point. I can't control the way I palm at his dick like it might grant me three impossible wishes. He stills my hand and meets me for another kiss. I allow his tongue to trace over mine as our teeth bump into each other in our frenzy.

He pulls away again. This time saying, "Okay."

One word never sounded so good to me before. He readjusts himself and follows me the rest of the way to his truck.

Once inside, I trace patterns with my nails on his scalp the whole way to the Ranch. I never noticed how sensual the music he listened to was until I was damn near vibrating with how much I wanted him. Soulful crooning and slow rolling percussion, keeps my libido peaked the whole drive home.

With any other man, I might still be trying my luck with stroking him. After putting my foot in my mouth several times tonight about alcohol, I need to be mindful of his boundaries. I respect his reservations. I know that safe driving is important to him, so I keep my touching to a minimum. It's very difficult with each subtly suggestive lyric making me squirm in my seat.

Finally at the Ranch again, we get to the side door. He presses his dick between my ass cheeks as I fumble around with my keys to find the right one. His hands hold me in place against him. Each of his kisses are warm and drugging along my neck and shoulders.

"It would be a lot easier to find the one I'm looking for if I could concentrate." I tease him, but it comes out like a breathy purr.

"I'll stop," he chuckles after one last kiss to my neck. I finally find which key is the right one. Inside the short hallway, I look him over in the low lighting from the lamp I've turned on.

We kiss some more, making it only a few steps at a time before we get lost in the dance of our tongues again. I'm past the point of being turned on or aroused. Desire is not sufficient to describe the kind of desperation I'm feeling buzz through my bloodstream.

Cory. Mine, for the next few hours.

I turn on my speaker, so that the sensual music from Jimmie Allen fills the space enough to mute what I plan to do to him here. Staying in my parents' house doesn't come with the luxury of going without.

Cory looks around my room as I turn on the few lamps in the space. I put my purse on the dresser and think about what he's seeing. This isn't really my space anymore. Some pictures are still up from high school. I haven't brought any of the decor from my apartment in here to update it.

Magazine cutouts of Yung Miami, Cardi B, Megan thee Stallion, and the queen herself, Beyoncé clutter one wall. The poster putty holding them in place, to create a collage of the goals and desires I had as a teenager to be just like them. In bed, I would stare at the wall and dream about what it would be like to live a lavish life similar to theirs. I had been close enough, and now I simply want to rip them all down. The P wasn't as powerful as they made her out to be. Using it had only gained me misery. I wonder about what their lives really looked like behind the scenes. Does it look anything like mine did?

I shake my head of the dismal musings that would get me absolutely no where. I have Cory here to myself. I fully intend to be dickmatized after all this teasing and primping.

Lying on the loveseat under my bedroom window, I beckon him over. He wastes no time with the few strides it takes him to get to me. He leans over me and I'm hit with the same delicious smell of him mixed with the familiar vanilla scent of my room. I'm even more turned on by his presence in a place that has never been used in this way otherwise.

It feels sacred to have him here.

Please, cherish me, Cory.

I've had a few friends here since I asked Teddy to never come back. I never had a man here besides him. The big *fuck you* I'm giving Teddy right now makes me even hotter and more desperate.

I wrap my legs around his back making his body collapse into mine. He growls and takes my ass into his hands pulling me so that my center lines up with his, perfectly.

Cory's lips crash into mine and I surrender to him. The fly of his jeans is driving me wild. I need to feel his skin on mine.

Breaking the kiss, I demand, "I want to feel you." He nods and lets me unbutton his shirt with sure fingers. I get to his pants, but he stops my movements.

Before I can pout, he says, "This dress, I love it on you but it needs to come off now." He nips around the neckline making my body feel like it will burst into flames.

I need it off, too.

I tug at the hem, lifting it over my hips and he helps me lift it over my head. Our eyes meet once I throw it to the floor.

The same recklessness I feel is written all over his face too.

Cory's here. With *me*.

He reclines into the seat and I stand before him in nothing but my heels and lace.

My curls fall around my shoulders, tickling my overly sensitive skin.

I spin slowly for him to see all of me. Feeling every place that his eyes roam, I shiver in anticipation. But also because I've never had someone look at me the way Cory does.

He bites his lip. "Damn, Reese. The fantasy doesn't compare to the real thing." Unzipping his jeans, he pulls his stiff cock through the fly, stroking himself slowly.

Ah.

There he is.

I had pondered what his cock would look like after having my hands on him so many times at this point. I knew he was big, but the sight of him stroking the thick shaft in his capable hand is almost too much to take.

A tease within itself.

Anticipation overtakes my awareness when a small bead of his cum appears on the broad head of his cock. He's so hard and glistening at the tip with the evidence of his arousal.

Lowering to my knees I get close enough to watch him with rapt fascination. My mouth waters at the prospect of letting him fill me.

My mouth, my pussy.

Hell, I'd let him fill my ass if he wanted.

I can't help myself, I swipe my thumb over his tip.

A hiss escapes his lips as he watches me bring my thumb to my mouth, tasting him. I hum my approval and reach for him to stroke him, mimicking the way he worked before.

He reaches for my face, holding my cheek with admiration. I feel a piece of my heart burn with the way he tells me he likes this, *likes me* in just that touch.

Spurred on by the affection, I get even closer to him to press his dick between my tits. Spitting onto us both, making it easier for his length to slide between them.

He groans and I feel the vibrations of his reaction down to the wetness soaking my thong, rolling down my thighs. I am so turned on right now that his heavy breathing is enough to bring me close to my edge.

I can't take it anymore and I need to feel him.

More.

I need more.

My tongue darts out to lick over his tip and he hisses out a breath again. Grabbing me by my arm, he urges me to stand. "Not yet, beautiful. I'm gonna come like that."

Placing his hands on the thin straps at my hips, I sway slowly, enticing him to take my thong off.

He turns me around, pressing my back forward. I grab onto the back of my loveseat. "This ass, Reese." He nips at the swell of my cheeks and follows it with a kiss along the bitten skin, squeezing my hips and thighs some more. Finally, he peels the thong down my legs and I step out of it.

Grabbing his hands again, I pull him to stand with me. Putting them onto my bra that's still wet from my spit earlier. It's sticking to me enough to rasp against my nipples when he pulls the cups down exposing them to the cool air.

His mouth finds my nipple and I cry out, "Yes, Cory. Bite me, please." He swirls his tongue once more and I beg, "Baby, I need your teeth." He nips at one softly at first, soothing it with his tongue before moving to the other, increasing the pressure with his teeth.

I press his face further into me, covering his nose with my breast. "More. I want more." He bites down in earnest now, grabbing me, and looking up to me with nothing but pure lust in his eyes. He takes my other breast into his hand and pinches the nipple between his rough fingers. "Yesss. I love it," I moan.

He picks me up and I loop my arms around his neck. His dick rests between my legs and I only get a tease of what I really want as he walks us over to my bed.

We fall in a tangle of limbs and he positions me on my back. More kisses down my chest and he pauses at the charm I have clipped in place. Sitting back onto his haunches, he rolls the tricolor beads between his fingers in question. I respond, "Later."

He nods but traces the chain with his fingertips from my neck to the middle of my chest. Following the two chains that hang from the ring my new charm is attached to. "I've been thinking about this so much, I never thought I would see it. Your body. Adorned with this. Just for me." He tugs at the metal and it sends goosebumps racing with the cold jewelry meeting my skin again. "I have to taste you again."

Before I can say anything, he's moved down my body throwing my legs over his shoulders. His face is close enough to my center that I can feel each breath ghost over my slit, growing more and more sensitive as he takes me in with his eyes.

He uses his thumbs to part my flesh and I writhe, desperate to feel his mouth on me. Strong arms hold my legs in place and I get no relief as he takes his time memorizing every glistening inch of me. I huff and stop wiggling, accepting that Cory will move at his own pace. "Did you want something, beautiful?" Each word sends his warm breath over my clit, making me throb.

"Well, there was talk of tasting…" I trail off as he licks my pussy from my opening to my clit. Sucking the sensitive bud into his mouth hard enough to make me grab his head with both hands. "Oh… My… God. Just like that." My nails rake through his soft, short hair as I buck into his mouth loving the attention he's spending on me. My back arches and he takes a lip between his teeth. The gentle way he holds it between his teeth sends the first tingles of my fast-approaching orgasm coursing through my body.

Releasing my lip, he slides one thumb into me and then the other. The thick digits have me calling out his name on an exhale as he works me closer and closer to bliss.

"Not yet, pretty girl." He pulls his thumbs out licking the left and then right, while I watch him in wonder and frustration because...

"Damnit, Cory, I was so close!" I whine and flop back onto the bed.

"I know, baby. But, I don't have a condom. There's one in my glovebox. I just need to go get it."

I shake my head. "If you leave, I will fight you. Look in my nightstand drawer."

He chuckles, but does what I said, pulling out the gold strip. I mentally pat myself on the back for always being prepared even when I had no expectations.

Hearing the wrapper tear, I lean up onto my forearms to see him rolling a condom on over himself. "I could have helped with that," I say with a smirk.

"I've got you. Stay just like that." He comes back to the bed, crawling closer to me on his knees.

He strokes himself never taking his eyes off me.

Just when I think he'll finally give me what I'm so needy for, I feel the dull thwack of his hard cock on my clit. I cry out at the pressure just building and building, my hand grabbing onto his thigh.

"Again," I demand. He smirks and I writhe even more, twisting my nipples at the delicious way he has me strung tight.

"You want this, pretty girl?"

How could I be more clear? I needed him inside me like an hour ago.

The sting of another thwack of his stiff cock to my clit fizzles through my bloodstream and I'm getting close. So, so close. Electricity is crackling through me. I'm hot and not hot enough all at the same time.

Before I can give him whatever smart retort I was going to say, he notches at my entrance. A brief moment of adjusting as I stretch to accommodate his size. He rubs my clit with his thumb and I'm whimpering for him when he slides his tip into me with a groan that has me clenching my sheets in suspense.

Cory's big.

So big that I question if I can make space in my body for him. It's a stretch and a good one at that.

It's all too much. Time slows and it's just us here.

Cory and Reese.

We lock eyes in the low lighting and can't help how I clench the hard length that's teasing me with his slow strokes.

He pushes into me deeper, using my thighs to move my body on his, watching his dick glide in and out.

"You want something?" He raises an eyebrow. I nod my head back and forth, feeling frenzied with how he's teasing me. "Tell me what you want."

"Hard. I want you to pound me. I need—" I'm cut off and my breath catches as Cory starts to thrust into me with short fast strokes that make my tits bounce.

I'm feeling weightless as he takes me hard and fast hitting the spot deep inside me, making me moan and keen for more and more of what he's doing. He runs a hand over my body, grabbing a handful of my tit and pinching the nipple again.

I never want this to stop, for him to stop.

He pulls out and flips me over. Lifting my hips, I eagerly push my ass back into him with my face in the sheets.

His hands twist in my hair, turning my head to the side. "I wanna see that O, pretty girl."

He thrusts into me again and again, grabbing my hips hard enough to leave marks as I come around his cock, spewing unintelligible words.

Cory chases his release a little longer. Each groan and *fuuuck yes, Reese* filling my soul with validation like nothing else can.

I feel him swell and his movements get more unsteady. He comes on a curse and I am more impressed with how long he lasted than the fact that I actually came too.

He pulls out slowly, exhaling loudly. His cock still stands as I make notes of every bead of sweat across his forehead and chest.

Laying boneless on my back, I hear him go across the hall to the bathroom to throw out the condom.

CHAPTER 26

Cory

"Come here," Reese beckons me over to where she lays on the bed.

A fucking gift.

I don't know how I got so lucky, but here I am with her laid bare for me to do what I want.

I enjoyed her telling me and showing me what she likes, how she wanted me to touch her. I loved every minute of her guiding me.

Now, I'm going back to what I love most.

Instead of falling into her arms, I lay between her legs, easing two fingers inside her wet pussy. Still dripping and swollen with the desire she has for me.

Did you hear that?

For me.

I did that.

She begins to say something, leaning up on her elbows. It dies on her lips as the sweet moans I want to play on a never-ending loop, escape her lips instead.

I suckle her clit back into my mouth with soft pressure, stroking that spot deep inside her that makes her arch farther into my mouth.

The sloppy sounds my fingers coax from her can't be drowned out by the country music playing faintly in the room. The way her pussy is talking to me beats any ballad or love song as far as I'm concerned.

I need to take this second orgasm from her and claim it as mine.

To claim *her* as mine.

Because this pussy belongs to me, now.

I'll never share it again.

A sane voice in the back of my head tells me to proceed with caution. I haven't known her long. Even more rationally, the murmurs of towns people creep up, too. I don't listen to any of that though. None of them know what it's like to have an angel like this at their mercy because she wants them there.

I do.

Reese's hand releases the sheets she had an iron grip on to softly comb her finger through my beard. Her eyes lock onto mine again. No discernible words are spoken, but she adamantly nods her head. Loving everything I'm doing and all those doubts leave my mind.

Mine.

She trails her finger down my jaw and holds my head in the place she wants. I increase the speed of my fingers and the pressure on her pulsing clit. She calls out my name then, "Cory! Cory. I'm going to come all over your face. Please don't stop. Don't stop."

There's no way I would.

This O is mine.

Just like this pussy. I'll drink from her until she tells me to stop.

I deserve the sweet nectar flowing from her, giving me life. For her, my only wish is that she never makes me give up my new addiction.

Her thighs tighten on my head. My ears pop with the seal her strong legs make against them. I admire how her body contracts and shakes as I allow her to ride out the second orgasm that makes me stiff enough to take her again.

Fucking beautiful.

This show is just for me.

Mine.

When she relaxes onto the bed I crawl up to lay behind her. Reveling in the slide of our sweat covered bodies for a moment longer. Holding Reese close to me with my arm over her waist. I roll the beads from the charm at her chest, loving how comforting the smooth stones feel in my fingers.

She chuckles sleepily and I ask, "What?"

"You wouldn't even be touching those if you knew what they represented."

"And why not?" I ask. She turns to look at me over her shoulder before turning back around.

"It's silly."

"It's not. What do they represent?"

She scoffs and takes a deep breath, seeming to prepare herself for the explanation. "The deep red crystal is Red Jasper. It's for courage and protection. The light pink is Rose Quartz. Most commonly known for compassion, forgiveness, and happiness. And the other is White Jade. It's for peace and calm." I listen to her voice, slightly raspy from what we've done but sated. I could listen to it all night if I was able to.

She hesitates for a bit before continuing on with a sigh. "All the crystals are for love, worn close to the heart. Chandie made this for me a few years ago." She turns fully this time and I'm able to see the charm more clearly resting on her body. They shine just a bit and I can't help but roll them in my fingers again.

I meet her gaze and she seems guarded once more. Like maybe I'll say something to upset her.

I consider my next words, carefully. "She wanted to protect your heart... and encourage love there too. That's an understandable desire to have for her daughter."

Her eyes soften. "Yea, it was." Her fingers find their way into my beard again. I lean into her hand, turning to kiss her palm.

I think she'll say more. When she doesn't, I ask, "Did it work?" My voice barely louder than a whisper.

"Hard to say. She only gave it to me before we came out tonight."

I lace her fingers with mine and we let the words hang there. Chandie gave her this charm before she went on her date with me. Approval from a woman's mother is important. It means everything.

And she gave it to me.

My mind is screaming at me to say something more. I don't want to be the fool to say that I want to keep her. I've said more than once that I'll care for her. Take care of her. It's more than just a sexual thing.

Don't get me wrong, the sex was incredible. I will never forget it for as long as I live and I can't wait to do it again.

Preferably, as soon as possible.

But I stay silent, which seems to be the only way that I can process when it comes to Reese. I don't want to make a fool of myself. More than anything, I don't want to scare her off. She is the closest I've gotten to feeling—whatever this is—in a long time.

She knows about my situation. Well, about my kids. Not much about my ex. Everything in me wants to tell her about it all. To open myself up to her and let her see all of my soul, my hurt, and my heart.

It's clear to me that Reese shows her interest and compassion with touch. When I gave her just a small opportunity to touch me, she hasn't stopped since. The only other beings that receive the same amount of physical attention are her horses.

I see the way she is with them. Her hands, magic on a mare that is otherwise skittish and agitated with any of the other ranch hands. I've never seen someone so fearless and strong. Her calm and confidence, calming them.

She isn't like that with anyone else. I don't mean the touching, but the same calming and open way she handles those horses.

Not her friends. Not Tony or Mack. The way she touches me is different. Significant.

That means something to me.

Maybe, I'm a simp and a fool. Maybe both of those things at once.

For her? For Reese? I will be, gladly.

She's looking at my face intently while we lie here in peace.

It could be awkward, but it isn't.

It isn't long before our mouths find each other again. We tangle in her sheets until I've tired us both out.

I'm nervous as hell to let another woman into my life, but in just a week, I've exposed myself more than I have in years.

This is a big deal for me.

I just wonder if it is a big deal for her.

Everyone's warnings had to come from somewhere.

Is it from a place of truth?

I can't see that being the case.

Being vulnerable to another woman who could destroy me seems to be the only way that I can function.

Reese is nothing like Vanessa.

"Hold me." Her request is whispered.

I pull her into my chest and hold her until I can hear her breathing slow. I told her that I would bring her home and I did.

I pull the blanket over her and slip out of bed. She looks heavenly with her hair spilling out over the pillows and a soft smile on her face even in her sleep. I want to stay here with her.

The last thing I want is to sleep in my cold bed alone, but I also have to be home for my sons when they wake up.

One day, I won't have to do this.

One day.

Just not today.

CHAPTER 27

Reese

"Hey everyone. My name's Reese. I'm here with Heather today. She's my sweetest girl." I rub under her chin and she leans into the affection. "Together, we're gonna help show you some of the basics; like how to approach a horse and some gentle and appropriate ways that you can show your appreciation for one." I give Heather a pat on her side, turning back to the kids. "Before we do that I would like for all of you to introduce yourselves to the hand you're with and the horse you've chosen. Today you'll be in groups of two. Remember to stay close to the front or side of the horse and resist the urge to yell or scream near these animals. We don't want to startle or upset them. Horses are very attuned to your emotions."

Mack walks with Artemis over to one group of two kids. Taylor walks with Raleigh to join Ellis and Fireball. Tony stands next to me with Daisy. He could be doing other things, but he decided that it would be his *honor* to watch me flail today. Though it was a tease, since he knows I don't flail.

The kids group up on their own next to the horse that they like. They are all arranged in a fan formation from where Heather and I stand. These kids are in the best hands with my team on their side. I'm far better with training the horses than with training people to ride them. So, I don't know how well that translates with little people mostly under the age of ten, but I'm confident in my abilities. I learned how to ride when I was seven years old after consistently begging my dad to teach me. They can't be any worse than my stubborn self.

My eyes snag on two boys who look almost identical to Cory. One has glasses with a short cropped fro and the other is basically vibrating with energy as he tries his best to stand still. I quickly avert my gaze as I don't want to make them feel uncomfortable.

I had almost forgotten that Cory would have his kids in this program. I had not really allowed him to talk about his children and now I see that was a mistake. Oh my god. This just got very serious—very quickly. Tony clears his throat and I shake myself from my thoughts to continue leading the instruction.

"Before our horses, Fireball, Raleigh, Daisy, and my dad's favorite, Artemis, were brought out today, our hands did an excellent job of brushing, prepping, and checking the hooves to make sure they were nice and clean. This is something you will also learn how to do at Mason Ranch. You'll see we also put the pads, which are like a thick blanket that goes in between the horse's back and the saddle, onto your horse for today, as well as the saddle itself. Finally, they all have their bridles on." I put my hand on the headstall gently, allowing Heather to turn her head for the kids to see what I'm talking about. "This attaches to your reins, which is one of the ways that you can control your horse once seated."

Each of the ranch hands points out the items I have just discussed up close with their young ones. There is some hesitancy from a few of them, but I see one of the mini Corys noting everything Mack is saying with concentration and focus. The smaller, busy one is touching each piece of equipment and saying "ah" in response to what Mack points out. "We'll teach you all how to do this prep for yourself, but I figured we could do something a little more fun for your first day." I walk to stand on the left of Heather. "Today, we're gonna show you how to use a mounting block to mount a horse. Let you feel what it's like to be on the back of these beautiful animals."

The kids start to murmur with excitement about getting onto the horse and I smile knowing exactly what that excitement is like for a young person.

Mack looks over to me and we lock eyes briefly, probably remembering our first time learning.

After that night at QB's, my trips through the fence had lessened. Partly because I had a certain single dad taking up my time and focus, but also because I wanted to give Mack some space. I came back to AR thinking that I would know all the answers and be some white knight. I wanted to be helpful and I wasn't.

Eventually, he texted me that he was sorry. I forgave him right away. I don't hold any grudges toward him. We both fucked up. Mack is the closest thing I have to a brother and I've already missed so much time with us not talking as much as I would want. He's changed and so have I. We can learn about who we are now together. For however long I'm in town, I want to mend these friendships in my life that I wasn't able to have anymore when I left.

I wink at him and he rolls his eyes with a smirk.

Giving my attention back to the kids, I say, "Don't get too excited everyone. We're going to be mounting only, not moving the horse at all. We have a bit to learn before you'll be ready to take to even a trot."

"Tony is our expert here." I wink over at him now which only makes him grin even bigger. He loves working with kids. He's a goofball, but no matter how much I know that and Drea knows that, she won't let him in. They drive me crazy with how perfect they are for each other. It's like... just open your eyes already! "He'll be helping me show the proper way to mount your horse."

Tony's deep voice rumbles out over the group. "Alright, who knows their right from their left, show of hands." Only a few hands go up. He laughs and changes his approach, "Okay. We're all gonna hold up our hands and make an L with your thumb and pointer finger, like this." They all follow his lead, including the ranch hands. I watch, walking Heather by the reins to the back of the corral. By the fence, I see Chandie coming over with a horse bucket.

She drops it with a dull thud when she reaches the railings. Leaning into it with both hands, she whisper yells my name so as to not distract the others. Making my way over, Heather immediately smells the quarter-cut apples. My mom moves the bucket even farther from the fencing, getting a chuff from the sneaky horse in protest. "Later," I tell her giving her a kiss on the side of her head and a couple of neck rubs.

"How's it going out here? You all look very focused." She smiles and I see her craning her neck around the nine-hundred pound spoiled baby still trying to inch closer to the fencing, all the while blocking her view. Chandie gives up and climbs onto the first rung to look over Heather's back.

I see Tony stepping onto the mounting block and swinging his leg over Daisy in slow motion for the kids to see the proper technique. Turning back to her, I say, "Pretty good, I think." Recalling my realization from earlier, I choose to add, "Who are the two boys with Mack and Artemis?"

She chuckles. "Oh, you noticed them, huh?"

"Why are you laughing? They just look familiar."

"I bet they do." She laughs some more. "Remind you of anyone you know?" Her eyebrows do a dance on her forehead and I can feel my impatience at this drawn-out answer growing.

"Mom, who are they?"

"Reese, you already know the answer to that question. They're Cory's boys. CJ and Brendan. The one with the glasses is CJ."

"Those genes run strong," I murmur. "You knew they were going to be in my clinic today?" I ask more loudly.

"Of course. I was the one who invited him to enroll them for the trial we're doing."

"Mom, why would you do that?"

"Why wouldn't I? My friend was going nuts with those boys running around her house all day. They're good kids, but they need something to do. Be in the sun, working off that energy." Well... I didn't think about Janet. It makes more sense when she puts it that way. "Trust me, this has nothing to do with you two dating."

"We're not dating."

"So what would you call him coming to the house to take you to dinner and not coming home til after eleven?" She raises a perfectly arched eyebrow at me.

Shrugging, I throw a thumb over my shoulder and say, "I think I should get back over there. You want me to bring that in?" I motion to the bucket with my right hand not holding Heather's reins.

"No, honey. Just leave it here. You can let the small ones give my babies a treat at the end of class." She gives Heather a pat before walking over to her car. No doubt to talk with Janet all about me.

I sigh.

That's the last thing I want right now, but keeping Chandie from spilling my business, is like trying to contain a river with a SOLO cup.

"Alright, everyone got it down? Let's break off into our groups again. The blocks are over by the fence, grab one and return to your horse." Tony claps his hands and one kid from each group goes over to do what he's asked. When we join him back at the front, I can feel a pair of eyes on me. The older brother, CJ, is watching me with curious eyes before his brother returns with a skip to join him, mounting block in his hands.

I may not have been talking with Cory about his children. I never thought that maybe he had talked to them about me.

With the way CJ looked at me, I think he knows exactly who I am.

Despite my growing suspicions, I continue the clinic trying my best not to think about just what these little boys know.

CHAPTER 28

Reese

"Relax." Andrea places a mug of Coors in front of me on a paper coaster. "What do you possibly think he could have told his young sons about you?"

"I don't know. I have been very pointedly avoiding most conversations about them!" I know I said I was all in. I know. Seeing them today was the first time that I realized these are real people. Yes, I knew children were people... logically. But... these are mini Corys! Actual small versions of him.

Not one man I've been with has had kids. Or... maybe they have, but never told me about them. That's definitely not the kind of relationship that I've been in before.

I gulp some of my beer thinking about how many children I *haven't* met. I don't know if that makes meeting my firsts now, any better or worse.

Ugh.

This is going to be very complicated. I don't know if I truly comprehended just how much when my mouth was making decisions my brain had not thought through yet.

Drea gives me a lifted brow before she's back to unloading beer mugs from the rack to their designated counter space. Disappearing behind the kitchen door for a moment, she returns with an order of cheese fries and nachos in her arms. She makes quick work of delivering the order to a booth on the other side of the bar.

I sip my beer, holding it in my mouth for the fizzing to distract my racing thoughts. It's not really doing that but... beer number two might be the one.

"So, what's so bad about him telling his sons about you? That seems like a good thing." Mel shrugs. She looks up from her phone where she's sending a quick text and smiling. "Shows that he thinks you'll be a lasting thing. It's kinda sweet."

"A lasting thing." I scrunch up my face in distaste like something smells bad. I take a gulp of the pale ale, slamming it back onto the table. "Me? Do you know me? Lasting is not my thing." And yet, you told him you were *really in this.* I haven't told any of them about that conversation we had in the woods. And now doesn't seem like the right time. The last thing I want is for more people to know how I fucked up by thinking I was ready for this kind of commitment.

"And you like that?" Mel slides her phone into her back pocket. Looking at their ordering tablet, she turns back to the bar top, pulling a few liquor bottles to start making a mixed drink.

"She loves it. Reese, the untamable. Reese, the one that got away. Reese—"

I cut Drea off before she can say something I really won't like. "Reese, the woman just trying to help her family out. Reese, who is only temporarily in Alpenglow Ridge."

Mel and Drea look at each other from opposite sides of the bar.

Rolling my eyes, I say, "You know, I may not have been here for a while, but the shared looks are getting old, real quick."

"What?" They say in unison.

Then Mel says, "You *haven't* been here in a while. But, the pickings are slim as far as men go. That has not changed since you left. This guy comes to town, just so happens to be working at your family's ranch when you get there. You two hit it off *and* he's talking to his sons about you? Why are you fighting this? It's like..." She struggles for the word or maybe just cuts herself off from saying what she means to say.

Drea chimes in, "Girl, it's like fate! He's cute and if you don't want a good man like that, then let him go." I flinch. Her words hitting their mark in my chest. I rub the spot and find difficulty in producing a response.

Why don't I just let him go? I had the perfect out earlier this week. My very best bet would have been to lessen the difficulties I'm bringing into my life. Even if Cory didn't have kids, he's still a divorcee. I know nothing about his wife.

Blah, blah, blah...

So, on and so forth.

The reasons are piling up.

I have one big glaring reason for why I should let Cory go. And *he* is not at all happy about my return. It's a miracle that he hasn't popped up again. Anything I know about a long standing relationship has come from Teddy.

The more I try to compare the two of them, the more I realize that I can't. I know all about Teddy's wife. And Teddy's son. Far too much for my own good.

But, I don't know anything about Cory's wife or kids. Ex-wife. And I can't protect myself because I've already made an exception for him. I've already let him into my head.

Into my bed.

My heart.

And that is dangerous.

He can't know me. Or who I am. Or what I've done. It hasn't even been two weeks, and I'm panicking.

"Fate is not real. Some things are just a coincidence. People with kids are always talking about and to their kids."

Drea looks at me more pointedly than before. "And you love to hear about Mireya, as one of her godmothers."

"Her worst godmother. More likely Mother Gothel," I reply.

Drea laughs, shaking her head and ducking off to the kitchen again to check on her orders.

"That's messed up," Mel says. "Is that really what you think? About yourself?" She waited until Drea was out of earshot to ask that last part.

"I don't know. Me and kids don't mix well."

"You led that clinic today. You said it went well." She does have a point. It did go well. And it was me who wanted to bring more young people to the ranch for this purpose. Teaching children the love of horses was easy. Everything else is…

"That is different and you know it. I don't even live here, and I'm not sure I am going to stay after dad gets this new program up and running. Children need stability and someone they can count on." I drink the rest of my beer, sliding it to the edge of the bar. Mel puts her hand on mine, stopping my hand's retreat.

Meeting my gaze, she says, "It's not different, sweetie. Being a parent, is learned behavior. Everyone has to learn. Some do it faster and better than others. But you don't just know everything overnight. It takes time and effort. If you can give your time and effort, then you are already doing amazing."

She lets my hand go and busies herself on the ordering tablet. I take that moment to breathe deeply while her back is turned to me.

Mel has always been *that* friend. She wants the husband and kids and house with the fence. *All that cheesy crap.* I thought her and Mack were going to have that forever kind of love because he wants that, too. She still lives in the house they bought together, but they never had any kids after they married. I always wondered why, but that is honestly none of my business. If neither of them is forthcoming with that information or conversation, I, of all people, am not going to pry.

Mel returns with a genuine smile in place to exchange my mug with another frosted one, fizzling with beer. "Do you figure you'll order any food to go with your Coors dinner?"

I sigh long and heavy. "I guess." I order chicken strips and fries, hoping they'll actually make it to me without coating the floor first. I really do love them from here. I don't know what makes them so good, but I am not one to look a gift horse in the mouth.

"Don't worry, the fun has arrived!" Chloe booms from the stairwell near the corner that leads up to her salon above. I hop up, skipping over to hug her. The smell of chemical hair products and heat swirls around us as she hugs me back.

"I just ordered. Are you getting something?" I ask, slinging an arm over her shoulder. We walk to the bar where I've been sitting.

"Nope. I'm only gonna stay for a little bit. Quincy made lasagna." She enunciates all the syllables in lasagna to emphasize how special this is for Q. He has a handful of dishes that he knows how to make from scratch. Whenever we talk on the phone, she gets so excited about it.

"Lucky. Now talk to me about the concert before they come back." I tilt my head inconspicuously toward the kitchen when we make it to the bar.

"What's there to talk about? Ty is going to be on stage. Mel is going to freak out and spread her legs, feel guilty, and go home alone. Drea is gonna wear something tight, and Tony is going to drool all over her, to which she will ultimately decline. Then, they both are going to call me to complain about how single they are."

My head spins with this shitstorm she's describing. "They what!" I respond too loudly before my brain can catch up to my mouth. She shushes, but I add, "Run that back. I missed all of that! I was asking more about the time and place type of details. This was... Girl, What?!"

"Keep your voice down, heifer! You heard me. That's the Cliff's Notes version. Don't even get me started on your little ass."

"My ass is not little." I scoff. Pressing a hand to my chest, I say, "Me, you don't have to worry about."

Clo raises an eyebrow. "Don't I? Miss I date daddies."

Laughing at her absurdity, I say, "Stop playing with me! I don't date daddies!"

"Let's not pretend like Rebecca has not told Janet, who has told Chandie, who told Sammie, who told me when I was touching up her red yesterday morning." I cover my face with my hands because there is no denying it now. "Sweetheart, I *am* the gossip mill. You better believe that I added that one to my apron just for this moment." She pats her invisible stylist apron in confirmation.

"It's that bad?"

"Bad? I'm hoping he traps you, and we can actually keep you this time."

"Ugh! Ew. Hold your tongue. That's enough! Don't ever curse my name like that." I laugh and she laughs with me.

Drea comes over with my food and asks, "What is so funny? You two are cackling like hyenas over here."

"Oh, nothing. Just about how you're finally gonna let Tony get a piece." Chloe responds with a straight face.

Drea clutches imaginary pearls at her neck. "Get a piece of what? I'm celibate."

"Celibate? Why?" This is the first I'm hearing about it, and I'm curious as hell.

"For your information, it's a very personal choice." I chuckle and pop a fry into my mouth. Drea continues, glaring at me, "You don't have to understand, but sometimes you have to make hard choices to protect the people you love."

"You love Tony?" I ask with giddy excitement. Finally, they need to stop these games.

"Girl, no. For Mireya." Drea pours another beer from the tap and leaves to deliver it to another table.

"See? I know about all of y'all. And that one," she waves a hand casually in the direction of Drea, "is trying her very best to avoid the fact that she likes Tony too. And Cinnabon," she points more aggressively at Mel, "is trying not to stir the pot. A people pleaser through and through. But, she should have gone after what she wanted from the beginning." She mmhmms to herself since I'm still trying to make sense of what I missed.

"It's a good thing I was not around for any of this drama. You three have your work cut out for you."

She tuts and pushes off the stool she was sitting on. "You have the most drama of all." Tapping her chest, she adds, "Gossip mill remember? Shampooing just right, will unlock even the tightest lips." She winks and says a general "Bye, guys." to the bar before leaving.

I don't even want to know what Chloe knows or thinks she knows about me if this is how easily she has clocked everyone else.

CHAPTER 29

Reese

"WHAT ARE YOU GOING to do?" Drea asks me even though her attention is on the two men off in the field on tractors, no less.

When I agreed to come help out the ranch, I thought, hmm... Dad will have me moving cattle from one grazing land to the next, training some of the boarded horses, maybe teaching a few classes... Hell, I have done those things in addition to all this... ugh. *Paperwork.*

And on a Saturday! It feels criminal.

Who knew there were so many files involved with cattle ranching?

In the distance, I see Tony showing Cory how to use the baler to bale and wrap all the hay he's just finished cutting in neat lines. And how am I supposed to concentrate when there are two sweaty and sexy men being distracting and sexy and sweaty? There is something too good about a man on a tractor. I think it's programmed in my country DNA to take notice.

Drea and I both sigh when Tony takes his hat off, scratching a hand through his smushed curls to put it on backwards.

Backwards.

He says something before he walks back to the barn and lets Cory finish doing his task. At least someone is able to get their work done.

"Dear Lord, save me." Drea says, fanning her face. She looks over at me, but I can't help her. I'm just as mesmerized.

I shake my head, putting my attention back on the stack of papers in front of me. "I have some idea, but nothing that I would want to try, if I'm honest."

I have to give it to Chandie; she was prolific in the recruitment process. The paper applications I've been entering electronically on our porch swing was going well. The one big problem is that several of these don't have a financial form attached at all.

When she told me these were complete, I thought she really meant *complete*. We're days away from the start, and fifteen of these kids have nothing submitted for payments.

"It can't be worse than Peak's, can it?" Drea asks.

Oh right. My *idea*.

In her mind, I'm sure it isn't. Where my thoughts are going, it definitely *is* worse than horny men trying to paw at me in exchange for a ten-dollar tip. My jar I had saved up from the past months working there is not going to be enough to cover what's missing here. I'm gonna need a lot more money and fast if I expect to keep these kids in the program.

Mireya plays with one of the barn cats that is currently sitting on the fence in our yard to the main grazing land. He licks a paw lazily while she fawns over how cute he is. "Don't pet him, Reya! They never wash those things."

"I beg your pardon." Throwing an arm towards the tabby in question, I explain, "He's a cat. He's literally having a bath right now."

"Uh-huh," she responds noncommittally. "The last thing I need on my plate is for Reya to come down with some barn cat flu or something."

I giggle at her mothering tone. "What the hell is cat flu, D?"

"Girl, I don't know, but I'm not trying to find out."

We laugh some more and sway on the swing while I clack away on my computer, and she looks at recipes on her phone.

It's excruciatingly hot on the Ranch, and if these fans weren't spinning at full power above us, I wouldn't deign to be out here. Sipping from my mason jar, I take another look over the spreadsheet I made with the current registrants.

All these kids are under the age of eleven. Some names I recognize, but others aren't ringing any bells.

Alpenglow has grown so much since I lived here before. Between new developments popping up along the edge of town and several farms choosing to allow property development instead of continuing their family's heritage of growing food for our area, it's getting to be so large. Not large enough, though. It's still an itty-bitty town.

I'm down to the last two forms. I hold them before they almost fly away in the swift breeze the fans have created. The names glare back at me in handwriting that must be Cory's. Tidy and small.

CJ and Bren Whitfield.

Cory's sons.

I thought that maybe I was finally able to catch a break. Not likely. And wouldn't you know, their financial forms are blank as well.

Thanks, Chandie. Your kindness knows no bounds.

Of course, she offered to have them come and did not bother to press the importance of completing the financial paperwork.

Feeling fed up, I call my mother, who is currently in Wyoming looking at lapidary materials for the next few days. She dragged my dad along with her, though he grumbled the entire time she packed their bags.

"Yes, honey?"

"Mom, what is up with all these applications that aren't actually complete like you said they were? What am I supposed to do with them?"

There's some talking that I can't quite make out, like she has her hand over the mic. "I'm talking with a vendor right now. Can I call you later? Just fill out what you can of the applications, and we'll figure out the rest. Okay?"

"Figure it out?"

"Yes." More muffled talking. "Do your best. We'll talk about it when Danny and I get back."

"But—"

"Love you!" The line clicks off.

I look at my phone, where her contact photo smiles back at me in utter disbelief. "Figure it out?" I ask again to no one in particular.

Drea looks up from her own phone. "I take it that did not go well."

"I may as well have not called her in the first place." I huff out a breath, now truly frustrated.

Taunting me from the top of the pile, Cory's sons' names stand apart.

I can only imagine Chandie bulldozing him into applying.

A smile starts to tug at the corner of my lips. That smile is quickly replaced by a frown. "What am I going to do? It costs money to run any business. I can't start off on the wrong foot with this. They put me in charge for a reason. How am I supposed to figure it out?"

Drea's bob billows around her face as she takes out the clip holding it back to reclip it into the same position. A tell that she is thinking deeply. She's been doing the same thing since we were young, though her hair was much longer then. "What did she say exactly?"

I tell her about the quick phone conversation, adding, "How am I supposed to start MHA in debt?"

"She said she would figure it out right? Maybe you should let them figure it out. Chandie wanted these kids here, and she trusted you to be the head bitch. Just use your best judgment. They picked you for a reason."

"Yea, because I'm their daughter."

She grimaces, "Maybe, maybe not."

"This can't fail on my watch, Drea. I have to find this money from somewhere."

"Reese. She said you three would figure it out when she got home."

The baler engine roars closer, and I take my eyes off of the computer to see someone nearing us. His tank top stretches tight over his body. The evidence of his long day of work, in the grooves of his muscles outlined in sweat. My gaze devours each rivulet that drips in lazy paths down his neck and arms.

I don't hear what Drea said because my focus is totally consumed by the delicious man riding along the last path of alfalfa hay he's baling up.

"Huh?" I ask, knowing full well that I won't hear her response either. My body is aching for something that I know this man can give me.

Release.

Who knew that the tractor and baler combination would make him that much more attractive to me? I feel like a bee searching for nectar. "Yea. Sure. Love you, babe."

"Not even going to address that," she grumbles under her breath. "Okay. I feel like I'm literally watching the start of a porno. Can you just let me know if you end up figuring things out?" I nod absently as she grabs her purse and keys from the side table. "C'mon babe. We need to get to g-ma's before I have work tonight," she calls to Mireya. Turning back to me from the stairs, a little bit louder, she says, "Text me."

"Okay." I give her a wave before I stride over to where Cory is now parked in the big green machine.

"Working hard?" I lean into the cab as he's pressing buttons to turn the rumbling machine off.

"Oh, yea. It's a scorcher out here today. I think I got the hang of it though." *Yea, you do.*

"Is this all you have to do?" I ask.

"For today. The guys are gonna come help trim the drives and add in more planters." He wipes his arm over his forehead.

It's like he's just baiting me at this point. I climb in and sit on his lap, straddling him. "Baby. It's hot. I'm gonna get you all sweaty." He holds my hips, trying to still me.

"Please do." I purr, pushing his sunglasses up to the top of his head.

He looks around to see if anyone can see us. "You've got that look."

"What look is that?" I say as I trace a finger over his damp chest.

"The 'I'm gonna devour Cory' look."

I smirk. "You don't like that look?"

He chuckles. "I more than like that look." His voice trails off at the end when my tongue trails from his collarbone to his neck. A slow, "Fuuuck," comes out on an exhale. "I don't even remember what I was going to say when you do that."

"Good. Listen to what I'm saying." He nods, eyes on my lips. "I want you. Now."

"Now?"

"Yes." I sit back to reach for the zipper on his cargos. "Can I have you?"

"Here? Reese."

I smile wickedly at him. "Who's gonna know?"

"Reese..."

"Can I have you? Yes... or no?"

He looks around again to see if anyone can see us. His eyes land on mine and he nods. "Yes. God, yes."

I grin at him and undo his zipper, reaching for him. He hardens in my hand when I've fully freed his dick from his briefs.

At the first stroke, his head falls back to the headrest. "That feels..." His eyes close and I continue my movements, tightening and changing my speed. He groans, and I get goosebumps as I feel my own arousal spinning up with his.

"Tell me. How does it feel, baby?" I shift so that I'm straddling one of his thighs. The jean shorts I have on allow me the flexibility to put a foot on the seat to stabilize myself. He watches me now, putting a hand on my calf as I work the both of us.

The baler rocks minimally and I know that after a while, people will start to notice what we're doing in here. There's no way I'm going to get what I want from him like this. Even with his hands dirty from working, holding me stable, I just can't get there. His hooded eyes meet mine when I stop everything I'm doing to tuck his dick safely back into his pants.

He opens his mouth to speak, but I sigh and say, "Come on, the shower is calling us."

"You don't have to tell me twice. I'm officially off the clock." I hop out of the baler, and before I know it, he's scooped me up in his arms, and we're headed to the house.

We walk in through the side door, and I'm kissing him in the hallway between pulling him toward the bathroom.

"Your parents aren't home?"

"Nope. It's just you and me here." I turn on the shower and drop my clothes to the ground, standing there naked in front of him.

He licks his lips when I get into the water stream. "Come on, Cory. I promise I won't bite."

Making quick work of dropping his clothes, he joins me in the shower for another passionate kiss. We take turns lathering each other up before his hand slips between my legs. I'm already so turned on that it doesn't take me very long to pant into my first orgasm. He steadies us both by putting a hand around my waist and the other on the shelf above us.

My toy goes clattering from the shelf, and we both look at it on the shower floor for a moment before he picks it up.

"So I've been competing with this?" He holds it to my aching center, teasing me just enough that I rise onto my tiptoes to control the pressure between my legs.

Still breathing heavily, I say, "Oh, there's no competition. Pinky is better."

"Careful, Reese." He turns the dial at the end, bringing Pinky buzzing to life. My thighs clamp around the toy, and Cory watches my eyes as I rub myself on it, chasing more friction.

"Prove me wrong," I say between tingles building low in my belly.

He puts the toy back and carries me to the room, grabbing towels on the way. After drying me off, he spends that time showing me just how wrong I was. Nothing compares to how quick and easy Cory gets me there. He took the time to learn what I liked and improve on it.

His balls slap against me with his fingers in my hair as we both near our climax.

I've let him take what he wants, but I have to get what has been on my mind since I had him in that baler.

Getting out of the bed, I coax him over to my loveseat again. He sits in all his naked glory, and I start to take note of things I missed before when we had sex here. His sons' names are inked under his left pec in an angelic font that denotes its importance. Even if I had never noticed it, I would have already known how important his sons are to him. The heavily shaded nature scenes along his arms and up his neck are both masculine and detailed in how lush the flowers are mixed with active native animals.

Smaller tattoos lie between his freckles, and each hold some clear meaning for him. I wonder offhandedly if he would get something inked for me.

I brush that thought away and climb onto his lap again. I'm still wet enough for him to slide into me easily. We both moan as I take him fully inside me. He kisses my neck and bites my harness as I slowly start riding him to find a rhythm I like best. My tits bounce in his face, and every now and again, he spares one a kiss or a nip. Holding my ass, he helps us both discover what we like. When I look into his warm, soulful eyes something clicks for me that never has before.

Sex with Cory is different.

Not just because Cory is a different person, but because he's... him.

In the past, sex was always a tool. My tool. *My weapon.* I could wield it in whichever way I wanted. Threaten to withhold it. Threaten to give it to someone else. Threaten to do it without them.

But with Cory, it's not like that. He doesn't expect anything from me. Nothing except my pleasure. He's never allowed himself to have it without me. He truly cares if I'm enjoying myself, and that's a priority.

He cares about me.

Sex has never felt so free except when it was with myself.

I want to be here with him. All I can think about is how much I love being here with him.

Riding him just like this.

Being close to him just like this.

Feeling his hands on me... just... like... this.

It's so easy to forget any worries I could have when he makes me see stars in the daylight. My orgasm rips through me like lightning and I burst into a million tiny pieces as the bliss shudders through me. He holds me close to him with both arms wrapped around my body. "Give me all of it, pretty girl."

Our hearts thunder in time with each other with our chests pressed this close together. His slow thrusts up into my pussy feel like heaven when he lays me down to meet his own finish.

My eyes never leave his as I watch him push into me over and over. Each time I think...

He loves me.

He loves me.

He... loves... me.

With him all around me, I forget about the formidable task I know I will have to do Monday.

For him. For this. It will be worth it.

I just hope he can understand and forgive me when everything is said, when everything is done.

CHAPTER 30

Reese, Four Years Ago

"THERE, THERE GIRL."

I walk slowly into the pen that I've just managed to get this youngling into. I close the small gate, holding the bucket in my hand out to her.

"Want something yummy? You've been running for a few days. Surely, the treat smells good." She backs away from me more and more until she hits the back corner. I can tell she doesn't feel threatened, but she is hesitant to let me near her.

I keep cooing to her in soft phrases, and we do this dance around the pen. Her curiosity gets the best of her, and she sniffs into the feed bucket. With her head mostly submerged, I'm able to put a rope around her. I rub her side and she lets me. I blow out a sigh of relief. It's not often that a horse will get out but with over a thousand acres of open land for them to roam, it can be a real pill to try to contain them again.

"Good girl. There's more where that came from." Her head is too big to get to the very bottom of the bucket, so I grab some of it holding it in my hand for her. "Not so bad, huh? If you can behave, there are more love and treats where that came from. We haven't named you yet. What do you think about Cheyenne?" No.

"Dakota?" No response at all. I think a little longer, scratching her back.

"Scarlett?" Her ears twitch and she sniffs into my hair. "You like that one? I like it too. I'll let everyone know from now on that you're Scarlett. And you'll come when we call you right?" Her big brown eyes give nothing away, but it'll take some time for her to get that trick down anyway.

Leading Scarlett to the corral, I introduce her to the area where the other young horses are grazing. I have just a few more things before I'm off for the day since—it's my birthday!

Last on the list is weighing out feed for the horses in the tack room.

"There's someone up front asking for you to sign for the sexiest red Mustang I've ever seen!" Taylor says. I almost knock the coffee can I'm using to the floor, but stabilize it on the table before it falls.

What? "No way! You're lying," I exclaim. Ripping off my gloves, I throw them onto the table. I run out front to the drive, and sure enough, there sits a shiny new convertible Mustang with a glittery red bow on the hood.

My jaw drops before I let out a big squeal that makes birds fly off the barn.

My dad comes running out of the house, searching for me, and my mom is not long behind him. "What is it? What happened—" he cuts himself off when he notices the car and the man who looks completely unperturbed by the ruckus I'm causing.

"Did you do this?" I ask, giddy with excitement and appreciation. "I love her!"

His brows bunch together, and he scratches at the slightly greying stubble on his neck. Looking to my mom, who shrugs, he turns back to me saying, "Reese, this isn't from us."

The man next to the car clears his throat. "I've got a couple of other cars to deliver today. Can you sign for this so I can head out?"

"Umm..." I look back to my dad, who reaches for the clipboard in the delivery guy's hand, but he moves it just out of his grasp.

"Says it's for Reese Mason. If that's you, I need some ID before I can release it."

"Yes! That's me! It is my birthday, after all!" I run into the house to grab my purse and wallet. I have no idea who it's from, but only an absurd person would say no to a free car that's this nice!

When I get back and take the clipboard to sign all the highlighted lines, I see Teddy's real name on the paperwork. Something like dread settles over me for a moment as I think about what this will mean for our agreement.

In the years since my eighteenth, our agreement has changed and evolved.

It was once high-priced liquor and edibles that felt like a party until I woke up used and bruised. Then it became a pill he may or may not allow me to take by myself.

When I faked ingesting them, I knew he was putting them in my drinks or food. Some nights, I would wake up in the middle of him shoving inside me and force myself to pretend that I was still knocked out. It was better to eat the entirety of my food, drink all of my drinks. Especially, if it meant that I wouldn't suffer through what I could consciously feel happening to me.

When I turned twenty last year, he became interested in something more... active on my part. I don't know if I missed the pills or the edibles more.

But nothing in this life is free. I named my price, and he paid it.

The dread is quickly replaced by excitement when I get into the car and notice the back seat is full of shopping bags. Not just any bags, though.

They're designer.

My favorites!

The new car smell mixes with the smell of fancy leather goods and expensive perfume that only comes from my most frequented department stores.

"Fuck, Reese, this is nice!" I startle at Mack hanging in the window of the driver's side.

Turning from how I was leaning over into the back seat, I'm about to respond, but not long after, Quincy is in the window on the passenger side. "Damn. Who is this from?" He fingers the bags in the backseat, trying to get a peek at what's inside. I smack his hand, and he recoils out of the car, laughing.

"A secret admirer," I respond, searching for the button that makes the roof drop down. When I find it, both guys step back, whistling long and slow.

The wind blows through my hair, and there is no helping the big grin on my face now. "Tell my dad I'm taking the day off."

I start up the car, kicking gravel up as I peel out of the driveway and head to the highway. Tissue papers from the bags billows out behind me.

I park in front of the condo I've become all too accustomed to. He's given me a key with how frequently I'm there now.

Since that first night with Teddy, I thought long and hard about what he expected of me. I think about it every time I wake up after missing hours of my life and feel exhausted.

Looking glamorous and expensive is my favorite thing. Having my hair and extensions done fresh every month. Plus, makeup and clothes to suit any occasion. And the jewelry, the jewelry is the biggest perk. I look and feel the part on his arm at fundraisers, on the occasional trip, and at dinners.

Not many get to live the lifestyle that's slowly becoming mine. When I'm back at the Ranch, I can see just how close I am to the life I had only dreamed of.

It doesn't seem that bad to trade just some control.

I just have to keep reminding myself.

He's set a standard for me that keeps only men who can afford my taste around me. I've been able to give up days on the Ranch whenever I need to spend more time with him or any others in Denver.

Tonight, is going to be the night he finally asks. I can feel it. I've been hinting for the past few months that we should move in together. Tonight is the night.

He insists that this is nothing serious. I know that he's seeing other women. What do I care? It's not stopping my bag.

But, he is possessive of me. I've been pretty good about keeping any other men out of his notice, though. If he's not my boyfriend, then I'm not his girlfriend. I'm single, for the time being.

He's usually working late and I need company when I'm up in Denver more often than not.

More is more, am I right? And I always want more.

I grab my bags from the backseat and shower before putting on the lingerie that he bought me. It's black with lace so delicate, I might rip through it just by breathing. I lay out on his bed in the master bedroom, snapping a picture from the neck down and sending it to him.

My mom gave me the most beautiful gold harness for my birthday, and it sparkles just right against my skin with the flash.

There's no reply from him after hours, but that's not uncommon with his schedule. It's a risk being here without him, but he bought me a car!

Not just any car.

A fucking drop-top Mustang.

I spend that time putting on makeup flawlessly, applying lashes, and straightening my hair to sleek, golden perfection. The last bit of argan oil I apply makes it gleam in the bathroom lighting. I finish off the entire look with a spritz of something yummy on my skin.

I take a moment to roll in his bed, hopefully leaving my smell there for him long after I leave. Plus, there's the added benefit of looking like I've rolled in bed. Perfect, but still a little bit messy.

It's not long before I get a text from Chloe in the group chat.

> **Chloe: I want the first ride in the Mustang! I'm calling dibs. What are you calling her anyway?**

Of course, Quincy already told her about it. I think for a bit.

> **Me: Obvi she's Sally.**

> **Chloe: That is a basic ass name, Reese! You can do better than that.**

> **Me: I am but a basic bitch.** [EMOJI WITH STUCK-OUT TONGUE]

> **Drea: Leave her alone. Besides, she's taking me first. I'm her best friend. And I made her that amazing molten chocolate explosion cake. She likes me best.**

Switching from one message to another I explore more options while I'm in town. A text from another man I met during an event I was at with Teddy still sits unread from this morning.

> **Jay: Happy Birthday... What are you doing tonight?**

Dry. Ugh.

> **Me: I'm busy.**

> **Jay: Are you in town? I'll pick you up. I miss you.**

Rolling my eyes, I reply,

> **Me: I know you do.**

> **Jay: I'll make it worth your time.**

They always want time. But, my time is no longer cheap.

Finessing is not for the faint of heart.

Emotions are worth something, but Louis is worth more.

I just turned twenty-one, so he better be prepared to make the milestone count. I won't see him tonight either way, but I could make time tomorrow.

> **Me: I'm listening** [RED HEART EMOJI]

The three dots appear as he's responding, but I lock my phone when I hear the door slam closed downstairs.

Teddy's polished shoes thud on each step he takes up the stairs.

Anticipation causes my heart to race the closer he gets to the master bedroom. I lay in a position that makes me look both exposed and vulnerable.

One of his favorites.

He opens the door and I put on my best smirk. He smirks back at me, watching me trail a finger up my torso from the door frame.

"Do you love it?" He asks, arms crossed.

The car? The bags full of gifts? This lingerie?

Does it matter?

The answer is the same.

I love being spoiled.

"Yes. So much, Teddy."

"Then why aren't you waiting the way we discussed?" The censure in his tone makes me scramble from the bed to my knees on the floor in front of him at the door. "Better." He runs a hand over my hair, and the validation runs down my spine in tiny prickles.

The attention and praise from this moneyed man made me feel more validated than anything else could. Something about the possessive way he desired me, felt like celebrity.

Felt like fame.

It had earned me infamy in AR and I ignored them all because when it was just the two of us, I could believe that I was more than the small town girl drowning in small town gossip.

I was so much more than her.

More men wanted me because I was on *his* arm. The jealousy of other women grew palpable at events. Not just from my high school peers. People noticed and either wanted me or wanted to be me. Teddy did that.

I felt powerful in his possession.

I felt adored. All I wanted was to be coveted in this way forever.

Being admired by one man was amazing...

But being valued by more men, all clawing for a piece of me was...

More. And I *always* want more.

I keep my eyes on the ground with my arms behind my back, hands clasped together. Seeing his shoes leave in front of me, he walks to a spot behind me.

First his shoes, then his clothes drop to the floor.

Fully expecting him to return for me, I startle when I hear the shower turn on and the heavy glass door close.

After fifteen minutes of kneeling like this, my legs are on fire, and my back aches from keeping my posture so still. But, I dare not move.

You might think that when we worked our way to this kind of submission, I would be used to the discomfort by now. That might be true if I wasn't still working the Ranch so often.

I have to be perfect for him in order to get what I want.

I'll ignore the pain because tonight will be the night, and I'll be making that call that I'm done.

That I quit country life.

That I'm no longer that horse-wrangling country bumpkin.

That I'm *his*.

There will be nothing to distract from being the only sub Teddy will need. If I don't work at the Ranch anymore, I can be here all the time. He won't need other women to make up for the time that I'm not here. We can be more than just this.

I'll belong to Teddy, and he will take care of me. So I wait as patiently as I can for his next demand.

Chapter 31

Reese

"He said it will be a few minutes."

The receptionist, Dawn, sits behind her desk again.

She's new.

Not the one who worked here before. "Would you like a water or coffee while you wait?" Her tone is dry and it's clear that she asked from protocol and not because she genuinely wants to offer them to me.

"No, thank you." *I'd rather you not spit in my coffee this morning.* I run a hand over my thighs when I sit in one of the overstuffed leather chairs in the lobby. I look around and try my best to remain calm though I want to walk very quickly so as to not attract any unwanted attention, out the chrome and glass door I walked in through.

Classical piano music plays and it feels sterile and cold in here. Comfort was not the goal in designing this space. I feel out of place in jeans and a tank top. My boots squeak with how tightly I have my legs crossed, and the sound echoes through the lobby.

Dawn looks over to me, and we meet eyes. I wonder to myself how old she is and if Teddy has gotten to her too.

I scroll my phone, trying to distract myself, when I hear the tell-tale sounds of the large oak doors opening, and the man I came to see steps out.

His light grey suit is pressed and he has a silk navy tie knotted tightly to his neck. We couldn't be more opposites if we tried in this moment. I feel my face heat with embarrassment at how underdressed and vulnerable I feel walking over to him.

It has been years since we were in the same room and I didn't look *the part*. His requirement of more from me was once the reason my core would clench. But now, his stiff suit and cold demeanor cause me to cross my arms around my body to stave off the shiver I feel from his icy stare.

"Ree, come with me." A command.

I stand with more uncomfortable squeaks. Dawn looks me over for what is probably the hundredth time as she stands behind her desk. She stood when he walked out. Her gaze bores into my back as I pass her into his office.

So he definitely got to her.

The door closes with a dull thud that reverberates through the clinical silence of his office which is missing the piano music from the lobby.

Teddy takes a seat behind the desk in an overstuffed executive chair. His light brown hair is parted and styled to perfection. The clean shave always made him appear more youthful to me. When I was younger, I thought he was some sort of suited hero who could save me. Now, I can only see what hides under that polished facade.

Opening my purse, I search for a few moments before I pull out the thin metal ring. It holds the two keys to the small apartment I've called home for the last three years. They clink onto the glass topped desk. "Everything is how it was when I moved in. You want to tell me how you knew I was at the house with someone?"

After having the most amazing weekend with Cory since my parents were gone, I woke up to a text from him on Sunday morning.

> **Teddy : Whoever he is, he can't have what belongs to me. Bring my keys to the office on Monday.**

"The doorbell. I still get the notifications." He reclines in the chair, steepling his fingers. I had completely forgotten that the doorbell camera on my side of the house was purchased and given to me by him when I still lived at home. "If you're going to sleep around on me, you could at least have the decency to do it at their house."

I can feel my anger rising, but I take a deep breath before I say, "You were spying on me? This whole time?"

"C'mon Ree. It's not spying when these are my things. I'm just keeping tabs." *My things.* Myself included. I roll my eyes.

"We had an understanding."

"Did we? I agreed to give you some space to think things through. I believe my exact words were, 'You'll be back when you want something, and here you are." He gestures around the office, though I was hardly ever in this place, specifically.

I flinch back into my seat. "I'm not yours anymore, Teddy. The moment you put your hands on me, intending to really hurt me, was the last time that what we had meant anything."

"Ree—"

"My name is Reese. You don't get to call me that anymore. You sent me that sick little note, and I really didn't appreciate it. The set was cute though."

He smiles, coldly. "You will always be mine, Ree. I let you play your games, and now it's time to get back in line. I purchased that set because I thought you would look mouthwatering in it. And here you are." He reiterates. "Did you bring it?"

I stand, causing my chair to scrape across the tiles loudly. "Games? What the fuck are you talking about? This is my life. I'm not the same young, naive girl. I'm not going anywhere but back to the Ranch. That's where I will be living. I'm not back."

"Did you bring the lingerie, Ree?"

Through my teeth, I respond, "Yes."

"Perfect. You won't need it, but I like that you thought of me. What's the number?"

Gritting my teeth, I pull the slip of paper with what my calculations came to from my purse, setting it on the desk. Even after adding up everything in my jar, I was short. There was a huge red number in our payment category.

My mom continued to say that we would figure it out and that I shouldn't worry about it. Each time I asked her if I should call or email to follow up on those financial forms, she told me not to. That we would figure it out.

Business is business, and a business in the red, can't keep being a business.

How could I allow this to happen when I had a way to make that money?

I walked away before because I didn't need him. I didn't need this kind of cash. What's one more mark on my wretched soul?

And here you are.

I had to make this call. This is but a small price to keep my dream alive for now. Something that may have been just for my parents before, but that became something I wanted so badly for myself as well. I wanted more than to help get things started. I wanted to be there to see Masons' Horsing Around grow, thrive, and flourish.

He slides the paper across the glass with a scrape. Teddy makes an appreciative sound from the back of his throat, and I shudder at the response.

"This was a bad idea." Standing from the chair, I walk to the door with my hand on the handle, ready to yank it open on my departure.

"I wouldn't leave if I were you."

"And why the hell not?"

"That's for me to know and for you to hope you never find out." A chill slips down my spine, and I turn to see he is only a foot away from me. His footsteps were silent like the demon he is.

He grabs my throat, pinning me to the door. "I fully intend to have you again. And I will have you right now. Dawn might get pissed, but I can always hire another assistant. You forget that everything you are now is because of me. You came after *me*. You got me. And now you don't get to decide when I will have what is mine. You promised me that you would always be mine. Shall I remind you why?"

"This was always an exchange. You don't own me."

"Don't I? Whatever I want from you, I will take. Whatever I want so that you can have all that you ask for. And this," He waves the paper I gave him in the air hard enough for it to crackle like fire, "This is a lot to ask for."

"Are you going to give it to me or not?"

"Oh, I will. But you will submit first."

I gasp, "Here?"

"Here."

"Why not later? I can just come over later." I choke out. Am I shocked that he wants to use me just like before? No, I expected as much.

But here? In this office? He never crossed that line with me. Before, I meant something more than his assistants. I was more than that. There was at least the false grandeur of being wooed with us in the past.

No one would ever be in danger of seeing the kind of things he requested of me. As far as they suspected, we were family friends... maybe his young girlfriend.

Now only a single door separates me from anyone who works with him from hearing or seeing me here being debased in whatever way he sees fit for the number I wrote on that paper.

He spins me around so that my back is pressed to the door. Putting just enough pressure on my neck. I can't breathe or talk comfortably. With his size and the fact that his thigh and body are pressed against me hard enough to restrain—I'm stuck where he wants.

Helpless and defenseless. Losing more air the longer he has me pinned.

I reach for my purse, but it's too far out of reach to get my blade for now. The strap in my hands could be a weapon, but I don't know if I'm strong enough to choke him with it. If I try and get into my cross-body purse it may fall and expose the blade. The worst thing you can do is present another weapon that can be used against you to an attacker. That was the first lesson of self-defense.

I internally curse myself for not being more prepared for his attack. True fear creeps in, as flashes of his cold eyes sear into me, from all those months ago.

"Do what I say. I don't want to ruin your face, Ree. It would be a shame for you to show up at the Ranch that way, now wouldn't it?"

He releases his hold on me. I suck in air with my hands on my knees, fighting the tears I feel coming to my eyes. "I will tell her. Your wife." I say it just loud enough for him to hear. My voice sounding small even to my own ears.

"As if she doesn't already know. I barely even live there anymore. She isn't stupid, *Ree*." He sneers the nickname at me. "Anyone can be bought. For the right price. She will play her part and keep her mouth shut. You of all people, should know that." He goes back to his desk and sits, looking just as composed as before. "Now, crawl."

This time, I can't fight the tear as it rolls hot down my cheek.

He's right.

And he has paid for me, in full.

I drop to my knees and do as he says. Just like before.

"Good. Now, strip." With each piece of clothing I remove, I feel a small piece of myself shattering.

Slut. The tank top drops.

Naive. My jeans join the pile.

Whore. My bra and thong mock me from their new location, off my body.

How could I not see this for the trap that it was? The moment I stepped into this building was the moment that I fucked up. I knew that it was only a matter of time before Teddy would come back into my life. That the desire I have for more would roar its insatiable need. This time, it's not just for me. I'm doing this for them.

It has been so many months, but I'll never forget what he expects of me.

I sit there on my knees, utterly naked in his office, with the shame rolling over me like cold, wet slime sticking to every exposed part of my body. My eyes are glued to the tile flooring.

He looks my body over, cataloging every small mark Cory made just a day before. I only feel more nauseous as the seconds tick by. I feel like I will blow chunks when the sound of Teddy's belt being undone rattles in the room.

I lift my gaze, and he holds my chin. "For each mark on *my Ree*, you get a new one to replace it from me. Hands on the desk."

I stand on unsteady legs and focus on the pens lined up neatly on his desk as he makes me count each hard slap of his belt to my ass and thighs.

The humiliation stings worse that the welts I know will rise up angry and red. I find myself thankful that he hasn't asked for something more painful from me. I told myself that I would never do this again. That I would never submit to this man who never cared for me again. The clock is ticking and there is only a short time until MHA will begin.

It's just pain.

It's just pride.

No one ever has to know.

Cory never has to know what I'm willing to live with and undergo.

By the time he gets to seven, my face is a mess of mascara and tears that pool on the glass. Pens askew.

Feeling him shove into me, I try my best to silence my cries until he finishes for fear that someone will hear us.

I don't bother cleaning up after him, and he doesn't try to clean me either. I know he would rather me drip his semen than let me have my dignity in his presence.

I put on my clothes as quickly as possible. Grabbing some tissues to clean my face as best I can, attempting to make my exit again.

"Ree, same time next week. And come better prepared."

CHAPTER 32

Cory

"Pasta sauce, penne, ground beef... I know I'm missing something."

"You should have listened to Aunt Jan when she told you to make a list."

"Yea, I know, CJ. But we'll figure it out, right?"

Bren comes sprinting down the aisle, missing the basket by mere inches. He rounds the basket, giving Gabe's lizard a squeeze before sprinting back down to the other end. Gabe giggles at his brother's teasing and eats more of the banana I gave him when we were in the produce section.

One thing I knew we needed was a salad mix. I figured it couldn't hurt to give him something to do with his hands as I tried to remember what I was supposed to be getting from this store.

Maybe I haven't paid for the yellow fruit yet, but I will. So, lock me up for a little treat and distraction for my toddler.

"Like a puzzle? What's missing?" CJ asks.

"Sure, we can think of it that way. Pasta and sauce are both on this aisle, so that's easy. Ground beef is on the other side of the store. I know there's something else." I pull my phone out of the diaper bag sitting next to Gabe, determined not to message Janet.

Maybe if I take my phone out of my pocket like I'm going to text her, it will jog my memory. Quite frankly, I'm exhausted. I had a long day of summer yard clean-ups at the two new properties my team secured. The last thing I want is an "I told you so" from both CJ and Janet, back to back.

"Maybe cheese?" I look up from my hands and get an eyeful of something much more delicious.

It's been a few days since I had Reese all to myself at her parents' house. I felt kind of like a teenager again, sneaking in and out of her place. But can't deny that it's been fun.

A knowing smile graces her lips, and I feel mine stretch across my face. I will never get over how much having her near me makes me feel whole again. It's like that weight gets a little bit smaller in her presence.

"Reese!" CJ gives her a hug around the waist, and she easily returns the hug. He stays there with an arm around her body until Bren races back to our side. He almost takes her down to the ground with the force of his hug. She giggles and rights herself, squeezing him close to her.

"Did you come to help dad grocery shop?" Bren asks her.

"Not quite, hot foot. But I overheard him, and I thought that he might need some cheese for his pasta. Maybe parmesan. That's my favorite." She gives Bren a wink, and he beams with the attention.

Oh, I get it, buddy.

Finally, I speak after being all too enamored with how well the boys have taken to her. Apparently, she was one of the instructors for their horse riding clinics on Thursday and Friday. She made an impression. My young boys might not know it now, but they are gonna have to get in line. She made an impression on me first.

It's been so long since I've had anyone do this type of thing with me. Where it's not just me juggling all the responsibility. Not that she is grocery shopping with us... Or that there is an us that includes her yet. I'm not giving up hope on her truly being all in though. I made it clear what I was looking for and she agreed. It's only a matter of time before I will be able to share this with her, too.

That cheese suggestion was perfect. I had almost forgotten all about what she said as I was daydreaming about having a family that included her. "Parmesan. I was gonna think of that... Eventually." I rub at the back of my neck.

She hums an agreement that tells me just how believable I made that statement seem. Her focus is too distracted by helping Gabe with some banana that's fallen into his lap. He takes it from her and pops it into his mouth. His little hand grabs onto hers, leaving sticky banana residue, but she doesn't recoil from his gooey gesture.

"You doing some shopping too?" I ask, lamely. Like a lame person.

Damn. Real smooth, C.

I notice that her small handbasket has a few items. That's *obviously* what she's doing here.

"Just picking up a few snacks." She lifts her basket to show me. I chuckle and feel my ears heating.

"Reese, my Auntie Jan put dad in charge of dinner tonight. She said that he wouldn't have too much difficulty with a red sauce out of the jar. It will be edible. Edible means that you can eat it. Isn't that silly? Food is to eat. But one time dad tried to make something called a stir fry, and everything was all burnt. Only the rice was good, so Jan ordered us a pizza. Usually, Aunt Sammie makes our dinner, but she's in Austin this week for work. So, it's dad's turn for dinner. Do you wanna have dinner with us?" Bren rambles out so quickly that I didn't have time to stop the train wreck of him oversharing all my business with his instructor.

My neck is now fully sweating in addition to my hot ears and I need to say something before she thinks I'm a shit dad.

Reese takes it all in stride, laughing some more at what Brendan has told her. She looks to me for guidance on what she should say to the invitation my son has, not so gracefully, given to her for dinner. I shrug like it's no big deal, but the heat is spreading to my armpits, and I'm thankful for the dry-fit shirt I'm wearing.

Why am I getting so nervous?

She looks back down to Bren and says, "I would love to come for dinner. Should I bring over a treat for dessert?" She scratches her chin in an exaggerated manner, like she's thinking it over.

CJ pipes up to ask, "Well, that depends. It's not gonna be fruit salad, is it?"

Her laugh sends sparks of satisfaction across my skin. She looks so at ease around the three of them. Gabe, still gripping her fingers, CJ's arm around her, and Bren basking in the attention she's giving him.

"Oh ew! Yuck. No fruit salad! How do you guys feel about ice cream?"

The three of them cheer, clearly approving of her suggestion.

"I can grab it for them when we're done here. No problem." I say.

"From here? No way. I'll pick up some from one of my favorite places in town. It's been a while since I've gone anyway. It'll be nice to pay The DreamCreamery a visit."

"Now, why couldn't he find a respectable girl in this town." I hear from over on the next aisle, just loud enough that I know Reese heard it too. Her smile has become brittle as she pretends that she didn't hear the not-so-subtle whispers.

"W-well I'm gonna head out of here, but I'll see you later on, right?"

"Six thirty!" I have to shout because she's already made it down the aisle.

She nods and gives a wave over her shoulder before disappearing from sight. And like the lame I am, I'm still standing there watching her go.

Why didn't I say something? I should have put that lady in her place. I'm tired of all the gossip floating around this place about her. None of it was true. How would they know? She *is* the respectable girl that I've found in this town. I stare after her, thinking of what I could have or maybe should have said.

"Cheese. We need cheese, dad," CJ reminds me after I had been staring after her for far too long in my thoughts.

"Oh right. Let's go grab the rest of the things we need."

<hr>

"WHAT A WONDERFUL SURPRISE!" I hear Janet say from the door. "Cory, Reese is here!" The boys all greet her with the same excitement as before. I hear them get excited when she shows them something she has. I hear the uproar over the ice cream when they realize what it is, and she's able to excuse herself to the kitchen with me.

I look at the digital clock on the stove and see that it's a few minutes past six. I've just started making dinner.

Reese comes into the kitchen to give me a hug. Her perfume wafts up around me, making my mouth water.

She pulls away, but I pull her into me for a kiss. The boys are all keeping busy in the living room with Jan while I make dinner.

She seems hesitant at first but deepens the kiss when she sees I'm not letting her give me a chaste kiss meant for church or something.

"Sorry, I'm a bit early. Just figured I could help you out. You seemed kinda stressed at the store."

"You noticed that?" I chuckle.

"Yea. That and I need to put the ice cream up before they all melt." She shows me the huge bag in her hand and I step out of the way for her to put the desserts into the freezer. "What can I help with?'

"You really don't need to. I've got some wine if you want. I'd like to have you in the kitchen to look at."

She sucks her teeth. "That won't do. I could at least boil the pasta."

"Okay, fine. But then you get to sit right there," I gesture to the breakfast bar on the other side of the island, "and be my muse."

"Your muse? That sounds like more work than cooking."

"For you?" I swipe a hand through the air. "It would be as easy as breathing."

Her cheeks redden and I give myself a pat on the back in my mind at the response. After pulling a band from her purse, she puts her hair into a ponytail. "In that case, let me get started with the pasta water." She gives me a kiss on the cheek, rubbing her lipgloss from my face and gets to work.

Despite my best efforts, Reese helped make the pasta, the sauce and garlic bread. It was a team effort in the end. I found that I liked having her in the kitchen with me, making a meal for the family. I thought that it would be uncomfortable to do this together, but it was fun.

Before I knew it, the food was ready. No wonder my dad wanted my mom in the kitchen. Reese was much more help than my mom was though. I could get used to this.

We all sit around the table eating and sharing stories until the boys need to get ready for bed. I leave for only a bit to bathe Gabe. When I get him out, Reese helps me get his pajamas and even reads to him while I work on bedtime for CJ and Bren.

By the time she finishes the story, Gabe has fallen asleep with his little fingers around hers. I watch them from the doorway as my heart melts a little bit more for this woman.

When she quietly backs out of the room, I allow her to bump into me on her way out.

"Ooop. Sor—" I cut her off with another kiss in the hallway.

"Thank you," I say.

She hooks her hair behind her ear, looking up at me cautiously. "For what?"

"For tonight. I... Thank you. You didn't have to do any of this but I'm so grateful that you did."

Her eyebrows scrunch as she searches my eye for a moment. Her smirk returns an she says, "Oh. That? Maybe I had an ulterior motive..."

I smile down at her, putting my arms around her waist. "And what would that be?"

Her hands fist my shirt and pull me even closer to her so that our bodies are pressed together from chest to thigh. "Which one of these is the room you're staying in?"

I pull her down the hall to my room and she closes the door behind us.

In the dark, I feel her take my shirt off and over my head. My hands find her waist again and its bare skin my fingers brush up against with her top gone too. I skim my hands over her back and up to her bra clasp, letting it fall to the floor.

Picking her up, I kiss her as we cross the room to the bed. I'm between her legs working her jeans off as quickly as I can.

"Thank you," I say again. Kissing from her ankle to her inner thigh, stopping only to bite at the sensitive skin there. She giggles and puts a hand over her mouth to muffle the sound.

Squirming her body closer to my mouth, she asks, "For what?"

This gift.

Helping with dinner. Bedtime. For being here. All when she didn't have to.

I didn't expect her to and I'm grateful for how easily the mundane tasks came to her. Like she was meant to be here doing them with me all along.

Meeting her eyes, I respond, "You."

CHAPTER 33

Reese

"Hurry Reese! I don't want to miss the sourdough this time! What was the point of getting here early if I can't get some?" When she says some, she really means more loaves than we could carry in both our arms combined.

Chandie power walks through the Alpenglow Ridge Farmer's Market. I do my best to keep up with her. She's easy to spot as the sun glints off her stone-covered headband, making it look like a small halo around her head.

My mom loves to cook for everyone on the Ranch and she prides herself on serving all the best ingredients. Lord knows, the woman could have a full conversation with a wall about how fresh and local everything is.

Every week during summer, the vacant lot on Main Street encourages local farms to set up tents and tables to sell their various goods. They have a few tents for small businesses like the Lewis Bread bakery my mom is currently making a beeline for. I tug the wagon she brought, trying to keep up with the sparkling woman on a mission.

While Chandie talks to Tommy Lewis about his stock of sourdough, I get lost in my thoughts about Cory. Two weeks have passed since we started whatever this is between us.

It's been... really fucking nice. I've been happy. Happier than I can remember being in a long time.

The initial week of the camp went well with the kids. *His kids.* Before I had made a point to never talk about them. But after meeting them for myself, they're not what I expected at all.

It's not the fact that they're young. I knew I wanted to work with children ever since I was one. Mack and I used to sit on the fence or hide in the stables to get close to the horses. I just knew I wanted to be someone who showed young kids how to love them the right way. I'd tell Danny about it all the time. I think that's what convinced him to let me learn all those years ago. Though I'm not a part of every aspect of the camp, knowing that I'm part of the reason that it's even happening makes my soul glow a little.

It's a lot of work, but I don't remember ever being this content since I left Alpenglow Ridge. I found myself giving up the few shifts I wanted to hold on to at Peak's. It wasn't difficult with how coveted those spots are.

Marie and Karla both got on my ass when they saw I wasn't closing with them anymore, but I'll just have to see them another time. Both aren't convinced that I'm coming back to Denver.

If I'm honest, I don't think I am either.

Cory and I text and talk on the phone almost every night. I was shocked that he left a bouquet of buttercups and anemone on the side doorstep one morning. They were beautifully arranged by him. He has such an eye for that sort of thing. I couldn't help but think that they would be perfect for a wedding bouquet.

A month ago, I would have panicked at the idea of imagining a wedding. But now? I still think about it every time I pass the spot on my dresser where they sat until they died.

To say that I like him, would be an understatement. When he's not working on the Ranch, I...

I miss him.

If I'm honest, I'm thankful that we both have been busy these last two weeks.

That life I was chasing, doesn't seem worth it anymore. I had all the glamour. The fancy designer names and meals and trips. The high-class events and even the high-class company.

But throughout it all, I was dying just a little more inside. Burying the pain of what I had to do in order to obtain the lifestyle I thought I wanted. I was never enough, they always wanted more of me. More of my soul, when my body wasn't enough.

Nothing in life is free. Everything costs.

With my most recent debt being paid in full to Teddy, I feel ready to leave all that behind me for something far better.

For Cory.

My mind is still reeling with how I can finally get from under Teddy's thumb. His looming threat can't go unnoticed.

I can't talk to anyone about it. Definitely not anyone here. I don't know if Chloe or Mel or Drea would judge me, but I might die from the shame and embarrassment.

Shame because of who Teddy is. Embarrassment because half the rumors circulating about me have at least some merit.

How do I admit that I am every bit the gold-digging hussy this town thinks I am?

There is no way that I can take those steps to separate myself from him entirely. The apartment was the biggest relief, but he owns more than just that. I don't know if I'm truly ready to let everything go.

Someone taps my arm, and I spin around, prepared to tell them to wait their turn. But, no one is there. Then, I feel a tap on my other arm and turn around, looking down, I see the blur of someone I know pretty well now.

Bren.

"He thought that would be so funny." I turn again to see CJ holding his little brother in his arms. The toddler is trying desperately to grab the cinnamon sugar pretzel hanging from the stand in front of me. Smudges from fingers I know to be Gabe's cloud CJ's glasses. I reach into my purse, pulling a microfiber cloth from my sunglasses case. I hand it to him.

CJ puts the toddler into my wagon with a bag I didn't notice he was carrying. The little one wastes no time pulling the little lizard stuffed animal from the bag to busy himself. He looks so content and happy to sit in my wagon. I lean over to squeeze his arm and brush some curls from his face.

"My dad was hoping he would see you here. Actually, Auntie Janet said Mrs. Chandie would be here buying up all the bread. I knew we'd find you here first." CJ informs me.

"Is that right?" I give him a smirk and he hands me the cloth back. "Well, I don't see your dad anywhere." I make a point of looking around as a joke, but then my eyes snag on broad shoulders and a beard that I would recognize anywhere. His beard is lined up with his haircut, both sharp and begging for me to run my hands over them. His eyes shine with appreciation when they meet mine. I feel the smile stretching my cheeks because I'm smiling like an absolute loon with the man being so near. It takes him only moments to cross the crowd and get to me.

His thumb traces the edge of my lips, fingers already weaving through the hair at my neck. "Is that for me?"

I nod, not trusting my own words. He leans close to me and before his lips meet mine, he asks, "Can I kiss you, pretty girl?" The nickname sends shivers down my spine as I recall the last time I heard it.

I nod more emphatically and his lips connect with mine. First with a soft brush that I thought I imagined. My eyes close and all the sounds around me, in this busy market, fade away. The second kiss is more firm. Cory's scent envelops me and it feels like it's just the two of us here. I allow myself to fall into this special place for us—where we make sense. There's a teasing sweep of his tongue on my lips before the kiss is over.

Blinking back into reality, his warm brown eyes are shining even brighter as he looks down at me. Before I can stop myself, "I missed you," comes tumbling from my lips. I startle at my own words. Not because the words were wrong, but because I didn't mean to admit them aloud.

Cory's hand brushes down my shoulder and arm to hold my hand. "I missed you too." He takes us in stride, with Gabe in the wagon and CJ walking next to me. Bren joined us at some point with a small sample cup of various fruits and a cracker with jam on it. He gives Gabe the cup with cut fruit and gives me a salute. I give him one back with a smile.

"We'll be back to load up your bread, Chandie." Cory calls to my mom.

"Alright, honey!" She calls back to him and returns to talking with Tommy.

Our hands swing naturally between us as the boys look at each of the table's offerings. "You know, green is probably my favorite color on you."

We pass a table with various peppers and onions from the Saunders' farm. All different shades of green, red, white, and purple produce lay arranged in crates. I look them over as I allow his words to sink into my spirit. I run a hand over the sundress I'm wearing. Go figure that a man who has dedicated his life to plants, likes green.

Lucky guess.

I smile to myself. "I think I like it better on you. Especially those green cargo pants." I hold my fingertips to my mouth and make a kissing sound. "Chef's kiss." Getting onto my tiptoes, I whisper in his ear, "Though these jeans are pretty scrumptious too." He looks down at his pants and I follow his gaze. But I lean backward. His strong thighs and ass fill them out perfectly. "Be sure to tell Levi, thank you for me."

At first, he looks confused before it dawns on him and he hugs me in close to him. "You better be lucky I figured that out." I giggle into his shoulder as he holds me. "I would have worn the green pants today and we could have matched."

Crinkling my nose, I push back on his chest. "Why would you do that?"

"What? Match with you?" I nod my head. "Because we're going steady." He says with a chuckle. His deep laugh resonates through my body. It's not the first time he's said it, but here? In public? Where anyone could hear and with his sons within hearing distance?

I start to feel self-conscious, like everyone in the market is watching us. I pull the wagon to the next table and feel the heat from Cory's hand on my back, but he says nothing.

It's just my luck that the next table is from the Stewart farms. "Hey, Rebecca." Cory is leaning over the table. The large trailer behind it is full of various greens, and there is also a stacked cart with cartons of eggs. I drop down to where Gabe is sucking on a piece of cucumber. The damp lizard sits on his lap and I pick it up, dancing it around like he showed me earlier.

"Oh Cory! I'm glad you made it. How are you?" Rebecca asks.

"I'm good. I put that yield report in your mailbox. Did you get it?"

"Yes, yes. Filed it away. I'm glad you're having an easy time with those deliveries."

"Not too bad, not too bad. Though a Denver boy like me can get lost easily on these county roads out here. Especially with all the construction still happening on those KB homes."

She tsks. "It is a hassle. But I had faith in you. If it weren't for those new homes, we would have to take our business much farther out than Alpenglow." Rebecca chuckles and I mock her under my breath, dancing the lizard around like he's saying the words instead of the woman behind the table.

"I don't know if you've met CJ and Bren yet." He corrals the boys between each arm. "Brought them today to give Jan some time with Sammie."

"I'm sure she appreciates it after Sam was gone so long. I've heard and seen the three of them in passing. But you boys aren't giving her trouble anymore, now are you?"

CJ and Bren both say no in that shy way that young kids do with strangers. I hear the table creak moments before Rebecca's voice is right next to my ear. "Who is this with precious little Gabe?"

I squeeze my eyes shut, willing the scowl off my face before opening them and turning to face Mack's mom. The shock is quickly overtaken by a scowl that is so similar to the one Mack is often wearing now. "Oh. Reese. What are you doing here?" Her look of disgust sears into me.

"Just browsing." Her eyes rove over my outfit like it smells bad and I bring an arm over my body to grab at my elbow. "I actually need to get the wagon back to Chandie." I turn to leave, pulling it behind me.

"Um… sorry." I hear Cory say before he's back beside me. He reaches for my face, but I flinch away, unsure if I can keep the tears at bay. The last thing I want to do is cry in this stupid market. He crowds me into a space between two tables that aren't being occupied, but are used as extra storage. With Gabe in his arms now, the two other boys busy themselves at the storage tables.

"What's going on, baby?" He leans down to meet my downcast eyes.

Gabe grabs at my hair saying, "Baby," in his cute little voice and I slip my finger into his hand, removing my hair. His hand is sticky, but I find comfort in the softness of his chubby little fingers. I rub my thumb over the smooth skin on the back of his hand.

"It's nothing, Cory. Let's just go to another table, okay?"

"It's not nothing. What is with you and Rebecca?"

"Small town stuff." He doesn't look convinced, but I'm not going to tell him everything in this moment. I don't want to tell him everything, *ever*. "Can we just talk about it later? It's not a big deal."

He nods his head twice, lips twisting to the side. "Later."

"I really do want to give Chandie her wagon back. Can I hold Gabe in the meantime?" He looks down at his son, who is practically climbing over to me anyway. Without hesitation, Cory shifts his toddler over to me. I hold Gabe in my arms, and he rests his head against my chest.

We walk around the rest of the market, and Cory picks up things here and there. Every now and again, CJ and Bren find us to show us a different sample they've picked up. At the McKenzie's table, they have fresh-cut florals and bouquets arranged in beautiful hand-blown glass vases.

Cory buys a small bundle of them that has been secured to a hair clip. "You just can't say no to cut flowers can you?"

"It's you I can't say no to." The meaning in his eyes isn't lost on me. I don't know if it's the genuine adoration or the hesitancy that makes me want to hold his heart with the tender care. For the life of me, I can't understand why anyone would fumble this man. He's so sweet and considerate.

"I like the sound of that," I say

Without saying another word, he brushes some hair behind my ear and clips it in place. A kiss to my temple brings a small smile back to my lips. He kisses the top of Gabe's curls too, and I notice that the smallest Whitfield has fallen asleep in my arms.

From the outside, we must look like the perfect little family.

Is that what I want?

Can I even have that?

I am only partially paying attention as we finally make it back to the Lewis bakery table. Chandie is still talking to Tommy, though the baked goods we saw before are mostly gone. The crate of sourdough sits untouched, as it appears she's bought all sixteen loaves he brought to sell today.

When I come into view, my mom and I lock eyes. I give her a look that tells her to say nothing about the small boy sleeping in my arms. She gives me a look that says she isn't going to and proceeds to ask, "Cory, are you coming to the launch party tonight?"

Okay. I didn't have a look for that.

"Launch party?" Cory asks. My face heats that I have completely let it slip my mind to tell him that was tonight.

Knowing Teddy would also be there, I thought that maybe I could find a way to brush it off as not being a big deal, and he wouldn't want to come. I don't know. I just completely dropped the ball on that, and now I'm in this incredibly awkward situation about it.

I do not want them in the same place. It could be fine for Cory... But terrible for me if Teddy sees us together.

My mom looks at me and tries to make the situation better by adding, "Yea, Masons' Horsing Around officially launched this week, as you know! We're having a few friends over tonight to celebrate a full roster. The counselors have all been selected, and we filled all fifty-five slots for the kids."

Thanks, mom. That helped exactly nothing!

Cory looks at me and asks, "You're celebrating tonight, too?" My guilty look can't be helped because, *remember*, I dropped the ball.

"I would love for you and the boys to come. Janet and Sammie will be there." Chandie says.

He looks even more affronted now with the knowledge that his aunt and her girlfriend were invited, and he wasn't.

I expect him to be upset but he just shakes his head. "Well, I'll be there to support my *girlfriend*." So much emphasis on the word, when he looks to me. "I probably need to start working on getting ready for that. Do you need me to bring anything, Chandie?"

"Nope. Just yourself, honey." Cory nods, calling his other sons over and picking up the diaper bag from the wagon. He gently shifts Gabe from my arms and into his. Kissing me once more on the forehead, he waves goodbye to us. Bren and CJ hug me before leaving with their dad.

As soon as they are out of my sightline through the crowd, I turn to Chandie. "What was that, mom?"

She looks confused but shrugs when I don't elaborate. Loading up her bread, I follow her back to the truck trying to figure out what the hell I'm going to do now.

CHAPTER 34

Cory

"HONESTLY, I THOUGHT YOU knew." Jan is pressing a pair of linen pants on the ironing board in her room. The boys are taking a shower in the other bathrooms. Gabe is playing happily with a dryer ball on the floor. The smell of spray starch and steam wrinkles my nose.

I'm lying on her bed, twirling my keys around my finger. Thinking about the way Reese reacted to her mom spilling the details about the party that she kept from me.

She *kept* it from me.

I try to ignore the sinking feeling that she didn't want me there for some other reason.

Like maybe she wanted someone else there *instead*.

"And what would make you think that, Janet?" We've been back at her house for a bit. I fed the boys lunch and let Gabe get a good nap in his bed. Hours have passed, and it's hard to not remember the cornered look Reese had at the market.

I thought that we had passed this point. All the while we were walking around talking about nothing, she could have asked me. Or even on the phone before I saw her today, but there was no mention at all. She's got me feeling like some dirty secret.

Not a secret, since she had no problem with being close to me and the boys today. Or any other time before now. It felt right. She felt right, with us.

Us.

I like how it sounds far too much. But, Reese is good with us. She belongs with this family.

"So, it's Janet now? Ain't you bout nothin?" She sucks air through her teeth. "Excuse me for assuming that at some point with your giggling at the phone, *your girlfriend* invited you to her launch party, at *her* house." She hangs the pants on the door to her closet. The bed dips near my feet and I look over to her.

"I don't giggle." She raises an eyebrow. "I laugh in a very deep timbre." She raises the eyebrow even higher. "That's not important. What *is* important is that she didn't invite me. Chandie did. Should we even be going to this thing?"

She thinks for a moment fiddling with her earring. Patting my leg, she responds, "We? I *was* invited." She laughs and I glare. Janet gives me a soft look. "Okay. If she truly didn't want you to be there, I don't think she would have let Chan invite you. Maybe she did forget. We never know what is going on in someone's life. Ask her tonight. Not in the haughty way you're picturing in your mind but with grace. Reese is a grown woman, not one of your boys."

"I guess you're right."

<hr>

CJ AND BREN SPOT some friends from camp right away and head over to play with them. Sammie grabs Gabe, and he goes to her easily, drinking from a cup I made him before we left the house.

People I don't recognize are everywhere here. That's not saying much as I only know the clients I've been working with and my family. My team has grown to five and I am in a place where I can be comfortable working less than a twelve-hour day. If I get one more person, I could even afford to work only on weekdays. Word of mouth helped me out just like I figured it would. Small towns love supporting small businesses. I wonder if I could have had this much success this quickly if I had tried to start Whitfield Landscaping in Denver.

When I follow the country music around the house, I take in the transformation the Mason's have done to the backyard. There are warm twinkling lights strung about with temporary poles placed all around to illuminate the vast yard. Guests mill about talking to one another. Plates of treats, I'm sure Chandie has prepared, are in each guest's hand along with drinks.

I know that a drink needs to be in my future, and soon. I don't usually partake, but tonight seems different. Something in the air.

Drea sees me from across the lawn and waves me over. I notice that both Mel and Chloe are standing with her.

"I'm glad you made it!" Drea says happily when I reach the group of women. "If you had gotten here just a minute or so sooner, you could've gone with the guys to get refreshments."

"Refreshments?" She scoffs. "Drea is already three drinks in. Ignore her. Q and the guys will be back, and they can show you where everything is set up." Chloe tells me.

"Three-drink Drea is a lot of fun." Mel gives me a chuckle and smiles, though I'm still looking around trying to catch a glimpse of— "She's in the back helping Chandie with Danny. He's a bit nervous with all these people around who haven't seen him since..." She trails off. She takes a sip from her White Claw leaving that statement hanging.

I see the large form of Tony blocking out the light coming from the patio door. Q is talking to someone I don't recognize as they walk over to where we are. Mel makes a point to step away from me when they get near us.

"Hey, man." Tony claps me on the back. "I thought you weren't gonna make it."

"I'm here," I grumble, feeling annoyed that so many of her friends have pointed out that they didn't expect me to show.

"Well you know Q, but this is my brother Ty." Chloe throws a thumb over her shoulder to the man I didn't recognize from earlier.

"Nice to meet you, bro." He offers me a hand that I shake. The same hand goes to rest at Mel's back and she relaxes into the touch. I instantly look for Mack, expecting him to throw another haymaker, but no one bats an eye at their closeness.

Deciding it's none of my business, I turn to ask Tony something. His head is lowered to Drea's ear, whispering. I ask anyway, "Where's the... uhh, food, I guess. Or the beer. I could use either."

"Yea, man. It's over here." I follow him after he whispers something else to Drea that makes her cheeks turn a shade of red that I can see even in the low lighting.

The porch wraps around to a side of the house I haven't been inside of. This must be the side with her parents' room. The large freezer is lit up by more string lights, and Tony hands me a Coors and grabs another for himself.

"You want some of the food?" He yells to me with the twangy music blasting from the DJ's speakers. I nod my head and follow him into the house.

It's quieter though not by that much. The large dining table now has a linen tablecloth and all sorts of food laid out on silver platters. Some travel burners are heating up large roasting dishes that I see Tony making a beeline toward. "No one makes better babybacks than Chandie. You better get some before people start noticing they're here." It shouldn't surprise me that he has already filled a plate high with ribs and is pouring barbecue sauce on with a ladle.

The thought of eating anything doesn't really sound appealing to me. I grab some cheese and what I recognize to be sourdough crostini so that I'm not drinking this beer on an empty stomach. We return to the group and I sip my beer, keeping my eyes peeled for Reese.

I still don't see her even after I see Danny walk out of the house with Chandie right beside him. He uses a cane to support himself. Chandie beams and sparkles next to her husband who looks weary but grateful. It's clear that he did not expect the size of the crowd gathered here today.

Rebecca sees me and comes over to speak. Everyone I was talking to before seemed to disperse when they saw her coming.

"Fancy seeing you here. I just keep running into you today."

"That's the thing about small towns right?" Saying that makes me think back to when Reese said we would talk later. I know it was meant to brush me off, but I can't imagine why Rebecca and Reese would have beef. They both looked disgusted to see each other. And with how nasty Rebecca was, I know there is more to this story.

Rebecca is going on about something that I've missed when she cuts herself off and pats my chest. "I don't think you've met Alexander yet." She waves an arm over her head, and I try to see who she is waving at. In all the time I spent working at the Mason's, I never saw another man on the Stewart's land besides Mack. I assumed Rebecca was single this whole time.

An older man comes into view looking irritated as hell. Mack is next to him, and the resemblance is shocking. They both have the same face and blue eyes. There is something about this family that just doesn't sit right with me.

When Alexander reaches us Rebecca says, "Alex, this is Cory. He's our newest contractor. He's the one who took over the sod collection this year. Really saved our bacon." She looks excited to introduce us, like it was essential that he met me. With how absent he is, I'm guessing I'll never see this man again.

"Excuse me." Mack doesn't wait for an acknowledgment before he leaves the conversation and walks somewhere else.

Rebecca scoffs and sways. It's clear now that she has been drinking. Alexander seems to notice it too and takes the cup she's drinking from. He has a sip for himself and looks at the cup as if it has offended him before pouring it into the grass beside him.

He still hasn't said anything, but I decided to introduce myself anyway. "It's nice to meet you. Those properties really bridged the gap for me. Thanks for taking us on."

Awkwardly holding the plate and beer in one hand, I hold my other hand out to him. He looks at it for a long moment before finally shaking it.

Alex grabs onto my hand tightly enough to be uncomfortable. I look down at our joined hands before looking back at his face. Cold blue eyes meet mine before he says, "I do enjoy solving problems. It's a shame that we haven't met sooner." His grip tightens a little bit more, and I wince. "Is that all you do around here?"

What the hell? "All I do around where?" I ask.

"Alpenglow Ridge? Are you employed elsewhere?"

I'm taken aback by the question and the fact that he still hasn't let go of my hand. "I'm working on more than just the Stewart's Sod properties if that's what you're asking."

He finally releases my hand and pats me condescendingly on the back. "You're gonna need it." He leaves without another word. Rebecca, seemingly oblivious to the weird exchange I just had with her husband, looks down at her empty hand and asks me, "Do you need another? I'm headed that way."

Lifting my can toward her, I say, "I'm good. Thanks."

She nods, walking to where the outdoor fridge is. I stand there still unsure of what happened.

"Funny how such a cool guy like Mack could come from such assholes, huh?" Drea tells me nearly making me spill my beer. "Sorry. I didn't mean to startle you, but you were kinda just staring off there. Most of us know to go the opposite direction whenever they're around."

"Yea, man. You good?" Tony asks. I nod my head and the music lowers in the party. We all turn to the patio where Chandie stands next to Danny who is sitting on one of the patio chairs. The mic gives a little feedback sound before she steps back, away from the speaker next to her.

"Hi everyone. I want to take this time to thank you all for coming to celebrate the official launch of Masons' Horsing Around!" Everyone claps, and she gives us a moment to do so. "Thank you, seriously, thank you all. We would not be here if it wasn't for the support from this community. Tonight is about more than just the launch of this incredible program for your young equine enthusiasts. It's also about our lovely daughter, Riesling." A murmur breaks out through the crowd and Chandie puts a hand over her eyes to try and see into the crowd better. "Reese, honey, come over to the patio."

The moment I see her step from around the crowd, they all part for her. Her golden hair falls in her natural curls framing her face. The form fitting champagne colored maxi dress hugs her curves and brushes over wedged shoes. She holds the hem out of her way to walk up the patio steps. The flowers I pinned in her hair from before are clipped in her hair though it's not pin straight as it was at the market.

She looks absolutely breathtaking with the lights on her.

I wonder where she was until now.

She beams at her mom and dad when she gets to them, giving them each a hug.

She looks so happy. So beautiful.

I can't wait to watch that dress drop to the floor tonight.

Tonight, I'm gonna tell her the one truth that has been more apparent than anything else.

I think I love this woman. Everything she has shown me has only made me care about her more. What I need at this point is to show her just how serious I am.

No, I know. I know that I love her.

I've joked about us going steady, but I'm fully enthralled by her. Would do anything to keep her. And I never want her to doubt that. I don't know what happened to make her question whether to invite me to this party or not. Showing her the truth of my heart will show her that I deserve to be here. I will always be there to support her in any of her endeavors in the future.

Chandie resumes speaking, though her voice is thick with emotion now. "After a long hiatus, Riesling has made it back to Alpenglow Ridge and was a vital part of this transitional period. Today is her last day as a silent partner."

Reese looks to her mom. Her face is no longer beaming with the big smile from earlier. She shakes her head almost imperceptibly, but Chandie nods in response.

"Today, you all are looking at the new chief operating officer of Mason Ranch and Masons' Horsing Around! Can we get a big round of applause for our new COO?"

Chapter 35

Reese

"Know that this changes nothing," Teddy says from behind me. I don't bother asking how he found out.

I'm sitting on the steps of my side door entrance to the house while he stands over me. Thankfully everyone is enjoying the party and has not noticed I'm missing or just haven't thought to look.

Everyone except *him.*

"What am I supposed to do? I fulfilled my part of this bargain with you. I am the COO now. They're going to announce it tonight. They need me here."

He grits his teeth loud enough for me to hear his molars squeaking together. "So, he knows about us? About these last weeks? Maybe I should inform him." His smug look makes my irritation grow at how condescending he really is. I glare at him because I've shown my hand and he would have no problem using it against me. Teddy doesn't stop there, he continues, "I don't like you this close to my wife. Or my son. I bought that apartment for a reason. But, you have done everything in your power to defy me. You're moving your things to the condo next week."

"No, I'm not. That is not what I want, not anymore. That's not what we agreed to." I back away from him into the house. There are a few guests in the kitchen but no one on this side.

"It is. You were always complaining about not living with me and now it's settled. I'll have movers come to get your things next week."

"It's not. It's not settled, Teddy. I'm not moving in with you. We had a one-time arrangement. You got what you wanted. Now leave me be. You have Dawn, and I'm not going to tell anyone about anything. You have my word."

In this part of the hallway, there is no way for me to leave unless he allows me to pass him. I remember how softly Cory held me in this very same spot. Being here with Teddy has tarnished that memory with the malice of his intentions for me.

"False. I saw your little boyfriend tonight." He scoffs. "Did you forget that you belong to me? You've had your fun. Whatever you thought you had with him is done. You're moving back to Denver. End of discussion." His command is low, but I feel ready to scream. I would if I knew it wouldn't alarm someone from the party and cast a bigger light on our argument happening here.

"No," I respond through my clenched teeth.

"No?" He raises an eyebrow, leaning over me to assert his dominance that little bit more. I nod my head, crossing my arms over my chest. "I fail to see how you think you have a choice."

"I do! This is done. What we had was never anything like what Cory and I have. You made it very clear that we weren't dating, that I wasn't your girlfriend. When I left months ago, this," I motion between our bodies, "was over."

Narrowing his eyes, he runs his fingers over a curl near my neck. My flinch is involuntary, when he says, "What would you call the last week of visits you've made to me for whatever it is you pulled from my account?"

"A last arrangement." I can't let him know how important that money was to me.

"That's where you're wrong. You will always want more. And I will be here to give that to you. That gardener can't do for you what I can."

Ignoring his insult to Cory, I stand firm in my conviction. "I'm not moving in with you, Teddy. We're done and I meant that. Or maybe you forgot what I said. Should I remind you of what you can stand to lose?"

The music quiets and I can hear my mom on the microphone talking outside.

He pushes off the wall with the hand he had above my head. "I'll be in touch. Keep your mouth shut as long as you're here." Teddy leaves from the side entrance before I can respond again.

Through the open door, my mom's voice reaches me more clearly. "Reese, honey, come over to the patio."

***

"Congratulations, pretty girl!" I spin to see Cory leaning on the support beam just behind me by the stables. Soft moonlight glints off his smile.

When he sees my face, his smile is replaced with a concerned frown, and he rushes to where I stand rubbing Heather's head.

After the big announcement, I had to get away from that crowd.

When I got home from the market, I was in the kitchen helping Chandie start to set up some of the decor and food that she was preparing for tonight. My dad let me know his plans to bring me into the fold for good. COO is beyond what I could have expected when I made the drive back to Alpenglow Ridge just a few weeks ago.

"I'm not gonna be able to do all I was before and dammit. I'm tired. I wanna relax with my wife and enjoy the fruits of my labor. If I'm going to put anybody in charge, I want it to be you, Riesling."

My mind is still spinning through why Danny would pick me.

Tony might have been a better pick or just someone with more experience running a business.

His confidence in me makes me feel hopeful but stressed all at once. I rub my forehead like it will fix the brain cramp I'm having. I was only supposed to be in Alpenglow Ridge temporarily. I belong in Denver now. Alpenglow Ridge can't be my home anymore. *He made that very clear tonight.*

"You don't seem happy." His voice pulls me from my downward spiral, and I look up to his handsome face.

I reach up, smoothing a thumb over the crease in his forehead. He holds my hand to his face, looking into my eyes for some answer. I don't say anything, trying to keep my tears at bay.

He takes my hand in his, massaging each finger as he studies my hands like he loves to do.

I want to find comfort in this. In him.

But my concerns are too big to be massaged away.

"I'm not," I say, finally answering him. A single tear falls, and I swear I can hear it drop to the wood chips.

Cory must hear it too. He pulls me into him without wasting any time to think first. I feel even more dumb. I just want to stop feeling so stupid.

Using my other hand, I bring his face to mine, kissing him softly with my apology.

He is not having any of that. Our lips become more frantic and I forget all about needing to breathe as I wrap my arms around his neck.

I want him to brand me with his lips, to feel every bit of emotion I have for him. Not the sadness, but the care I have for him.

To live in this moment between just the two of us until everything else goes away.

For him to feel how much I want the life that I've glimpsed could be mine with him.

I want a life with him. To truly be *going steady*.

His gentle teasing. His concern for me. I even want the three adorable sons who bring him so much light. I want some of that light to shine down on me and brighten the materialistic desires I've only been indulging with more dark, degrading acts.

The truth about me, that I never want him to know.

The truth about how I've been saddled with finessing. Manipulation after manipulation weighed more and more heavily on my soul just to get what I thought I wanted.

My tears are coming at a steady pace now and I have to pull away. I need air.

The concern he has is a tangible thing as he wipes the moisture from my face and I know I can't hide it from him anymore.

I can't keep living in both places and keep him too. I sit on the bench across from the stables. Wrapping my arms around my middle, I try to stem the crying but my sobs can't be helped anymore. The dark path of my makeup and tears run down my face to my dress and I don't care if it's ruined.

He drops to his knees in front of me trying to take my hands into his again. I shake my head. "Baby. Talk to me, please. Why aren't you happy? This is a huge accomplishment." A little part of me cracks. *Why did it have to be him?* "What's going on?"

I finally speak and it comes out watery and broken. "I can't live here. I can't stay." He flinches like I've hit him. I wipe away another tear and meet his eyes.

"I don't understand." His confusion breaks me even more because I want to tell him everything. I know I can't do that when what I have to say will mean the end of us. I just know it.

"I can't explain it to you." *I can't tell you if I want to keep you.*

"You aren't happy about becoming the COO? I thought you loved the Ranch. The horses and kids." He doesn't specify, but I know he means him and his kids too. It's in his eyes.

Cory isn't stupid.

He has to see that I'm not a sure thing. Like everyone else could see, I am only a fleeting idea. Men want me when I'm cute and fun. To have a good time. *To use me for what they want.*

When he sees what I really am, he will leave, just like the rest of them.

Except one. The one who had tainted me so thoroughly that I can never have anyone else. He ruined me.

"I do. That's not the issue. It's never been about the Ranch." *It's me.*

"So what then?" He begs me with his eyes to open up to him. But I can't. *I want to keep you.*

I shake my head and more tears fall. He raises my chin and wipes more tears from my eyes. His gentle and patient attention only makes me more upset. "It's too much, Cory. It's too much for you."

"Just tell me baby. We will figure it out."

We.

He and I.

This can't go on anymore. I have to end this because there can't ever be a *we*. He can't be the one to be with me. He deserves better.

He deserves someone who deserves him, and that girl is *not me*.

Sighing deeply, I say, "My ex. Not exactly an ex, but this man I was with... He doesn't want me back in Alpenglow Ridge." Cory goes still. A deer in headlights. Another man I've pulled in to give me what I want. Prey.

Shredding hearts is the only thing I'm good at. And his is only moments from destruction. He doesn't even know how much yet.

"And why doesn't he want you here?" He asks carefully.

"I can't talk about this, Cory." *Please don't make me hurt you.*

"Are you still seeing your ex?" He asks me through clenched teeth.

"No. Not like that. We had an agreement. We're done. I thought we were done. We are done. I honestly don't know. He's so controlling. He won't let me go."

Cory stands. "Who is this asshole? We will go file a report tomorrow. He can't just terrorize you and get away with it." He holds out a hand for me.

I stare at it, but don't take it, choosing to hold my middle instead. I honestly feel like I will be sick. I rock softly, working up the courage to say what needs to be said.

Finally, I force the words out. "It's more complicated than that. He owns my car. My apartment was in his name. Damn near everything I own was purchased by him. He owns me. The money that I told my family was funding the final portion of the camp here came from him. And I took it, knowing the consequences."

"What the hell? I don't understand. What fucking consequences?" His voice booms around me. I wince and sink into myself even further.

The music is still going strong over on the lawn so I know no one could hear him from the stables. A few of the horses near us stomp around in their pens. His energy whips around me, and I can feel the pieces of his heart cutting into me like shards of glass. But I keep forcing the words out.

"I told my parents that the last fifteen kids were paid for, but they weren't. She offered the spot to these kids knowing their families could not afford the tuition. So, I made an agreement with him to cover their costs." A sob rips from me, and I can't keep it in. I rub my nose across my arm, not caring about how gross and disheveled I must look now. "He thinks that it was just going towards more designer bullshit I'm usually buying. But, it wasn't. It was for these kids." *Your kids.*

He scrubs a hand over his head and then his face. Pacing back and forth in front of me manically. "Okay. It's just money. I'm sure your family can work something out. We can find a way to pay him back."

We.

I shake my head. More tears fall. "He doesn't want money, Cory."

He stops pacing to look down at me. Hurt shining in his eyes. I can tell that he doesn't want to ask the question, but he does anyway. "What does he want, Reese?"

"Time," I whisper.

"Time?" I nod my head slowly.

"Time to do what?"

I shake my head.

He asks again, "Time to do what, Reese?" His voice is getting louder again. "What does he want, Reese?"

"Control."

"What kind of control? Just tell me what the hell this is. What is so precious for you to lie to me about? What you've been keeping from me."

"It's a power exchange," I yell back at him. "He pays me, and I let him use my body for whatever he wants." I feel truly sick now. I have never had to spell out what we do to anyone else. Spelling it out so crudely, sugar coating nothing. It is what it is. There is no easy way to explain to your boyfriend that this is how you paid for his kids' camp tuition.

This is what I did to him.

"Does he hurt you?" His voice is monotone.

Looking at my hands, I think back to my most recent times with Teddy. "Sometimes," I admit quietly.

Cory backs away from me. "You let him... He... Reese, no." Each time he breaks off a sentence, he backs further away from me. This is what I knew would happen. I knew he wouldn't like what was underneath the pretty face. "So he pays, and you just let him use your body. You spread your legs like a prostitute?"

"You don't understand. Just let me explain."

"Explain?" He's yelling again. "You just spread your legs for this guy who doesn't even care about you. He pays, and you agree."

"Cory—"

"No! I don't want to hear about why it was okay for you to lie and cheat on me when I asked you so many times. You had so many opportunities. And you lied!"

The truth of what I'm willing to do to get what I want.

But I want him.

"Cory, please." I can't take the words back now. I can't put them in a box and ship them away like I want.

"No." He grabs at the back of his neck. Shaking his head as he paces farther away from me. "What the fuck, Reese?"

"Please," I sob.

"I don't... No. Why would you let him do that? I thought..."

My sobs are louder. "Please. Just let me explain."

"Is this the kind of shit you're into?"

"Cory, please. Just listen to me. "

"My girlfriend." His eyes gleam in the moonlight, watery from the hurt I put there. "And his girlfriend, too."

"He's not my boyfriend," I rebuke in a small voice. "Please let me explain."

"Let you explain how you've been cheating on me, letting some sick fucker do this to you? I don't think so. You're sick, too. I let you around my sons. Into our lives. All the while you've been doing..." He waves his hands around in the air. "You've been with someone else."

I'm yelling now too. My frustration at the situation bubbling over. "I tried to tell you. Hell, I know you've heard what they say about me in town. I'm not wifey! I'm not just some replacement for your wife to take care of your kids and cook for you every night. I had a life before you. You never wanted to hear about it. That's not what you wanted to hear."

"I wanted to get to know you better. I wanted you to tell me about your life not hear it from some gossip in town. You can't build a relationship on rumors, Reese. You didn't tell me about any of this. I thought they were just that–rumors."

"You didn't want to know how I lived before I met you. They never do."

"They? I'm talking about me! My kids. My family. How would you know what I wanted to know? I should be able to make that choice for myself, not based on half-truths." He glares at me in disgust. "When?"

"When what?"

"You know what." He continues glaring.

"Please Cory. I didn't cheat on you. It's more complicated than that."

"When, Reese?" He yells and I flinch. I shake my head. I can't tell him. I can only break so much, and the truth he knows has already done enough damage.

I drop to my knees and hold my face in my hands. I can't do it. I can't put this final nail in the coffin. I won't say anything else.

A keening noise comes from me as my knees scream from the pain of wood chips digging into the skin through the thin fabric of my dress.

I hear the sound of his shoes crunching the wood until only the low thump of the music from the party remains.

Pulling myself up from the ground with the bench, I brush chips from my dress. Doing my best to clean up my face. I make it back to my house through the side door and thankfully run into no one before I can sneak inside.

CHAPTER 36

Reese, Ten Months Ago

RED COATS MY FINGERS when I swipe them over my mouth.

Blood?

Teddy stands in my living room. Hand still in the air from where he struck me.

He... Struck... Me?

"What did I do?" My words are a shaky whisper. I sound weak and small.

I am weak and small.

"Tell me *how* Jay saw you at The Capital Grille with someone who was not me." His red face should have been a dead giveaway for how angry he truly is.

Jay. The same man who was begging for crumbs of my attention for the past several years. I thought that might have been him at the restaurant, but my attention was on Michael.

Michael had just booked a trip to New York for the two of us. I had begged Teddy to take me, but with all "the work" he has been doing lately, I haven't seen him for more than a few hours every day.

I decided to look elsewhere.

I had gotten sloppy.

And Jay had decided to tattle.

Teddy's words cut through the small space, "Not just eating there! But touching? You touched another man. Is what I give you not enough?"

Is it?

It wasn't enough. I don't want the attention of all these men, who only want the status that having me can bring them.

I want real love.

I want a companion.

I'm tired of competing to be important to someone.

I love the trips, the cars, the clothes. But at some point, I have to love me too.

The silk night dress I answered the door in feels too tight, as my body reacts to the pain of his blow. The studio apartment he got for me was not nearly as nice as the condo he lived in.

Not grand or exclusive.

There isn't even an elevator for the building and I have to climb up all these stairs to get up here. No balcony. The appliances aren't even stainless steel. Not even a walk-in closet. It might as well be welfare housing.

He has been "allowing" me to live in this studio since he won't allow me to properly live with him. I can stay the night or the weekend, but "he requires his space."

"You hit me." I can hear the strength returning to my voice, as anger simmers just below the surface of my heating skin. Clenching my teeth, I say, "You just fucking hit me."

"Answer the question, Ree." His cold blue eyes regard me in the most soulless manner I've seen to date. When I am on my knees, obeying his commands, he makes me feel cared for.

Some pain is inherent with the biting, spanking, and occasional whipping. For *his* pleasure.

But, this?

This is different.

"No. You answer mine."

"Ree. You're testing my patience."

"You haven't seen me in three weeks! You've been testing mine!" I yell back at him.

"I have been busy. I've been working. Or did you think all your shit just came from thin air?"

"Then tell me how is it that *Nicole* can get time with you, but I can't."

Here I am suffering from the petty actions I played at to feel desired. Trying to get back at a man, who had his assistant keeping his dick wet, while I wait for text response from him for hours.

He wanted me, had me, and now he's moved on.

The only tell that he has been caught is in the clenching of his jaw. I see it tick once, and twice more before he grabs me. His grip around my arm is tight enough to bruise. Those glacial eyes have dilated in his outburst of rage.

Quicker than I can blink, I'm on the couch, sinking into cushions that offer me no comfort. "And you think that gives you the right to give someone else what belongs to me?" Spittle hits my face. His restraint vibrates in my arms, as I try to get out from under his hold.

He shifts, releasing my arm, as more hair falls onto his sweaty forehead. His forearm presses into my throat, and I squeeze my eyes shut, refusing to utter an apology when I've done nothing wrong.

I've been perfect for him. *Perfect.*

Hair. Makeup. Nails. Clothes. Shoes. *Perfect.*

If he needed me on his arm at an event, I was there. Shitting on all those old wives and escorts.

If he wanted a companion for dinner, I was there. Stilettos high and sharp enough to cut someone's throat.

If he needed someone on their hands and knees, submitting to his every desire. Pill or no pill.

I. Was. There.

That all changed when I decided to visit his office one day a week or so ago. I brought dinner to surprise him since he was supposedly working late.

I walked into the lobby to find his assistant's desk empty. When I looked on her computer screen, admittedly being nosy, I had to put a hand to my mouth to muffle my gasp.

Their in-office messenger was still open on the screen, demanding, "On your knees in five."

The sounds were low from the heavy oak door, but I heard them clear enough. Nicole was getting the time that belonged to me.

Teddy had passed me over for the last time.

At one point, maybe I could have accepted that there were other women in his life. But now? With everything I've endured, dissociated from and changed for?

I can't be just *an option* anymore.

Jay was smart enough not to disclose to Teddy that I was at dinner with Michael Wade. From Wade, Casey & Stewart. His partner. Michael was all too happy to even get close to "a lovely, young thing" such as myself.

I had felt his lingering glances behind his wife's back at many of our shared events. My guess is that cheating on your wife is the requirement for making partner at this law firm.

A wife, I will never be.

Lord knows, Rebecca can't stand me.

Though she has never said anything to my face directly, I make sure to avoid her and the snarling biddies she keeps around her in Alpenglow.

With his forearm still against my throat, I'm finding it harder and harder to breathe. I bite out, "You're not my boyfriend, remember?"

"I'm not. And you would do well to remember it. Regardless, you belong to me."

We struggle, and I manage to kick out at his leg causing him to stumble off of me.

I labor to get off of the couch, leaning back onto my kitchen counter for support. "This is done, Teddy. We are done. I can't live like this. I'm not some pet that you can keep in this fucking crate until you want to play with me. I need more!"

"What more could you possibly want? Anything you ask for, I give to you, Ree! Every goddamn thing. You knew what this was. You knew what I required."

My voice is still raspy when I reply, "I thought it was enough. But, it's not." Moving quickly, I rush to my room to grab as much as I can and start stuffing clothes into a suitcase.

Teddy comes in behind me pulling things out of the bag as quickly as I'm shoving them in. "What are you doing?"

"I'm leaving. I'm going back to Alpenglow."

He kicks the suitcase from my reach, standing in front of where I'm kneeling at my dresser. "No, you aren't."

"Yes, I am. I should have never come here to be with you in the first place." A single tear falls and I wipe it away.

"I'm not letting you go back there. You're mine, Reese. We have a good thing going here." I clench my jaw and begin piling clothes in front of me again. "I'm not letting you go."

"You won't see me either! So which is it? Am I yours or are you not my boyfriend? What is this?"

"It's what it's always been."

"Well, I don't want it anymore. I don't want to find out that you're sleeping with your assistant when I try to do something nice for you. Or spend so much time alone that you don't even know what I'm doing with my life anymore. If you paid any attention to me, then you'd know why I was at Capital Grille and you wouldn't have to hear about it from Jay!"

Teddy's voice is eerily calm when he responds, "We made a deal, not a commitment."

"So, why am I the only one that is expected to fake faithful?"

"That was a part of our deal."

I shake my head, faster and faster. My disappointment rising at the situation I'm in. This man is not the man I thought he was. I never knew him at all. He *never* cared about me. He would never take care of me like I wanted.

"I want out, Teddy. I don't want to live like this anymore."

"I'm not letting you go. I'm definitely not letting you go back to Alpenglow Ridge."

"You can't keep me here. I'm not staying with you for even one day longer."

"Ree, be reasonable." He sits on my bed, looking down at me on the floor. "I'm not gonna allow you to go back home where you can put my reputation in jeopardy. I've worked hard to get where I am and to give you what you want. One fight is not a good reason for you to leave."

"Why not? You have someone else. Just let me go." When he doesn't respond, I say, "Well, let me put this plainly. If you don't let me go, Colorado's leading corporate attorney will be in the headlines everywhere. Pictures, video, and years of evidence to support just about any allegation, I choose. I can paint whatever picture I want, and it won't be a pretty one."

Tilting his head to the side in an unsettling way, he asks "Are you threatening me?"

Refusing to back down, I square my shoulders. "Did you hear what I said?"

"Fine." He pops his neck. "I'll give you some space. But, you'll stay here, in this apartment, since I'm already paying for it. You won't be moving back to AR." He walks through the bedroom threshold, turning back once more he adds, "I know you'll be back when you want something."

CHAPTER 37

Reese

IRRITATED BY THE NASTY feeling rolling through my gut, I get ready for a shower.

I try my best not to think about all the ways Cory's whole demeanor changed since we were here last.

Unclipping the dangling charm from my harness, I lay it carefully on my bathroom counter. My dress slinks to the ground and I toss it into the hamper.

Feeling dirty and used.

Again.

No matter what I do, my mistakes come back to haunt me.

I try and use the aromatherapy from my shower to force some calm into my body. The steam wafts up around me, but I feel like I'm choking.

Choking on the false positivity and delusion warring with one another in my mind.

The delusion that my truth wouldn't scare anyone away.

The false positivity that my heart is fine.

Some part of me thought that Cory was different.

Some very foolish part of me thought that a man would stick around after I shared my body with him, shared my story. That they could find more than my body valuable enough to stay.

He had every reason to run.

I've only dug myself deeper into the hole that is Teddy. I can't blame Cory for going. I knew he deserved better, but I still thought that maybe he could love me even if I am ruined.

I will not cry. I will not cry. I will not cry.

I will not cry anymore about this. It's as much as I deserve.

I don't even know what I would be crying for.

That's a lie. I know exactly what I'd be crying for.

Sadness for how I hurt Cory. For how I will miss that little glimpse at true happiness.

He got what he wanted and now he's done with me. Why would he fight *for me?* End of story.

Time to turn the page.

I scrub at my scalp, face and body. Focusing on getting as clean as possible. Washing away any evidence of the seemingly sweet man who took me on one of the best dates of my life. That wasn't embarrassed to have me around his kids. That told me he wanted more from me.

I have to rid myself of any trace.

When I get out of the shower, I feel only slightly better. Rubbing my vanilla body cream in, I look at my reflection. Eyes puffy, cheeks blotchy, and skin rubbed raw.

I feel gross all over again.

This is my problem. And I get the answer wrong every time. I choose wrong every time.

I don't even bother with blowdrying my hair, opting to throw it into a bun. It'll be a problem for future Reese.

Laying in bed, I anticipate a text from Cory telling me that he got home okay—or something even after everything I shared tonight. It's the decent thing to do. What he normally did.

Instead, there are a few texts asking me where I'm at from my mom and the girls.

A knock on my door has me sitting up. I expect my mom to pop her head in the doorway.

It's Chloe's face that appears instead. "Can we come in?"

"Yea, I guess."

Chloe, Mel and Drea come into the room, all arranging themselves on my bed.

"Are you okay?" Drea asks.

"Clearly not." I exhale, laying back on my pillows.

Drea winces. "You know what I mean. Do you want to... talk about it?"

"Talk about what?"

"We saw Cory grab his kids and basically storm out of here in a huff. Did something happen between you two?" Chloe says.

"Nope." I say into a pillow.

"You sure. Today was a big day. COO?" She pauses. "And a break-up?" Pushing the pillow down from my face, I meet Chloe's eye, and she looks at me knowingly.

"You can't break up if you aren't dating." I respond.

"Don't give us that bullshit. What happened? We're here for you." Drea says.

"Yea. If you can't talk to us about it. Who are you talking to?" Mel says.

No one. And I'd like to keep it that way.

"Well, I'll start." Chloe lifts a hand. "Men suck."

I scoff. "You're married to your high school sweetheart. What do you know about men sucking?"

"Oh, I know that they suck. Just because I'm married doesn't mean I don't have eyes and ears. I work in a salon, remember? I hear about the trifling stuff they do all the damn time. And Quincy is not without flaws solely because he's married to me."

"Fuck it, I'll go second" Drea lifts her hand. "Men suck. I'm still celibate, and I'm happy about it. After Mireya's dad, I thought it was a him-thing. The dating pool is laughable in Alpenglow Ridge and even more laughable online."

"Okay. I'll go third." Mel lifts a hand. "Men suck." I look at her face and see the honesty in her eyes. "I know I haven't shared much with you about the divorce, because I know how close you are to the Stewarts." I am about to cut her off when she says, "Let me say this because I saw something tonight that would alarm anyone if they knew what I knew. And I want to start this by saying I would never judge you. The women in this room would never judge you." She places a hand on mine over the comforter. "I saw Alex introduce himself to Cory tonight. At first, I thought nothing about it. But the interaction looked very intense. When I saw Cory follow you out to the stables, I worried. I thought that maybe Alex said something to him. So I followed after Cory."

I feel my face get hot and my chest burns. I open my mouth to speak again. But no words come out.

Mel continues on anyway. "I overheard the conversation, though I didn't mean to be nosy, honest to God. Reese, I wasn't trying to snoop, but I worried." Her eyes get watery and she squeezes my hand, getting me to look up from the stitching I'm picking at on the comforter. "I won't say what I heard if you truly don't want them to know, but I think you've been carrying this for a long time. And after thinking on it, I think I know just how long."

I nod my head, and Mel resumes talking, "When Mack and I were dating, he would sneak me over to his house at night. His dad was rarely home, and his mom slept like the dead after her pill. But one night, I heard him talking to someone on the phone, when I was getting up to use the bathroom. He was, umm... Taking care of himself..."

"Okay, gross. Where is this story going, Mel?" Chloe pretends to cover her ears with her hands. I look back down, squeezing my eyes shut, knowing exactly where this story is going.

"I tiptoed over to the door, just being nosy. And shit, Alex is hot for a dad, and he looks just how I imagined Mack would look when he gets older." Chloe and Drea cringe, but Mel waves them off. "Whatever, I was... curious. When I got close enough to his door I heard Reese's voice coming from the phone."

I feel the first tear roll down my cheek.

This night only gets worse.

It's silent in the room. I can't take the unknown anymore and raise my head. Drea's mouth is wide open. Chloe's hand is over her mouth. Mel's eyes are glassy, but she has not let go of my hand.

"She called him Teddy. I don't know what she was doing on the other side, but I hurried back to the room with Mack and never told a soul. I've known who he was all the while." Now her tears are falling, too. "I failed you as a friend, and I never knew what was really going on. I resented that you sided with Mack in this divorce. With the kind of friend I've been, I don't blame you." She shakes her head. Chloe hands both of us tissues from my nightstand.

"No, Mel. That's not what happened. I just... Mack is like my brother, and you were always so wary around me." I stop talking, realizing—"You've been wary around me because you knew I was with his dad this whole time. You never said anything, keeping my biggest shame a secret. Does he know?"

"Does who know? Someone, please fill in the gaps. I don't get it." Drea says.

"Can I tell them, Reese?" Mel says

I shake my head, "I will. Mack's dad is Alexander Theodore Stewart. To keep what we had a secret, he told me to call him Teddy..."

I tell the three of them about the day that our relationship changed. When the gifts started. When he started turning the relationship into what it is now... and about the submission. Every sordid detail of our history laid bare for these three women. For these women who have been my friends for the longest time, even when I held everyone at a distance.

When I finish with what happened tonight, I feel just a bit lighter, but raw and aching. Hearing the full extent of what I got myself into, and now what I have inadvertently gotten Cory into, makes me feel sick all over again.

"Well, damn." Chloe says. "This is... something else. Why didn't you feel like you could tell me this?" Before anyone else can say something, she adds, "You two are cool or whatever, but it's me. I hold everyone's secrets."

I give her a look. "Chloe, you update me on a regular basis about everyone's business. Gossip Mill, remember?"

"Yea, everyone else. I'm not talking about my girls. Plus, who are you gonna tell? You've been in town for like a day."

Rolling my eyes, I say, "I've almost been here for a month, Clo."

"And it looks like you're trying to leave again."

"She's not wrong." Drea, who's reclined against my headboard, scooches closer to me until our arms are pressed against each other. "You don't have to run from this. From us. We would never judge you. Fuck that guy. It's us versus anyone else. I'll always have your back. We," she motions around the circle of us, "will always have your back."

Words and sounds of agreement echo amongst them.

"Teddy, Alex, whoever he wants to be known as, can't keep doing this to you. We will figure it out, okay?" Mel raises her eyebrows at me. "We're your girls. We'll come up with something between the four of us." My friend still looks close to crying, but I feel closer to all of them more than I have before.

Mel lies between Andrea and I. Chloe lies across the foot of the bed. For the rest of the night, we brainstormed about how I could possibly get myself out of this mess.

CHAPTER 38

Reese

"I THINK I FEEL well enough to get my shotgun out for him."

I chuckle and look up at my dad, who rides on Artemis while I walk with him at a steady pace. "I don't think that will be necessary, daddy. It's nothing. You can't just shoot any man who upsets me."

"That may be, but you don't look like you're having a good time. I warned him beforehand." He gives me a conspiratorial look, adding, "We'll just say it's self defense."

I chuckle again at his antics, rolling my eyes playfully. "And what makes you think that I'm not having a good time? I'm out with my favorite man and steed." I lean over to Artemis, whispering, "Don't tell Heather though."

"Riesling, you look like you didn't sleep a wink. What time did you get to bed?"

I did sleep, though. After the girls and I talked, I felt better. They left when it got to be too late, and I was down like a brick. My dreams were not pleasant. At least I don't remember them. When I woke up, I tried to cover the bags with a little concealer. The purple hue was gone, but there was nothing I could do for the puffiness. Makeup can only go so far.

"You know I don't have to tell you any of that." He gives me a look and I give him one right back. I relent, "I got to bed late, but I just have a lot on my mind."

"Like what?"

If I had known he was going to be so chatty this morning, I would have prepared better.

Who am I kidding?

How could I have prepared better?

"I don't know. This is all real." I wave my arms all around me. "I'm really moved back to Alpenglow Ridge now. I'm taking over the business. That's…" I trail off seeing Cory's truck coming down the drive from where we're at. I clear my heart out of my throat and continue, "A big step. When you asked me to come home, I thought I would be here for a short while. And now, I'm really here full-time. I've even given up my shifts at Peak's, but soon enough, I know that commute will be too much to bear, and I'll have absolutely nothing tying me to Denver anymore." And maybe that's a good thing.

If it weren't for the threat looming over my head. For now, it seems that Teddy will back off since I haven't said or done anything to alarm him while I've been here. But who is to say how long that will last?

When he confronted me at the party, I thought that maybe he was going to declare that he did truly care for me. Not that it would matter and not because I wanted him to. His possessiveness over me just isn't appealing anymore. It's not cute. Everything that I gave him, meant nothing. I meant nothing. All the clothes, jewelry, etc meant nothing. *Means nothing.*

Especially when I've lost Cory.

My dad's voice cuts into my thoughts as I realize I've been staring at Cory getting ready to work. "You should've been home a long time ago. I feel partly responsible that it took something as drastic as my health declining to bring you here again. For that, I'm sorry."

My eyebrows pinch. "What are you sorry for?" I ask him.

"For not fighting for you. I knew you ran from here, and I never pushed you to fight back. To fight for your home. Making this addition has always been our dream. Ever since you were a little girl. I want you to know that I am happy with whatever you choose, but I want you to find the same joy in running this place as I did. My father passed it down to me, and I didn't want to take on this kind of responsibility. But, I grew to love it. I see the same love in you now, even if you don't yet. Just like Pop Pop saw in me."

"I do love it here. It's a lot of work and so much to learn all at once. If I had stayed, I would probably be more prepared to be the COO you need right now."

"Can't change the past, Reese. If it's too much, then tell me. I don't want to overwhelm you. I know it's a lot."

"Don't worry about any of that. I want to be there for you and keep this place afloat in any way that I'm able. These horses are my joy. I can't believe I was so far from my heart and survived." I rub Artemis' side and guide us toward the barn again.

When we get back to the stables, I help him dismount and get Artemis set up to roam the corral the hands have set up. Several horses are already being walked over to the area.

"We're the same, you know?" My dad says.

I smile and raise an eyebrow at him. "How so?" I say and pick up the saddle and saddle pad.

"We're happier around horses." He grabs his cane and holds out his arm to me for a hug. I go to his side and lean into my dad's body. He hugs me fiercely. Artemis seems to sense this is a bonding moment and he steps over to us. We both lean into his side including him in this moment, as well. "Happy you're back, Reese."

"It was never my intention to stay gone for so long. I just thought it would be better to stay where I was after I left." The comfort of his embrace makes me forget all about the stupid concerns I have about the man who doesn't care for me and the man who saw who I was and then ran.

I came back to Alpenglow Ridge with one purpose. They asked me to be here for this program and now to take over this Ranch. That's where my attention and focus are going to be from this point forward.

All things considered, I'm winning right now. I've been able to come home, be with my horses. I have my friends and family back. We're closer than we have been in years. The loneliness I felt seems like a distant memory. Finally being honest with Chloe, Drea and Mel has been the best part of being home.

I thought Cory could be a part of that, too.

Sigh.

Like my girls said—men suck.

As my dad said, this is our dream. The very first group of young people will be here for us to show them what it means to be a friend to horses. Also how they can learn to ride, at least with assistance, and for some—on their own. Some kids will find and foster their love for these majestic creatures with our help.

With my help.

My heart swells at the idea of being a part of that in any way.

"You pictured something different for your life. Always chasing this hot thing or that flashy new purse or whatnot. All that stuff fades, Reese. You chase that, and you'll be running for the rest of your life. We want you to be happy. I know you hate when I say I want to see you settled down, but I don't know what else to call it. The pasture will stay green when you take care of it. It's a little more work, but it's worth it."

My brows crease and I frown, his words hitting a little too close to home for my liking. "I don't follow." He holds me away from him by the shoulder, assessing my face. "What?" I ask him. "It's a lot of horse analogies this morning."

"Well, let me make it clear, if you want something to grow, you take care of it. The grass, the relationship, your heart. If it's worth it—you'll nurture it."

I scoff, "Now, I really don't know what you're talking about daddy."

"Sure, sure. I've seen how you look at him."

"Well, I'm not looking anymore."

Cory and another man walk along the fence with a cart of planters filled with colorful blooms. They talk, and Cory gestures with his hand around the property while the other man nods. When he turns to head back to his truck our eyes meet for a moment. He averts his gaze and walks with more purpose to his truck with his hands in his pockets.

My attention snaps back to my dad.

"You sure about that?"

"Yep."

"Sure." He scratches at the stubble on his cheek, looking completely unconvinced. "Do you want to... Uh, talk about it?"

Do I want to talk about how Cory just completely ignored me? Or about how I will have to be more strategic in avoiding him on the property because he still has work to do here?

No.

I do not.

Men suck and I don't want to think or talk about him anymore.

When my heart catches up, I'll be fine. But until then, this is my motto for anyone who asks.

I scoff. "Talk about what? What's on the agenda for today?"

CHAPTER 39

Cory

FUCK.

I knew it the moment that I said what I said. There is no way that I can take back those words. The hurt in Reese's eyes won't leave my mind.

It swirls in my head, along with all the rumors I willfully ignored. Refused to believe.

I told her that I was ready to commit to her. To bring her around my boys more. That I was serious. Hell, I thought I was going to tell her I loved her that night.

All while I never knew about what she was doing behind my back.

My angel. My gift.

More like my curse.

Laying in my bed, I run my fingers over the birthday card again. I wish for the millionth time that I could talk to my parents about my life. To ask for their guidance.

What do I do?

I was wronged.

She cheated on me.

So why do I feel like I hurt her? Why am I still thinking about how I could have done better? Handled the situation differently.

She said he wanted her control. That he hurt her. What does that even—

God, I don't want to finish that thought.

Reese gave me her word. She had every chance to make things right. But she didn't take it.

Her text with Teddy rings like a bell in my skull. I haven't even gotten clarity about what the fuck is going on there. Is he the guy? Or is it some guy I haven't heard of.

I barely know this woman.

But I trusted her.

I did.

Will he try to touch her again? Is she safe?

Fuck.

I didn't want to learn what it was like to live without her. I didn't want to put an end to what we were building. I was a fiend for her attention and the radiance that poured from her.

My mood wouldn't improve because I refused to move on from her.

My mind continues to play tricks on me, Reese with random men over and over in my sleep. Of her letting some man touch her.

I wake up exhausted and feeling strung out like an addict who hasn't had their fix. The horrible thing is that I want another hit. I want to get high off the drug that is Riesling Mason. When I'm with her, she makes me happy. She makes my sons happy.

We fit. Everything clicked so easily with her. I almost wish she hadn't told me.

Does that mean that every negative piece of gossip I heard was true?

I lope from my room to the kitchen, where Janet and Sammie are already moving about. "I wish I had gotten cold brew. You look like you could use it."

"Thanks, Jan." I grumble, sipping coffee from the island stool. I'm reminded of the nights Reese would come over and make dinner with me. I shake my head at the memory.

That Cory had no idea.

He was happy. I wished she had never told me anything, so I could have lived in the blissful bubble of ignorance.

"Maybe you should just call her." Sammie says over a shoulder as she scrambles eggs on the stove. "Nothing that can't be solved with a good conversation." Her chipper voice grates on my sleep deprived nerves.

"Talking is what got me here in the first place."

Sammie turns, red hair flipping over her shoulder. Her hazel eyes narrow when she demands, "Explain."

Janet sits next to me on the island. "Yea. Explain. You have two women here who could give you some advice." She elbows my arm. "And we won't even charge you by the hour." She winks. I take in her tan cardigan over a white top and jeans. She's dressed and ready for the day, while I'm still in sleep pants and eye crust.

I sigh. "She cheated on me." I sigh again, setting my coffee on the counter. I lean onto my elbows so I can grip my forehead with both hands. "She cheated on me and then told me all about it at the launch party when I went to congratulate her about the COO spot."

The echos of cartoons are the only noise in the room. I look up from my coffee to see Janet and Sammie having a silent conversation over my head. They stop when Sammie sees me lift my head.

She clears her throat, plating a copious amount of eggs among the six plates she lined up on the counter. Bacon comes out of the oven next, and English muffins after that. "Come eat, boys."

Sammie moves two of the plates to the dining table, and she chops up the third plate of food for Gabe.

Bren and CJ sit, digging into their food right away while Sammie helps Gabe into his booster seat at the table.

"Thank you for making them breakfast," I say when she returns to the kitchen. "I probably could only manage toast right now."

"Don't mention it," she replies, sliding a plate in front of Jan and me. She kisses Janet before sitting next to me on the island with her own food. "Food helps you think better."

"I need to *stop* thinking. Maybe sleep for the next few days." They look at each other again over me. "Can you two stop that? I'd like to eat without your weird telepathy happening over my head."

"You are so grumpy. Maybe it's because you lost someone you really care about?" Janet responds sarcastically.

"Yea. I did. Weren't you listening? My girlfriend cheated on me." I enunciate each word slowly for her, hoping I don't have to repeat myself again...

"What did she say exactly?" Sammie asks.

"I don't know." I drop my fork onto my plate. "She said her ex controlled her and that he owned her or something." I shake my head. "That he hurt her."

"What?" They ask at the same time. Both of their faces are twisted up in disgust.

"Yea. They have some sort of agreement, and he doesn't want her to stay in Alpenglow Ridge."

"But that he hurt and controlled her?" Janet asks, concern etched in the lines of her brown face.

"They had some kind of agreement, Jan. She was—" I grit my teeth, my appetite gone thinking about last night again. I push my plate away. "She was sleeping with him for stuff. Said that her apartment, car, and clothes were all from him. She went to him for money to pay for some of the kids' tuition at the Ranch."

"She said it was her ex?"

"She said it wasn't her ex—that she didn't cheat on me. What else would you call—" I look over to the table to make sure the boys aren't listening, but decide to lower my voice anyway, "What do you call hooking up with someone else when you're in a relationship with me?"

Sammie sighs. "Have you seen her social media, Cory?"

"No. What does that have to do with anything? I don't need to see her with someone else."

"That's not what I'm saying. You wouldn't find that anyway." She pulls her phone out of her pocket and swipes around. Holding it up for me to see. There's a big difference in the woman she's showing me. The woman on the screen is not the angel I met in the hallway. "Do you think that Reese was at a resort like this with the money she was making from Peak's?" The crystal blue water glimmers in the sun behind her. She smiles into the camera with a sheer coverup over a white bikini. Her blonde hair flutters in the breeze as she leans on the doorway of the gazebo in the sand. The cocktail in her hand had a small umbrella in it with fruit on a skewer sticking out. She looks sexy and carefree as someone takes her picture.

Sammie takes the phone back and shows me another picture. In this one, she wears a beaded gown and pointy heels. Her ears, wrists, and neck all glare in the flash of the photo. My balls tighten just a little with how you can peep her thigh and calf through the high split in the dress. The background is a lavish marble staircase where the crystal chandelier to her left glares in the flash. "What about this picture, do you think she could afford any of the things you see in this picture from her tips at Peak's either?"

When Sammie speaks, it takes a few moments for me to break my stare from the glittering woman in the post in front of me to answer her. "No, she couldn't." I don't know anything about fashion and I've never been anywhere as nice as these pictures. They look fancy as hell. I knew she was out of my league, but I didn't realize exactly how much until I saw these photos. The woman I know stands in stark contrast to the woman I'm seeing here.

"We all knew that she left Alpenglow for something more, especially after that Mustang showed up on the Ranch. When she started sharing things like this on her socials after she left, we figured she had found what she was looking for. All the glamour and bougie shit she had a penchant for. But then..." Sammie looks at Janet. They share another look that I can't discern.

"Well, then that all stopped. Chandie was the first to notice. For a few months, there were no posts. That would probably not be a big deal for someone like you or me, but this girl was posting almost every day. Chandie worried, but she never got any answers from her. Then Danny had a heart attack, and Reese finally came home to see him." She shakes her head. "She was different, Cory. I don't know how different, since we barely saw her for years. It could have just been from the pain of how we almost lost Danny, but we think it was something else."

Sammie chimes in, "These glamorous photos where she looks like a fancy celebrity were from a year ago. When she started sharing things again, it was in a Peak's uniform, encouraging people to come see her for lunch or dinner. Something drastic changed."

I think back to when we went to dinner in Denver. I asked her about what she did for work before she worked at Peak's. She shut the conversation down completely. Was this why? Now I wonder even more if this Teddy guy who threatened her had anything to do with everything as well.

"Cory, I've seen you two together. What you're telling me doesn't sound like the woman who was here cooking for your kids." Janet squeezes my hand and I look up to her. "It sounds like she was in an impossible situation. He has all this control over her, and she told you about how he hurt her. What did you say when she told you?"

Scrubbing a hand over my neck, I tell them, "I don't know. I freaked out. I asked her when they had last been together, and she wouldn't tell me, so I left."

"Yikes," Sammie says. "She tells you about her abusive ex treating her this way, and you just left."

"She cheated on me..." Even saying the words, I feel like a fool. I squeeze my forehead again. My brain only saw the betrayal and nothing else. I didn't know what happened because I refused to listen to her story. I didn't know anything.

"You need to talk to her, Cory." Janet says, taking my hand from my forehead.

Fuck. "I know."

CHAPTER 40

Reese

"I WON'T ASK FOR any details, but we know he's gotta have that BDD, right?" Everyone is in Chloe's bathroom getting ready for the concert tonight. I am too, though I don't have any plans to join them, but it's nice to get ready with my girls anyway.

The smell of smoking hair products and perfume is thick enough to choke on, with all four of us primping and prepping for the night.

"Don't you mean BDE?" Mel tries to correct Chloe in her tinkling voice.

"No, Cinnabon. His shitty ex-wife stayed for three kids! He definitely has BDD. Big Daddy Dick! How else do you forget that you don't want kids? Look at Reese. She went from not being able to stay in town for a few hours to thinking about getting a condo."

"Shut up, Chloe!" I swirl my fluffy brush into the shimmery rose-colored powder and dust blush onto my cheeks. "Stop talking about Cory's dick. No one said anything about a condo."

I don't want any part of this conversation to continue. I blocked his number, so I couldn't hear anything more from him. I didn't realize how often we talked until there were no more calls or texts coming in. I was also beginning to miss seeing the mini Corys. I see them at the Ranch, but it's not the same.

What was I supposed to do?

Though I want to know more about this supposed shitty ex-wife but I'm not gonna ask her with everyone here. She's far too *free* with the information.

Clo shrugs. "It's only a matter of time. Consider it wishful thinking."

Drea gives me a look to say *I got your back* before changing the subject. "Okay, well let me add my two cents. Mel, I haven't seen you this happy about going to a public event with a man since... hell never!" She bumps into Mel's shoulder.

"He's not a man, he's Ty. We all know him. We're just supporting a friend."

"Right." We all chime in, dragging the word out to emphasize just how much we believe her.

"Are you sure you don't wanna come tonight? It'll be fun for us all to go out again! How often is it that I have a sitter, and Q gives us all the night off?" Drea says.

"I'm sure." I've got a date with some sappy rom-coms that will hopefully cause me to cry enough to make my mascara run. I can't bring myself to be around everyone having a good time tonight. "Everyone has someone, you know? I just wanna chill at home. Maybe eat some ice cream."

"Not true. Q and I can keep you company. It'll be just like old times!" Chloe says.

Drea sighs loudly. "Ugh. No one wants to be around you two lovebirds when you start sucking his—"

"Stop! It's not high school. We aren't like that anymore!" Chloe rebuts.

"You are too!" Mel adds. We all laugh louder. "I'm sure they'll be ducked off in some dark corner tonight. At least none of us have to cover for them now."

"Like we didn't have to cover for you?" Chloe bumps into Drea, who bumps into me. My lipgloss wands slides from my lips to my cheek, smearing my perfectly done contour.

"Hey! Now I have to completely redo this!" I whine.

"What does it matter? You're not coming anyway." Chloe says with an eyebrow raised. I shoot her a sharp look, and she mouths *sorry* and blows me a kiss with a wink.

Wiping the gloss from my cheek with a makeup remover wipe, I reapply the makeup that was messed up. When I'm done I say, "Like I need a reason to look flawless. Maybe I have other plans."

Drea puts a hand on my arm, "And what exactly are these plans that are so important you need to get this cute for it? Ice cream doesn't care if you have a full face."

"I don't get why y'all are surprised that I'm cute… I'm always put together and looking good. And smelling so good, you'll moan just a little bit when you hug me."

"That good, huh?" Mel looks over at me, waving a strip of eyelashes to dry and get tacky.

"Yes, ma'am!" I waft some of my perfume toward my nose, humming loudly in approval.

"Ugh. I need some of that then! Gimme!" Mel grabs at the bottle and I step out of the bathroom.

"Ah, ah, ah, Tinkerbell. This is powerful stuff. I need to be assured that you're going to use this for good and not for evil."

She steps out of the bathroom to chase after me. "I promise, Reese. Just gimme a mist! I need all the luck I can get."

I keep her out of reach with a hand on her shoulder. "I thought *it wasn't a man. Just Ty.*" I mock her earlier words.

"He's not the only guy that's going to be there."

Chloe adds, "Like you'll be looking at any other guys, but help a girl out, Reese! Stop gatekeeping."

"I wasn't kidding. Mel can't handle this kind of power." I say.

"Mel is right here! Mel wants the power!"

I eye her, considering. "What do you need power for? Ty has been in love with you since you moved here. All you have to do is bat those eyelashes at him, and he'll drag you back to his place." I tap a finger to my chin. "Potentially over his shoulder."

"She's right," Drea says from where she's leaning over the counter, close to the mirror, putting on mascara.

"Like I said before, You don't need luck. Ty has been bugging me to, and I quote, 'invite my friends' to this concert since he booked it. He definitely didn't mean Drea or Reese." Chloe explains.

I scoff. "He didn't *not* mean me."

Chloe ignores my assertion, continuing as if I've said nothing. "You showing up tonight is all you're going to need, Cinnabon. I know Ty better than anyone, and I remember exactly what he was like when we were young. Hell, I know what he's like now, and you're all good babe."

Mel bags up her makeup meticulously like it's the most interesting task she's ever done. I clock her silence. Chloe looks at me, clocking her silence too. Though Drea wasn't really there when we were juniors, she can feel how pregnant this pause is becoming.

Feeling us all staring at her, Mel finally looks up. She struggles to speak for a while, mouth opening and closing, but no words come out. We all converge on her for a group hug anyway.

I know that the divorce has been hard on her and she's trying to move on. It would be hard for anyone in a town this small. With her life so heavily attached to this place, she would never leave to start over. I feel for her. I squeeze her tighter, to which everyone else squeezes too.

The doorbell rings, startling all of us as we release Melody from the four-way hug.

"Oh, he's here. Good." Chloe says with a fluff of her bob once more. She exits the bathroom again, and I follow her since I'm done fixing the lipgloss smudge anyway.

"Who's here?"

She casually responds, "Cory."

I pull her into her bedroom, which is the last doorway before we reach the stairs. Quincy's voice is loud enough to be heard upstairs, and I wonder what it is they're talking about. More pressing, "Why the hell is Cory here, Chloe?"

She looks at me like I've grown antlers, "Because I invited him, obviously."

Dumbfounded, I take a few breaths before I go off on my friend of many years, and the only person I trust to do my hair. It would be a tragedy to burn this bridge, but I am very much so considering shaking the shit out of her. Through clenched teeth, I ask her, "Why *exactly* did you invite him here?"

"How could he take you to the concert if he didn't pick you up?"

I blow out another breath, searching for calm. "Chloe," She looks at me with an oblivious expression on her face. Like she doesn't know that she is meddling in business that she ought not be meddling in. "I'm not going to the concert. I told you where I would be tonight."

"Honey, I heard what you said." She smooths my hair over a shoulder. "Besides, we all want you to go, and you're already dressed. Wouldn't you hate for this cute lil' top you're wearing to go to waste?"

"You know that's not the point."

"But imagine how nice a concert with your very best girlfriends would be and then ending the night with BDD? That sounds like an amazing Saturday night, to me." When she sees I'm still not convinced, she adds, "Okay fine, he pled his case with me, and I'm willing to forgive him. Can you just hear him out? You don't have to go if you don't want to. Grown woman and all that. I will not pull my puppy dog eyes out if you still think he's not worth it."

Rolling my eyes at her on-brand meddling, I rearrange my boobs in my *very cute lil' top*, as she put it, and make my way down the stairs. I straightened my hair last night, so it's billowing around me as I take each step down the stairs. Cory sits on the couch that faces my descent. By the time I make it past the landing, he's already standing, gaping at my outfit. I see his fist clench at his side, but I choose to ignore where I already know his mind is going.

I said I would hear him out. So, he better have something good to say.

Chapter 41

Cory

"I guess you're here to apologize," Reese says, tone dry and arms crossed.

Quincy coughs to cover a laugh before leaving to his kitchen to give us some privacy. His thumbs up from the doorway before he disappears is not as reassuring as I'm sure he meant it to be.

Reese looks amazing. Her honey blonde hair is sleek and shiny, hanging long around her face and shoulders. The ends curl enough to frame her generous chest just like the first time I saw her. Jeans that look like they're painted on with how tight they are over her hips and thighs. It's been a while since I've seen her this close in person. It hurts my heart that I can't touch her right now. To hug her to me. To run my fingers through her soft hair.

Under her piercing stare, I feel just as much like prey as I felt that first day too. Whatever I need to do in order to get in this woman's good graces again, is never asking too much. Her presence alone, makes me want to worship her on my knees. If she wants me to grovel I willingly volunteer to be in trouble every day.

Punish me with your pussy in my mouth and my fingers buried deep inside you, my angel.

I shake my head, realizing I've been undressing her when I'm still *the idiot* who left her crying on the stable grounds when I didn't know the full story. "I just want to talk. I realized how dumb and irrational I was being. Being in a relationship is new and hard for me. I have a lot of trust issues after Van."

"Okay, so talk."

"Did I mention that I'm an idiot? I realized that. But I recognized that I was panicking. I was panicking because I thought that maybe I would lose you to someone else. That you might pick some other man over me. I couldn't sit with myself thinking I did nothing to secure myself with you. I don't want another man to be an option for you while we figure this out. I couldn't see what you were plainly telling me. I couldn't see that you were hurting and asking for me to understand. You have baggage, but I have baggage too. Fuck. You drive me crazy. From the first moment that I saw you, I knew that I would do anything to be in your gaze, to gain your affection, to be worth your time." She rolls her eyes. "You think I'm joking, but I'm not Reese. I just want to be close to you. Learn all about you and your past. Find out what you like and don't like. You caught me in your web, and you weren't even trying. I want to be your prey. Catch me and keep me, please."

"Damn. That was sweet." Mel and her other friends are on the stair landing, leaning over from the wall. Mel clamps a hand over her mouth, leaning back out of the way with her other eavesdropping friends.

She shakes her head at them, grabbing my hand and pulling me outside. At first, I think she's going to tell me that she's done and that this is over before it can really start. But, she sits on the concrete stairs in front of the house. I follow her lead and sit down next to her.

The cool evening breeze whips through here, and the essence of whatever perfume she's always wearing makes me lean in closer to her. I sigh at the comfort of smelling her signature scent again. It's been a week, but not having the assurance that she would see me again made me nostalgic for all the parts of her I would miss.

"Cory, I don't know how to feel about any of this. I didn't want complicated. I didn't want this to get complicated. There is a lot I'm dealing with in my life, too. From your words, I want to fall into your arms. I want to stay there and let you surround me. But when you left me after I told you the truth about my situation. It broke something in me. I just don't know if I can do this."

I rub a frustrated hand over my hair. "I'm sorry." I turn to face her but she's looking at her shoes. Her red toenail polish peeks from the wide band of her sandals. "Reese." I gently use my hand to hold onto her chin and turn her head to me. "I'm sorry. I don't know what I'm doing. But I don't want to lose you."

"I get it, Cory. I understand why you were mad. I lied to you. I kept a lot of myself from you. But, I didn't cheat. What he and I had was business. A business that I want to be done with. That, I am done with whether he likes it or not. Before I worked at Peak's, what we did behind closed doors was how I kept a roof over my head, food in my stomach, and yea sure, all the lavish things I could want. There were many, many perks, but there were many drawbacks as well. At one point, I thought that what we were doing could lead to something romantic, but that was never the case. He was a client, if you want to make things more palatable. Nothing more."

"I think I understand that. The client thing. I have to be honest and say that I don't like it. But if he's hurting you, threatening you... Reese, let me help you."

She searches my eyes, then looks down to her feet again. "How can you help me? You're disgusted by what I am. What I did."

"Reese, I'm not. I promise I'm not. You did what worked for you. I get it. I saw what kind of lavish life you were living. I don't know that I would choose to do something else if that was the benefit of your agreement with him. I just want you to be honest with me. Can I tell you something honest?" She nods her head and I take a deep breath.

"When my wife left, I thought years of us being apart would be enough to heal that part of me that feels like I'm not good enough and every woman will eventually leave me too. That's not on you. It has nothing to do with you. But I saw a text," I debate if I should tell her the whole truth of things now. But ultimately decide that I had to lay everything out for her to see what I've been going through. I can't ask her for honesty when I'm not willing to give it in return. "The other day, when your parents were gone, I saw a text from Teddy. For whatever reason, your phone unlocked and I saw the text he sent you saying that you were his. I brushed it off because of what you said the first time I saw a text from him. Is he the man who is threatening you now?"

She shakes her head and stands up. "You went through my phone?!" She looks disgusted and like she can't recognize me. I stand, too, but I don't advance to touch her like I want to.

"No, I would never do that. I heard it vibrating and I went to silence it for you because you weren't up yet. I had no idea any of that would happen, but I didn't know what to do with that information, so I lumped it in with the first text in my mind. First, the text from my truck after what was a pretty good night we shared. Then another text from him saying that you're still his after we had sex all night... I didn't know what to think. You told me he was nothing, and then when you said everything at the party... I don't know. It broke my fucking heart to think that maybe you were playing me."

She scoffs. "You don't know what you're talking about." Her eyes are glassy and her arms are crossed again.

"Please, baby." I reach for her hand, but she steps back. "I just want to help you. If you're in trouble, I can't just ignore that. I want to protect you if I can."

"I told you before that it's complicated. I don't even know what to tell you because I don't know if I can be open with you about this again. Not after how you reacted at the party. This is too much. You have every right to your feelings. I know you do, and you have your sons to protect, not me. God. It's all too much, Cory. Go to the concert, have a good time or don't. I can't go with you. I can't do this." She goes into the house again, but I stand there, stunned.

I grab at my chest, trying to hold my heart inside where she cut me deep. These aren't the answers I expected. This did not go how I saw it going at all. I ripped myself open and she gave me nothing in return. Am I the fucking idiot I feared I would be?

There is nothing else I can do. I'm not going to that concert without her. I get into my truck and drive in silence back to Jan's.

CHAPTER 42

Cory

"Cory! There's someone at the door for you." Janet's voice echoes down the hallway.

For a second, I find myself wishing that it's *her*. I can't even bear to speak her name right now. I'm still hurting from her leaving me on the stairs last weekend. My heart is still aching from how I miss her. She left me there raw and even more uncertain, just like I left her at the party.

Reese was wrong about me. I said those things out of anger and called her out of her name. But that's not me. I was blindsided, and I panicked. I fucked up.

I'm not disgusted about what she had done. It took some time to wrap my head around it. But, I'm not that guy. I'm not someone who judges people like that. I don't want to be like them. To disrespect her ever again.

Now, I'm just upset that she lumped me in with those people who didn't deserve to know this part of her. When I knew what was going on, well, more about it, everything started to click into place for me. The rumors. I could see how the vitriol that was whispered about her was both true and untrue.

She made a way to live the glitzy life Sammie showed me. What she did with her body was none of my business. If that's how she was making it happen, I couldn't help but be impressed. I worked my ass off and never even came close to that kind of lifestyle. My girl had men eating out of the palm of her hand, and she had picked me to open her heart to.

Had.

I don't know if I could handle it if she was still doing whatever it was behind closed doors if we were still together but... that was something we could talk about. I would want her to talk to me about it. There is something that she isn't telling me.

I know it.

What would make her leave a posh life like that? It wasn't just her dad or Masons' Horsing Around. Something else happened to her.

And I'm scared to know what it is.

My mind is jumbled with the possibilities of what would make her change her lifestyle. Why this dude would threaten her to stay out of Alpenglow Ridge, away from her family...

She doesn't want me to be a part of that solution, and I have to respect that.

I'm grateful for my new workload keeping me busy. My team is seven contractors strong. The first person I wanted to celebrate with was Reese. That was my biggest problem because thinking about her only brings me more misery.

Walking to the living room, I see that CJ and Bren are watching a show about robot dogs on the TV. They're eating a snack Sammie made for them. She sits on the couch, reading from her Kindle. I'm also grateful to be here close to family. Janet and Sammie have been there for me and the boys more than anyone else has in a long time.

Janet only has the door open a crack, so when I get there, I am shocked to see who's looming outside, looking as hesitant as ever.

"Vanessa, what are you doing here?" My tone is clipped when I step outside the door. I close it behind me so that my sons can't see their sorry excuse for a mother by accident.

"I should have called—"

"Yea, you are supposed to call. That's in our paperwork. Now is not a good time."

"I know, Cory. Okay? I'm sorry I didn't call, but I knew you wouldn't let me see them today."

"Your visitation hours aren't until tomorrow. I didn't expect you to be here for them, just like the last three weekends."

Van takes a step back from me. "Don't treat me like that. I'm trying."

"Trying what?" She says nothing, so I keep talking, "I really don't have time for this. Like I said, it's a bad time."

"Can you just talk with me for a second?" I've had just about enough of these talks with the women in my life.

Not that Van is even in my life anymore. The last thing I want is more bad news. To shoulder the bad decision of yet another woman in my life. But this is the mother of my children. The fact that she drove out here is reason enough for me to at least hear her out.

"Fine. Come around back." I lead her to the bench in Janet's backyard.

She looks the same as always. Her hair is longer, but her eyes look brighter, and she seems different. Something about her is new.

Wasting no time, I ask, "What do you want?"

"Just to talk." I motion for her to continue. "About what I've learned in therapy."

I'm stunned for a moment because I begged Vanessa to talk to a therapist for years, and she always scoffed at the idea, reassuring me that she was fine.

She continues, "I've been in therapy for the last six months."

My jaw is hanging open at her admission.

"When Pete left me, I was depressed. More depressed than I had been before. I had dark thoughts, and I was not well. I've learned from my therapist that these are intrusive thoughts that stem from the guilt I've been feeling about the boys. I couldn't be around anyone. Did you know I've been staying at my mom's?"

Still shocked about the fact that she is in therapy, I respond honestly, "No, I didn't."

"Yea, I've been there for the past year. I think I was depressed long before Pete left me. In our conversations, Georgia, my therapist, tells me that I have to learn to forgive myself."

I was following until she came to that part. "Forgive... yourself?"

My incredulous tone brings her eyes to mine from her nails that she was picking at. "I never forgave myself for allowing you to shape my life."

I push off from the bench and stand. "What is this bullshit you're saying, Vanessa. Why are you here?"

She keeps talking like she hasn't heard me. "When we got pregnant with CJ, you started talking about our future and getting married. I went along with it because I didn't know what to do. But—" her voice is as quiet as a whisper now, "I didn't want to have our baby. I wanted to have an abortion. I didn't want the future you wanted."

"You what?" My tone is harsh and I try my best to rein in my growing anger. "You fucking came here to tell me that you wanted to get rid of our baby?"

"No, Cory, just listen. This is hard for me."

"Hard for you? I'm the one raising our kids! How is this hard for you in any fucking way?"

"Cory, I just wanted to keep you happy. My family was not going to let me come home after we had a baby out of wedlock. You decided what we were going to do, and I was young. I didn't know that I could say no, that I should have found another way. You were my everything. If I upset you, then what? I didn't have anywhere else to go. So, I stayed. I stayed in our marriage, and I kept having our babies. I wanted you to be happy, but I was struggling every day. From one bout of postpartum depression to the next. You barely even noticed. So happy with the family that you wanted so badly. I lost myself. I was gone."

"Of course, it's my fault." I roll my eyes, and I bite my tongue because I know what I will say is not going to help either of us.

"It's no one's fault. I'm just telling you what I experienced."

"And me begging you to see someone, picking up the slack around the house, providing everything for us, was me doing what?"

"I'm not saying that I'm not grateful for all that you did. For all that that you are doing now. Cory, I'm still healing. I have been struggling with depression for the last seven years. It's not anyone's fault, and I'm not pointing fingers at you."

"Can you get to the purpose of this visit then?"

She takes a deep breath, making a point to meet my eyes. "When I asked for a divorce, I thought it was just that I didn't want to be with you anymore. I was no good for the kids the way that I am. The way that I was. You were always so much better with them. But, I'm healing. I've been taking this medication that has made life more bearable for me. It's improved everything. I tried two others before this one, and it was much worse before it was better." She wipes at her eyes. "Do you know how terrified I was for them? In my care, as unstable as I was, I would forget to feed myself the appropriate number of times a day. I cringe just thinking about life back then. My mood swings would come and go, and if you weren't there, I don't know how I could have done it. How I could have been a good mother for them." Her eyes are watering up more with the confession.

I resist the urge to comfort her. "Your mental health has always been important to me, Van. But, this is not my problem anymore. I'm happy you're doing better. I'm happy for you healing. I truly am. What you're telling me does not make me feel more confident. I have to protect CJ, Brendan, and Gabriel. They need security and stability. I already feel bad enough moving them out of Denver. "

"I never wanted you to leave."

"But you didn't stay either. What about what I want? You come here and tell me that I coerced you into a life you didn't want, made you have babies you didn't want. What am I supposed to do with that? What about what I wanted?

"You know that's not what I'm saying."

"Do I? I just wanted a family. I wanted us. And you apparently never did. I loved you and you're telling me the whole time you were just there with us out of indecision."

A pattern of me wanting to be in something committed and long term emerges before me. Vanessa never wanted to start a family with me. Reese doesn't want to be a part of my family now.

And I pushed them both despite their desires.

"I'm sorry, Cory." She says.

Feeling irritated and increasingly upset, I ask, "Why did you come here?"

"I wanted to come to you and talk to you about it. But if we can't come to an agreement, I'm going to petition for more time with the boys. I want to see them. They are my sons."

"You what?" Now I'm yelling. I can't keep my anger from boiling over. This woman who just told me she never wanted our kids, now wants more time with them. "Tell me you're joking, Van. You haven't even been making your scheduled visitation time since we moved here."

"I'm not joking. I told you I started a new medication, and it's working wonders. I feel like me again. They need their mother. I'm the only one they've got. As long as I'm still breathing, I want to be a part of their lives."

I scoff again. "And your therapist told you that?"

"It's in my heart, Cory. This is what I want. I can't change the past. I can't be there when I wasn't, but I can be there for them now."

I rub a hand over my head. I don't know what to do. "I need to think about this. You dropped this all in my lap, and it feels like an ambush."

"It was not my intention. I knew you would not have expected me to be here tomorrow, and I didn't want to waste my time with them talking about this."

"I told you this was not a good time for me. I will think about it. But you better not say anything to the boys tomorrow. Nothing is set in stone, and as it remains, you have visitation for the weekend, and that's it."

"I understand, but I won't wait forever."

Her words feel like a threat, though I'm sure she didn't mean them that way.

I was telling Reese that I had baggage, and here it is, at my doorstep. I have to figure out how to explain to my sons that their mom is coming back into their lives. I have to decide how I can make this work and trust her again when I have no indication that she can, in fact, be trusted. Vanessa does seem better off than before. I just wonder if there is a motive or a reason why she's all of a sudden trying to be in our lives again.

She leaves, and I walk back into the house. "Who was that?" CJ asks. "Was it Reese?"

"Is she coming over for dinner? I miss her having dinner with us dad." Bren says.

Sammie gives me a sad look, and there's nothing that can stop how my heart cracks a little for them. I opened theirs up to a woman who has left us, again. Maybe Vanessa truly is back for good, but I don't want her here. I *want* Reese. And I can't be with her, she doesn't want this.

Having no idea what to tell them, I change the subject entirely. "Do you want pizza or burgers for dinner tonight?" Cooking would be too much for me and my racing thoughts, as I try to process what the conversation I had with Vanessa will mean for my life moving forward.

CHAPTER 43

Reese

"Here are the keys."

Teddy looks at me expectantly. "And why are you giving these to me?"

"I won't need them anymore." I drop the large tote bag I'm carrying on the desk, as well. The rest of his gifts from over the years are in Sally out front. The most expensive of them in this bag I've just relinquished over to him.

Years of my life, a summation of the past eight years now gone. It feels good to not be burdened with them anymore.

He stands from his chair, leather squeaking. "Do you think that this is going to settle things with me, Ree?"

Knowing he would try to intimidate me, I stand my ground. "Maybe not. But, it's a start. You like negotiating. So what is it going to take for you to let me go? Completely."

He scoffs, rounding the desk. Teddy stands in front of me and I have to lean my head back in order to keep my eyes on his. "You think this is a negotiation? It isn't. What part of *you are mine* do you not understand? How silly will I look to let you go when you've been made so perfectly for me? Crafted by my own hand. Til this day, I have yet to find anyone who submits as beautifully as you do."

My back begins to sweat again, but I stand firm in my goals.

I want this to be over.

I won't be his.

My heart already belongs to someone else, despite my best efforts.

I should have left long before this got out of control. "It's always about your image. These suits, the hair, the gifts, me. You wanted control, and I'm not giving it to you anymore. I am no longer your submissive." Feeling emboldened by the ticking in his jaw, I continue, knowing that he will not like what I have to say next. "Send me the bill, but be prepared to take this public. I will not shy at unearthing all your dirty laundry. What's important to me now is not the same as when I was a teenager. Hell, not even the same as a year ago! I want more than the transactional attention you gave me. I'm worth more than the monetary gain I received from you. I'm done. I mean it." Crossing my arms over my chest, I take a step out of his space. He looks irritated enough to do something about it. "This is done."

We hold stares for a few beats before he shakes his head incredulously. He walks back to his chair and sits. His irritation was now masked in a calm demeanor that would fool any average person, but I know he is about to deliver his next blow.

Crossing an ankle over his knee, he speaks again. "And you think that gardener is going to give you what you want? You think that *single dad of three* can give you the life that I can?" He laughs, a wicked sound, before meeting my eyes again with his empty ones. "You'll be back."

He must have done his research. Looked Cory up. Something about the way he's telling me this has me feeling uneasy. But I refuse to show him any weakness. "Whether he can or cannot is none of your concern anymore. I just want out. I will not be back."

The door is slow to close, but Teddy says nothing more on my departure.

Dawn trips over herself, trying to get back behind her desk. Like she wasn't just listening from the other side of the door for the entire conversation. Her face is smug as I walk to the elevator and wait for the cab to reach the tenth floor I'm on.

"I'll be taking very good care of Alex while you're gone. He'll never want you back." Dawn sneers at me.

So, my suspicions were true. She must have been listening in on our whole conversation in there. It had to hurt being compared to me—and not measuring up. I don a smirk with all the confidence I feel leaving this office untouched.

Flipping my hair over a shoulder, I say, "Sweetheart, I hope you enjoy yourself." I couldn't care less if he was sleeping with all the staff he employed. It was none of my concern anymore. If I'm honest, it never was any of my concern. My heart had never belonged to him.

On my slow descent to the ground floor, I pull my phone out of my back pocket. I have never been more thankful that my parents still had me on their cell plan. I would be remiss leaving my phone on Teddy's desk, too.

One day that would be an expense that I was responsible for, but hey, baby steps.

I scroll to the contact I'm looking for and smile. It connects, and her tinkling voice comes in over the line. "Are you okay?"

"Yea. I'm okay." I kick some gravel with my boot and drop down to the curb. "Are you still in Denver?" There is some ruffling on the line that sounds an awful lot like bedsheets. Pulling the phone from my ear, I press the speakerphone option so that I can check the time. "It's a little late to still be in bed." Melody teaches dance at Alpenglow Ridge High three days out of the week and works most nights at QB's. It's Friday and I know she has a shift tonight.

I hear a door close and she comes onto the line. "Do you need a ride?"

I let her change the subject as I stare lovingly at Sally parked not even thirty feet to my left. I let out a long sigh. "Please. I will even buy you lunch if you take me back to Alpenglow Ridge."

She laughs and a male voice calling her name comes through in the background. "Drop me a pin, and I'll head over in the next five."

"Thank you, Mel."

⬩◆⬩◆⬩

RAPIDLY APPROACHING HOOVES MAKES me turn to see who's coming.

I came out with Tony and Taylor to drive the cattle from one grazing area to the next. Thankfully, they are too preoccupied with their task to talk to me. We're looking for cows who have strayed between trees and down in one of the creeks. They can be rambunctious and stubborn at times, but it's good to keep my mind busy. I whistle loudly, startling a group of six, who become more apparent as they begin to move around.

I was enjoying the ride with Heather. Taking her on the old trail in the back that I thought I saw a few cows hanging milling about. There are not many days where Heather and I can get a chance to ride on our own.

After the initial bout of riding clinics, we've been taking a break. A precaution so the horses used for demonstration with the kids don't get overworked or stressed. Heather has been so good, and I think she loves being around the kids. They truly are a special group.

Legend's mane whips out in furious waves that match the equally furious facial expression on Mack, who is approaching us. He slows just before he will spook Heather.

"Where are you going so fast, hot foot?"

"Get off the horse, Riesling." He dismounts and stands with his hands on his hips.

Why do people only call me by my full name when they're upset with me? "Okay…" I bring Heather to a halt and hop off. "What is this about?"

"You wanna tell me why I saw Sally parked outside of dad's house today?"

I wince just barely, but Mack's horrified expression only grows more horrified when he catches the reaction. He rips his hat off, throwing it across the field. Legend toes into the ground at Mack's outrage.

"So it's true." A statement. Not a question.

"What's true?" I try to place a hand on Mack's arm but he shrugs out of the contact.

"Don't play stupid, Reese. Please do not stand there and act as if you haven't been keeping this bullshit up for years. Like you haven't been lying to me for years!" He's fully yelling now, and I take several steps back toward Heather. "Oh, no. You are not running from this. That's not an option. What the actual fuck?" He covers his mouth with the back of his hand. "How long have you been fucking my dad?"

His crude words slap me across the face, and I feel my face heat at his accusation and disgust. I want more than anything to not be here and to not have this conversation.

I never thought that this would get back to Mack this soon. He hardly talks to his dad anymore and goes to see him in Denver even less. Of all the years his mom and dad have been basically separated, Mack never took his dad's side.

"Mack. It's complicated. I—"

"Well then uncomplicate it! How long?"

"A while."

"Why?"

"Mack, I never wanted to hurt you." My throat feels dry and unused now. I shift from foot to foot. "We kept it a secret for that reason."

"I never knew why my mom didn't like you. I could never figure out what changed. But, you've been sleeping with her husband for all these years. I don't blame her. How long?"

"I think we should talk when you calm down. You're going to say something you don't mean."

He laughs cruelly. "You think I'm going to be calmer about you being the reason my parents aren't together? That I will calm down about how you destroyed their marriage."

I gave him the opportunity. I tried to de-escalate the situation. But I'm not trying anymore.

He wants to talk then I will tell him the full truth. "Your dad approached me, came on to me. Ruined his own marriage! If you want to point fingers, then point them at Teddy."

He looks shocked. "That's... Oh my fucking God! How did I not see it sooner?" He scoffs and it's so similar to his dad that I flinch. He drops to the ground, first sitting on his butt and then laying fully prone. "This whole time. This whole time, when you said something about Teddy, you were talking about my dad." With an arm over his eyes, he blows out a breath. "Since you were seventeen."

I can feel his whole world fracturing. The realization cracks through our bond like an earthquake. Everything we've talked about over the years is being revealed in a new light.

I sit down next to him. "Since I was seventeen."

"Why?" His voice is broken, and he sounds defeated.

"At first, he just wanted to keep an eye on you. He said he just wanted to know that you weren't getting into too much trouble... then things changed."

Sitting up, Mack looks at my face. The sadness swims in his blue eyes, threatening to spill over. "Why didn't you tell me?"

"I don't know." It comes out like a whisper. Clearing my throat, "He seemed genuine at first. Like he really just wanted to keep tabs on you. As I got older, he wanted more. I was naive, starry-eyed and he knew that. Baited me with the shit I wanted and kept asking for more and more from me."

Mack looks me in the eyes, and I swallow. He reminds me so much of when we were younger in this moment. "I need to know the truth, Reese. Not this tiptoeing around what really happened. Please."

I take another deep breath and exhale loudly before sighing it out. Telling Mack the truth about his father was daunting more than anything. I knew that he didn't care for his dad much. But to find out what I'm telling him so many years later would affect anyone in a significant way. Throughout the talk, he asked an occasional question. Mostly, he was silent except for the teeth grinding and knuckle popping.

When I'm done, Mack wraps his arms around my shoulders. "I'm sorry."

For what? For yelling? For accusing me when he didn't know the truth?

"It's not your fault," I say.

"I don't care. You're my sister, and I didn't protect you. I knew you were running. I knew you didn't feel safe and I never—" he gets choked up, and I feel the tear hit my tank before he wipes his eyes with the back of his hand. "Reese. I am so sorry. Fuck. I—"

I rub his back. "It's okay. It's over. We're over. Sally is there because it's one of many ties I've severed between us. I never wanted you to find out. Or anyone."

He holds me by the shoulders, forcing me to look to his face. "Reese. You can't blame yourself. I did stupid shit at seventeen. Hell, I'm still doing stupid shit now. I just wish you would have told me so that I could have beat his ass sooner."

"You what?"

"When I saw your car, I went into the condo. He was drunk and told me that he had your car because he owned it just like he owned you. I decked him. I didn't ask any questions, but I just saw red. I didn't even think it would be this bad. Now I wish I had got another punch or two in. Maybe a kick to the gut. Disgusting prick."

"Mack, he's your dad! You can't just fight him." Though, there is some sick sense of satisfaction with the image of Teddy being clocked in the face.

"I can do whatever I want. He deserves that and more. He's lucky it was not worse."

I chuckle, surprising myself after such a heavy conversation. "You know you can't just fight every person who upsets you? One of these days, it is going to get you put behind bars."

"Yeah. I probably deserve it. But to protect the people I love, it's worth it."

I bump a shoulder into his, "Still my brother then, huh?" In this moment, he feels like the person I grew up with more than he has in the past few weeks. Maybe it's because I can look at him, knowing that I'm no longer lying to him. But he will have to process the hurt from the truth about his own dad. I reach for his hand, and he easily intertwines it with mine.

"Yea. I guess you're stuck with me." He gives my hand a quick squeeze. "Now, I desperately need a whiskey after all that." He stands, pulling me up with him.

"I need to help the guys get this herd through the gate first, then we can pop a bottle."

"Fine." He playfully rolls his eyes before smiling, "But I get to pick which kind," he responds, mounting Legend again.

CHAPTER 44

Cory

"You look like you've seen better days, pal."

"You could say that." I slur into my beer.

"What's on your mind?" I look up from my pint to the owner of this place. His four eyes swirl in my vision, and I look back down to my drink, figuring that it will be easier to concentrate on.

"Well, where should I start? My girlfriend..." I manage sloppy air quotes around the word. "is gone. My ex-wife is trying to take my kids from me and I can't remember where I put my keys."

"I don't know about the first two, but Drea took your keys when she saw you wobble your way to the bathroom after the last beer. I take it that you're not a big drinker since this is only your third." He raises an eyebrow, or maybe three at me.

"As a matter of fact, no, I'm not." The words run together and I sit a little straighter like that will sober me up. "Shit. How am I gonna get home?"

"I'll take you." I turn over my shoulder to the owner of the tan hand currently resting there. I scowl up at the last face I wanted to see tonight.

"Well, I figured my night couldn't get any worse, and then you showed up."

Mack chuckles. "Lemme have a coke, Q. And his keys."

Quincy fills a glass with the bubbling dark liquid from his soda gun under the bar top. He slides it over to Mack and next, my keys. I attempt to intercept the fob sliding across the counter, but overshoot it. He lifts his glass out of my way and pockets the keys easily.

"What do you want, Maxwell?" I sneer, turning in my stool to face the man.

"You got a problem with me?" Mack grins.

"Many."

He laughs. "And what would they be?"

I slam my nearly empty beer on the bar top. Holding up a hand, I tick off my reasons using my fingers. "Well, you want my girlfriend, ex-girlfriend. I'm constantly hearing about you and Legend from the boys every night and your fucking smug face." He is still grinning when I finish.

Grinning, smug bastard.

"That all?" He says around a chuckle.

"Why are you here? I'm trying to enjoy my beer in peace."

"Like I said, I'm here to take you home."

"You're not trying to date rape me, are you?"

He laughs even louder. "Um, no. You're a good-looking guy, I guess. But, I prefer women."

"I'll take an Uber."

"Ha. Yea. On a Wednesday? In Alpenglow Ridge? I doubt it. This is not Denver, brother. You'd get home faster by walking."

"I'll walk then."

"Oh, come on. I'm not that bad."

"Why are you trying to get me in your truck so bad?"

"We need to talk."

"Oh really? What about?" I finish my pint, tipping my head back. I nearly fall out of my stool, but I grab ahold of the bar just before the stool betrays me.

"I've been where you're at buddy. I don't know why you hate me so much because we have a lot more in common than you think."

"You and me? Now, that," I slap a hand on my knee, "is a good joke. We are nothing alike."

"C'mon, buddy. My wife left me." He gestures to himself. "Your wife left you." He gestures to me. "We're looking to drown the pain with a good drink. I'd probably be reaching for something a little stronger, but it's still the same."

I point a finger at one of him, saying, "I don't drink. So, beer is good enough."

"Hey! I meant no offense." He holds his hands up now as if I'll attack him or something. From my understanding, *my buddy* here is the one known for being volatile and rearing to throw a punch—not me. "Just pointing out that we could be friends. I'm a pretty good one."

"Oh yea." I drag out the words. "Because you and Reese are such good friends." My tone is petulant, and I know I sound childish. But I don't care. This jackass has been making his plays since I got here. It was likely him that Reese had been hooking up with.

But that doesn't sit right. He couldn't be the guy. I'm just being petty.

"We are. I've known her my whole life. She's like a sister to me and I would do anything for her."

I shake my head and get up from the bar. "I'm gonna go take a leak." I do use the bathroom, but I take the side door and start walking out of the parking lot toward my aunt's house.

"Hey man! What the fuck?" Mack runs out of the bar after me. I haven't gotten far, but he catches up with me easily. I sigh and roll my eyes.

"Dude, what do you want?"

"I'm trying to be a good guy and help you out, man. It's way too dark out here for you to be walking on the side of the road."

"Good, maybe it'll hurt less to be roadkill." *Instead of her prey.*

Mack steps out in front of me. "You don't mean that. I know three boys who need their dad. You can't just abandon them."

"They have their mother now. And I haven't had parents for a long time. I turned out just fine."

"I can't let you do this."

"And what are you gonna do about it? Jan's house is only four miles from here. I'll walk."

"Like I said before, it's not safe. What's your problem with me anyway? Just get in the truck. I could have already dropped you off by now."

"You could also have already driven to your house by now."

He huffs indignantly. "Why are you fighting me on this?"

"I don't want to get in your goddamn truck, Mack. I just want to walk home and think."

He presses, "Think about what?"

"About how I'm a fucking idiot who falls so hard for women who have absolutely no inclination to commit to me. About how my sons love this woman they think can replace their fair-weather mother. Or maybe about how I thought I knew someone, and they left me to fucking die in the truth that I knew she was too good to be true." I'm yelling and I can't stop. "Why would she lead me on? What did she gain? Why can't I give her what she wants to make her stay? Why am I not enough?"

"Well, fuck. That is..." He blows out a breath and claps my shoulder. "That is some tough shit. For whatever reason it is that you don't like me, that's irrelevant. We have so much in common. You'll see. You may not be able to see it right now, but talking helps. We can think and talk on the way to Jan's. Lemme just get a vest." He sprints to his truck, boots clomping in the gravel, and returns with a neon reflector vest on.

"Let's start fresh." Holding out a hand to me, he says, "Hey, I'm Mack."

I roll my eyes, but shake his hand. "Cory."

"My wife left me after she had a miscarriage of our first baby. Just fifteen weeks along. She told me after she had gone to the OB and came home without our little miracle. She didn't want to talk about it. She didn't want to tell anyone. And she made me promise that I wouldn't talk to anyone else about us even expecting. I lost my baby and my wife all in a matter of days. Now, she's seeing other people and moving on. And me? I just started sleeping without a bottle of Jack in my hand."

"Shit, man." I scrub my hand over my face feeling sobriety come into frame. "You never knew?"

"About the pregnancy, yes. I knew. The loss... I found her on our bedroom floor crying after she ignored my calls all day. I panicked. Reacted badly.

She shut me out and my life crumbled. Everyone in town treats me like I was the reason she left our marriage, like I abused her or something."

"Shit. I'd be nursing a Jack bottle, too."

"Yea. I'm the idiot who respects her wishes in not telling anyone. The fucking idiot who has held his tongue, and my own friends look at me like they don't even know me anymore. I guess I have changed. But when Reese finally came home, she never treated me like that."

I grit my teeth at the mention of her name. "If this is some long speech about how you knew it was her all along, I'm gonna throw up."

He laughs softly. "Nah. Definitely not. Said before, and I'll say it again—Reese is family. What's your deal with her anyway? Last I heard, you two were all touchy-feely at the farmer's market. Now you're drunk off three beers walking home with me."

"There is no deal with her."

"So..." He throws a thumb over his shoulder, "You were drinking about something else?"

"Sure."

"Uh-huh. That's not how I heard it."

My eyebrows raise and I stop walking. "What did you hear?"

"So there is a deal!"

"Of course, there's a deal! She's gone, man. Won't even take my calls."

He winces and I start walking home again.

"Hey! Wait. I need to tell you something, and I know she won't like it, but I think for both of your sakes, it's important that you know."

"Man, there's nothing to talk about. She doesn't want me. I need to focus on my kids and keeping them on a good path. Too much on my plate, on my shoulders. I know she wants more than I can offer."

"For real. Just listen. I promise you want to hear this."

At the seriousness of his tone, I stop walking. Crossing my arms over my chest, I give Mack my undivided attention. "Go on then."

"Reese got involved in a seriously fucked up situation when she was way too young to understand how messed up everything was." I shake my head, already prepared to ignore whatever else is coming next. "No, really. At seventeen and with someone that she thought she could trust. Someone we all thought we could trust." His face looks pained. "Hell, I thought he was a piece of shit long before I was made aware of quite how large a piece of shit he truly is."

"What are you saying?"

"Teddy was," he sighs, "He was basically grooming her, man. He took advantage of her ignorance. Convinced her that many things were normal when they weren't. Reese had been involved with him for so long, not knowing that she could do better, deserved better."

"But," My mind tried to catch up with everything that Mack was saying. "You're wrong. She was still seeing him for money. They had an agreement. She was finessing him, man."

"No. I'm not wrong." He points to his busted up knuckles. "I know them both. It is taking everything in me not to go back to his house and show him just how fucked up all this shit was." He speaks through clenched teeth, his irritation growing. "He made it seem like they were in some sort of exchange." He shudders and gags a bit. "Reese has always been like a sister to me, but she never told me about this. He made her keep this part of her life a secret because he knew they were not in a healthy relationship of any kind. Cory, did you not hear me? He started pursuing her when she was seventeen."

"Yea. So what? Teenagers mess around when they're young. I lost my virginity at fifteen."

Mack shakes his head."Probably to another fifteen year old. Teddy was forty-three."

"He what?" I can't believe what he's saying. A forty-three year old man was pursuing a seventeen-year-old Reese.

All that she said to me that night comes crashing into my consciousness.

"He doesn't want money, Cory."

"It's a power exchange."

"Does he hurt you?"

"Sometimes."

"Please, Cory. It's more complicated than that."

I try to swallow down my disgust, but the more I think about what she confessed, the more nauseous I feel. She was seventeen. The small amount of food roils in my stomach, but I force out the next words. "How do you even know that?"

The apologetic look on Mack's face is the only warning that I know I will not like this answer even more than the ones he's given me so far. "I know that because I confronted him about it, and she told me everything. Teddy is my dad."

"Your... Dad?" I question. My mouth is dry and I swallow as the guilt begins to claw it's way up my throat more acutely.

Time slows.

The man I met at MHA's launch party. Flickers of our argument are garbled as my brain recalls each piece of that conversation that should have been more alarming to me. Each piece that should have made me pause and see what my angel was trying to tell me.

Is that all you do around here?

You're gonna need it.

He couldn't be. No.

He can't be the man who Reese...

Oh, God.

"I need to—I need to..." I toss my phone to the ground and drop down into the grass off the side of the road. Cold moisture seeps into my pants, but I don't care. Disgust at my behavior rears its ugly head once again.

I just need a moment to think. I put my head between my legs.

He doesn't want her back in Alpenglow Ridge. *I bet he doesn't.* Not around his wife and son. Her best friend.

"How could he do that? For all these years." I hold my head in my hands.

"Believe me, I thought the same. I wish I had hurt him more for what he did to my best friend, to my mom."

"No wonder Rebecca hates her."

"I never knew. I tried to get her to tell me what their deal was for the longest. She never would budge. Probably too scared to say anything."

"I fucking hate this man."

"Well, what can you do? I can't keep beating the shit out of him. But him and I haven't been good ever since he moved out of the house and left my mom. I knew he was sleeping around. She knew it too. Just never knew who it was with." He shakes his head. "I'm sorry you got tangled up in this."

"Me too." I curse and kick at the grass. "I just miss her so much."

"Give her time. I know she cares about you, man. I've never seen her like that with anyone."

He stands from the ground and holds out a hand. "Time heals all, brother."

I take his offer, dusting on my jeans. "How long could it take to heal this?"

CHAPTER 45

Reese

"Can I talk to you two for a bit?"

"Of course, honey," Mom says. My dad puts his phone down, and Chandie mutes the house flipping TV show she's watching. "What's up?"

My hands feel clammy, but I need to do this.

It's been three weeks since I've seen Cory. But I see his boys every weekday for clinic, Bren and CJ anyway. I've only caught a few minutes or so with little G when Janet is the one to pick them up.

CJ has told me that their mom has been coming around more, doing stuff with them. I'm happy for the three of them because it seems to make them happy. Maybe he's got back together with his wife. My crazy shit driving him to his ex. I wouldn't blame him for doing that.

I would be lying if I said I didn't miss him more and more every day. At night, I swear I can feel the brush of his hand on my face, the smell of his beard oil, or the small tug of his fingers in my hair at the nape of my neck. More than anything, when my harness shifts, I can almost imagine it's his curious fingers tracing along the metal chain.

My dreams are no better—haunting me with visions of what our life together could have been.

"I wanted to come clean about something involving the business."

Chandie sits up straighter on the couch. Danny takes his reading glasses off and sets them on the table.

Taking a deep breath, I tell them, "When I told you all about the last registrants for this cycle of MHA, I lied about the funding."

"You lied? How?" My dad asks, his serious conversation posture in full effect.

"I paid for their spots. I paid for their spots with the money I got from an... unsavory exchange."

"What do you mean unsavory? It wasn't drugs, was it?" Chandie holds a hand to her chest, clutching the pendant she's wearing.

"No, no. Not drugs. The man I was involved with asked me to do something that I was no longer comfortable with for the money. I'm telling you this because we have the next round of camp spots opening. Where there are some young ones that will be returning, some will not be because I am no longer in a relationship of any kind with that man. The number may be lower this time, and I wanted you to know that it's not because of anything we've done or because the program isn't amazing."

"Honey, what? What were you doing for the money?" My dad looks about ready to explode. My mom puts a hand on his leg, keeping him in his seat.

"I would rather not say, but I wanted to let you know that I'm working on a new plan to bring in more students."

"Now, just wait a minute. Slow down. How many students were you paying for?"

I shift from foot to foot, trying to decide if I should be honest or not. "Fifteen," I mumble.

Danny looks to mom and then at me. He doesn't show any emotion other than confusion on his face, but I suspect he's still trying to figure out what exactly I'm talking about.

"Oh that's nothing. The nonprofit that we are partnering with would love to see us offer scholarships. Those fifteen spots can be offered on a merit based scale. Wouldn't that be wonderful, D?" She looks to my dad.

"Nonprofit? Scholarships?" I ask.

"Well, yea. Honey, this 501c3 has their own goals and such. We just provide the facility. It was never about what we could stand to earn. Outside of the horsemanship aspects you and the others have been providing, it's their program that is really the heart of all this. You didn't think it was me or dad coming up with all the activities these kids have been doing did you?"

"I didn't think it was you, but..." I stand there, going over every conversation I had with them in the past month about this camp. Each thought speeding past me, faster and faster. "Non-profit..."

"Honey, I told you we would figure it out. Anything that wasn't paid for, would have been accounted for by the organization. I don't totally know how that all works, but I told you not to worry about it."

I stand there for a few moments more before I sit in the armchair. "Why didn't I know any of this?" My voice is just a whisper.

"Well, you did know we were working with a partner for MHA, maybe you just didn't go that deep into the paperwork or something... Honey?" My mom grabs my hands, which are wringing together. "Are you okay?"

"Okay? I'm... I don't know. I need to think. I'll talk to you later." I stand from the chair and head out to the truck, needing to get... I don't know really.

I drive slowly through the town.

Needing space.

Trying my best not to spiral out of control.

I don't know anything. I thought the money was important because the money has always been more important to me. More important than my relationships with my family and friends. More important than my own happiness.

Everything I did... It all could have been avoided. I never had to take anything from Teddy. I could have ended things sooner if I had just been honest with my parents about the tuition sooner.

If I had been honest with myself.

I felt too scared of being a failure and having to go back to him.

Goddamnit! And I did that anyway.

Got myself into a bigger hole.

Fuck.

I lost Cory all for no reason.

I lost the only man who loved me.

He never said it, but I knew.

And I ruined it all.

I roll my windows down needing more air.

I feel like I can't breathe.

Before I know it, I'm turning into the senior center parking lot. The movie has already started, but Patrick lets me buy a ticket and park in the back either way.

I rest my head on the steering wheel and begin to cry. Big sobs wrack my body, and I let the self-recrimination eat away at me.

A knock on the passenger window makes me jump. With a hand over my heart, I look up to see Cory standing there. He motions for me to roll the window down. I wipe at my eyes and do what he asks.

"Are you okay in here?" He shakes his head. "I can see that you're not, but can I sit with you?"

Still wiping at my face, I unlock the door. He gets in the truck and I look him over briefly. Green cargos and a black shirt. He looks so much the same and altogether different.

A comfort and pain, all wrapped into one.

There's a large part of me that really wants him to leave. But an even bigger part that wishes he would hold me. He doesn't do either of those things. He just pulls a tissue from his back pocket and hands it to me.

I clean up my face, mumbling, "Thanks."

"Where's Sally?"

"Gone." I fold and unfold the tissue in my hands.

It's been three weeks of no communication, and I could feel the Cory-sized hole even more acutely with the man sitting right next to me. The familiar smell of him swirling through the cab. I wonder if it will linger after he's gone.

He hums a sound. I'm not going to elaborate because it's none of his business anymore. When he left me that night and then at Chloe's house... he lost those privileges.

He loops a stray curl around his finger. "The black looks good. It'll take some getting used to."

Dying my hair back to its natural color was the biggest change I've made to my hair since I was eighteen.

Being dumped for the first time in my life came with the added benefit of breakup hair. Chloe was hesitant, but she relented.

"I'm not taking you back to blonde after this. Once you go black you're not going back." Chloe chastised.

"I'm sure. That was the old me. I'm different now."

And I did feel different. I felt like me. An unusual thing to think when I've been me all along. This version though...

This version is enough and she deserves more than what money can buy.

She deserves happiness too.

"Why would you need to get used to it, Cory?" My bitter tone is more biting than I really intend.

"I just wanted to say that I'm sorry."

My mouth hangs wide open. Of all the things I expected him to say, this was not one of them. "You're... sorry?"

"I am. I shouldn't have run out like that..." He shifts in the passenger seat, clearly uncomfortable with what he is about to say next. "I should have talked to you. I shouldn't have judged you and said those things. And I shouldn't have used your friends to talk to you before that concert."

I look back to my tissue that is crumbling in my hands now that I've started tearing holes in it.

I don't know what to say to that. I didn't know how to explain things before, and I still don't know what to say now. I stare unseeingly at the old film playing on the back of the senior center building.

The movie audio could be heard from a specific station on the radio so everyone can privately watch in their own cars. I chose not to even look for the station because I wasn't here to watch a movie.

I was here to sulk and cry in peace.

Silence stretches between us, filling the cabin with all the things we aren't saying right now.

"I missed you… Miss you. Mack found me at the bar and told me everything. I didn't want to hear what he had to say because I was still so hurt. But I was there drinking. They took my keys and he walked me home."

I look up to his face. The sun is setting, casting us in warm light. I'm instantly reminded of our trail ride and the way he took me to heaven on the picnic blanket I packed.

Now, he looks tired. His eyes aren't as bright as they usually are, puffy and dark from not sleeping well, I imagine. Hearing that he was too drunk to drive home makes me feel even more like shit. But I can't lie to him, "I missed you too." I blow out a long breath. "I really wish you had talked to me though. Let me tell my own story."

"I know. Trust me. You weren't answering my calls and he found me at QB's. But hearing it from him…" He clenches his jaw. "I wanted to punch him and his dad."

So he does know everything. "For what? What did he say?"

"It's not what he said. I just want to hate Mack so badly, but he's actually a cool guy. I can see why you two are close. I was jealous of how familiar he was with you while I was still just trying to get to know you. I thought that…"

I scoff, "You thought he was trying to get with me, didn't you?"

"I did." He hangs his head. "I thought there was no way I could give you what he could. He knows you better than I ever could. But now I know that it was never like that between you." He shifts again. "I still want to fight his dad for what he put you through. I can't afford to catch a charge like that though."

A lone tear runs down my cheek, but Cory wipes it with his thumb before I can use the ripped up tissue in my hand. "I was old enough to know better. I still lied to you. You deserve more than that."

"Baby, I know. I wish you didn't keep this from me. I wish that you had told me from the jump. I want to be there for you." He chuffs. "I would not have liked it. But, maybe I would have handled things much better. We could have figured something out together."

"That's not me anymore. I'm done with that life... that lifestyle. I want something different now."

"I know, pretty girl." The affection in his tone almost breaks me. The way he says pretty girl has always made my lower belly squeeze in anticipation.

"We can't do this again." I say.

He drops his hand from my face. After he wiped my tear, he rubbed circles on my cheek. Fingers entwined in my hair, just like he used to. The loss of his touch guts me in a way that I'm not prepared for.

"What?"

"I think it's for the best, Cory. You have your family to think about. Their mom is back in their lives, and maybe you should fix things there for them."

"Really? Vanessa is back for the boys. Not for me. Like I told you before, we would never have worked out. She said as much when she barged back into their lives." He crosses his arms, sitting back in the seat. His jaw ticks and I stay silent. He closes his eyes and the labor of his breathing would be alarming if I didn't know Cory better. His patience knows no bounds. "Don't you think that I should have a say in what I want? On who I want?"

"You don't want me. You like the idea of me. The idea of being in a relationship with me. I'm still figuring my life out. Trying to come to grips with the choices that I've made. Trying to forget how the way you looked at me changed absolutely when you found out about Teddy. To forget those words you said. That 'sick shit' I was into impacted my life in more ways than I ever knew." I unlock the doors and start the engine on the truck. "I need time to think. And I need space."

"What about what I want, Reese?"

"I can't, Cory."

"So, just like that, the conversation is over?"

"It's for the best."

"The best?" His voice reverberates around me but I don't shrink. "The best for who? What about CJ, Bren, and Gabe? What about me? Is it best for all of us to miss you every time we go to the farmer's market and every time we have dinner set for you to join us? How is it best for everyone to be miserable while we are apart?"

"It's best because I need to process Cory. Everything in my life has changed! I can't be a partner to you. I can't be a mother to them. Fuck. I barely even know what I'm doing with my job at the Ranch. I just need time. Please, Cory. Stop making this harder than it needs to be."

I can't take his compassion and patience right now. My heart is already cracking and splitting with all that I've learned. I will shatter into pieces if he says one more thing to make me question myself.

He opens his door and steps out. Before he can slam the door behind him, he says, "I'm sorry that you're going through this. I truly am, Reese. But don't think for one second that making yourself into a martyr will change how people see you or what they will say. We fucked up. Both of us have made mistakes. Suffering by yourself will not make them go away. And beating yourself up while you're alone will not make it any better either. I'll always be here to support you, and that won't change. When you figure out what you want to do, you have my number."

With that, he closes the door and leaves my heart in pieces.

CHAPTER 46

Cory

"AND LET ME KNOW if there is anything that you need. Even if it's for something small. I'm only going to be ten minutes away, max."

"Don't treat me like the babysitter, Cory." *Kind of a glorified one at this point.* But, I don't add that point because it's not going to help me or my nerves to pick a fight with Vanessa right now.

"Alright. Come give me a hug, boys." I wave them over. It's clear that they all look wary of being left with her. I feel a little guilty for not being here. But, as Vanessa has reminded me, time and time again, she is their mother.

"Are you gonna go see Reese?"

"Reese?" Vanessa asks, though her face is neutral.

"No, Ceej. Not today. I wish though, buddy." He nods solemnly, pushing his glasses up on his face. CJ gives me another hug. "It will be okay, dad. She'll take you back." The comment kinda takes me by surprise, but I chuckle and give him a squeeze back.

"I hope so, buddy," I reply. I can feel Vanessa's eyeroll from here, but she says nothing else.

Bren is already waiting by the door. She's taking them to the park today. The town is having a water balloon party now that the kids can play in the water features they have turned on in the park. His big water gun, courtesy of his mom, is slung over his back.

We will have to talk about how against the play guns I am when they return. After much deliberation, I knew I had to give Van a chance to make it right with the boys. She and I will never work again, though. After she dropped that bomb of telling me I forced her into a life with me, we will never try to make it work again.

Whether or not I'm with Reese, I won't reconcile with Van.

I came to Alpenglow Ridge for peace and to figure out just where I was going with my life. I fully accepted that there was nothing between Vanessa and I. I did not expect to still be trying to make space for her anyway. I wanted to believe that she would be back in their lives, but I couldn't have hoped it would be this soon.

I am happy for the boys. I truly am.

Hell, I'm even happy about being able to have someone who I can rely on to co-parent. Maybe not today. Maybe not this month, but I can see that Van is trying to be a better mother to them.

She has been here when she said she would be, and I have not had to race across town to pick up her slack since she came to me the other day. This is only the second weekend, but I can feel the difference. It's night and day.

She's not quite the woman I met in my twenties, but she is much closer to that person now than she was when we lived together.

With all the good things in my life, I still feel what's missing. Who's missing. It's times like this that I wish I could be an alcoholic or a workaholic. The Riesling Mason sized opening that I can't fill with alcohol or work demands that I make things right with her.

How can I make things right? After weeks of rereading our texts and seeing her post updates in Alpenglow with her friends, I just feel empty.

She pulled me in and now I don't know where to go.

I don't want to see other people.

I want to see her. I want to be the one to make her smile again.

"Oh. My. God." Janet says.

"What is it?" Sammie asks.

"Sam." I sit up in my bed and stop my fingers from twirling my keys. The two of them are in the living room by the guest room I've been staying in which is just close enough to hear what's being said.

"Oh my. Now, why would Rebecca post that?" Janet says.

"I guess she had enough. I'm gonna call Chandie." Now, I'm up and out of the room, with Reese's mother's name being mentioned.

"Call her for what?" I ask.

Janet puts her phone down and pats the couch next to her. "Cory. I don't want you to freak out when I show you this."

"Why would I freak out? What is going on?"

"It's about Reese. I know you're still all torn up about her. This would be upsetting to me if it were about Janet." Sammie clacks her nails against her teeth, seeming to think a bit more about what she is going to say next. I'm sitting on the couch, but there is no way I can be comfortable with all this build up. "Maybe you should call her."

"Call her for what?" I ask, getting impatient at how they're talking around me.

"Oh, it's online. He'll find out soon enough." Janet picks up her phone again, unlocking it. She hands it to me and when my eyes take in what is on the screen I feel my stomach turning.

I scroll and scroll through post after post of photos and videos on the screen.

There are no captions, just a dump of what looks like years of footage.

Her gold harness glints back at me in a menacing way. I can't help but keep looking, keep watching. Janet and Sammie are saying something, but I can't hear it, for how fast my heart is racing in my ears.

It's Reese. *My pretty girl.*

But, not.

These photos are clearly meant to be private. Meant to be for her and whoever the white filming hands belong to.

Compromising positions, toys, lingerie, bruises and her mouth open in pain or ecstasy, I can't tell. I see in high definition exactly what was going on behind closed doors. There is no talking around it or speculating now. Here is the full scope of what she was involved in. I can't stop looking at what's in front of me.

Then I put the phone down, because none of this was meant for me.

For my eyes, or anyone else.

How could Rebecca do this to Reese?

"How can we get these down?" I ask more firmly.

"Cory, I don't know. I reported the posts, but you know that stuff takes some time." Janet says.

"So, these are just everywhere?! There is no way that Rebecca can get away with this?"

I pull out my own phone, trying to get a hold of her, but it's going straight to voicemail.

Trying Reese's phone next and the same thing happens. She's probably turned off her phone after everything that's going on. Or maybe I'm still blocked.

Fuck.

This is bad.

"You didn't know." I hear Janet say. When I look up, she mouths Chandie. "God, I'm so sorry. Let me know if there's anything we can do to help. I reported the posts, and so did Sammie. But—" There's a pause as Chandie says something on the other line. "I understand. We're here for her. This is just awful."

If the sneers and rumors were bad before, I know they are going to be horrible now.

Everything in my body is telling me to go to her.

To comfort her.

This is beyond an invasion of privacy.

She needs someone by her side.

I stand from the couch, ready to do something about this.

What? I don't know.

But there is nothing I can do stewing in it at the house.

"She asked for privacy, Cory. I know you want to go to her, but they just want to be with family right now. Can you imagine what this is like when they just made Reese the face of their children's camp? Don't go over there like some white knight. When she is ready to see you, she will."

But I know, Reese. I saw her yesterday. I know she was already having a hard time. She needs someone on her side fighting for her. I know that person can be me. I could be the person to do that for her.

She asked me to give her space and I'm going to respect that.

But she never said I couldn't send her anything to help.

"Where are you going?" Sammie asks as I'm leaving out the front door.

"To the nursery."

Chapter 47

Reese

"I figured I should be the first to show you this."

"Show me what?"

Chandie says nothing else before she puts her phone in front of me.

The first thing I see is lace.

The second thing I see is my blond hair glowing in the flash of the camera.

"No," I whisper.

I scroll and see more photos of myself in increasingly more exposed positions. Tied up, tears running from my eyes, spread open for anyone who is friends with Rebecca Stewart. Her Facebook profile is littered with photos and videos of me with her husband.

"No!" I yell. "What the hell?!"

"Honey," my mom's voice is broken, and the sorrow breaks through the red I'm seeing like a knife. "Is Alex the man you've been seeing all this time?" Her watery eyes don't hold the judgment I feared. It's more carefully concealed outrage. For me or the situation, I can't tell. My thoughts are too chaotic and jumbled for me to make sense of it in any way.

I drop down to the floor.

The world is shifting under me and I can't stand anymore.

I can't bear to decipher the look on her face any longer. "Yes."

She sits on the floor beside me and hugs me. I've curled up with my head between my knees and my arms wrapped around my legs. "I reported the posts, but it still takes some time for Facebook to remove it. Rebecca isn't answering her phone. Honey. Tell me what happened. What can I do?"

"I don't know." And I don't. Why would Rebecca do this? Why? "Does dad know?"

"No, he's still out with the cattle, but I'll intercept him. This might send him into a panic."

"Might?! Mom."

"Okay. We don't have to talk about that right now. Please breathe, Riesling. We will figure this out."

"My life just imploded. Everything I tried to achieve, up in flames because Rebecca finally got tired of Ted—Alex's bullshit."

"She knew? I'm sorry. I've heard her whispers in town. Her and I never were the same after you left... I never put those things together before. I just—Honey, I don't know what's going on." She goes silent for a beat and asks, "Was Alex the exchange you were telling us about? These photos... Is this how you paid for those kids?"

"I—" The words are cut off because I don't really know how to answer that. The truth is yes. Everything with Teddy led to the final deal I made with him. As much as I thought being here temporarily would fix things—fix me—that could have never been the case.

I am the complication.

What made me think that moving back into my parent's house next to his wife would be simple?

A wife who has singlehandedly fueled the nasty rumors and sneered at me at any given opportunity.

The very person I avoided for years whenever I was in town for any period of time.

The front door app pings on my mom's phone, and she curses when she sees who is there. She raises the phone to her mouth, speaking in a tone I know she uses when she is trying to be patient. "How dare you step foot on my property."

"I just want to talk." Rebecca's voice makes me tense under the arm that my mom still has wrapped around me.

"How about you take down those posts, and I will think about not shooting you where you stand, witch." As close to the word I would have used as she will get. Even in her fury, my mom remains in character. She despises the use of curse words in her house.

"Chandie, I did not post those. Someone has locked me out of my account, and I can't access it. I didn't know what happened until I got your voicemail."

I mouth "voicemail?" to my mom and she just shakes her head.

Chandie leaves for just a moment to let Rebecca in. Rebecca returns back to my room and I feel the depth of her true innocence in how disgruntled she looks.

When she sits in my loveseat, I ask her, "How long have you known?"

Rebecca huffs out a breath. "A few years. I didn't know it was from when you were that young. I feel sick. I thought it was when the car showed up next door. I... I feel disgusted in knowing what Alex did to you. You have to know I never knew it was like this. I had suspicions, but I found out just how long from the posts today."

I nod my head. Standing from the floor, I urge her out of the room. "I know that this is not your fault, but I can't have you here all the same. I accept your apology, for now."

My mom walks with her to the door and they argue as I go to lie back on my bed.

"Anyone home?" Chloe says from the doorway.

Tears fill my eyes and I break down. Everything I thought I stood to gain by coming home.

I worked so hard to do this right.

"Reese, we're here for you." Drea's voice comes in.

"This is fucking awful," Melody says. "Sorry, Chandie." She calls down the hall.

"No, it is fucking awful. Can you girls stay with her?" Chandie calls back, not waiting for a reply as she heads out of the door.

They all agree, coming to sit next to me on the floor.

"I'm so dumb. This is all because of me. My life, the camp. It's all going up in flames." I throw my arms up and rest my head against the bed behind me.

"It's not. Babe, this is some illegal shit. You could sue Rebecca for how she just put all this online without your permission." Clo says, brushing her bob into place with a little brush she pulled out of her purse.

"Who cares about that? I thought I could be the sweet small town girl who took over her parent's ranch if I just left everything in Denver. That is never going to happen. I knew she thought I had stolen her man. I knew she hated me. But this? No one will ever want to have me around their kids again. She claims she didn't do it, and I believe her to some extent. She still has to secretly be happy about it all either way." There's silence after I spelled out just how terrible this truly is.

Drea cuts into the silence by adding, "Well, at least you looked really good." Mel elbows Drea. "What? She did. So what? Maybe you are a pornstar now. Those girls make bank!"

"Not helpful, Drea. She's not a pornstar. She's Reese." Chloe corrects.

"A woman who had her trust betrayed by a man she was in an agreement with, and his wife sought to go after her by posting all that stuff from his phone." Shaking her head she says, "How did she even get all those pictures? I don't care what you say. I think she did it," Mel says.

"I don't know. They hardly see each other anymore. I doubt Rebecca knows how to *hack* anything. Maybe she hired someone. I don't know."

Mel's brows scrunch. "You think she hired someone to get all these... you know?"

"I have no idea. Honestly, he never was any good at keeping his phone locked or keeping anything like that private on his devices. I found out about him and his last secretary because he just messaged her on the company instant messenger. Literally, anyone could see it. Including me."

"Wait a minute." Chloe throws her brush back into her purse. "You caught him with a secretary? At his office?!"

"Yes. It was why I ended things. Before our most recent agreement. He got... he fucking hit me when he found out I was seeing other people too.

He never even denied hooking up with her. Ugh. We were so toxic. I should have known this would blow up in my face. I can't imagine a more public way for it to go down either. Rebecca is friends with probably every person in this town on Facebook. The parents are going to throw a fit. And they should."

"You are not at fault here, Reese. Anyone could have been hacked like this. You were targeted! Those pictures were private, even if you were sleeping with her husband." Mel winces but adds, "She can choke on dirt for all I care. This was not the way to go about getting revenge for that."

"Thanks, guys, really. I appreciate it. That I have you. I don't know what to do anymore."

"Nothing to do." Chloe says, digging around in her massive purse again. "Tiny wine for you." She hands me a small bottle of riesling. "A tiny wine for you two." She says handing Mel and Drea a bottle as well. I grin at the golden liquid and crack it open.

"It's only ten in the morning, Chloe!" Mel protests.

"It's five o'clock somewhere! Besides, this is basically like a mimosa or something." Drea adds, screwing the lid off of her bottle and tossing the lid into the trash can next to her. She holds her bottle in the air.

I raise mine too, and Chloe raises her bottle with ours.

Rolling her eyes, Mel opens her bottle and clinks it with the others.

"Bottoms up." We say in unison.

I cough at the sweet wine and ask, "Why wasn't this liquor? On second thought. Mimosas would have been better."

"Well let's go to QB's. Brunch is in our future." Drea responds tossing her empty bottle into the trash too.

"You all don't open till 11," I say.

"Don't remind me," Mel pouts, laying out on the rug. "I have to clock in at 5."

"Well, I own the place. I'll cut you off at two so you can still serve tonight." Chloe says with a wink.

"I love y'all." I know that alcohol probably isn't going to fix anything, but I could stand to brunch with my ladies to at least take my mind off of my life falling down around me.

<hr>

WHERE DO YOU WANT me to put these?"

I look up from my nails and see the vase in my mom's hands. The anemones bloom beautifully in the center of the bouquet. She gives me a soft look, but I don't take the bait. I'm not going to talk about the flowers with her. I don't really know what to think of them myself.

"You just can't say no to cut flowers can you?"

"It's you I can't say no to."

"You can just put them on the dresser with the other one."

She nods and walks over to the dresser. "Honey, there is no more room for these."

I put my nail file on the nightstand and she's right. The other six vases are already taking up the full space on the dresser. "Umm... let me have the note and you can just put them somewhere else in the house, I guess."

It's been about a week since everything went down and Rebecca's account was hacked. I haven't been able to do what I normally would with Masons' Horsing Around. There are only so many rom coms I can watch while my friends all carry on with their lives. I hide away in my house, hoping not to run into a concerned parent or any other skeevy propositions from men in town.

She sits at the foot of my bed. "Are you gonna call him back?"

"I don't know." I didn't. I don't know what to say. Each of the notes on the flowers has been more beautiful than the last. Not only did he figure out that all variations of ze poppy were my favorite, but the wide array of colors he's sourced to create these bouquets really made me miss him. The notes, though short, are what I look forward to keeping. Each one I've stored away in my nightstand drawer, reading over them again at night when I'm in bed alone.

Reese,

Some cultures believe that the poppy or anemones are a symbol of an incoming storm when the petals close up. There is a storm coming. I know that you have so much to face and there are loved ones around you. I hope that these will add to the protection against any ill will you may endure.

I'm here for you always,

Cory.

Reese,

Some cultures believe that the poppy or anemones are a symbol of fragility. Let me hold you and care for your vulnerabilities. With me, you will never have to worry about breaking. With my hands and my heart, I'll hold you together.

I'm here for you always,

C

Reese,

Some cultures believe that the poppy or anemones are a symbol of anticipation. I anticipate the sound of your voice in my ears and the feeling of your heart beating against mine.

I'm here for you always,

C

Reese,

Some cultures believe that purple anemones are a symbol of protection. Let me keep your heart safe and protect you. Let me wrap you in my love and be the thick skin to deflect any menace.

I'm here for you always,

Cory

Reese,

Some cultures believe that the poppy or anemones are a symbol of renewal. I came to Alpenglow Ridge to find my new beginning. I found you instead. You made me feel alive and loved. I hope to be a part of your renewal, too. We are not our pasts. You can start fresh with me, with us.

I'm here for you always,

C

Reese,

Some cultures believe that pink anemones are a symbol of death. Accept this symbol as the death of the love you pursued before and the rebirth of what we can have with it gone. Let's celebrate our opportunity to create something new, just us two.

I'm here for you always,

Cory

The newest bouquet has several large white anemones that look pristine and angelic. I stare at the small white envelope in my hands. My name is written in the small, clean letters I would recognize anywhere at this point. My mom watches me and I feel the weight of her gaze. "Could I have some privacy?"

"Oh." She gets up from the bed and walks over to the door. "I think you should at least call him, Reese." I give her a look and she says, "Okay. Fine. I'll put these in the kitchen." She leaves, closing my door behind her.

I look at my name for a few more moments before I finally tear into the envelope.

> *Reese,*
>
> *Some cultures believe that the white anemone is a symbol of sincerity. The delicate appearance of these blooms made admirers wary of destroying their fragile petals. Only those who knew how to care for and handle these flowers could keep their beauty intact. My intentions for you are pure. I will handle you with care. I will protect your petals and prove to you that I deserve the privilege of admiring your beauty, inside and out.*
>
> *I'm here for you always,*
> *Cory.*

I don't feel the tear but it lands on the card. It wells up over Cory's name before sinking into the paper. Wiping at my eyes, I read the note again. And again.

He must have seen those pictures online, there isn't a single soul in town who hasn't seen them. All my ugly secrets and the depth of what I was doing over the years plain and clear. And yet, every day, I receive a new note and bouquet from him.

My friends have been taking me to do things outside of the house like getting food or just going on a trail, being sure to share online and show that I am not beat down by the leak of those photos. They are removed from Facebook, but the memory of them is still on the breeze in murmurs I hear at the convenience store when I'm getting gas or at the deli when I'm getting a sandwich.

I'll never escape my past.

But Cory... he isn't scared of that.

Chapter 48

Cory

"We know that there have been some concerns that you would like us to address after what happened last weekend." Chandie says from her porch. Danny sits at the table, giving a grimace to those gathered here.

"Is Reese in trouble, dad?"

"No, she's not in trouble. But, she's sad."

"I miss her being at camp last week." *I miss her too.* I look at Bren and see the sincerity in his eyes.

Giving his shoulder a squeeze, I say, "I know bud. Maybe she'll be back soon." For their sake, I hope so.

We're sitting in folding chairs on the Mason's lawn with the other parents of kids in the MHA program. Gabe is sitting in my lap, and my two oldest sit on either side of me. Some kids are playing loudly behind us while they wait for all the parents to take their seats.

"Last weekend, Rebecca Stewart's Facebook account was hacked by an unknown person. Many photos and videos were shared to her profile without Rebecca's permission or the permission of the individuals present in the posts. This is not only hateful and invasive but also illegal. This is a legal issue and will be resolved as such. No one involved consented to have the media shared. As you can imagine, this has been a difficult time.

"Over the past week, we've deliberated over the best course of action moving forward. We understand if in light of this happening, you would like to pull your kids from the MHA program. You will receive whatever your unfulfilled balance is on your account. No questions asked. Simply send me an email, and it's done." She looks over the people gathered. A few people leave in the back. I hear the murmurings of the crowd but don't turn to see who left, I likely wouldn't know them anyway.

My focus is on the woman sitting on the porch steps. This is the first time I've seen her in a cowboy hat. The edges curl up on the side, and it's pushed down low in front of her face, but I can still make out the details. I've never seen her look so sad and dejected. I want to go to her, but now is not the time.

Melody and Andrea are sitting on either side of her. Chloe and Quincy sit on the steps behind them. Mack is standing guard it seems, to the side of the stair post. The corner of my mouth lifts just a bit at seeing her surrounded with so much support.

I wish I was a part of it.

"With that out of the way, you should know that Riesling will be stepping back from the child facing role she has played. She will be working behind the scenes to ensure that we continue to provide a fun and safe way to care for your young people this summer. If you have any questions, we will be here to answer them as best we can."

"She should not have been around kids in the first place. Now the world really sees what she is. A skank."

I turn to face the older couple behind me, giving the full strength of my scowl to the woman who commented. "Watch what you say around my kids and about my girl. Is there gonna be a problem I need to solve here?"

The woman rolls her eyes at me, saying, "I'm just telling the truth of things," and leaves with the man she's sitting next to when she sees I'm not budging.

"What's a skank?" CJ asks me.

I huff out a breath. "It's a very mean thing to call someone and you shouldn't say it."

"But why would they say that about Reese?"

"Because that woman is a hateful person. Some people will judge others based on the things they assume about them. It's not right. We don't do that."

He nods and lowers his head. Bren leans over my lap tapping CJ. "Look! She's here!"

"Reese!" My kids bolt over to the woman in her tight jeans and tank top. Wine red boots drawing my eyes just as much as they always do. Her friends look on with smiles when Reese stands from the stairs to greet my sons. She gives them a tentative smile before the two of them are squeezing her. Gabe holds my hand, but is diligently making his way over to where his brothers are.

"Hey," I say lamely, like a lame person, when we reach her at the porch steps.

God, she looks good. Radiant even in her turmoil. My mouth waters at the sight of her. I hold my bottom lip between my fingers, hoping to stop the outpour of questions and nonsense that could come out after that charming line. *Get it together, Cory.*

It's been so long since I saw her in person. I almost forgot how her keen eyes could drink me in so languidly. In a matter of moments, I know she's taken stock of everything I'm wearing and all the little details, too.

Can she see how little I've been sleeping? How I've cleaned up my beard and haircut just for her?

Or maybe she's noticing the longing in my eyes that I can't contain when it comes to her. Suddenly, the cargo pants and tee I'm wearing don't seem like enough to see her for the first time in almost a month.

"Hey," she replies. "Thank you for the flowers... and the notes. They were both beautiful." She shifts from foot to foot before toeing the grass with the tip of her boot. "Look, I'm sorry I never called you back. I've just been..."

"Busy?" I question. I didn't expect her to accept or acknowledge the bouquets I had been preparing and sending to her. Part of me knew that she wasn't going to fall right into my arms, but I wanted to encourage her even if I couldn't be with her. I never wanted to see that light inside her dim because of something so horrible.

"Spiraling, actually." She looks down at my boys still hanging on to her. "The notes really helped me. I guess what I'm saying is more than thank you. What I'm saying is that I'm grateful even if I didn't show it right away."

I crouch down to eye level with CJ, "Can you take the boys over to the fence to look at the horses graze while I talk to Reese real quick?"

CJ gives me a reluctant look, but nods. "C'mon Gabe! Let's go look at the horsies, okay?"

They leave and I stand again, facing the woman I've still been missing. "Is there anything I can do to make this at least a little bit better?" I gesture to the crowd of people now talking among each other and to Chandie. From what I can tell, they aren't at all bothered by this meeting. The people who left truly were. Reese has more people on her side than she thought.

A small smile. "Maybe."

"Tell me. Name it, and I'll do my best to do it for you." Whether I'm coming off as earnest and sincere or desperate, I don't know. But my pride took a nose dive a long time ago when it comes to Reese.

Though if it sounds suggestive and she's down with it, I wouldn't mind that either.

"After all this, you still honestly want to be associated with me?"

"Are you kidding? I have been going out of my mind missing you—long before those pictures were leaked. Waiting for you to come to me. I wish I could have been there when everything went down... Jan said you wanted to be with family. I hoped that you would have called me. I understand why you didn't. I support you in the outrage, Reese. This was the biggest violation of privacy, no matter what the circumstances are. No one deserves to have their private photos shared against their permission." I cup her face fiercely, turning her head so that she faces me head-on. "We will do whatever we can to get this shit taken care of. Do you hear me?" Releasing her face, I take a step back and grab at the back of my neck, feeling self-conscious after rambling on as she stands here, just listening to me.

Her smile grows larger and she says, "So, you're kinda obsessed, huh?" Then she puts my hand back onto her face.

I huff out a laugh. "Just a little."

She considers me for a moment and I try to wait patiently for what she will say next. She rubs a thumb over my beard, saying, "I know a little spot over on the river. Maybe you remember it?"

"Yea, I think so." I grin because I remember it *very* well.

I've replayed that memory more times than I can count, dick in hand. A man has to make do with what he has to after all. Any time I shared with Reese seemed like too little time and it was my biggest regret.

Reese waves her other hand over her head and the boys come running from the fence. "You wanna do something fun?"

Bren and CJ smile broadly at each other.

When we arrive at that special spot just beyond the trail, I lay out our picnic blanket and the kids play near the river bank while the horses graze. She lays her head on my chest, black hair splayed all around her, and I rub her fingers in mine. The smile on Reese's face is enough to make me finally relax and breathe easy.

She looks down at my ministrations. "Why do you do that?" I give her a questioning look and she clarifies, "Massaging my hands, my fingers."

I consider for a few moments before I say, "At first, it was just because I needed to control your hands from wandering when you were tipsy at Quincy's bar." I raise an eyebrow at her and she laughs softly at the memory. "Then, I recognized how much you liked it. You basically melted and I can understand that, working with your hands all day. I guess... I just wanted you to feel relaxed and comfortable around me, so I kept doing it."

She's quiet for so long after that I don't expect her to answer me. What she says surprises me more than I could anticipate.

"I love you, Cory." She sits up on the blanket and I let her hands go. But Reese takes my hands in hers. I remain motionless, for fear that I'm dreaming this whole thing up. If I am, I don't want to wake up.

"I think I've known for a while, and I just never felt like I deserved the love that you were always trying to show me, even in the little things you did for me. Even in my darkest light, you were trying to be there to hold and protect me. Whether I wanted you there or not. But, I know now for sure. I love you and your sons and I never want to be without the four of you in my life ever again. I've been miserable dealing with all this, but more miserable missing you guys. Some part of me still believes that you deserve better. I'm still selfish enough to admit that I don't care. I will try my best to be the woman who deserves you anyway."

Nothing could keep me from tugging her into me after hearing those words. All I've wanted is to be a part of her world, of her life. My vision blurs, but I wipe her tears before my own can fall. "I love you, Riesling Mason. None of that stuff matters to me. You are everything! It would be my honor to be your man. For you to be a part of our family, for real."

We kiss and her tongue searches for mine as she climbs onto my lap. Reese holds me to her body with her fingers in my beard. I nip at her lips and our mouths meet. Desperate to make up for the time we lost.

"Ew!" My sons say, and reluctantly, we pull apart. Brushing some hair behind her ear, I give her one last kiss after she settles next to me on the blanket again.

I chuckle as Gabe wiggles between the two of us. He wraps his arms around Reese and settles for a nap I guess because after a few minutes of us talking, he's out like a light.

The day starts to wane and everyone is getting hungry, so we head back to the house for a dinner Chandie has prepared for us. She and Danny share a look after looking over the full table with my sons and her daughter all eating and talking.

When it starts to get late, I take everyone back to Janet's for bed, but Reese stays to help the hands for their evening duties.

I woke up this morning not knowing how the day would end. As I go through the nighttime routine with the boys, I unlock my phone, knowing that my love will pick up when I call.

CHAPTER 49

Reese

"I KNEW I'D FIND you out here." I would recognize his voice anywhere.

"What are you doing here, Teddy?" I look around the stables hoping that anyone is still here working late.

No other person in sight.

I came to love on Heather, Artemis, and Daisy after taking us up the trail today. I've always found peace around them. The perfect ending to a perfect day. Though I'm having to step away from the camp aspect of things here, I still have so much to love about my decision to stay in Alpenglow Ridge.

This asshole isn't going to ruin it, even if it's the death of me.

"I'm just here to visit Legend." The odd sense of deja vu hits me when a gust of cool air blows my black hair around my face.

Like nature, herself, knows something is not right here.

I didn't have the sense to run before. But today, I'm older and wiser.

"Visiting hours for our stabled horses ended at eight."

"I know. Staff is all gone for the night." He grabs my arm, pulling me close to his body. "I've got you all to myself. Just like old times." The acrid smell of whiskey burns my nostrils, and I turn my face from him.

"You've been drinking. Go sleep it off next door. I'm sure Mack will let you in." I wasn't sure, but I'd rather him try that than to stay here right now. I fidget, testing his hold on my arm but there is no give.

He gives a humorless laugh. "The same son who punched me in the face last time I saw him. Not likely, Ree."

The name makes me shiver in his grip. "Well, you're not welcome here. Leave while you still can."

"Or what? You gonna leak more photos of us."

This motherfu—"Why would you think I would do that? Have you been drinking that much?!" I yank my arm again, but he's dragging me towards the driveway.

"Don't worry about how much I've had to drink. Grab that shovel, and let's go."

I do what he says because I don't want to antagonize him further. He may not be wasted, but he has definitely drank more than a few today.

When we reach my truck he says, "Throw it in the back." The loud clang of the shovel feels ominous. There's only a few reasons why he would need a shovel out here. "Get into the truck and drive west."

Whatever he came to do, I don't want to involve my parents. It would have been easy to scream out, but I don't think they could hear me from the other side of the house. Especially if they're sleeping.

Think, Reese. Think!

I take too long trying to come up with a plan. "Drive!" His scream reverberates around us in the cabin. Something presses into the side of my neck, and I freeze. "Drive to the stockpile." I don't even bother turning around to face my attacker. "Getting involved with you was the worst mistake I ever made. You tempted me from the beginning, and I, like a fool, gave in to your every whim."

The effort it takes for me to refrain from speaking weighs on me. But, the very real threat of losing my life makes me show the restraint necessary for my current predicament.

Stay calm. Stay calm. Just breathe.

"And what did I get but a fucking knife in my back!" He yells into the truck and I flinch. "Michael had no qualms in telling me about how you and him had a thing going too."

"We had dinner, once."

"Shut up. I know you're lying. You always said you would tell everyone. Are you happy now? Happy that you ruined my reputation? Micheal is having the board come to a vote to have me removed. Me?" He scoffs, the gun digging into my neck harder. "Fucking removed. Can you believe it?"

I say nothing because I have no idea what he's capable of right now. "My wife," he sneers, "Was all too happy to serve me divorce papers this morning. That frigid bitch hasn't been near me in years. And now? Now she wants to leave with half. What a fucking joke. You two work together on that *leak?*"

"Work together? Alex—" He cuts me off with a tsking sound.

He corrects, "Teddy."

I don't bother saying his name at all. "We did not work together. Neither of us knows who put those pictures online."

"Convenient." He punctuates each syllable with a press of the gun into my neck harder.

Cory's contact pops up on my dashboard screen. The soulful ringtone blaring like an alarm through the confined space. His sweet eyes smile at me from a selfie he took on my phone when we went riding, but I can do nothing to answer him right now.

I say a silent thank you that he's not here and his boys are safe at home.

The pungent smell of manure hits my senses through the vents pumping A/C in the truck. The odor, plus the rapid beating of my heart, turns my stomach and I feel like I will vomit at any moment.

"Park and get out here."

I do as he says, grabbing what I need from my purse that's thankfully still in the center console. Shoving it into my back pocket, when he gets out of the truck. He yanks open my door, pulling me toward the foul pile of shit. "Get over here."

I take slow steps over to him. It's obvious to me that he didn't have a clear plan coming here. He looks around, lip curled back, appearing more deranged than sane. His rage fueled him up to this point. I just need to think my next steps through.

I just need to think.

He pulls at his hair, looking frustrated and unhinged when he points the gun back at me. "All this shit is your fault. If you never tempted me, I would still have everything."

"You can still have everything. It's just a job, Al—Teddy. You can make it right. It's not over." I try to reason with him.

"Oh, but it is." The safety clicks as he focuses on me. "It's over for you. I can play the mourning boyfriend, reinvent myself for the public."

"How can you mourn a living person, Teddy?"

His condescending look, says it all. With pity in his voice, he responds, "You won't be living."

I look at the gun in his hand and feel my body shaking with true fear now.

"This is your plan? What are you going to do with the body?" I shudder. *My body.* The best thing I can do is keep him talking so that I can come up with a way out of this alive. I just need some time to think.

Reese, please. Think of something. This can't be the end. I have so much to live for. My mind conjures the image of Cory, Bren, CJ and Gabe clearly. Them, laughing and smiling together. What I stand to lose if I can't figure out how to get away from Teddy...

All of that joy, that light, will be gone.

I won't lose them.

An idea starts to take shape and it's risky but I have to try and make it back to them. Nothing Teddy has ever given me has been as special to me as they are. I want a chance to prove that to them. I want a chance to show them that I'm worthy of their love.

I'll be damned if this asshole will take that from me.

"Why do you think we came to the manure pile? No one will find you in this. Doesn't get picked up for months. I will be long, long gone by then. Don't think of trying anything, or I won't hesitate to shoot you." He walks over to the truck and grabs the shovel. Throwing it to the ground by the pile, he makes a gagging noise. "Start digging," He commands.

"Teddy. Just listen to me. You don't want to do this. I can help you fix everything." I take a few steps toward him. I have no intention of digging my own shitty grave.

"You will," his deranged smirk taunts me.

Keep him talking. Keep him talking. Keep him talking.

"Teddy, baby." I purr, putting on the act for him. The shell I was—for him. Praying that he can't hear my nerves. "We could try this again. Everyone knows we are together now. Not a secret. We can be a real couple. Don't you remember how good we were together?" I take a couple more cautious steps toward him and he lets me. The gun hangs at his side.

Big mistake.

"Always with your games. You want me, and then you don't. But you will always be mine. And now no one else will have you ever again but me."

He aims the gun at my chest.

I reach into my pocket, just like I practiced so many times before. He barely notices, either from the alcohol or from his own self-assured confidence, I'll never know.

The cool metal in my hand greets me, like an old friend. "You ready for retribution?" I say in my head.

"You are mi—," he says, but I whip my arm around and strike just as Teddy pulls the trigger. I feel the blade puncture his suit jacket and pressed shirt, already on a path to twist and pull out. My ears ring and my hand is slippery, but I hold tight to my switchblade as I grit my teeth on an ever-present "NO," that comes from my soul.

My body falls to the ground at the impact of being shot and the sound of my name being called reaches my muffled ears just as the pain begins to make itself known.

The feeling of warm blood running down my arm to my fingers is only of fleeting recognition. I cry out from the ripping of muscle and bone as the bullet enters my body. In the grass, my vision is fuzzy, but I never let go of my weapon.

He... Shot... Me?

CHAPTER 50

Cory

IT'S BEEN TOO MUCH time.

She should be home by now.

I shrug off the idea that maybe I'm being clingy.

One thing I know about Reese is that she loves attention. If I am being clingy, that's exactly how she wants it.

Taking my phone out of my pocket, I select her contact and press the small phone icon.

It rings and rings before ultimately going to a non-personalized voicemail message. I call again with the same result.

Something twists in my gut, telling me to treat this more seriously. Something is not right. If I were blocked, it wouldn't even ring.

I drive to the ranch. Though it is only a few miles from me, it feels like hours as I creep down the dark country roads.

When I get to Reese's house, alarm bells are ringing as I see that her truck is not parked horribly in the spot where she normally parks it. Where it was parked earlier.

There is a shiny black Mustang similar to her old car. I have a feeling about who it belongs to, which only makes me more nervous. I don't fucking like this.

I park and get out of my truck to look for any clues about where Reese could be.

In the distance, I can see the illumination from headlights going down the path away from the barn.

That must be her.

Why would she be going out there this late at night? It just doesn't seem right.

I'm running toward her before I can give it a second thought. I try to keep to the areas of their property that don't have much light so that I don't alert anyone of my presence. There are only a few safety lights that have all been triggered from them driving the path.

Staying close to the fence until I can get close enough to them, I hear Alex droning on about something. I can't hear over my own heavy breathing, and my heart sinks when my suspicions are proven true.

Alex brought her here. Why?

There is no chance that whatever is going down here is friendly. I dial nine-one-one and hang up before I creep around the side of the truck opposite of them where he can't see me.

They're facing off by the large pile of manure and she takes a step toward him. "...no one else will have you ever again but me." He says and aims a gun at her heart. I'm moving from behind the truck and running toward them.

I have no weapon.

No plan for what I'll do.

But I know I can't let her go through this with no one by her side.

I'm here for you always. I wrote those words to her, and here are the actions to back them up.

Alex says, "You are mi—" but his words are cut off when Reese takes a chance ramming her hand into the gut of the man holding the gun and I hear it go off.

The loud bang of the bullet being released from the chamber echoes around me. Time stands still for a moment as I see her fall backward into the grass at the impact of being hit.

"Reese!" I don't think. I'm running to where Alex lies, clutching at his stomach while he's also trying to reach his firearm again.

It's no use because I'm there, kicking the gun out of his reach before he can do any more damage.

I press my boot on his hand clutching his side. He cries as I let the full weight of my body rest on his wound. "If you come near *my girl* again—it will be the last thing you ever do, fucker." I take my foot off his stomach only to raise my foot and deliver a swift kick to his side. I leave him to suffer in the product of his own miserable choices.

Then, I'm over to where she lays in the grass. There's blood everywhere. Her shirt is soaked as she holds an arm to her body.

"Baby?" I ask. "Please, please. Baby, are you awake?" I brush the hair sticking to her sweaty face and kiss her forehead. Her eyes are squeezed shut and she looks like she's in incredible pain. I tug her body closer to mine, trying to see how she's hurt, but she wails.

I don't know what to do. I don't know how she's injured and I don't want to make anything worse.

Blood oozes from a wound in her arm, and I sigh in relief that the bullet didn't hit something more vital. The headlights from her truck give us some light but not much.

"Cory?" She asks, eyes still screwed shut. I pull her body closer to mine. I can feel her trembling. She says, "You came to save me," through stuttering breaths.

I cup her face and tears roll down my cheek. "Of course, I came. I love you, I knew something was wrong. I should have never let you stay here alone. I should—"

She shakes her head faintly saying, "Shhh." I try to grab her hand, but it's clenched around something. I can't tell what it is for all the blood.

I stroke her fingers anyway, trying to coax her into loosening her grip.

I huff a laugh, taking it from her to look it over. "A knife?" I look back to her smirking face. "Where did you get this?"

"A lady never reveals her secrets," she says between stuttering breaths.

A sense of pride comes over me as I look down to Reese in my arms. Will I ever stop being impressed by this gorgeous woman? Probably never.

The sound of the ambulance rings in the distance. "Come on, pretty girl. You have to stay awake. That's your ride."

***

"I'M SO GLAD YOU'RE here. The flowers are beautiful, Cory. She's awake if you want to give them to her yourself." Chandie looks tired, but I know she's been here all night with her daughter.

I only left the property when the ambulance had her safe and secure to come to the nearest hospital, which is a couple of towns over. Chandie rode with her to the hospital and assured me that she would be safe with her now.

The police asked me several questions on the scene when they found Alex as I showed him where he was.

A second ambulance was called for him, and I can't say that I'm relieved that he survived long enough to be stabilized.

I came back to Janet's for the night. I didn't get any sleep after I showered all of Reese's blood off of me.

I was too busy counting down the hours until I got any notification from Chandie that Reese was going to be fine and that I could come and see her.

Her mom huffs out a long sigh and says, "There is also something that I think you should know."

She ushers us over to the opposite side of the hallway from Reese's room and my stomach sinks. "What is it?"

"There was information gathered to suggest that they know exactly who shared all those photos of Reese and Alex." She chokes up a bit and I rubbed her arm.

Taking a deep breath, I ask, "Who did it, Chandie?"

"Apparently, Alex had been sleeping with his assistant, as well. Dumb bastard never even password protected his phone. She sent all their pictures to herself. That was the only lead they needed to find out it was also her who got into Rebecca's account."

She squeezes my arm. "Don't tell Reese yet. I don't want to upset her, but I just thought that you should know... after everything." She sighs. "I'm so happy you were there, Cory. I've known this man for over thirty years. I never knew... I may not even have a daughter anymore if you weren't." She shakes her head again.

"It's me who is lucky. She's strong and resilient. Everything will be okay. I know it, Chandie."

She nods, giving me a hug. Danny comes to Chandie's side and removes her. He holds out his hand and I take it. "We really are so grateful you were there." He shakes my hand adding, "We'll be right outside." Danny nods toward the room and I head that way.

Nothing could prepare me for what I'm seeing as I walk into the recovery area. Reese lays in a hospital gown with her hair piled on top of her head. She looks fragile and small with her arm in a cast.

She still looks beautiful and it takes my breath away to see her alive and not covered in blood like before.

"Hi," I say despite my dry throat. I'm overcome with emotion and I'm exhausted from not sleeping well last night, but she's alive.

She's alive.

"Hey," she says, pushing the table from over her to sit up. "Are the boys with you?"

I come to her side and help her, adjusting the thin pillow behind her back. "No," I respond. "I can bring them by later if you want."

She flashes me a sad smile, "I don't want them to see me like this. Not yet." She lifts her casted arm into view.

Placing the flowers on the table, I stand next to her bed, feeling awkward. I look for a hand to hold, but neither seems like a safe bet. I settle for placing my hand on her calf. "I'm so happy you're okay. Well," I look at the tube and monitors attached to her, amending, "I'm just happy you're alive."

"Smooth, Cory. Real smooth." She teases.

I laugh despite the situation. Everything that has happened in the past twenty four hours flashes through my brain. A high with getting her back and then the lowest of lows thinking that I could lose her forever.

Looking into her beautiful brown eyes, I say, "You look like prey."

She licks her lips before her smile brightens, "More like roadkill."

"I've got to work today, but when you're out of here you'll call me?"

"Only if you leave me your letterman." She nods to my jacket and winks.

I take it off and place it next to the vase I brought.

She shakes her head, "No, no. I want it now."

I bring it to her laying it on her body like a blanket. She shifts down into it, burying her nose into the fabric. "Are you smelling it?"

"Of course. It smells just like home."

Like home.

I get as close to her as I can to kiss her forehead. "I love you, Reese."

Heading out of the room to get to work, I hear, "I love you, Cory."

There was a moment last night where I never thought I would hear her say it again.

I turn back at the door. "I love you."

CHAPTER 51

Reese, Two Months Later

"I never knew what this would feel like."

I look at Cory's ex-wife, who has come to sit next to me on the bench behind Jan's house. "What do you mean?" I ask.

I was watching the mini Corys play before Vanessa's visitation time started today. Over the past few weeks, she and I have been ships passing in the night because I really just didn't want to deal with whatever she could dish out. From everything I've heard about this woman, she is the big bad.

Have I not been through enough?

"I guess being replaced." She chuffs a pitiful sound.

Okay. I was not expecting that.

The last thing I want is to play this petty game of "who took who's man." If she feels that way, I want to put an end to it as soon as I can. "I could never replace you, Vanessa. They will al—"

"Spare me the diatribe. I know that I brought them into this world, but I failed them. Many times. I'm happy that he found you. That they have you now. They never looked at me the same way they look at you."

I think about what she's saying. Does she mean just the boys or Cory too? It's hard to tell. Vanessa doesn't act like the jealous ex I suspected she would be like. I don't want to think about what it's like to lose someone like Cory. Or his sons for that fact. I love all four of them with everything in my heart.

What must it feel like to see me standing in the place she may have thought she was going to fill?

"You know, it may not be what you want to hear, but I don't think you failed them. People make mistakes." Hers were massive. But it's not my place to judge anyone on their past blunders. I've made many myself. "I can't say that I know what it's like to be pregnant or have kids, but everything happens for a reason. Here you are now, trying to make it right."

Truthfully, everything in their marriage has nothing to do with me. I'd rather leave all that in the past. I feel immense pride that Cory has opened up to me about his life with her and his struggles with their changing custody agreement now. He's my partner, and I'll support him in every way I can, no matter how uncomfortable it can be sometimes.

"My mom wants me to hate you so badly. I almost listened to her. You're right. Here I am. And I want to be there for them."

"Reese! Did you see my flip? I flipped right off and— Bren notices Vanessa sitting next to me and continues after a big inhale, "Mom, did you see me? Did you see my flip?"

She smiles at him. I smile at the two of them. I don't feel jealous, just happy to be a part of this when it was almost gone forever.

"It was fantastic, B! We need to get you into the Olympics soon." Vanessa says.

Bren beams at us both before bounding back toward the swing he's been flipping off of. Afro curls flying back behind him in his haste.

CJ sits under an Ash tree in the corner, reading a comic, living in his own world. He gives us a wave after Bren speeds by him, ruffling the pages of his book.

Gabe toddles over to my knees with his lizard in hand. He puts the stuffy on my lap and climbs onto the bench between his mother and I to drink from his cup. The small boy watches his brothers as they play. I lean over to kiss his forehead and he leans into my side.

Never in a million years would I think I'd be sitting on a bench with my boyfriend's ex-wife watching their kids, and it be cordial. Casual, even. I would be lying if I said I minded it one bit.

"THIS IS AMAZING PROGRESS, Reese. You have been honest with yourself and put in the work to see these positive changes in your life. Do you see the transformation?" My therapist asks me.

With Cory, it took several days to unpack all the past trauma I have been through. For it all, he held my hands and allowed me to stop when it was all becoming too much. Several times, he would curse and need breaks of his own when he learned about the parts of my life that included Teddy. Those parts that Mack would not have been able to tell him. We cried together for that young girl who was led down a path she couldn't see a way out of. We cried for the pain I swallowed and never let go of. But we both felt better having everything exposed and open.

"I do." I nod my head and twist my hands in my lap. She doesn't force me to elaborate, instead choosing to let the silence hang in the air. On my laptop screen, she waits patiently for me to lead our discussion.

It's been a few weeks since Teddy shot me. After everything that happened in the past month and really over the past eight years, I knew it was time to talk to someone. Lidia Rafael-Dominguez specializes in sexual trauma and post-traumatic stress counseling.

Positive changes.

The legal ramifications that Alex "Teddy" Stewart faces with Dawn are just the tip of the iceberg. Thankfully, they both were inexperienced and left so much for the police to find regarding my case. Both of them are facing a year in jail with heavy fines on top. His reputation rests in pieces. He's unable to play the mourning boyfriend with two witnesses who can attest to his murderous intent. My turmoil with Alex is long from over, but it feels like the beginning of justice. I'm thankful he survived to face it.

I've had Cory and my friends to lean on in this trying time. With their help, I've kept somewhat sane after everything went down. I couldn't have dreamed up a better support system once you factor in my mom and dad.

Mack has to face more than the sordid past his father and I share. Now he knows his dad tried to kill me, as well. My friend cannot seem to catch a break. My heart truly aches for all he has been through in the last year.

My brace itches, though my arm is mostly healed from the humerus fracture the bullet caused. I haven't been able to ride in weeks, but it's left more time to apply for a business program online.

I formally stepped down from the COO position with MHA. It was an easy decision to make and my parents understood. I'll be back when I feel more confident in my business aptitude. In the meantime, I've become very familiar with paperwork and learning more about how to operate the business from my dad. I have big dreams for Mason Ranch and once I get my bearings, I'll be back as head bitch to put more of my plans in action.

"I have so much to look forward to that I am grateful for," I add. The transformation she talked about earlier starting to become more clear. I am in a much better place now than I have been in years past.

"That's good." She smiles at my smile. "Well, our session is just about done. Do you want to meet at the same time next week?"

"Yes, that will be good for me," I say and I close the laptop after we say our goodbyes.

Placing the computer on my nightstand, I take the small white card from its spot next to my lamp and lie back in bed.

Just like the other bouquets that Cory arranged for me, the one he brought to my hospital room had a note attached to it. I grin thinking about how he was there for me when no one else was that night. The cardstock has already softened from how much I've read this thing.

> **Reese,**
>
> **Nothing shines brighter than a smile on your face. Nothing makes me happier than a laugh from your lips. Nothing makes me more complete than your love.**
>
> **I love you,**
>
> **Cory**

My phone buzzes next to me and I pick it up.

Cory : Should I pick you up for the party?

I tell him that I'm riding over with Chandie and Danny. Cory has officially moved out of his aunt's house and into a place of his own. An Alpenglow Ridge resident now. He's been so hush-hush about it that I only know it's in town. I'm excited to see it at this point. Even the boys have told me that they love it and that I will too.

I'm anxious to see his new place. My doctor told me that activity was ok at this point and I'll start physical therapy in the next week. But still, Cory has been resisting my advances because he doesn't want to hurt me.

That time is over today.

"You ready to go, honey?" Chandie asks me from the doorway.

I grab the gift bag from my dresser. "Yep. Let's go see this new place."

Epilogue - Cory

"Dad, I need to tell you something."

"What is it Bren?" I drop to a knee in front of him so I can hear him over the music and people that have showed up to celebrate my new place.

"I invited someone to our warming house party."

"That's great, man. Just don't run through the house. If you're gonna play, do it in the backyard."

"I don't think she's gonna run through the house, dad. She has really good manners."

"She? Who did you invite?" I ask.

"Me." My gaze travels up toned legs to a very familiar green dress, landing on the gorgeous face of my very favorite person—now without a cast, but a brace instead.

Who I actually invited, not him.

"Reese." She gives me a tentative little wave. It takes me a moment longer to realize that I'm still on one knee in front of her. Bren darts out of the way and I call, "Don't run in the house," after him, though he's long gone.

Her glow is back. Even brighter than before, though her hair is straight and black now. Just like when I saw her for the first time, my heart races in my chest. I can see the harness winking in the kitchen light above as my gaze travels down her body again.

She looks fucking delicious.

"Oh, um, this is for you." She hands me a gift bag with tissue paper sticking out of the top. I can't tell what's inside from the bag. "It's a mug. I put the gift receipt inside."

"I'm sure I won't need that. Thank you."

"Congratulations, must be a relief to be out of that old bat's house, huh?" Her dad says, coming into the kitchen behind her.

"I heard that, Danny!" Jan calls from the dining room, where I now realize she's been listening in. He chuckles and gives me a couple of pats on the arm.

"Yea congrats, honey." Chandie says, giving me a kiss on the cheek. Leading her husband by the arm to the dining room, where Janet and Sammie are talking to a few of their other friends.

We stand awkwardly by the kitchen island for a bit, unsure of what to say. Though we have been talking since the attack at her Ranch, Reese has been keeping mostly to herself to recover. With the continuous influx of new business and subsequent new employees, I've been just as busy.

She breaks the silence saying, "It's really so nice, Cory. Bren tells me that they all have their own rooms now."

I have been looking at places for a while and this one was too great of an opportunity to pass up. "Yea. I got lucky that the Carr's are moving to Wyoming. Everything has been newly renovated. I can give you the tour if you want?"

"I would love to look around." Taking her hand, we walk through the kitchen to the stairs.

The first room we look at is CJ's which already has Marvel posters and a bookshelf with his comics and figurines stored neatly in rows. The daylight streams in through the windows and I see Reese taking in all the details. "I could probably have guessed this was his room without you telling me."

I laugh at her assessment, "It's true. The boy does love comics."

The other bedroom upstairs is Bren's. It looks like a tornado hit it, with clothes and toys strewn everywhere. I snag a small pair of underwear hanging from the footboard and throw them into the hamper.

"Definitely Bren's room," she says with a giggle.

"I asked him to straighten up in here before everyone came over." I shrug and close his door as we walk through the other areas upstairs including a little room I'm in the process of turning into a small home gym.

"This house is much bigger than I thought it was from the outside."

"Just wait til you see downstairs. And the yard. I haven't had much time, but I will make it look like I actually live here. Old man Carr didn't really care about anything but green grass. It is a nice lawn, so I'm not being ungrateful. It's just missing..."

"Some color," she finishes for me with a knowing smile.

"Um... yea," I chuckle and bite my lip. "It needs more color."

We walk back downstairs and the absence of chatter from before rings through the house.

From the dining room, I can see that everyone has moved outside to enjoy the sun setting over the mountains. Like the incredible view from the Mason's back porch, we have the same setup where the back of the house faces the mountain range perfectly.

"C'mon, I'll show you Gabe's room." I hold Reese's hand again as we walk through the hall which remains bare as I haven't put any art up yet.

I've painted one wall in his room green and various reptile stuffed animals sit on floating shelves I've hung. His room is the closest to mine, so when we leave, Reese asks, "What's over here?"

"That's the master. You wanna see it?" I raise an eyebrow.

"If you don't mind." She says with an eyebrow raised back at me.

"Not at all." I'm grateful that I did straighten up in here and it still smells like the products from my shower earlier.

She walks over to the bed resting a hand on one of the footboard poles. Her fingers trail the bedding and she turns on one of the lamps from the nightstand.

My dark grey bedspread and pillows are arranged neatly. There are no picture frames anywhere. My work boots sit by the door and the infamous letterman jacket we seem to be trading back and forth lays over the microsuede chair in the far corner.

She sits at the foot of my bed, nodding slowly. She pats the bed next to her. "You look uncomfortable. I promise I don't bite. Unless you want." She adds with a wink.

I grin at her teasing from where I'm leaning in the doorway. Wasting no time, I join her on the bed. My hand drifts along her jawline. The feel of her soft skin entices me to brush her hair over her shoulder to trace her long neck. She shivers, looking into my eyes. "So you're officially a country boy living in Alpenglow Ridge now, huh?"

"I don't know if I'd say that. There are some perks about AR, that I've come around to."

She leans in to kiss me but before she presses those full, soft lips to mine, she asks, "Like what?"

"You."

"Can I kiss you now?" Her sultry eyes focused on my lips.

I nod my head and she kisses me fiercely. Her mouth trying to take ownership of mine and I don't resist her.

She climbs onto my lap and I can feel the heat of her through my shorts as she settles her weight onto me. My hands lift her dress up over her hips, at first so that she can get comfortable.

She breaks our kiss to pull it up and over her head, being careful to not catch it on her brace. The little pink lace thong she wears catches my eyes, but the matching tiny lace bra begs for my mouth.

I hold on to her, nipping a trail from her neck to her tits catching the chain in my lips every so often. She grinds down on me and my dick is begging to get more of her attention but I don't want to rush her. I know that she's been impatient, but she wasn't there cradling the love of her life as she bled out in the night. I don't want to hurt her.

I tentatively bite her nipple through the fabric. The sexiest moan caresses my ears. I want to hear it over and over again. I bite the other, deciding right then that I need this bra off, and I need it off right now.

I recognize the charm right away.

Mine. I smirk down at it, licking the skin around it and Reese pants, "You're wearing too many clothes, Cory." When I don't get up right away, she huffs, "Stop treating me with kid gloves! I want you and I don't want to wait anymore to get fucked hard by my boyfriend."

Boyfriend. That's all it takes and my restraint snaps.

I flip her onto the bed, standing between her legs. I tug the t-shirt over my head and she makes quick work of unbuttoning my shorts, pushing my boxers down with them.

My dick springs free in front of her. She looks up into my eyes as she pushes me by my thighs away from the bed. She slides down the bed. I look back to my bedroom door to make sure that it's closed.

Small miracles. It is.

Those alluring eyes capture mine again as she grabs ahold of me. I wrap her hair around my fist and watch as she licks all around my tip. Focusing on breathing through my nose, I let her take her time teasing me with lavish licks around the rim of my head. "Just like that, pretty girl. Drive me crazy."

She smiles around my dick as she takes me deeper leaving little pink rings from her lip gloss on me. I grab the base of my shaft pulling it from her mouth. She moans, letting her tongue trace along the underside of me. "Stick out your tongue baby." She listens and I slap my dick down a few times and she digs her nails into my thigh.

"You want it in your mouth?" She nods.

"In your throat?" She nods more fervently and wraps her lips around me, sucking me deep. She grips my thigh as I begin to work up to a rhythm that she can keep up with.

She gags and a tear begins to roll. I wipe it with my thumb. "Fuuuck Reese. Look at you choking on this dick like it's yours." She holds onto my thigh, keeping the suction tight on me, when I try to pull out. "It's yours. You like that, huh?" She starts bobbing, but I swear I'm gonna bust right now if I let her keep going. I feel my nut tightening in my balls, but I keep breathing, holding on to my release.

Using her hair around my hand, I halt her motion. She looks up at me, defiantly using that little tongue to lick the thick vein back and forth.

"Don't I get a taste?" I ask. "I've been waiting so long for you, pretty girl." And I have. I mean more than just the past few months, but for long before I even met her in that hallway.

This woman is my blessing.

She releases my dick with a pop, wiping the corners of her mouth. "Come taste me then." She hops back onto the bed, rubbing her clit over the little lace thong on her knees. Her eyes never leave mine as she begins to moan, throwing her head back with her mouth in a little "O."

Crawling over her, she giggles and makes her way up the bed. I pull her thong off, tossing it into the room somewhere. Wrapping her legs around me, I feel how wet she is as my balls tingle in anticipation when my dick slides through her lips with ease. I let her down and spread her thighs to get a better view of her pretty pussy, begging for more attention. I slip a finger inside her and sigh. "Baby, you're dripping for me."

She nods with a smug smile, "Your dick in my mouth did just the trick. I've been thinking about it every time Pinky has come to the rescue." A growl rumbles through my chest, thinking about how she's been coming on that toy instead of me for the past few months, and my mouth waters.

I can't wait any longer to taste her. She needs me. My tongue flicks over her pussy and I push my finger back inside her.

Her thighs squeeze my head and I use my other hand to give me enough room to lick over her clit. Teasing her as I add another finger. "You're so tight," I groan over her bundle of nerves. She shivers again, bucking her pussy into my face trying to get more friction. "I've missed this."

"Cory, please. Just lick my clit. I need—" She gasps when I suck it into my mouth and curl my fingers inside of her. "Like that baby. Please don't stop." She chants as I eat her like she's my favorite meal.

Because she is.

"Every time I have this sweet pussy in my mouth, I can't get enough. Are you gonna come for me, pretty girl?"

She shudders into my mouth on a cry she muffles into my pillow as her orgasm rips through her.

She drags me up her body kissing me and stroking my dick until she can slide it inside.

We both sigh as she adjusts around me.

"Baby..." I look into her eyes with the question I know she can guess.

"I'm on birth control. I want this." I still, and she grabs my face with her fingers in my beard. "I love you."

I'm truly gone for this woman. "I love you, Reese."

Whatever she wants, it's hers.

I stroke into her slowly, cherishing her body until we're both spent and panting on the bed.

<hr>

"CAN I OPEN THIS now?" I ask when we make it back to the kitchen after cleaning up.

"Yea... I definitely think you'll like it." She winks.

I toss the paper onto the counter and take the white box from the green gift bag. A deep laugh burst from me when I finally pulled the mug from the box. "World's Best DILF, huh?"

Reese laughs a bit at herself and nods emphatically. "I'll say," she smirks.

"I can't say I'm mad that my girl has a plan." I grab her by the waist, bringing her close enough so her chest heaves against mine with her laugh. The joy and relief in her eyes makes my heart squeeze even more.

Satisfied and content... with me.

I put that look on her face, and I want to keep it there.

We walk out into the backyard, and no one balks at us hand in hand.

CJ and Bren make space for us at the largest table. They carry on in their conversation as if nothing has ever come between us.

Because nothing ever will again.

The End.

Thank You for Reading!

Thank you for joining me on this journey through Saddled with Finesse. Your time and support mean the world to me, and I hope you've fallen in love with the characters and their story as much as I have! **Want more from Cory and Reese? Read their steamy bonus epilogue here to find out how Cory proposed to Reese.**

https://zeakayleighgalan.com/saddled-bonus-epilogue

Share Your Thoughts

If you enjoyed this book, leaving a review is one of the best ways to support authors like me. Reviews help other readers discover stories they'll love, and your voice matters! **Leave your review on Amazon or your favorite review site!**

Keep the Love Going

Saddled with Finesse is part of the Alpenglow Ridge series. Dive deeper into the world of Alpenglow Ridge with these other books in the series:

Verse to Acclimate: Years after heartbreak tore them apart, a broken small-town girl and country music's rising star must face the scars of their past to find out if love is worth a second chance.

Tropes: Second Chance, Best Friend's Brother, First Love, He Falls First, Mutual Pining

Whisk til Peaked: Trapped by a snowstorm in a luxury resort with only one bed, a single mom and her loyal best friend must confront unspoken desires and buried secrets that could shatter everything they hold dear—or finally bring them together.

Tropes: Best Friends to Lovers, Single Mom, Snowed in/Forced Proximity, He Falls First

Roped on the Ridge: She woke up with no memory, a past full of secrets, and a cowboy who refuses to give up on her... even when the truth threatens to destroy them both.

Tropes: Amnesia, Roommates, Black Cat x Golden Retriever, Surprise Pregnancy

Hope by the Horizon: When a guarded hippotherapist clashes with charming ranch hand, their undeniable chemistry ignites a journey of trust, healing, and unexpected love—if they can overcome their pasts. [FREE NOVELLA]

Tropes: Boss/Employee, Reformed Playboy, Grumpy/Sunshine, He Falls First

You can find all my books on my website: www.zeakayleighgalan.com

Stay Connected

Want to be the first to hear about new releases, exclusive content, and special offers?

Sign up for my newsletter at www.zeakayleighgalan.com/news

A Special Treat Just for You

Keep reading for an exclusive sneak peek at the next book in the Alpenglow Ridge series. Get ready to meet new characters, revisit familiar faces, and fall in love all over again.

Thank you for being part of this journey. I can't wait to hear what you think!

Hugs,
Zea Kayleigh Galan

Sneak Peek

MELODY

Checking my dress for the last time, I grab my clutch and exit the vehicle.

Walking to QB's, I feel my curls swinging along my back and shoulders as I do my most confident strut to the door. Head held high and hips swaying, I find an ease in pretending this event hasn't worried me.

You finish a thing the way you start a thing. Strong. My mom's words call to me from a memory.

I'm here for my friends, and it will be fine, I say to myself as I near the building.

Two easels flank the main doors as streamers blow softly in the breeze. A collection of Polaroid photos pop out from a bokeh background on the canvas. The top left shows Cory hugging Reese from behind, laughing. She leans forward with a big toothy grin, laughing too. The middle shows Reese holding Cory's chin while she kisses his cheek. The last photo on the bottom right shows them staring into each other's eyes with the kiss print bright on his cheek.

They look absolutely adorable on these candids! They are the cutest couple. It's obvious to anyone with eyes that they are obsessed with each other. I almost can't believe it took Reese two years to finally say yes to his proposal.

I take a deep breath and pull the doors open. It's still pretty quiet since guests don't start arriving for another half hour. I have been in this bar far more times than I can count, but the decorations in the entry have me feeling a little lost.

Making my way into the main bar area, I walk through the employee doors to the small server's station, looking for any of my friends. No one I'm looking for is there or in the office. My stomach grumbles and I give up looking.

Okay, new focus.

Following the delicious aroma of barbecued meat, I find the buffet table on the far left side of the large bar area. A few of the normal tables have been removed from the floor to make space for the new addition. Opposite the food is a microphone stand and a few chairs that are set up like there will be a live band. Reese didn't mention hiring anyone, and I just assumed she'd have a playlist or something.

I don't think about that further because my stomach grumbles again in an obscene way. I look around to see if anyone heard the stomach complaints. A few of the bar's normal servers are helping with the party, but they aren't close enough to me to have heard. I blow out a heavy sigh of relief and take in the bar's new decor for the event.

Bouquets of anemones are arranged in short, clear vases everywhere. A mixture of purple and white anemones are arranged with cobalt blue delphinium and tree fern wisps. *So beautiful!* Must be Cory's doing. There are some along the bartop, on the bar tables, and a few hang from the beams near the walls. Streamers of blue and purple are hung around the doorways and from the posts at each end of the bar. Around the edges of the buffet table are the same streamers and vases. More of the couple's polaroids hang in various places around the low-lit room.

My fingers fidget with my necklace as I look all around me. I'm in awe of the work Chloe has done for the bar outside of the florals. What was once the luxe man space of QB's is now an elegant event space to celebrate Reese and Cory's engagement. Chloe has always had an eye for this sort of thing. My old room at Daddy's always made me think of her.

And *him.*

Heaping potato salad onto a forest green paper plate that is already overflowing with food, I decide to just grab a second plate. Tender brisket, smoked sausage, and two kinds of chicken legs are piled next to the mac and cheese and grilled corn on the cob.

Chandie outdid herself!

Would having the baked sweet potato and potato salad be overdoing it? Eh, better to be safe rather than sorry, so I put the sweet potato half on my second plate, along with some buttered dinner rolls.

Do I regret missing both meals today?

Yes.

But am I happy that I have extra room to taste everything on this table?

Also, yes.

Walking from the buffet table, I spot Chloe arranging name cards near the main couple's table by the performing area. She looks beautiful in her long mermaid dress, which is the color of sapphires. Her sharp nude pumps peek out of a split that runs up the maxi-length dress to her knee. Chloe's long bob flutters in wide curls that swoop away from her face in a side part. A comb with little blue sparkling gems pulls back the hair on her right side behind her ear. "I wanna be you when I grow up, okay?"

Looking up from her task, she does a little jump with her arms tucked in before she wraps an arm around me and squeezes. "Cinnabon, you know there's only one Chloe Bridges." Gesturing to herself from head to toe, she sighs deeply, like the information just pains her to relay to me.

In her mind, it probably does.

The Chloe Bridges is both glam AF and the craftiest chick around. I bet she made all these decorations... with her hands.

I roll my eyes and give her a bump with my hip. I put my plates down on the table, saying, "You know what I mean, Clo."

Each of the cards she's placing has either a picture with Reese and a guest or Cory and a guest. I see the picture of Mack and Reese hugging on the little card Chloe places by his seat. I can feel my eyes starting to water.

I'm happy for Reese. So happy for them! But I don't want to see Mack and have to be okay. To pretend that hurting him doesn't still hurt me. I have always cared for Mack, and I have so much love in my heart for him.

But it wasn't enough.

Nothing was enough.

It's hard living in the same town as him. Our lives are so close to each other. I'd like to celebrate my friend without him though.

Clarity of just how uncomfortable tonight will be runs down my back in a shudder.

"You will find someone, Mel." Chloe starts rubbing my back in soothing circles. She moves a curl back into place before continuing. "Or maybe you will find peace in loving yourself. Reese will appreciate the support tonight but, baby, this..." She motions to the general area of my face with her hand. "The sad eyes need to go. You look stunning and I need you to put the Mel smile on and celebrate!"

The Mel smile.

Right.

I know she means well. She and Mack were friends long before I came into the picture. Hell, they all grew up together. At this moment, I can recognize my selfishness. Tonight is about Cory and Reese.

They shouldn't have to choose which of us gets to hang out with them. What Mack and I had, it's over. It's just awkward now. I'm an expert at figuring out which of the group outings he will be at or not. If Cory is there, Mack likely will be too. Subtle questions about the activities can help too. I don't know how often I've been "sick" or had a class "run long" in order to skip out on the events he is also attending. I don't have the answers Mack wants and I'd hate to have my friends pick up on what actually happened between us. I fiddle with my clutch bag for a beat before I give her a suspecting look.

"Don't give me that look! I'm not picking sides. You both needed to move on. You wanted the divorce. That is all I need to know. I'm not in the middle. Get lost in the ambiance I created for celebrating tonight. Please?" She presses her palms together in front of her face mock-pleading with me. Her bottom lip pokes out a bit, and I know what I have to do.

I reel back and push my hair over my shoulders. Rolling them back, I put my hands on my hips and draw my knees together so that one foot leans to the side. I changed my stance entirely to mimic my very best old Hollywood starlet. "My apologies, darling. Does this suit the ambiance better?"

I'm barely able to hold the pose before we both erupt into laughter.

When I first moved to town, I told Chloe about how my old dance instructor would make us all do this pose before our jazz ballet performances. It was ridiculous then, and it still makes me laugh to think how it did make me feel more confident. It at least helps me get rid of these nerves.

I hug my friend because she really has been there for me in so many ways. She squeezes me back before we both check if we smudged the other's makeup.

"As a matter of fact, I think that will—"

Reese cuts Chloe off by coming over to the two of us, placing her hands on our shoulders. Her face is unsmiling when she looks at my friend saying, "I take it that you haven't told her yet. You said you would tell her, Clo."

Chloe's eyes dart to me quickly before looking back to Reese. They have a silent conversation involving eye bulging and head nodding.

I step out of her hold and face my friends. "Well, can someone tell me? I don't care who." I check my phone and see that the party is only fifteen minutes from starting.

It's Chloe who finally looks at me saying, "Don't panic, okay?"

"You must know that telling someone not to panic, signals them to absolutely panic!" I'm flapping my hands out to the side of my face as if the fanning will cool down how hot it's getting in here.

"Good point. I'm gonna just rip it off like a bandaid!" Reese steps between Clo and me like she's shielding my friend from harm.

Chloe steps from behind Reese. "No. I will. Ty is playing for the event. He and his band will be the entertainment for tonight, and it is not a big deal."

"Oh."

Much worse than I thought.

Much, *much* worse than I thought.

Mack, I can expect. I know him. Tyson... I don't think I can handle. The last time I talked to him ended in... catastrophe.

"Yea, like she said. It's no big deal." Reese gives me an encouraging smile, arranging some curls around my face. "He's gonna play some songs, and that's it. No big deal."

"Oh." I go back to flapping at my face and breathing in and out slowly.

"We didn't want you to freak out. Mel, we know that breakup was hard. But... we are all adults... and we can be civilized. It's not a big deal anymore." Chloe says, but there's a roaring in my ears that's growing the longer I stand here.

Why does everyone keep saying it's no big deal—when it very clearly is!

"You didn't want me to—yeah, okay. I'm gonna just run to the bathroom real quick. Excuse me."

I hear my heels click on the wood floor faster and faster as I go to the bar restroom and push past the door.

How can I still be so upset?

I stare at my reflection. I look flustered under my makeup and my eyes are glassy.

I don't want to deal with any of this tonight.

The drama or the men.

This is for Cory and Reese, who are like family to me.

Shit.

I should have expected Mack would be here. He and Cory have become like best friends,

Of course, he would be there. No big deal at all.

It's been years.

Holding on to that sentiment as tightly as I can, I take ten deep breaths. I blot my face with a cool, damp paper towel, hoping the placebo will take effect. When I feel calm enough, I straighten my shoulders and exit the restroom.

I'm two steps down the hallway when the setting sun nearly blinds me as the side employee doors open.

I stop and hold my hand up to shield my eyes. Continuing to walk toward the main bar entrance again.

With equipment under both arms and the guitar strap I would recognize anywhere crossing his chest, Tyson shuffles into the building.

My feet are glued to the spot because I don't know what to do. The surprise on my face is mirrored in his.

No *big deal.*

KEEP READING...

<u>VERSE TO ACCLIMATE HERE!</u>

Acknowledgements

The first person I need to thank is Bryan. You have been my very best friend for so many years now. I love you more than words can express. I don't know where I would be without you, mi rey.

My babysita, mini me, and biggest cheerleader is next. I love you N. You are always there to celebrate, way too early, and I love you for it. You remind me that even small victories are worth big celebrations.

To my mom. Thank you for showing me that words have meaning. Writing is catharsis and illumination. Most importantly, thank you for showing me that sharing your truth through language is worth the hustle, every time.

To my gram. Welcome to smutlandia. Thank you for your unending support and everlasting faith in my ambition. Your generous heart and compassion for others are some of my best qualities. Thank you for showing me that joy has no expiration.

To Karime Garza. Your friendship and presence in my life are never something I will take for granted! My favorite black cat and most honest friend, may we forever share our soapbox and find our next favorite reads together.

To my beta readers. Abby, Britt, Brooklyn, Faith, and Karime! I love you all for taking a chance and helping me make it through this release. Without you, I would be lost! Big, big thank you ladies!

To my BIBLIOBABES! I love you all so, so much! Your support pushed me to finally publish this story and I will never forget that. You're the best friends a girl could ask for!

To my ARC readers. It means the world to me that you dedicated your time to reading this book and sharing your opinions of it with others! I am so grateful!

To you! Hi! Thank you for reading my words! I hope that you enjoyed them and will stick around for more of the journey! I would hug you if I could! Hopefully, we will hug one day!

Also by Zea Kayleigh Galan

Alpenglow Ridge

SADDLED WITH FINESSE — Can their unexpected kiss ignite a love strong enough to overcome the shadows of her past and give him the fresh start he's been searching for?

Verse to Acclimate — Years after heartbreak tore them apart, a broken small-town girl and country music's rising star must face the scars of their past to find out if love is worth a second chance.

Whisk til Peaked — Trapped by a snowstorm in a luxury resort with only one bed, a single mom and her loyal best friend must confront unspoken desires and buried secrets that could shatter everything they hold dear—or finally bring them together.

Hope by the Horizon — When a guarded hippotherapist clashes with charming ranch hand, their undeniable chemistry ignites a journey of trust, healing, and unexpected love—if they can overcome their pasts. (Read FREE https://zeakayleighgalan.com/free-novella)

Roped on the Ridge — She woke up with no memory, a past full of secrets, and a cowboy who refuses to give up on her... even when the truth threatens to destroy them both.

Shades of Vengeance

<u>Into the Blue</u> — A cold-hearted crime boss discovers that he can't let go of a dancer at his nightclub after she is attacked by his rival.

<u>Written in Red</u> — A dark stalker romance coming 2026!

Thomas Family Saga

<u>Perfect Harmony</u> — An ambitious lawyer needs a fiancée to climb the ladder and his best friend agrees, but somewhere between the ring and their kiss, pretending starts to feel like the truth.

<u>Fierce Harmony</u> — A rivals to lovers small town romance coming 2026.

About the Author

Zea is a passionate storyteller who brings romance to life with heartfelt emotion and unforgettable characters. A lifelong lover of love stories, she weaves her background in anthropology into crafting tales where swoon-worthy heroes fall hard for their strong, relatable heroines.

Living in the picturesque mountains of Colorado with her husband, daughter, and a spoiled, posh cat, Zea draws inspiration from her surroundings to create warm, vibrant settings readers want to escape to. When she's not writing, she's indulging in her other loves: cooking, hiking, designing clothes, or curling up with a romance novel and a plate of sweets.

Zea is dedicated to connecting with her readers and invites you to join her on this journey of love, laughter, and happily ever afters.

Want to be the first to hear about new releases, exclusive content, and special offers?

Sign up for my newsletter at

www.zeakayleighgalan.com/news

www.instagram.com/zeakayleigh

www.facebook.com/zeakayleigh

Signed Book Shop

www.ingramcontent.com/pod-product-compliance
Lightning Source LLC
Chambersburg PA
CBHW030743310726
48969CB00005B/1297